FLESH AND THE WORD 4

"MICHAEL M____: A CASE STUDY OF DOORBELL TRADE"
BY C. BARD COLE

A sensual hip-hop bike messenger drops by, gets off, and walks out just soon enough to keep the author in a perpetual state of longing, asking the eternal question, "Does he love me?"

"ONE FOR THE ROAD"
BY CANAAN PARKER

A memorable lover named Marco the Magnificent (and is he ever!) gives the author one last screwing—a climactic experience that may never come again.

"THE MASTURBATOR"
BY JIM GRIMSLEY

Between visits from doctors and nurses, a bored sick man occupies himself with vivid fantasies of friends in bed with friends.

"DOCTOR FELL"
BY MICHAEL BRONSKI

The author reveals the shocking details of his S/M sex play—with a partner into piercings, cutting, and blood sports.

These—and many more—
uncensored and hot, true stories

MICHAEL LOWENTHAL is a writer and editor in Boston. His stories have appeared in numerous anthologies, including *Best American Gay Fiction 1996*, *Men on Men 5* (Plume), and *Friends and Lovers* (also Plume, which he edited with John Preston).

EDITED AND
WITH AN
INTRODUCTION BY
MICHAEL LOWENTHAL

F L E S H

AND THE

WORD 4

GAY EROTIC
CONFESSIONALS

A PLUME BOOK

PLUME
Published by the Penguin Group
Penguin Books USA Inc., 375 Hudson Street, New York, New York 10014, U.S.A.
Penguin Books Ltd, 27 Wrights Lane, London W8 5TZ, England
Penguin Books Australia Ltd, Ringwood, Victoria, Australia
Penguin Books Canada Ltd, 10 Alcorn Avenue,
Toronto, Ontario, Canada M4V 3B2
Penguin Books (N.Z.) Ltd, 182–190 Wairau Road,
Auckland 10, New Zealand

Penguin Books Ltd, Registered Offices:
Harmondsworth, Middlesex, England

First published by Plume, an imprint of Dutton Signet,
a division of Penguin Books USA Inc.

First Printing, May, 1997
1 3 5 7 9 10 8 6 4 2

Ⓟ REGISTERED TRADEMARK—MARCA REGISTRADA

LIBRARY OF CONGRESS CATALOGING-IN-PUBLICATION DATA
Flesh and the word 4 : gay erotic confessionals / edited and with an
introduction by Michael Lowenthal.
p. cm.
ISBN 0-452-27760-4
1. Gay men—Sexual behavior—Literary collections. 2. Erotic
literature, American—Men authors. 3. Gay men's writings, American.
I. Lowenthal, MIchael.
PS509.H57F567 1997
810.8'03538—dc21 96-48595
CIP

Printed in the United States of America
Set in Garamond No. 3 and Futura

CONTENTS

ACKNOWLEDGMENTS

FOR THEIR ADVICE AND ENCOURAGEMENT, I'D LIKE TO thank James Ireland Baker, Brian Bouldrey, Clifford Chase, Bernard Cooper, Vestal McIntyre, and especially Michael Bronski and Scott Heim. My appreciation also goes to Julia Moskin, Matthew Carnicelli, Jennifer Dickerson, and Yvonne Orteig.

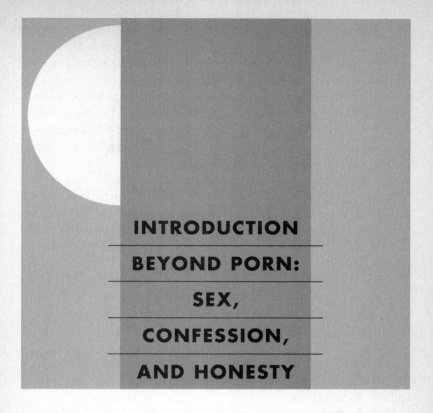

INTRODUCTION

BEYOND PORN:

SEX,

CONFESSION,

AND HONESTY

WHEN I WAS A HORNY, TORTURED ADOLESCENT, JUST DIS-covering the pleasures of flesh, I kept a small spiral notebook in my desk. The notebook was not the typical teenage angst-prattle diary, nor the repository for the love poetry I was composing for boys in my class (I had a separate journal for that), but simply, exclusively, the place where my most secret transgression was confessed. Every time I masturbated, I made a hatchmark on the current page. The marks accumulated in clusters, every four verticals stabbed by a dramatically diagonal fifth. I used whatever pen or pencil happened to be handy at the time of my self-abuse; the pages were a motley jumble of blue, black, red, and graphite gray.

Looking back, I see that the scratchings possessed the kind of unplanned, primitive beauty we ascribe to ancient cuneiform tablets. They were human communication in its most elemental form: *I was here; I did this.* But at the time, I could view the tally only as evidence of my desperation, like a prisoner of war's calendar etched into his cell wall.

Jerking off was an addiction, and I, having toddled the addict's proverbial first step toward recovery, had admitted I had a problem. Two and three times a day, I whipped myself into a blissful frenzy that, as soon as my heartbeat subsided, transformed into marrow-aching guilt. I was out of control.

The spiral notebook was the solution I concocted to cure myself. Whenever I felt the urge to bring myself off—so the theory went —I would open my desk drawer, remove the notebook, and face the scorecard of self-degradation. I would be so appalled by the profusion of blemishes against my soul that I would resist acting on my desire.

I was dutiful. I entered mark after mark, scrupulous as a scrivener. Before each wet-palmed session I paused, pulled out the notebook, and studied my sordid history. But somehow the antidote didn't work.

The problem was, my confession turned me on.

I would look at the multitude of colored slashes on the page and remember all my previous jerkings, the volumes of semen I had spilled. Each vertical line was an erection, seductively beckoning. More than that, though, I was aroused by the very concept of my notebook. I was entranced by the idea of a boy so sex-obsessed that he would go to these lengths to wean himself. It didn't matter that the boy was me. The depravity itself was a stimulus, and the fact that it was written down.

My tabulation was my most guarded secret, and yet, being written, it was also in some way a public record. Like any diary, its existence meant that a part of me must have wanted others to know. I imagined people—my mother, my schoolmates—discovering the document. Would they know what the code signified? Would it inspire them to masturbate, too?

And so, inevitably, fantasizing along these lines, I would drop the notebook, tear open my jeans, and torque myself to new levels of pleasure.

*   *   *

If my own sexual confession thought-controlled me so thoroughly, imagine my delight in discovering other people's tales out of school.

At first, any sexual writing sufficed. The already pleasurable experience of reading (which is, after all, an essentially masturbatory activity), combined with the heightened pleasure of specifically erotic content, transported me. I still remember the page in my edition of Judy Blume's *Forever* in which the main character is introduced to Ralph, her boyfriend's penis (page 80). I could draw you a diagram showing exactly where on my mother's bookshelf her spine-cracked copy of *Fear of Flying* resided.

Books, in my intellectual Jewish household, were sacred objects. And so to find my own sexual fantasies legitimated by their appearance on bound pages was a revelation. The words themselves thrilled me, their shapely curves as appealing as those of any centerfold's physique. I would hold the book and think, heart-poundingly: *I can't believe they printed that!* I imagined the author conjuring the word, then the typesetter setting it, the proofreader proofing it . . . a virtual daisy chain of naughty strangers.

Would that I could reclaim that unadulterated rush. . . .

The problem, of course, is that the thrill of the forbidden lasts only as long as something is indeed forbidden.

As I grew older, came out as a gay man, and began buying explicitly sexual books and magazines, porn became routine. In fact, it became part of my business. To support myself as a freelance writer, I edited collections of erotic writing.

This should have been my dream job: sex and writing, two of my favorite things in life, combined. (And believe me, I'm not complaining about having a "job" that allows me to write off *Torso* as a research expense for my income tax.) But I discovered that once the tingle of "I'm getting away with something" dissipated, once I had to rely solely on the *content* of the material I was reading, the vast majority of porn left me, well, limp.

Pornography is often considered the most transgressive form of writing, the "literature that dare not speak its name." And yes, in our prissified, see-no-evil, yet deeply sex-fixated culture, erotic writing is necessarily provocative. Sex can be used to sell Calvin Klein jeans, or Samsung microwaves, or cigarettes . . . but use sex to sell *itself*, and suddenly it becomes unspeakable.

The great irony, though, is that while the *fact* of pornography may trespass against society's rules, so much of the actual writing is anything *but* boundary-breaking. The vast majority of published pornography is—like any other kind of genre writing—formulaic, stale, cancerous with clichés.

For me, good sex is a sucker punch. It knocks me in the back of my knees, tilts me off-balance. A perfect orgasm feels like it snuck up and bit me from behind. And so it should be with sexual writing. That's why the paint-by-numbers porn endemic to stroke magazines just doesn't work for me. When the trucker/professor/coach is introduced, I know it will only be three paragraphs before the hitchhiker/ freshman/shortstop appears, and I know exactly what they're going to do. The gushing simultaneous climaxes are as predictable as they are unlikely.

Given the preponderance of bad erotic writing, my occasional participation in the industry became a kind of torture. I found myself increasingly immune to the possibility of arousal. Each new cookie-cutter story I read compounded my resentment at the writers who had stolen one of my most basic pleasures: being turned on by literature.

Some mornings, I would sit down with a sheaf of submissions, wincing through lines like "his throbbing baseball bat skewered me to the hilt," my own equipment shriveling as if I'd just plunged into an icy lake. I'd force myself to keep reading for a couple of hours, then get the day's mail and sit down for a break.

And on certain lucky days, an amazing thing happened. . . .

I would slice open a letter from a friend in San Francisco, or New York, or Florida. And there I would read—in honest, unselfconscious prose—that friend's account of getting fucked at Blow Buddies, or jerking off with a Hasidic boy he met on the subway, or roving the dark corridors of the baths. The tales were unpremeditated and utterly riveting.

I was especially intrigued because some of the mind-blowing admissions were from acquaintances whose published sexual writing left me cold. I realized that when they were recounting their own true experiences, unencumbered by the burden of being "pornographic," their writing was naturally—almost irrepressibly—erotic. The sex they described didn't have to be monumental to do the trick. Even if the account ended with frustration—"the one that got away"—or the admission of impotence, I still inevitably got off. The honesty itself was a turn-on.

And so, craving more confessions, I conceived of *Flesh and the Word 4*. I wrote to gay writers whose work I admire, inviting them to submit first-person, nonfiction sexual memoirs. I didn't care about the specific content, I told them; they could write about sex they'd had, sex they'd witnessed, sex about which they'd merely fantasized. The only thing I insisted was that the confessions be candid.

There is a long tradition of "true confession" pornography. The best-known contemporary example is probably *Penthouse Forum*, in which readers purportedly write in to the magazine with accounts of their sexual adventures. These "true" letters, however, are thoroughly commodified and contrived, oftentimes by paid freelancers. Sex radical Boyd McDonald was the preeminent chronicler of gay examples of the genre. In his magazine *Straight to Hell*—and later in books like *Lewd*, *Flesh*, *Meat*, *Cream*, and *Raunch*—he collected anonymous letters from gay men around the world. As with *Forum*, however, the authenticity of the experiences can be questioned, and with their crass tag lines ("Does Man Want Butt Hole Used As an Ashtray?") and stroke-lingo dialogue, the vignettes are steeped in the conventions of pornography. Slightly gussied-up successors to McDonald's chapbooks, including the *My Biggest O* and *My First Time* anthologies recently published by Alyson Books, suffer from the same tendencies.

The collection you're holding represents a break from this tradition, because here sexual bravado and explicitness are not nearly as important as emotional forthrightness and creative accomplishment. In fact, this book has much less to do with trends in pornography than with the current surge in the literary memoir form.

If the eighties were the era of the tell-all biography, the nineties are the era of the tell-all autobiography. Literary memoirs like Mary Karr's *The Liars' Club* are landing on the bestseller lists. Bookstore shelves are filled with true accounts of dysfunctional families, alcoholism, mental illness, suburban anomie. Confession is "in."

A May 1996 special issue of the *New York Times Magazine* depicted on its cover a large book with the words "True Confessions" in bold type; included were "real-life stories" by some of America's most prominent and promising writers. In his introduction to the issue, James Atlas points out that the confessional line in American literature is clearly traceable through some of our best writers, from poets Anne Sexton and Robert Lowell to Walt Whitman's "Song of Myself." Autobiography, he notes, is a "democratic genre," allowing everyone—"the famous and the obscure," those enfranchised and those pointedly not—to have their say. It makes perfect sense, then, that in our age of multiculturalism, memoir would be the *genre du jour*.

Some critics have questioned this trend, charging that "auto-pathography" is simply the latest excess in our self-indulgent Oprah-fied culture. It's bad enough to hear these embarrassing revelations on talk shows, they say, but does our literature need to be "sensationalized" as well? Do we really need to know, as he writes in his memoir *Secret Life*, that poet Michael Ryan had sex with his dog? Shouldn't such sordid details remain privileged knowledge between patient and therapist?

Gay men can't help but hear such suggestions with a deep sense of trepidation. Until very recently, we were told the very same things: "Can't you just keep it private?" "Save it for the psychiatrist's couch." It was not a predilection for sex with dogs but rather our most basic desire to be loving, sexual beings that was considered pathological.

For gay writers, then, perhaps the memoir as a literary form has even greater significance. Memoir is the literary embodiment of the political slogan "Silence=Death." After a long history of not being able to speak and write about our lives, gay men are now defiantly claiming the right to tell all, to tell it like it is, to confess.

In the realm of specifically sexual writing, some might argue that gay men have already told plenty. Recent years have seen a remarkable proliferation of sexually explicit magazines and anthologies of erotic writing. But the hard-won freedom to publish openly sexual work may, paradoxically, have moved us further from the emotional truths of gay life. Freed from their professional and personal closets, many gay erotic writers seem only to have traded one mode of hiding for another: now they hide behind twelve-inch penises and superheroic pecs. The memoirs in this book are an attempt to move beyond such blowfish porn, into territory at once more recognizable and more astonishing.

Stripped of their fictional defenses and their pornographic smoke-and-mirrors, the contributors to this volume bare themselves at their most vulnerable. I encouraged the writers to ignore the conventions of erotic writing, perhaps to forget that they were even trying to be erotic. And so you will find that in some of these memoirs, the sex never happens, or perhaps happens only in the writer's imagination. In some of these memoirs, the dicks are small or can't get hard. In some, the authors end up with their feelings hurt. But every fervid confession is searing nonetheless.

Some of the activities and attractions are shockingly explicit: one writer gags himself with his own penis; another slices his partner with scalpels; another devours feces; another licks his lover's Kaposi's sarcoma lesions. But there are also moments shocking in their tenderness and familiarity: adolescent crushes, first fucks, sex in the "marriage bed."

I have no guarantee that every detail recorded in this book is exactly "factual" or remembered with courtroom accuracy. I'm sure some fudging occurred in the course of each writer's attempt to shape his story. But absolute veracity is not the point. As Toni Morrison has pointed out, there is a crucial difference between "fact" and "truth." The memoirs you will read in this collection are undeniably "true." You can feel it when you're reading them: the excruciating, exhilarating yank of the human condition. The pull is all-powerful because it is exerted not only on our genitals but also on our hearts and minds.

These erotic memoirs are whispered secrets that bother our ears but seduce us with their tickle. They are roadside accidents from which we can't avert our gaze.

They are the most elemental form of human communication, proclaiming: *I was here; I did this.*

—Michael Lowenthal
Boston, Massachusetts
August 1996

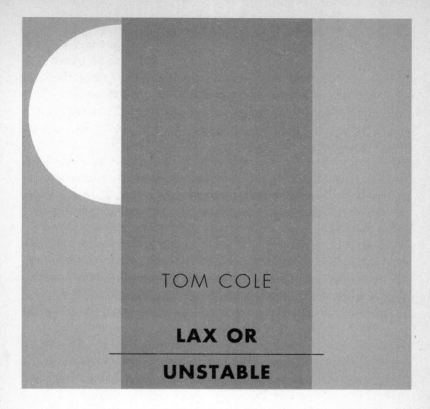

TOM COLE

LAX OR

UNSTABLE

I GUESS YOU COULD SAY I WAS SEXUALLY PRECOCIOUS. I discovered my parents' vibrator when I was eight. It was of the old-fashioned type. Gray and heavy with tight long springs for handles that later, when I grew them, would snag my pubes. It was like my brain was exploding. I used it so much my legs were sore and it was hard to walk for days at a time. The vibrator used so much electricity that when plugged in, it made all of the televisions in the house go fuzzy. So, when any of the family members were using the vibrator, everyone else in the house knew it was being used, because in my house, the television was always on, and there was a television in every room. A strange sort of scrutiny.

My parents had a copy of *The Joy of Sex* which they hid, not very well, under my father's bed. Some pages were folded in, so I

knew the type of sex my parents liked best. The print on the handjob page was all worn down, and by now I bet you can't even read
the writing. The entry mentioned rhythm and gripping the balls
while you stroke. There is one technique called the tornado in which
you hold the penis between your hands and twist it as if rolling a
ball of dough into a strip to make cinnamon buns. I hate giving
hand jobs.

I remember looking for something to stick my penis in when
I was a child. I found a toothbrush holder in the bathroom that
seemed to be the correct size. It was in the shape of an aqua-blue
fish, with its mouth open wide. The problem was that once I stuck
my dick in the fish's mouth, it grew far too large to come back out.
I panicked. I was trapped. I knew I shouldn't have done what I did,
but I couldn't keep from trying it. I swooned, passed out, my head
banging on the toilet. During my blackout I had a dream that lasted
forever. In my dream I was aboard a hijacked plane. The hijackers
tied me up and measured my penis. They were measuring everyone's
penis. We were all lined up, shivering, with our hands tied behind
our backs. Mine was too small. The pilot said I had malgrowth and
that I would never get hair under my arms or opaque semen or a
large penis because I had masturbated so much, and with a vibrator
at that. One of the stewards came up to me. He pressed his finger
into my anus and said, "I like 'em tight." It was at this point that
I came in the fish.

When I regained consciousness, I was staring up at the toilet
with my mother banging on the door asking if I was all right and
telling me she didn't know how many times she had asked me not
to lock the bathroom door. The fish was still gripping my penis with
all its might. I looked to the toilet as if it could give me some sort
of advice. I was hoping that somewhere down there in the plumbing
a talkless voice might emerge telling me what to do next. The toilet
lid in my house was clear Plexiglas. You could watch your bowel
movements spiral inward as if caught in an inverted tornado. I was
caught, I was driven, I was repulsed. My father banged down the
door. My mother put her hands to her nose. We had to crack open
the fish with a hammer as if it were a piggy bank. Semen spilled

into the sink. Everyone got to see the size of my penis. I said with all earnestness that it was an accident. That it just sort of fell in. That I hadn't zipped up my pants and it just sort of fell in.

The first time I sucked my own penis was at the age of fifteen. I was a student in a public boarding school in North Carolina. I was in the communal shower, which was a large tiled box. It was exciting because anyone could walk in at any moment. I lay on my back and lifted my legs behind my head until my toes touched the tile wall. I inched my toes down until my cock was in front of my lips. At first I could only get the tip in, but as my ligaments loosened, I was able to push half of my cock in my mouth, tickling the back of my throat. As I thrust my hips back and forth, I looked at the tiles on the wall and hypnotized myself by counting them. At one point I knew exactly how many tiles there were in that bathroom. Then I would come in my mouth, the semen dripping down my throat like oysters or glue. As I slowly rocked forward, my muscles and joints aching, I felt like an amoeba, able to reproduce on my own. I was naive. I thought that wherever the sperm landed, a baby would form. I thought perhaps I would be the first person to give birth through the mouth. I liked sucking my own cock. I couldn't imagine putting someone else's in. My back would be lined with a grid, an imprint from the tiled floor. I looked as if I had been branded, or as if someone had painted a Mondrian on my back— some squares redder than others, my textured skin wrinkly from steam.

This became a ritual for me. I would suck myself off every night at around eight. I practiced my routine. After a while I could swallow my cock whole. I thought about starting my own sword-swallowing act.

I became obsessed with my weight. The skinnier I got, the better head I could give myself. I purged regularly until I would vomit involuntarily when brushing my teeth. I perfected an unusual gag technique. I would purge on my own cock, tickling the back of my throat with the head, barfing all over my neck and chest, a mixture of bad institutional food and semen. I would stand under the shower forever, forcing the chunks down the drain with my big toe. I felt as if I had been emptied of all my fluids, a strange douche. Even now, my erogenous zone is my throat; and I'm aroused by digested food.

I went to the doctor. My flexibility has been diagnosed. I am ligamentously lax or unstable.

JAMES
IRELAND
BAKER

MUSTARD SEED

I GREW UP THE SON OF A METHODIST MINISTER IN AUSTIN,
Minnesota, a small town known chiefly as the site of the original
Hormel meat-packing plant. Though my neighbors often pointed
with civic pride to the fact that the Miss Minnesota Pageant was
held at Austin's Riverside Arena every summer (an event which
seemingly, if temporarily, lifted the town onto a more exalted level),
life here was generally listless and depressing—circumscribed, as it
was, by the plant. The air smelled constantly of pig shit and bacon;
the football team was called the Packers, and few Austin boys left
town for college, but followed the paths of their fathers, and their
fathers' fathers: marrying local girls, siring children and working
their way through the hog kill.

I felt trapped here, a would-be aesthete watching Ann Sheridan
movies and listening to David Bowie, but I didn't have a name for

my sense of dislocation until the day a classmate cornered me on the playground and called me "faggot," adding: "You fags are all alike. Why don't you go back to where you came from?"

The idea that fags had been shipped, like slaves in galleys, from Fagland or Homocity was patently ridiculous, of course, but not without its own freak logic: The homes into which gay men are born are seldom the homes where we actually *belong*—and I did feel, acutely, that I'd gotten lost or been misplaced in this sad, oppressive ghetto where the squeals of dying pigs could be heard on the wind in the summer.

For a while, I believed that my sense of being stranded, a stranger in familiar lands, was wholly my fault. Austin was not the problem; the problem was that *I* had failed to adapt. The problem was that I was not the boy I was supposed to be. The problem was, of course, that I was gay.

At the time, I was devoutly religious, but when I examined my troubles I decided that perhaps I was not religious *enough*: I had, for instance, never actually accepted Jesus Christ as my "personal savior." Remembering the stories of salvation certain Christians—cripples, perverts and the terminally ill—claimed to have experienced after consciously asking Christ to live in their hearts, I asked my mother if, in doing likewise, I would become a "different person." She said, emphatically, yes.

"*Who*, then?" I asked.

She didn't have an answer. She made it sound as though I would remain who I was, but become more religious. I, on the other hand, took the idea quite literally; by "different person," I meant Elizabeth Taylor.

Down on my knees in the darkness of my bedroom that night, I prayed to Jesus, asking Him to save me, telling Him that I wanted, more than anything, to be "normal." I waited, prayed and waited some more. I looked around, expecting to see or feel something—anything—but there were no lights, no stirrings in my soul, no sound other than the ticking of my bedside clock. I shrugged, deciding that, like antibiotics, the result of prayer might take time to kick in.

I climbed into bed, telling myself that in the morning I'd

emerge into a new identity as though into a tailored suit. But when I woke I was, disappointingly, still Jimmy Baker. Believing now that Christ did not exist—or had, for whatever reason, decided not to help me—I embarked on a wholly secular quest to transcend the tyranny of my identity and my surroundings. I read Kafka, became a vegetarian, wrote short stories about Paris, took French classes in high school and, perhaps most importantly, started jogging.

Every day I took the same route, running past the Mobil station, along the asphalt path that cut between the small, seldom-used local airport and the cornfield, down Road 10 to the old dump that was cordoned off by a thick chain, on which a sign read: NO TRESPASSING. KEEP OUT. Though I had passed this dump every day for years, it wasn't until the spring of 1980, when I was seventeen, that, on a whim, I decided to explore it.

There were ancient ovens, chrome hubcaps, stripped car tires, broken safety-glass windows, rusted bumpers, wire hangers and—inexplicably—piles of bowling balls. I'm not sure what I expected to find in this eerily quiet wasteland, but what I found changed my life: Inside a doorless refrigerator, a photo of a woman's breast peeped out from within a plastic Rexall Drug bag. Still catching my breath, I leaned down, opened the bag and discovered a *Playboy* from the 1960s (pastel, airbrushed centerfolds), a *Hustler* from the early 1970s (shaved women covering each other with baby oil), and—the item that meant the most to me—a water-damaged, newsprinty novel entitled *Mouse's First Love II*.

I opened this book and read:

"Suck me off, Mouse," Grunge sighed heavily, unzipping his pants. "Really gnaw on my thick prick. Let me feel your lips on my skin flute. Really." He began to laugh wildly in that irritatingly seductive way of his. "I want you to suck it."

and I read:

I felt his throbbing dick in the back of my warm, suckling throat. I felt myself rising to the occasion and then I felt his hands on me, freeing my engorgement from its nest within my jeans.

and I read:

He voided himself into my convulsive welcome.

I was literally staggered. Bad as the writing was, the sheer cheesy physicality of it gave me an identity, a location, a *body*. It also gave me, briefly, guilt: As I stood reading, I suddenly realized that I was in an open, public place. Feeling watched and judged by God Himself, if not by junkyard dogs, I looked around, then packed the porn in the Rexall bag and carried it stealthily home. When I finally reached my bedroom, I shut the door—there were no locks—and hid the magazines under my dresser.

I took the novel out and lay down on my bed.

Mouse's First Love II was, as it turned out, the story of two boys, Mouse and Grunge, who meet while hitchhiking; are forced to have sex with a sadistic truck driver; end up screwing a Hollywood producer for money; and finally fall in love with each other. There were words like "shaft" and "head" and "sucked" and "lick" and "wild" and "juice" and "blood." There were scenes of oral sex and anal sex and analingus and "hot, wet" kissing.

In the following weeks, this novel invaded my thoughts, my consciousness reeling with—and suffocated by—sex. I couldn't walk to the refrigerator to fetch a glass of milk without imagining Grunge "voiding" himself into Mouse's "convulsive welcome." Driven by these visions, I was soon jerking off three and four times a day, wanting nothing more than to be left alone with my thoughts and a jar of Noxzema.

In late July of that year, I found a job—my first—washing dinner dishes at the local Country Kitchen for a woman whose late husband had been a minor baseball player in the major leagues (his autograph was, it was later determined, worth sixty cents). As the heat became oppressive, the houses up and down our block turning into wooden ovens, our neighbors left, family by family, for vacations in Disneyland, New Orleans and Galveston. Because of my new job I was, for the first time in my life, happily exempt from my family's annual summer trip to our isolated cabin in northern Wisconsin. On July 29, my parents left in their Corvair van, my younger brother and sister waving to me from the back window, leaving me with a twenty-dollar bill and a cat to take care of.

I was finally alone and so, I imagined, I would order pepperoni pizza from George's every night, watch *Night Flight* until 3:00 or 4:00 A.M. and masturbate whenever the hell I wanted. What I did not imagine was spending all my free time with the only other person left on our street, an aimless eighth-grader named (I'm not making this up) Roderick.

At first he meant nothing to me. He had a short, compact body, dirty blond hair that hung over his forehead in neatly cut bangs and a straight, thin, colorless scar under his left eye. He had blue eyes and beautiful skin, but he wasn't particularly attractive and he was also, somewhat disturbingly, diabetic. He injected himself with insulin three times a day and carried Space Food Sticks with him to school in case he went into insulin shock, which had happened— famously—in a wood shop class one December afternoon. My brother, Josh, returned from Ellis Junior High that day with the terrifying, glamorous news that our neighbor was a heroin addict and that he'd just gotten "sick." The rumor was that Rod's mother (who reportedly sunbathed nude and drank vodka martinis) gave Rod heroin she'd filched from her irresponsible lover, a chain-smoking local doctor.

"He was just having an insulin reaction," I said authoritatively.

"It was *heroin*," Josh insisted.

"There *is* no heroin in Austin, Minnesota."

"Whatever," he said, warning: "Just don't ask him about it. And, whatever you do, don't talk to Rod about his mother."

I had no reason to believe I'd ever talk to Rod about *anything* (his "heroin addiction," his mother's nudism, the alluring scar under his eye), especially since he was only fourteen, an age difference that seemed insurmountable—but Rod, like me, was left alone that summer. His friends were on vacation with their families; his father worked all night at the hog kill; no one knew where his errant and infamous mother had gone. So Rod, who ordinarily would never have spoken to me (as I would never have spoken to him), suddenly became my best friend.

Early every stifling afternoon, after I'd gotten up and showered

and eaten, I would call Rod and he would come over. He always
wore the same thing: no shirt and a pair of jogging shorts. We would
jog, watching heat rise off the pavement as we passed the Mobil
station and the Big K Motel. We would cross the two-lane road and
run through the airport parking lot. We would run on the path that
cut between the airport and the cornfield until we reached Road 10,
which we followed all the way down to the dump.

As the days passed, I noticed that Rod hardly ever laughed, but
that when he did his eyes crinkled up and his mouth became absurdly
crooked. I noticed his teeth, too, long and white, and the way he
cut his fingernails. I noticed his nipples. I noticed his eyes. The more
time I spent with him, the more I became conscious of a shift within
my innards, a groundswell of tenderness for this boy I hardly knew.
I began to think of Rod and his body in terms of *Mouse's First Love
II*, merging the impressions I'd gathered from his company (he was
unimaginative and unadventurous) with the lessons I'd learned from
pornography (sex is everywhere, everyone wants it all the time, suck
my dick and fuck my ass), until I began to embroider reality, adding
nonexistent sex scenes to our afternoons as if in italics, inserting
words in Rod's and my sentences in parentheses:

"I want to smell your skin," I imagined saying to him as we
finished our run outside the dump one day. *"I want to taste you,"* I
*said, and when he nodded I leaned forward, held the back of his head in
my hand and brought my lips to his. As I stroked his hair with my hand,
I licked his tongue and said: "I want to suck your dick."*

What I actually said was: "Je voudrais sucer tu penis."

"What?" he asked.

"Nothing," I said. "Hey, I found dirty pictures here once." I
motioned past the chain.

"What?"

"Pictures of naked ladies, I mean." Pause. "Want to see them?"
"Sure."

In the Gospel of Matthew there's a scene where Jesus Christ
casts out demons from a boy. The boy's father explains that his
(smooth, stunningly handsome) epileptic son is constantly falling
into fire and water and that the disciples can't cure him. Jesus, like

an impatient doctor who's been on call too long, damns His gener-
ation as "faithless and perverse," and abruptly—easily—performs an
exorcism. When the disciples want to know why they themselves
were unable to accomplish this, Jesus says: "Because of your little
faith. For truly, I say to you, if you have faith as a grain of mustard
seed, you will say to this mountain, 'Move from here to there,' and
it will move; and nothing will be impossible to you."

I figured I had at least the faith of a mustard seed, and anyway
I didn't want to move mountains. What I wanted was Rod's penis
in my mouth. I did not think this was asking for too much.

"Please, Jesus," I prayed that afternoon while Rod was at home,
injecting himself. (Christ had already ignored my attempt to save
my soul, but perhaps, I reasoned, he might want to save my body.)
"I'm asking you, please, Jesus, let me have him. Amen."

I went to my dresser and took out my magazines.

My parents' room was the only one in the house equipped with
air-conditioning, so that's where I always slept—and where I took
Rod when he came over that night. We were on my parents' bed,
staring at *Hustler*'s images of glistening women playing tennis in the
nude. Their bodies were hairless and their clams completely raw. I
expected that Rod would be entranced by these women, by their
breasts and buds of flesh, but he seemed only mildly interested. Disappointed by his listlessness, his utter lack of affect, I decided to
provoke him.

"The guy who took these pictures," I said. "What do you suppose he was thinking?"

"He must've wanted sex pretty bad."

"Maybe it was just his job."

"Maybe."

"Would *you* like that job?"

"Sure."

"Taking pictures of naked ladies?"

"Sure."

"Maybe your mom could pose for you," I said quietly, but he
either pretended not to hear or he actually didn't. Instead, he yawned,
said he was tired and wanted to go to bed. I asked if he wanted to

spend the night and, when he said yes, I assumed that we would (fuck our brains out) sleep in my parents' bed together. I was puzzled when he lay down on the wicker couch.

"You're sleeping *there?*" I asked.

"Sure."

"You can (fuck me) sleep in the bed, if you want. There's plenty of room."

"But it's your *parents'* bed."

"So?"

"So which one of us will be the mom?"

I didn't really understand this question (and consequently had no answer for it), so I ignored him. He pulled his share of the bedding and the pillows to the couch—and then he took off his clothes.

The only light in the room came from the illuminated orange globe near the wicker couch. The globe showed the world as it had been mapped inaccurately by early explorers. Its light was low, making Rod's skin look like a kind of celestial milk chocolate combined with, say, the blushy red you sometimes see on peaches. But the color of his skin was only the beginning; there was also its texture, so fine and soft I was certain that, like pigs or dogs, he had no pores.

I wondered where his sweat came from.

He undressed nervously and, sensing his self-consciousness, I put my head down on the pillow and pretended to close my eyes. In truth, I was squinting and could therefore still see him—and what I saw was that he was watching me. When he decided that I was sleeping—or at least appeared to be—he unbuttoned the top button of his Levi's, unzipped them and pulled them off.

Then he did something I have never forgotten: Carefully, with an endearing combination of clumsiness and grace, he *folded* his clothes and piled them, one by one, on top of each other. And then he turned the globe off.

I thought about Mouse.

When he pulled off his underwear I could see the carbon blackness of his pubic hair, a wiry thicket that seemed neatly trimmed, but was in fact merely nascent. He had the kind of body where the hair was all in place— a small triangle of hair above his crotch, wisps of sweaty hair under his arms, hair on his head . . . and that was it. His testes were small, pale,

pink and hairless, and his penis, not as large as I'd imagined, was tender,
lean and full-blooded.

Something was opening up in me, something I couldn't control. I dropped
to my knees and crawled to his crotch and was leaning, mouth open, toward
the lustrous gland when—

I couldn't sleep. The air conditioner made soporific humming
and dripping sounds, but my fantasies were keeping me uncomfort-
ably erect. The only light in the room was now coming from the
streetlamp outside. I lay still on the bed until my eyes adjusted to
the relative dark, and then I rose to see Rod sleeping without blan-
kets on the wicker couch, shirtless, in his underwear, his eyelids
looking somehow both heavy and light, the tips of his white teeth
barely visible past his moist and slightly parted lips. I kneeled before
the couch and stared at his crotch, trying to trace the curves and
shape of his penis under the fabric.

"Hello," he said in his sleep.

I jumped. "Oh, God, you scared me."

"There was a party. I saw a diamond, and they had . . . a radio."

"Really?"

"At the party. There was dancing."

"What party?"

"Oh, gee."

"Voulez-vous coucher avec moi ce soir?" I whispered.

"Na, na, na, na," he sang tunelessly, still sleeping.

When we woke the next afternoon, we didn't say a thing, but
trudged off in our underwear to take our separate showers. There was
a shower in the bathroom on the first floor, and another in the basement. Rod went into the basement and I, knowing there were no
curtains on the window looking down from the driveway into the
basement bathroom, put on jeans and a T-shirt, snuck from the house
and lay face-forward in the small garden my mother had planted in
front of the window. I pressed my face against the screen.

Rod was in the shower, singing.

When he stepped, dappled with water, from behind the shower
curtain, I strained to see as much of his body as I could. He had a
slight erection, what my cousin had once called a "whiskey dick,"
but more erotic than his stiffness was the care he took as he dried

under his arms, the crack of his ass, his thighs, between his toes, under his balls. The deliberateness with which he put the towel in each ear and twisted it, cleaning both the ear canal and the backs of his ears, was maddening.

I wanted to scream, but did I? He looked up, catching—so I thought at the time, so I remember now—my eye. He seemed scared at first, then embarrassed. I was too serious—and too in love with him—to laugh it off. Instead, I felt trapped, immobilized, humiliated.

He stared back, briefly, and then, as if he'd never noticed me —in fact, maybe he hadn't—he returned to the calm, slow, patient drying of his skin.

That afternoon, when Rod left to inject himself with insulin, I took out my father's manual Hermes typewriter and wrote my un-suspecting beloved a letter.

Dear Rod,

I typed:

I know this might seem weird, but I just really wanted to tell you that I like you a lot and think it would be nice to ~~suck,~~ ~~love~~ get to know you better. I hope this does not seem strange, and I am not a gay, but I ~~want you~~ think about you ~~all the time~~ a lot and would like to ~~suck your penis~~ help you out in life. I hope you know that even though we don't know each other that well I do care about you and I will always ~~love you~~ be there for you if you need me. You have a friend in me forever.
~~Love~~ Sincerely,
Jim

That night in the restaurant's tropically hot kitchen, I poured industrial-strength detergent into the large stainless-steel dishwasher and rinsed the remains of patty melts, pancakes and cigarettes from dinner plates before filing them into the racks. As my eyes and nose filled with hot steam, I imagined Rod having an insulin reaction and

I imagined saving him. I imagined trying to feed him emergency honey from a silver spoon, drooling it into his mouth as he convulsed. I imagined not being able to get the honey off the spoon. I imagined resourcefully pouring the thick golden syrup into my own mouth, locking my lips to his, thrusting my tongue down his throat. I imagined him swallowing the honey and saliva, sucking it off my tongue, then brightening, looking at me with love and wonder, knowing I had saved his life.

I imagined giving him injections.

It was 99 degrees when, at 2:00 A.M., I returned, smelling of grease, from the Country Kitchen, praying to Jesus as I pedaled, sweating, past the Hormel plant: "Please, Jesus, please, please. I have faith, I have faith, I have faith."

Rod was waiting on the front steps. He was wearing cutoffs, Keds sneakers, a blue shirt and a baseball cap.

"You coming in?" I asked.

"Sure," he said. "I was hoping I could stay over."

Ask, and it will be given you; seek, and you will find; knock, and the door will be opened to you. For everyone who asks receives, and he who seeks finds, and to him who knocks it will be opened.— Matthew 7:7–8.

The first thing I did when we entered the house was grab the letter from the typewriter, tear it up and throw it in the garbage. Rod went upstairs to my parents' room and I took a shower, washing the sweat, grease and the smell of industrial detergent off my body. The night air was so hot that when I stepped from the shower and toweled myself, I didn't feel cold, so I wrapped the towel around my waist and traipsed upstairs to join Rod, who was lying on my parents' bed, *Hustler* open on my mother's pillow, the air conditioner on.

"You like that magazine?" I asked.

"Sure."

"You ever had it?"

"What?"

"Sex?"

His nose wrinkled. His limbs were all over the bed, like pick-up-sticks, as though they'd been thrown there. "No," he said bluntly, but I could tell that he was thinking about it.

"You don't run around the house naked or anything?"

"No." He seemed offended.

"But you're naked right now, right?"

"I'm wearing clothes."

"But underneath your clothes, you're naked, one way or another, all the time, right? I mean your penis, for instance, is there right now, isn't it? Whether you like it or not, it's just inches away. And, anyway, your mother—"

The flesh around his eyes tightened. His damp, drooping bud of a mouth puckered. "What *about* her?"

"Well, she sunbathes nude, doesn't she? She takes baths and then she dances around the house in the nude, doesn't she? And she's fucking Dr. Carlson, who gives her heroin and—"

He sprang off the mattress, wobbling a little as he leapt at me, hitting my bare chest with the palms of his hands—one, two—pushing me away from him with every stroke—three, four—and finally lunging forward, wrapping arms around my chest, kicking my legs out from underneath me. Five. Before long I was on my back, Rod straddling my chest, holding my slippery, still-moist wrists to the floor, one on each side of my head. I felt his bare thighs against my waist, felt his skin against my skin. I was suddenly serious, body rigid, hardening. Worried that everything I felt for him would betray itself in the obviousness of my incipient erection, I pushed against him, trying to overcome his lock on my body. When his left hand slipped, my right hand flew, hitting him across the mouth.

"Goddamnit it," he said, forcing my wrist back to the floor.

I could see his tongue churning behind pursed lips—and then he spat in my face.

"Fuck you," I said.

"Take it back!" he said through another mouthful of saliva.

"No," I said, and when he let another long, bubbly stream drip from

his lips, I opened my mouth wide, caught it—and swallowed. He took his hands off my wrists and, knees still straddling, leaned forward, inch by inch, until his lips were next to mine. He held them there for seconds, then opened his mouth.

What happened was this: I took "it" back, told Rod to calm down and tried to calm myself. I stood up, carefully concealing my erection, and walked downstairs to the bathroom. The entire first floor of our house was dark, so that the light from the bathroom made a path across the hardwood. Leaving the door open, I let my towel drop to the floor and stood before the toilet, my erection in my hands. I didn't hear a sound, but when I looked up from the toilet bowl I saw Rod standing in the doorway.

"You all right?" he asked.

"Sure."

"You've got that funny feeling, don't you?"

"Yes."

"I can see you have that feeling."

"Sure."

"So." He smiled, suddenly. "What are we gonna do now?"

I picked up my towel and we went upstairs, talked about nothing for a half an hour—and fell asleep: Rod on the wicker couch, me on the bed.

In the middle of that night I woke, terrified that I had passed up the one thing I had prayed for, convinced the opportunity would never occur again. I climbed from bed, kneeled before the couch and stared at Rod's face. He looked exactly, I imagined, like the epileptic boy immediately after the expulsion of the demon. He had the dewy glamour of the newly exorcised, his tanned face like porcelain in the blue light. *I pulled the blanket from his waist and tugged the elastic band of his underwear down over his genitals. I saw his penis, limp and motionless, and I leaned over, licking his tight smooth balls, traveling with my tongue up the slim shaft of his dick, finally taking the ripe bud of his head into my mouth.*

He opened his eyes, surprised—shocked, even—and seemed momentarily repulsed, but he was hardening and I was moving faster. Everything was inevitable now. "Man," he moaned, eyes flickering back into his head, as though he were on the verge of passing out. "Oh, man, what is that, oh, Jesus, nice." He put his left hand behind his head, cradling it against the wicker arm of the couch, and put his right hand on my neck, guiding me over his dick. "Suck it."

I could feel him pulsing, body jerking.

"Drink," he gasped, then shuddered and voided himself into my convulsive welcome.

He woke, suddenly, and seemed to see me staring at him. "Je suis chaud comme un lapin," I said.

"What?" He sat up, panicking.

"Nothing," I said, returning to bed, more or less certain that he wouldn't remember any of this in the morning.

The weather broke, beginning to seem increasingly like autumn and less like molten summer. School loomed; vacations ended, families returning to Fourth Avenue near the airport. When Rod's real friends reappeared in the neighborhood, he was no longer interested in spending time, or staying overnight, with me. We stopped jogging to the dump in the early afternoons. I hardly ever saw him again.

One day my father took me out into the driveway, where, on the unwashed chrome bumper of our Corvair van, I saw fat words fingered in the dust:

JIM IS A FAG!

My father wanted to know where this had come from. I affected nonchalance, said it was just a joke Andy Landherr had played—that we were old buddies and that these taunts went back and forth like a stupid game, Andy calling me a fag and me calling him one back. My father seemed unconvinced. In truth, I was fairly certain that Rod had returned to his "normal" self and, realizing how close the two of us had come to carnal knowledge, had imputed all the motivation to me. Perhaps he understood French. I wiped the words away with my arm.

My senior year arrived, and after that I moved away to a small Midwestern college, where—without my family, without an extended community—in a suicidal fit of desperation born of (eternal hopefulness) a nervous breakdown, I prayed, again, to Jesus, asking him to cast out demons, asking him to make me normal. "For truly,"

Jesus said to me, "if you have faith as a grain of mustard seed, you will say to this mountain, 'Move from here to there,' and it will move; and nothing will be impossible to you."

I wanted to move mountains. I wanted to change my life. I didn't have the faith.

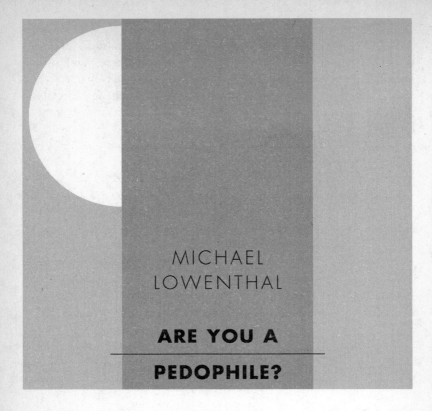

MICHAEL LOWENTHAL

ARE YOU A

PEDOPHILE?

ARE YOU A PEDOPHILE IF YOU LUST AFTER TEENAGERS AND even preteens, cultivating avalanche-force crushes on your favorites; if you stalk them, and learn where they live, then loiter across the street to glimpse their gangly perfection? Are you a pedophile if you call these boys on the telephone, once a day, twice, contriving to find one who'll come to your house and look at your penis, or show you his, or maybe let you touch and suck it?

What if you yourself, when you do these things, are only a boy, fourteen years old? Or twelve? Or half that age?

First was Dusty Wilson. I can't remember exactly how old I was when we started fooling around, but I couldn't have been more than seven, because that's when we moved to Maryland. Let's say I was six. Dusty would have been six, too.

Dusty was alluring not because of any particular feature—at that point, had I established my "type"?—but simply because, as The Best Friend, he was available. As I remember, he had bland brown hair cut by his mother into a natural football helmet, which, despite its unremarkable color, managed to clash with the striped polyester-blend T-shirts he always wore. Even at that tender age he had old-man eyebrows, two fuzzy caterpillars appliquéd above his eyes.

Perhaps Dusty's most exciting feature was that his house had an indoor swimming pool. I think his father was a dentist.

The game we began to play bore a close resemblance to the *Lone Ranger* episodes we watched daily on TV, although our plots—if this is possible—had even less variation than those predictable black-and-white reruns. In every enactment we were buddies, pard'ners, on some horsey mission Out West. After the requisite encounter with danger—tomahawking Injuns, black-bandannaed bandits on a hijacked stagecoach—one of us would end up gravely wounded. Usually this meant buckshot deep in the flesh.

Even then, I knew this was not the standard finale for American boy adventure games. According to tradition, we should have emerged from each scuffle triumphant, declaring victory for the forces of Good, and if injured, only slightly so. But conventional victory held little appeal; defeat brought more intriguing rewards. I had devised our version's perennially catastrophic ending to maximize the potential for "playing doctor," a game that on its own terms would have been suspect but that under the guise of our Western adventures was acceptable.

During long hours studying my body in the privacy of our apartment bathroom, I had become enamored of the veins that wormed on either side of my abdomen. Bluely visible just beneath my pale skin, as if perpetually about to break the surface, they portended of things almost, on-the-verge. When we swam in the pool at Dusty's house, I noticed that he, too, possessed these enticing veins. Sneaking glances as he concentrated on impending deep-end dives, I saw how the veins traced down and disappeared under his swimsuit's fraying band. Although I could deduce from my own body where Dusty's veins must lead, I wanted to confirm this with hard evidence.

And so, with a precocious and conniving sense of biology, I developed a theory—which turns out to be not too far from medical truth—that infection could spread through the bloodstream. Infection, or so I argued, was the inevitable accompaniment to the injuries Dusty and I sustained in our Lone Rangering. Just think how dirty those lead pellets must be after being fired from some rascal's shotgun!

Thus, while the exact locations of Dusty's wounds shifted from episode to episode, the results were always the same. The game would wind up this way:

Dusty, groaning, clutching his hand: "Oh, no. They've shot me. Clear through. Check out the size of that hole."

Me, grabbing the limp appendage, gentle but firm: "Let me take a look. When I lived back East, you know, I was a doctor."

I spend a minute dutifully pretending to clean the wound, while Dusty winces and writhes convincingly. I bandage the hand, wrapping imaginary gauze between thumb and forefinger. I'm doing my medical best.

Then I turn serious and lower my chin like Walter Cronkite reporting the death toll of some distant disaster. "I'm sorry," I say. "It seems the infection has spread."

"Really?" Dusty asks. "It doesn't feel like it. Actually, I feel fine."

"No," I insist, "it's definitely spreading."

I point to the veins in his skinny wrists, then follow the blue line along the inside of his forearm, over the plump hot dog of his six-year-old biceps, into the swoop of his armpit. The vein disappears under muscle, but as I lift Dusty's shirt, and as he flinches from the cold touch of my hands, I explain how the vessel actually continues down his torso's length, skirting the heart, burrowing near his belly button. "See here?" I say, fingering the slight bump of color just above his jeans. "This is really the same vein." (Miraculous!)

I press and prod Dusty's flesh, copycatting my real doctor at the yearly physical, humming enigmatically with every poke.

"It looks pretty bad," I conclude.

"Are you sure?"

"Oh, yes. It's moving very fast. There's only one thing I know to try."

Then—and it still amazes me that he succumbed to such an obvious ploy—I would unbutton Dusty's pants. Tugging them down to his knees, I would lean over and study his secret parts: the blushed pinkie of a penis, the tiny scrotum clutched against his body like a bloated tick. There was the faint bitter smell of chlorine.

Trying to maintain professional detachment, I'd trace the meandering purple wisps in his erection. "You can see how it's darker here," I would say. "That means it's getting worse. But I think there's still time to save you."

The cure was to pull on his dick from the base to the tip, milking out the dangerous infection. I always remained within the gentle bounds of our role-playing, careful not to cause any injury that would require consulting an actual doctor, but with practice I learned how much I could yank the skin without making Dusty gasp, which angle induced the widest smile. With its size and shape, its firm but still spongy flesh, Dusty's dick reminded me of a baby dill pickle. I resisted the urge to bend down and steal a bite. Instead, I'd savor its energetic pulse in my fingertips, every squirm of Dusty's stalky limbs, conscious even then of the inevitable day when he would question the plausibility of my diagnoses and call it quits.

In lieu of a visible orgasm, how did I know when to stop? I guess I simply decided when he had had enough, when the life-threatening elements had been safely expelled.

"There," I would say. "You're all better now. That was definitely a very close call."

"They've been getting really big lately. Like, twice as big. You think I might have cancer or something?"

We were sitting on the floor of Adam Glickman's attic bedroom—Adam, Gil Miller, and me—woozy from the Heineken his father had allowed us in honor of Adam's bar mitzvah that morning, our pants and underpants heaped by his hamster cage, boners wobbling like Weebles that would never fall down.

Adam and Gil were thirteen; I was a year younger (twice the

boy I'd been during my fumblings with Dusty Wilson), but renowned for my medical expertise.

"Let me see," I said, bending for Adam's crotch.

He cupped his balls delicately, as you might a fragile hatchling
fallen from its nest. They were big indeed, bigger than mine, tight
against the pimply skin of his sac. They reminded me of the hard
plastic eggs in which Silly Putty arrived.

"I think they're fine," I said. "Your balls growing is just the
first sign of puberty. It's nothing to get upset about."

I was the one with reason to be upset. I knew I should have
seized this opportunity to feel Adam's balls, to pinch them, hard as
I could, and see if sperm would squirt out like ketchup from the foil
packets we exploded in the school cafeteria. But I had missed my
opening.

Would our show-and-tell session now sputter to an anticlimac-
tic end? Would it be another six years before I was offered the chance
of flesh?

If Adam had had his way, it might have been. We had agreed
on a mutual jerk-off, but still consumed, perhaps, by his fears of
physical deformity, Adam pulled his Jockeys back on and clambered
into bed. That left me and Gil.

I had never thought of Gil Miller as even vaguely sexy. He was
not noticeably ugly, but seemed to exude an overwhelming wrong-
ness: too fat one moment, too skinny the next, the way a hologram
never looks quite right, no matter which angle you choose. He possessed some inexplicable quality that could turn conventionally cute
attributes—freckles, say—into nauseating blemishes. On his pasty
cheeks, the spray of sun-induced dots looked like stovetop spatters
of grease after a hamburger's been fried.

I resented Gil for his family's ostentatious wealth. They were
always the first in the neighborhood to have each new status symbol.
They rushed to buy a refrigerator with a built-in ice machine, a VCR,
a complete Atari entertainment set. On their den's mahoganied wall
hung a framed photograph of Gil's father shaking hands with Rich-
ard Nixon.

But when Gil squirreled into his sleeping bag, then tugged the zipper down a foot and invited me inside, I didn't hesitate. I was volcanic and would take what I could get. Adam's proximity might have stifled me but instead served as incentive: If Gil and I got things going, maybe Adam would change his mind and join.

At first we faced each other. The heat of two bodies—two revved-up, blood-rushing bodies—turned the sleeping bag tropical. Gil reached blindly down to my crotch, and if fingers had the capacity to gasp, that's what his did when they reached my dick.

"It's so big," he whispered, his breath stale and carbony in my face—or maybe it was the smell of campfires trapped in the sleeping bag's cotton weave.

"It's not," I said. "It's normal." But when I groped for his erection, and felt something, and was uncertain for a moment if it was his dick or a finger, I understood our difference.

"Roll over," I commanded, my voice suddenly barbed with a drill sergeant's impatient superiority.

"But then how can I—"

"Just roll over!"

How was it that an older kid could be so tiny, so hairless, so impotent? As with Dusty, I became aware of myself not only as the horny innocent boy aiming to get his rocks off, but as someone else, someone strangely adult. This was *my* show; I was director as well as star.

I tucked my boner into his butt crack, where, oddly, there was more hair than I'd felt above his penis. The bristles scratched my circumcision scar. I began to rub and grind.

"What are you doing?" Gil asked.

"Just wait," I said, too engrossed to explain the obvious: If I rubbed long and hard enough, there might be sparks.

I curled into him, reached around to pinch his fetal prick. I loved the control, enfolding him, the bug in my Venus's-flytrap. I squeezed tighter and redoubled my thrusting. Gil whimpered, more from fear, I think, than from pain.

A creak of springs above us brought my attention to Adam, who leaned his head over the bed's edge and stared as if Gil and I were exotic zooed beasts, rendered safe only by the distance between us. "You guys," he said, as I pushed once, twice, a third time into the clammy slot of Gil's behind, my hard-on a needle tracing his record groove, releasing perfect music. "You guys are *weird*."

On Adam's last word I stopped, deep in Gil's fleshy grip, and spray-painted my private graffiti on his burning skin.

A backwash of semen, with no place to go, coated me with my own sticky warmth. It was the first time I'd ejaculated in another person's presence, and it was different from coming by myself, better, more like peeing in its continuous fluid pleasure but also more violent, more like gunfire, like death.

"Gross," Gil shrieked, squirming to pull away. But there's only so much room in a sleeping bag. I lazed into him, my body leaden with satisfaction.

"What did you expect?" I said. "I thought that's what you wanted."

"I didn't know you'd make it wet," he said. "You didn't say *that* would happen."

And his innocence, his inexperience, made me start to get hard again.

Two days later, Gil was in my bedroom. No Adam. Just us.

Was there some pretense? Homework? After-school cartoons? I don't remember. Nor do I remember undressing. The scene begins with us naked, in bed.

"Can I show you something?" Gil asks, his voice shivery.

"Sure," I say. "What? What is it?"

"It's something a friend of mine showed me."

Gil's friends are all my friends. I wonder who this friend could be.

He slithers down my body, tenting the sheet above him so he remains invisible. I want to see him. I want to see his greasy freckled face as he does whatever secret thing he's planned.

Suddenly there is the wetness, the hot foreign wetness that steals a crucial part of me and clones it into a hundred throbbing replicas, then plants them back on my body so that my groin is an undersea forest of ticklish anemones.

Whoever taught Gil to give a blow job taught him well. His

mouth has the consistency of overripe peach flesh. Juice drips. His tongue laps it up.

I giggle, nauseous with giddy bliss. *Mr. Owl*, I'm thinking. *Mr. Owl, how many licks does it take to get to the Tootsie Roll center of a Tootsie Pop?*

Pop. There it goes. Into Gil's mouth. Then onto his cheeks when he pulls away. The sheet falls and I see the creamy smears on his nose.

"Why'd you do that?" he says, swabbing himself clean.

"I couldn't help it," I say. It's the truth.

"You ruined it. You ruined everything."

Ruined what? I think. How could anything that feels so good cause any harm?

"I'll do you, too," I offer, but Gil is already off the bed, pulling on his pants, out the door.

I called. I called and called. Gil's father, who seemed to stay home an awful lot for someone who hobnobbed with presidents, always answered, and always told me Gil was busy—raking the lawn, studying. I wondered what lie Gil had concocted to enlist his dad's protection.

Finally, one afternoon I caught him. He must have been expecting someone else to call. He picked up, and his squeaky prepubescent voice entered me like adrenaline.

"Can we get together?" I asked.

"I don't want to see you," he said.

"We don't have to do anything. We can just talk."

If I could just get Gil alone with me, I was sure I could have him again. We would do things differently this time. This time I'd find out exactly what he wanted.

"I have to go," he said. "My father's coming into the room."

"Please," I begged, "just for a little."

There was a pause. Gil's breath burst through the wires in painful spurts, like an unpracticed emcee testing a microphone. "Not in your house," he finally said.

"Okay. Not my house. The schoolyard? In five minutes. See you there."

Our houses sat five hundred feet from each other, on streets bordering opposite sides of the elementary school we'd both attended. We were in junior high now, but still considered the playground our rightful turf.

Gil arrived on his Huffy dirt bike, the latest overpriced toy his parents had lavished on him. It was an absurdly short distance to have biked. At first he circled me, coasting, backpedaling for balance. The knobby tires chattered on the hardscrabble infield.

"You're making me nervous," I said.

"You're making *me* nervous," he said. But he stopped, lowered his left foot as a kickstand. He wouldn't go so far as to dismount.

"Why are you being like this?" I asked.

"I told you I didn't want to come."

"I don't get it. Did I, like, miss something?"

Gil said nothing. He scuffed his Keds in the dirt. His body was doing that hologram thing again: good-looking, repulsive; visible, invisible.

I was aware that boys weren't supposed to do what Gil and I had done, but I considered this a reflection of adult stinginess, not any inherent vice in the act. Adults forbade all sorts of pleasures— drugs, masturbation, driving—the vehemence of their policing in direct proportion to the desirability of whatever was being withheld. The way I looked at it, Gil and I had pulled a fast one on the world. While everyone else was eating spinach, we'd snuck into the pantry and tasted dessert. I couldn't fathom why—now that we'd discovered each other's willingness—he would of his own accord choose to call things off. It was like finding a map to buried treasure, then burning it before you had the chance to dig.

I straddled the Huffy's front wheel. "You're the one who started things," I reminded him. "*You* told me to get in the sleeping bag. *You* wanted to show me that sucking thing."

"Let me go," he yelled. He torqued the handlebars, trying to break free, but I grabbed them and I was stronger. My crotch pressed against the bike frame's metal fork.

He shouted again, "Let me go!"

The rubber handlebar grips twisted against my palms. I felt the dry searing pain not just in my hands, but all over: the thrill of holding him captive.

"I thought you liked it," I said. "Let's try again. Can't we? Just once?"

"Get away!"

This time the tire knocked my knee. I toppled to the ground. Gil kicked my leg away and stomped on his pedals, accelerating across the playground with a spuming dusty afterburn.

There was no use chasing him. I limped home, not bothering to brush off my clothes, and locked myself in my bedroom. There, on the same old bed on which I'd doctored Dusty Wilson, the same sheet Gil had hidden under a week before, I unzipped my pants and jerked off. I thought not of the hallucinatory warmth of Gil's mouth; not of our tangle in the sleeping bag, my dick in his feverish butt. What I thought of—the memory that made me wet my own chin with an arcing gush of the liquid that had so disgusted Gil—was the feel of the Huffy's handlebar in my palms, the yanking friction burn when he'd struggled to pull away.

Gil's rejection confused me, but didn't lessen my resolve. The question was not if I *should* have sex with boys, but *how* I could best snare a co-conspirator. Someone younger, I decided. Someone more convincible.

Jason's house abutted a third side of Somerset Elementary's perimeter. He was two years behind me, a sixth-grader, which meant this was still actually his school, and that I wielded the allure of an alumnus, a junior high bus-riding sophisticate.

Every afternoon, after the bus dropped me off at the top of the hill, I would jog home, wolf a snack of cinnamon toast and orange juice, and walk across the street to the school grounds. Jason's backyard came right up to the asphalt basketball court, separated from it by a six-foot-high chain-link fence. I would loiter near the fence, pretending to study the Four Square courts and the giant dodge'm circle painted on the black pavement. Within five minutes, Jason would appear at his back door.

He had impossibly straight, nougat-blond hair that, unlike my stiff unruly waves, parted and reparted itself with a casual shake of his head. God, I wanted that hair. I wanted to weave it into a silky cocoon to sleep inside. I wanted to collect fallen strands from his pillow and use them to floss my teeth.

Jason's other features were equally entrancing: his pale blue cough-drop eyes, his architecturally perfect nose. His smile strained the capacity of his eleven-year-old face, like a seedling overwhelming its greenhouse cube of soil. He was ready to be transplanted, transported, to be taken to some new and better place. At least that's what I told myself.

The first few times we met, I made it seem as though I was just bored, looking for some competition. Hey, did he want to shoot some hoops? Jason would find his basketball, toss it to me, then scale the fence for a brief game of one-on-one. Neither of us was good enough to land the sphere through the metal net very often, even though it was handicapped for elementary-height munchkins. But I couldn't have cared less about the score. Just being so near to Jason, jostling with him as we fought for the ball, was ecstasy. Sometimes the mere scent of him was enough to distract the trajectory of my shots. He smelled like dirty laundry, like a musty rumpus room, like being crushed under a group of boys in a tackle-football pile.

I can't recall exactly when I first broached the topic of sex. It was probably after a session of basketball, perhaps a game I'd let him win, while we were sitting on the low wall beside the school maintenance shed.

We dangled our legs, banging sneaker heels against the concrete. My feet were big for my age, big enough to elicit admiring comments from shoe salesmen. But Jason, two years younger, had feet equally as large, and on his smaller, wiry frame, they verged on the grotesque. At the same time, they clunked with irresistible charm, like a galumphing puppy's outsized paws.

"Those are huge," I said, pointing to his forest green Pumas.

Jason shrugged. "They're new. I outgrew the other ones."

"Well, you know what they say. . . ." I elbowed him in the ribs, guffawing. He laughed along for a second, but I could tell he didn't have a clue what I'd meant. "Is it true?" I asked.

"What?"

"Is your dick really enormous, too?"

A rash of embarrassment rouged Jason's cheeks. He looked down to his lap, where his hands were folded protectively. Had they been like that a moment ago, or had he just moved them there?

"Well is it?" I persisted.

"I don't know. I don't have anything to compare it to."

"You've never seen another guy's dick?"

Jason shifted on the rough concrete. "I haven't . . . not when it's, you know."

"Hard?" I asked.

Jason nodded.

I just shook my head, hoping Jason would infer from my silence that his inexperience made him some kind of freak, unworthy of my eighth-grade attention. Then, when I offered to help him overcome his deficiency, my proposition would seem selflessly generous. He wouldn't be able to refuse.

"You could try mine," I finally said.

"What do you mean?"

"My dick. It's hard right now. Want to compare?"

Jason swallowed like someone trying to keep down his first illicit swig of booze. He looked toward his house. "I . . . I can't."

"Not here," I said. "We could go somewhere."

Jason jumped down from the wall. "I've got to go," he said, and ran for the safety of his backyard.

The next day, Jason met me at the chain-link fence as usual. Good, I thought; he's realized he wants it. I decided to act normal, pretending nothing had happened. If I let his desire dangle awhile, let him see I wasn't to be taken for granted, then the next time he wouldn't be so quick to turn me down.

"Ready to get beaten?" I said. "Best two out of three."

No response.

"Come on," I said. "Go get the ball."

Jason lowered his head. A few blond hairs fluttered like feathers. He kicked at a patch of lawn where the grass had been worn away, revealing blood-colored mud.

"What's the problem?" I asked.

"I don't think I want to play," he said.

I chortled, trying to make him feel ridiculous and unreasonable. "I don't have to hang around with sixth-graders," I said as if my companionship were a precious commodity. As if *I* weren't the desperate one.

"All right, just come to the fence," I tried. "I want to whisper something."

Jason didn't budge.

I could have climbed into his yard. I could have caught him and forced him to do anything. But I thought of Gil Miller: the angry cloud of dust as he'd fled on his Huffy, the ensuing year of chilly silence. I never understood exactly why Gil had shunned me, but I'd decided it had something to do with overeagerness, breaking the boys' creed of cool. Before Gil, I'd thought all you had to do was show how much you wanted something, and you'd receive it as reward; but now I wondered if I'd shown him too much. Now I knew there could be more power in *not* wanting than in wanting.

Jason turned and walked back into his house.

For six or seven days we met like that. Jason refused to climb over the fence and play, but he still seemed interested in my company. Buffered by a four-foot safety zone, he listened to my questions:

"Do you jerk off?"

"Can you come yet?"

"Have you ever seen anyone else come?"

Jason never responded much. He shrugged and twisted and bit his pinkie nail. The only time he answered with a distinct, emphatic "no" was when I asked if he had ever touched his little sister *there*.

Then one day, he didn't show. No lights were on in the house, and I figured maybe he was out with his mother on some errand. Perhaps he had a doctor's appointment. I pantomimed an imaginary foul shot and headed home.

The next day, too, he didn't come. This time I could see him through the kitchen window, a wispy shadow behind undulating curtains. I called out his name, proposing a game of one-on-one. I rattled the fence. When I yelled his name again, the shadow disappeared.

The failure with Jason injected me with self-doubt. I had been able to dismiss the Gil debacle as a casualty of my inexperience, but now I was forced to confront a pattern of rejection. I couldn't understand it. I craved sex like salt, searched for it in every nook and cranny of my life, and I'd always assumed every boy felt the same way. Why, then, would Jason—like Gil before him—decline the opportunity?

I was especially shaken by Jason's refusal, even with the fence between us, to bring his face near mine, as if my very breath on his skin would be dangerous. *Was* I dangerous? Was I so repulsive that no boy would have me? (My own boy-lust was so overpowering that it never occurred to me some guys just weren't attracted to other guys.)

My response was Newtonian: I reacted to self-doubt with an equal counteraction of brazenness. I immediately sought a new subject on whom to test my technique.

Matt Webb was another neighborhood kid, in Jason's class at school. He was small and mousy, with a nose curiously bumped, as though broken in some intrauterine boxing match. His feet were not nearly as large as Jason's, but they were still too big for his body. He didn't walk on them so much as they walked him. Unable to balance properly, he wore down the soles of his Adidas until the rubber squidged out like a fallen soufflé.

Sometimes, when I lay in bed at night, sheets tangled between my knees, just the thought of Matt's misshapen sneaker soles was enough to make me come.

It turned out we both held the job of walking our respective dogs. When our paths crossed one day after school, we stopped to let the pets get acquainted. My Siberian husky, Masha, lunged to sniff his golden retriever's rear end. The dogs' unabashed flirtation inspired me.

"Why do dogs lick their own balls?" I asked, the oldest joke in the book.

Matt shrugged.

"Because they can!"

His guilty laugh made me certain he was a better candidate than Jason—more mature, ready for tutelage.

I learned the exact time Matt set out for his daily walk, the three neighborhood routes among which he alternated. I adapted my own routine accordingly. We became dog-walking partners.

My jokes progressed from autofellating dogs to real, human sex. I dropped *boner* into conversation as often as possible. I hinted at knowledge I might share. Matt seemed suitably intrigued. He loped along beside me, his thin lips curled into a rapt, embarrassed smirk.

Once, I almost touched him. I could see the bulge in his right pocket, which I knew, since I'd seen him pull them out often enough at the end of his walks, to be his house keys. But I pretended not to know.

"What's that?" I asked, drawling the words with innuendo.

"What?" Matt asked.

"That." I pointed to his pocket. My hand hovered centimeters from the denim pouch. I could have plunged, could have burrowed my fingers in and collected his body-warmed lint.

"My keys," he stammered, showing me. Then he turned quickly away, jangling the tiny metal shapes that locked him nightly out of my reach.

In addition to our walks, I started calling him. The physical separation, the lack of eye contact, emboldened me to be even more explicit than I was in person. I asked if he'd ever measured his dick, if he had tried to suck himself, if he was circumcised. He refused to respond, but neither would he hang up. I could hear his ragged breath on the line. I knew he wanted more.

"When you're taking a shower," I asked one evening, thinking of Adam Glickman, "do you ever, like, check yourself? I was doing it the other day, and when I looked down, my balls were like twice their normal size. I wigged out, you know? I got it into my head that I had punctured a hole somewhere, and that hot water from the shower was pouring in. Pretty soon it was just going to swell up and explode and my balls would be, like, smithereens. But when I got out to dry off, I looked down again, and they were back to normal. I guess it was just the heat making them, I don't know, relax. Has that ever happened to you?"

"It's time for dinner," Matt said. "I've got to go."

When I called the next day, Matt's father answered the phone. I put on my most ingratiating Eddie Haskell voice. "Hi, Mr. Webb. May I please speak with Matt?"

Mr. Webb's cough was strained, mechanical. "Matt can't talk now," he said. "He's doing homework."

"Of course. When would be a good time to call back?"

"There is no good time. Don't call here anymore."

The phone clicked like a gun hammer cocking back.

I panicked. Had Matt told his father about my advances? His father would tell my parents, my teachers; I'd be dead meat. But then I thought of a worse possibility. What if Mr. Webb, on his own, had sensed something peculiar in my persistent attentions toward his son? If it was Matt who had accused me, I could deny everything, his word against mine. But if Mr. Webb had so readily detected, even in a thirteen-year-old, the rapacious mind-set, then maybe I really was a freak.

Kevin, the next and last, didn't need a father to intervene on his behalf.

He was only one grade below me. I was fourteen then; he must have been thirteen. I had noticed Kevin that summer at the town swimming pool. He swam butterfly for the team, and wore a purple-and-white regulation Speedo faded almost see-through by sun and chlorine. When he hopped, glistening, from the practice lanes, his suit would balloon comically with trapped air, and he would pat his crotch back to normal with a series of sputtering farts.

Even when he was done, though, his Speedo bulged in one telltale spot. Apparently, he hadn't learned to tuck his dick cashew-like over his balls as the other guys did. His jutted straight out like a handle, like something you could grab and crank to jump-start an engine.

At the pool I kept my towel handy, careful to hide my own embarrassing bulge. But at home, I posed in front of the bathroom mirror, arranging and rearranging myself in my swimsuit. First I would pretend I was Kevin, aiming my howitzer dick. Then I was his father. I barged in, chided him for his lack of shame. *Don't you know everybody in town's staring at you? It's indecent! Here, let me show you how to do it.* And I would stuff my dick roughly between my thighs, imagining it was Kevin's, until my suit's Lycra pouch bloomed in a sticky star.

When school started that fall, Kevin turned up at my bus stop. I flashed him looks as we waited, but he averted his eyes. When the bus arrived he quickly claimed a place next to Alison Crosby. I settled into the seat directly behind him. The bus lurched forward and I did too, almost sinking my teeth into the fuzzy nape of his neck. I blew a surreptitious stream of air, watched gooseflesh rise.

That afternoon I tailed him home. He lived not far from me, at the top of the street the police closed after winter snowfalls as a designated sledding hill. I memorized the address.

Our town had its own mini–phone directory, arranged geographically. I paged through, found his house, his name, his number. It all seemed far too easy.

His mother hollered for him and he came to the phone. I explained who I was. "From the bus? Remember? I sat behind you?" I didn't breathe heavily into the receiver. I didn't ask about his masturbation habits, the length of his erection, or the presence or absence of foreskin. I was absolutely polite.

Kevin said, "I know what you're doing. I don't want to talk to you."

Before I could defend myself he'd hung up.

The next morning he wasn't at the bus stop. The bus came. We boarded. The usual chatter. Halfway to school we passed him on Little Falls Parkway. He was riding his bike, his backpack humping beneath his jacket like a bizarre reverse pregnancy. He didn't look up. I never talked to him again.

Skulking around the neighborhood, scoping boys, scaring them. A dirty old man at six, twelve, fourteen. If what I had desired had been more socially acceptable, would I have been more appropriately romantic? Or would I still have coerced boys, plotted devious means of entrapping them? Were my tactics born of desperation, or did I enjoy the psychological deflowering?

During college, when I returned to my mother's house for holidays, I would walk the streets of the old neighborhood, past the houses of the boys I had stalked, then return to my childhood bed and masturbate to the memories. What if Kevin or Jason or Matt— or one of their younger brothers—had emerged and offered himself? Would I have consummated the obsession? Or after so many years of my settling for just the chase, had the chase itself become too essential to the attraction?

What about now? Should I tell you I jerked off five times in the course of writing this? That I almost didn't write it, because these are among my most precious sexual recollections, and I worried that consigning them to the page would sap their potency?

Even if I haven't propositioned a single underage boy since those early attempts—and, probably, I haven't—does my continuing fixation mark me as a predator? Am I a pedophile now?

And how about you? Did you get turned on reading this? Did it make you think of sex you've had with boys, or wanted to? Sex you've stolen or tried to steal? How about it? Are you?

DARIECK SCOTT

WHY I NEED

TO BE

GANG-BANGED

TO BE

TURNED ON!

SEVERAL MONTHS AGO I WAS AT MY GODMOTHER'S, clearing out some boxes of personal effects that had languished in her basement since my college graduation. With my godmother and my sister standing behind me, watching, I reached inside a dusty calendar-box and, to my surprise, pulled out a dirty magazine. That it was a porn mag was embarrassing enough; that it was a *heterosexual* porn mag, rife with shots of women displaying their bare breasts and gaping vaginas, was reason to faint. My godmother and sister, both of whom know I'm gay, gasped when they saw the cover. Neither spoke while I hurriedly tossed the thing into my pile of "saves," and though I shrugged and faked a laugh, I felt unmasked, revealed as a far more sexually perverse person than either would have imagined.

Called *Erotic Letters*, the magazine cover featured a blond woman sandwiched between two naked white guys; all three were nude, and their bodies glistened as if oiled with Vaseline. I had bought this lovely piece of filth when I was still struggling to be straight (ha-ha). One of the two men, slim and sleekly muscled with fine brown hair curling on his chest, I now recognize as one of my many "types." Above the cover photograph, a headline boldly promised to reveal WHY I NEED TO BE GANG-BANGED TO BE TURNED ON! Inside, this "true" erotic letter was accompanied by a two-page photo spread of another woman, crouched on all fours on a locker room bench. A tall blond man, naked except for the gold neck chain dangling in his chest hair, held his fat, half-hard dick at her lips, while another fellow took up position to pork her from behind. Three other dudes, one of whom had a vague resemblance to Kareem Abdul-Jabbar, stood in various states of undress, grinning. "My entire body had turned into one giant pussy and I was hot!" read the excerpt in a red-boxed insert.

It was cheesy stuff, a predictable rehashing of familiar male fantasies. Yet days later, as I read the letter in the privacy of my bedroom at home, I found myself becoming more and more aroused— and before I reached the story's end, I was flat on my back, my pants bunched at my knees and a stream of cum running down my torso.

The following is an account of how fantasies of heterosexual gang bangs—preferably involving randy, hairy young male athletes —have been a cornerstone of my development as a gay man. It takes place in two different settings, inside the American military base in Ansbach, West Germany (1979), and outside the American military base in Leavenworth, Kansas (1982). The names have been changed to protect the guilty (especially me). The attitudes of the males portrayed herein toward women—well, girls, since we were in our teens—is inexcusable, and I offer no excuse for it.

The two men: they were boy-men, I should say, exuding a musky physical masculinity as yet unmatched by emotional development. Angelo and Zay, I'll call them. Angelo was tall, while Zay was shorter than me, but aside from this difference in height they were uncannily similar, so much so that their presence in my life, their nearly identical sexual offers made three years and an ocean apart, seem more than coincidental. Both were slim and tightly muscled, standout athletes in football and basketball; both had large, occa-sionally buoyant Afros like eraser-heads stuck on pencils; both were of a light, sparsely freckled brown complexion that waxed at milky coffee and waned at a mellow tan; both had a quiet but mischievous manner; and both were possessed of a nubile magnetism that made dozens of girls fall at their feet with rapturous desire.

The long trail of broken hearts Angelo and Zay left in their wake gave most guys a chance to wallow in envy and to exploit the dejection of the casualties. I sniffed along the path for a different reason: to stake my own claim to the very pleasures the girls had won and then lost. No one seemed to suspect. I was quiet, excessively studious (my claim to fame), far from magnetic but capable of flashes of charisma, and the fastest sprinter in school (my second claim to fame). Under cover of this admirable and aloof facade, I stalked my male peers, obsessively and ravenously. I collected well-timed glances at their exposed, athletic bodies like wild game and dragged the prize carcasses home for private feasting. This hunt was so clandestine that I myself didn't become aware of it until many years later. As a sprinter, I never approached the fame of football or basketball players, but because I could outrace lots of guys who thought they were something in the 100-meter dash, I was respected by the in-crowd. I worked assiduously to hold on to this hard-earned regard. I dated girls, occasionally commented on girls, longed (or so I thought) to fuck girls.

That I was not, in fact, fucking girls, that I could scarcely even imagine myself doing so, ate away at me, poisoning every accom-plishment on the track or in the classroom. Fantasy became my only refuge against feelings of inadequacy and loneliness—a vast catalogue of jack-off fantasies where the boys I covertly lusted after cast aside cloak and dagger and behaved like satyrs, like lust-machines, fuck-ing, fucking, fucking.

Never in these dramas that took me to climax two and three times a night did *I* appear as a recognizable being. None of the girls was recognizable either; guys like Angelo and Zay were the stars of the show. Today memory has smudged the details of their faces, too, but I still remember well what it looked like to see them ramming their big dicks into tight little pussies (not that I'd ever *seen* a pussy, mind you, tight or otherwise), and the image, captured from behind, of their butts and balls in motion, circling sensuously, arching out, slamming back in. Those boys must have shot more jism in my dreams than they did in their own. They were raunchy and aggressive, my fantasy lover-boys-once-and-twice-removed, in control of the action but gloriously out of control of their frenzied desires. Inevitably in these fantasies my stud and I came at the same point, shortly after he gripped the bloated shaft of his johnson in hand, gave it a slow, preening stroke, and then poked its wide head at the faceless girl's asshole for a bone-shaking butt-fuck. The image shook *me*, at any rate. I had to conjure no more than two or three downward sweeps of his ass, give the merest flickering thought to his testicles bobbling between her thighs, the hair of them tickling, stinging her flesh—and I was gone. That the act of sodomy perpetually served as my conclusion is, of course, a telling detail. To flesh out its history and meaning, I have to turn to memories of a third friend of mine, Davis, who, while endowed with none of the beauty or aphrodisiac virility of Angelo or Zay, possessed powerful charms of his own.

One gray afternoon in ever-gray Ansbach—shortly after I had met and become enamored of Angelo—I accompanied my friend Davis Williams home during lunch period. Davis, once himself a frequent star in my nightly stroke-off fantasies, was on his way out. Angelo was much more handsome and far, far more popular, and being at that time a pure whore for good looks and high status, I had already let Davis slip from my mind.

No one was home in the Williams apartment; the shades were drawn, the living room dark and tranquil. Davis abruptly excused himself and fled to the bathroom down the hall, and I sat on the couch to wait for him to fix my lunch. Davis closed the hallway door behind him. I didn't hear a toilet flush, but in no time at all I looked up to see Davis's shape reappear in the beveled glass of the door. The door swung open.

Davis's fingers were wrapped around his hard dick, and his dark-chocolate balls swayed outside the zipper of his blue polyester pants. As he moved relentlessly toward me, he yanked his foreskin back and forth. "I *love* doing crazy things," he announced.

I had seen this thick, veined visitor before. One night a year earlier I'd slept over at Davis's house. In the hours before dawn, as we sat talking about sex and gossiping about who was doing whom, Davis calmly suggested that since all this talk was making us horny and all, and you know, since there weren't any girls around and stuff, why shouldn't I play his "girlfriend" and he play mine? I was taken aback—though playing his girlfriend was precisely what I had secretly desired for weeks. Still, I was all too aware that Davis's bedroom shared a wall with his parents'. To convince me, Davis whipped back the covers of his bed to reveal his naked lower body and showed me his stuff; I looked it up and down, and found myself powerfully drawn to the smell of his crotch as it wafted over to my nose. But I couldn't bring myself to take action—not much action, anyway: I do think that maybe I touched it and maybe he touched mine.

This time, though, Davis was going to have his surrogate girlfriend, and he wasn't taking no for an answer. I sat stunned, transfixed by the sight of his dick, and suddenly there he—they—were above me. Davis dropped one knee to the cushion of the couch. My lips were already parted in shock (not to mention that intoxicating crotch aroma) so I just naturally leaned forward, opened wide, and with a flick of my tongue took the thing into my mouth like a good girlfriend should. A part of me stood off, observing from some perch near the ceiling, aghast with horror and condemnation. The other part liked the taste of Davis's dick pumping in and out of my mouth and surrendered greedily to every vicious judgment that my observer flung from above: cocksucker, whore, faggot. Each insult seemed somehow to liberate me, incited me to greater depravity; it wasn't long before I lay stomach-down on the couch with my virgin eighth-grade behind raised in the air to receive Davis's forceful dicking (my memory of this is that it felt so good to have him on top of me that the entry didn't hurt at all; but that isn't possible, is it?). And it wasn't long after that that Davis fell upon his back and threw his legs up in the air for me to fuck him.

How it is that his parents arrived home and failed to detect the smell of three ejaculations and adolescent male sweat, plus stains of ass-juice on the couch cushions, I don't know. I do know that while Davis fixed me a very bland sandwich, and while we rather sheepishly walked back to school for fourth period, the pungent odor of our freshly fucked young black-boy butts was so powerful for me that it drowned out all else.

Soon enough, though, what we had done began to assume larger—indeed, biblical—proportions. Consumed with shame for what I had allowed to happen and terrified that Davis might tell our mutual friends, I shunned him, and when his family left Germany to return to the United States two months later, I was relieved. I vowed to my vengeful Old Testament God never to do "it" again, never even to think of it.

Skilled at repression, I was able to keep that vow for years, in letter if not quite in spirit: as a compromise, I made anal sex central to my boy-screws-girl fantasies. When Angelo mounted Girl X from behind and gave it to her Greek style, it was the smell of Davis and me fucking each other, the memory of that smell, that helped bring me to orgasm, every time. This peculiar hybrid of hetero sex scenes and sublimated homo passion disguised me from my harsh inner critic's censorious eye and proved a durable vehicle for expressing sexual desire—which brings me, finally, back to the nasty, ruthless allure of the heterosexual gang bang.

Angelo

Angelo, apart from being sweet-natured, tall, and cute, had his lineage going for him. He was the youngest in a trio of Coleman brothers who dominated the school's basketball team and dominated the school's hallways with their Afros. Because of his older brothers' stardom, Angelo drew an excessive amount of attention from the school's girls, who, like me, couldn't resist gorgeousness and prestige in the same package. Indeed, Angelo's package was the first thing I heard about him. In English class the seating chart surrounded me with three foxy black girls who shared girl-gossip with me just as if I were one of them. One day they were talking excitedly about a new find. Jane said, "Did you see him in gym class? His legs were wide open and he had on those little shorts." It always threw me, how dirty girls were in talking about guys. Tara said, "Yes, girl. And his thing went from here to there." She traced a long, sweeping U in the air with her finger. Denise assented. "It wasn't a dick, it was a snake, girl."

If I were canine, my ears would have shot straight up. "Who are you talking about?" I asked as if I didn't really care. "Angelo Coleman. He just came to high school, and they already putting him on the varsity team." "Mmmhmm, and he will be on *my* team, soon."

I made a face of disgust to keep up appearances, but when the bell rang, I hit the hallways searching for Angelo. Later, I had collected enough glances below Angelo's belt to ascertain that he was indeed carrying an ample length—though likely no more ample than that of a dozen other guys. In that era we all wore tight pants and we all did a pretty good job of arranging the contents to our advantage. But scoping out a Coleman crotch was like the thrill of star-fucking: the mere fact of the guy's fame added two or three inches, in girth and length. Whether he deserved it or not, Angelo came to monopolize my sexual fantasies over the next several months. My vision of him was almost always from below, tethered to his feet along with some nameless, faceless female sex slut, the two of us begging to receive his gifts. Standing straddle-fashion above us, the phantom Angelo would peel those tight pants off his slender hips, serving up a dense tangle of pubic hair, followed closely by a coffee-colored snake that dangled halfway down his muscular thighs.

Another effect of Angelo's being a member of royalty was that he pulled a lot of "trains."

Papa Coleman and his family lived on a small auxiliary base in Crailsheim, forty kilometers away from the main army installation at Ansbach. Only a few other military families lived with the Colemans out there in the boonies, and since the teenagers of this group were mostly male, it had become something of a regular practice in Crailsheim for the guys to share the few female distractions around. Many were the Monday mornings when the Colemans and their Crailsheim friends disembarked from their hour-plus bus ride to Ansbach talking in low voices about the "train" they'd run the previous weekend.

Running—or, as the parlance had it, "pulling"—a train involved bringing several guys together with a girl who was remarkable either for her adventurous sexuality or for her hapless susceptibility to male lies. One of the guys, the good-looking or suave one, would approach a likely candidate and with guile, persistence, and probably alcohol, persuade her to drop her pants while a number of other dudes lined up behind him for a ride. (I'd have figured that by the time the "caboose" had done the deed, Girl X would be a traumatized mess; but I was acquainted with several girls who'd gone on these debauched little journeys, and they appeared to be surprisingly nonchalant, sometimes even proud.)

I never angled an invitation to stay over at the Coleman house, nor did I ever happen to be in their company when, as I imagined it, a wave of lust and a curiously accommodating female body swept down from the sky like lightning. My curiosity grew. I began to want to witness one of these "trains." I wanted, especially, to watch while Angelo took his turn. I wanted to be right up next to him as he did it. This was not a simple desire, not merely voyeuristic; nor was it only a masked wish to play girlfriend, to lie as I imagined the girl lying beneath him, gasping for breath with her (my) hands on the sweat-slick globes of his ass—though surely this was part of it. As much as that I wanted to experience Angelo himself as the sensations coursed up the length of his dick and swirled around in his hips; somehow, I thought, in being present for this scene I could possess Angelo completely, occupy him in the glory of his masculine power, at the same time as, in identifying also with the girl, I could pour out my pent-up passion for him and allow it to consume me.

So it was that a surge of terror hit me when the moment came to fulfill my desire—terror that I would stand revealed at last for the lust-sick gay-boy I really was. In retrospect, I needn't have feared. Angelo wanted me, too, in his way.

On the very last day I saw him, Angelo was visiting my neighborhood, having stayed after school for a farewell to his Ansbach buddies (of whom I was proudly one) before his family moved back to the States. As evening came, I found myself one of only two well-wishers who remained at Angelo's side. The other was Norman, an awkward, overweight, light-skinned fellow whose inept forays into athletics were regularly ridiculed behind his back. Norman and I were both the sons of African-American officers, few in number on that post, and so our parents often threw us together. As a general matter he embarrassed me, and I never resented his presence as much as on that evening, when I wanted Angelo all to myself.

We were loitering outside the DYA—the Dependent Youth Activities center, a small, useless block of cement that housed some pinball machines and an alcoholic coordinator. A girl named Jenny was also there, and Jenny was, of course, flirting with Angelo. To my mind this was a hopeless task, since Jenny's appeal rested largely in her two tiny nubbin-breasts (padded with tissue to round them out to the size of apples) and the Farrah-flip of blond hair on either side of her face. The acne pimples glossed over with too much white powder didn't help much, either. (I'm being harsh, I know, but that's how I thought of her. The only girls who got my respect in those days were pretty and/or smart and/or African-American, and since Jenny fit into none of these slots, she remains in my memory painted in the unkindest terms. She, like Norman, was coming between me and my man, and I didn't like it.)

Norman and I stood a few feet off, leaning against the wall of the DYA as the sun fell and Jenny did her best to work her wiles. Angelo grinned and teased her. He touched her arm with his long fingers, laughed, and at one point seemed to corner her with his lanky body. She looked up at him and didn't move. I couldn't hear a word passing between them. Angelo's tight amber pants were plastered to his narrow behind. All at once he broke away from her, she drifted inside, and he came over to where Norman and I waited.

"Well, man, in two days you'll be back in the world," Norman said for the thirteenth time.

"Yeah, I'll be in the clouds lookin' down on you mugs," Angelo said. He angled his hand in the air like a plane in takeoff.

"Yeah. Things won't—it won't be the same around here, man. We won't have Angelo to show us how it's done, man," Norman blathered. "We'll miss you."

That shocked me, because it was emotional and true, and Norman was supposed to be a guy like the rest of us. "Yeah," I said gratefully. My heart was pounding.

Angelo smiled; it was a smile midway between genuine appreciation of our affections and the salacious smirk he wore in my fuck fantasies. "Well," he said in a suddenly low and slightly nervous voice, "as a going-away present to me, why don't you two come join me and ride this train?"

I was stunned. If Angelo had pulled me aside from Norman into the deepening shadows of nightfall, unzipped his amber pants, and let the contents spill into his hand for my attention and worship, I could not have been more fulfilled, more vindicated.

Yet I neither refused nor accepted. Frozen, shut down, I don't think I said anything. Norman did some hemming and hawing, the result of which—apparently—was that Angelo dropped the idea. Or maybe Jenny somehow nixed the idea. Maybe she cast an eye toward Norman and me and thought, *fuck, no*. I would have been able to empathize; the thought of sharing Angelo with Norman and Jenny both was nauseating. The combination of this nausea and the terror of getting what I had wished for (when I knew what I wished for was *BAD*, in about seventy different ways) made a ghost of me at that fateful hour; if I answered Angelo at all, it must have been barely audible, so delicate a whisper that he could only construe my response as a negative.

But if my mind and body disappeared, my ears did not, and they rang with his words for days. I remember watching the clock on the following Sunday, and calculating just when his plane would lift off. *Why don't you join me and ride this train?* I kept focusing then, and I focus now, on that "going-away present" bit. How could the three of us fucking Jenny together have been a gift to *him*, to Angelo Coleman, object of desire for nearly every girl in school? I had an inkling that I quickly squelched, but that today seems clear and incontestable: that there was desire in Angelo's request, desire for me (and for Norman, too, I guess, though even now I shudder at the thought). There was risk and vulnerability in what he said, for it was clear to all three of us that he could have had Jenny by himself. To ask that we be there with him was to reveal that it was not the riding alone that enticed him but the train itself, and whatever the train meant to him. I was not, it turned out, entirely alone in my fantasies.

This may seem obvious—but for me this revelation was as new and wonderful as it was unsettling. Where Davis's cunning and brazen seduction left me feeling used and guilty, Angelo's invitation, however much it paralyzed me, felt to me like genuine affection. I don't think that before he said those words I had ever experienced love coming from another male in a form that I could receive. Today Angelo lives in my memory less as a stud than as a sweet, kind, almost angelic welcoming presence.

Then, too, what he also bequeathed me was an ever-keener desire to do the gang-bang thing; and when the next invitation came my way, I didn't hesitate to accept.

Zay

Zay Winston dwells in my memory as a mischievous grin and sexy body hair. Apart from his Afro (already out-of-date by the time I met him; but this story takes place in Leavenworth, Kansas, where up-to-the-minute fashions were not exactly commonplace), he had sideburns that curved to the outer regions of his cheeks, five-o'clock shadow to rival Don Johnson's (we're talking early eighties now), and the thing that almost always captures my lustful attention: hair creeping up above his shirt collar. Since Zay and I ran track together, I had the pleasure of checking out his hairy legs, too, and the fan of hair spreading over his trim, sinewy brown chest. And then his crotch and his ass—especially his ass. Once when his back was turned to me in the locker room, he bent down and I stared, never having seen such an abundance of hair on anyone's butt.

Like Angelo, he had a quiet but highly active sexual drive. This drive drove him to occasionally absurd—and, for me, irresistible—behavior. Apparently one night Zay, drunk out of his mind, had unzipped himself in a crowd of girls and whipped it out right there for everyone to see. "Ain't I got a nice one?" Zay had supposedly said. Then there was the fact that he was dating a white girl. What little knowledge I had then of interracial couplings seemed always to be absolutely soaked in nasty sex and uncontrollable lust. When I watched Zay and his girlfriend grind on each other between classes in the hallways, the myths we pass around like currency in American culture would spring to mind: black men's and white women's secret lust for one another; the huge size of black dicks; the whorish ways of white girls. I objected vehemently to these offensive clichés—but at the same time, I couldn't resist the excitement they stirred in me.

Zay's border-crossing into the steamy environs of racial and sexual myth was not the only such foray. One day in journalism class

Victor, the white boy who sat next to me—he was a gorgeous crea-ture, a wrestler with high cheekbones and full lips and a talent for wearing Levi's exactly as they should be worn; oh, I had a *major* crush on him—one day Victor turned to me and whispered, "Last night I had sexual relations—with a black girl." Well, *that* got me going. He proceeded to tell me how (1) he had been driving around town one night with his fellow wrestler Ray, a black guy, and Vanessa, a very cute and very peppy black girl who was an officer's daughter, when (2) she put her hand on Victor's knee and said, "Let's get this Oreo going" (I admire her brazenness to this day), and (3) he was afraid Ray, who wanted Vanessa, was going to kill him, but after they dropped Vanessa off, Ray told Victor to go for it—warning him to keep the liaison a secret, because if they were found out, "No white girl will ever sleep with you again." Victor actually believed this, but the risk of being forever barred from white pussy didn't stop him from getting two-thirds of an Oreo going with Vanessa at the next opportunity. "And the blood *poured*," he said, while I lis-tened, rapt. I was given the blow-by-blow for the week or two that this dangerous secret affair lasted; at one point Victor even cooked up a little scheme where he would publicly date a white girl while I publicly dated Vanessa. "And then," he said, "when we get to the bedroom . . ."

In a town that was as ample in its supply of racial bigotry as any other white-bread, countrified village in the Midwest, the high school students, especially the athletes, were busy as beavers sampling the wares of the other side. Despite Victor's example, however, the samplers were almost inevitably black guys and white girls—a cou-pling which began to make its way into my sexual fantasy life, and which brings me to the story of Zay.

Zay was a sprinter like me, the team's second-fastest in the short races. Since the Leavenworth High track team was so small, he and I became friends—although, of course, this was not entirely happen-stance, since having zeroed in on his hirsute butt-cheeks, I naturally had to zero in on him.

The youth of Leavenworth spent Friday and Saturday nights cruising the one or two main strips of the town. On any weekend evening you could expect to find a large proportion of people from school lounging in the Burger King parking lot, at the video game arcade, in the so-called mall, or lined up in their cars at the park. One spring night near the end of track season, Zay and I were driving together in my gold Trans Am with the eagle sticker on the hood. (This make and model of car was, along with my collection of *Jet* magazine Babes of the Week, part of my meticulously crafted heterosexual cover.)

I was thrilled merely to be at Zay's side, but he was getting bored. Stretched out in the passenger seat of the car with his hands clasped behind his Afro, he looked like he was going to fall asleep. To salvage his attention, I said—unconvincingly, I thought—"I wish there were some girls we could hang with."

Suddenly Zay became animated. "Karen Bell! That's what we need tonight, man! You heard about Karen Bell?" I had not. "Karen Bell, man, the junior? She's this white girl who likes to get fucked by black guys. You know what I mean?"

I didn't exactly—but I wanted to know. "How do you know that?"

"DeVaughn told me." (DeVaughn was a fellow track team member, though, like Zay, his real claim to fame was as a football player.) "He was over at Mark Dennison's apartment" (Mark was a guy who'd graduated a couple of years ago) "and him and Ray Wilkins" (the same Ray who missed an Oreo in Victor's car) "and Billy Jameson, Scott—all those dudes were chillin'" (the dudes in question were all football players, all African-American). "And then I guess they got some ideas into they heads, man, because Mark called up this Karen Bell girl and told her that they were there. And she came over."

He gave me a meaningful look. "They all sat around in a circle in front of the TV, and she went around and sucked all of 'em off. Then they took turns fucking her. I hear Ray Wilkins was about to go wild. He wanted to do all kinds of shit. They had to pull him off her."

"What was he trying to do?" I asked. My thoughts had snapped immediately to an image of big Ray, trying to lodge his dick in Karen's asshole.

"I don't know. But you know how big that motherfucker is."

He laughed. "And then Phil Wallace" (another African-American) "told me that he went by and picked her up at her house, and they parked right down the street from there, and he and his cousins fucked her in the backseat."

"All of his cousins?"

"Two or three of them. Some of them boys wasn't but thirteen! It doesn't matter to that girl who she sucks, long as he's black. Long as *it's* black."

"Mmmm," I murmured. I began to feel hot and uncomfortable, thinking of all those guys together. I turned the idea over and over in my mind before I was able to say it: "So, uh, where would you find—do you know how to get in contact with this girl?"

"Nnnot . . . really," he said. He straightened in his seat and smiled. "Why? You want to find her? Tonight?" He was teasing me, I'm sure. I didn't drink, didn't smoke pot, and was rarely if ever seen at a party; he probably figured that I wasn't serious. But he didn't know about my experience with Angelo.

"Yeah. Let's find her." I tried to rein in my excitement so that I would sound resolute but nonchalant, like, *Why not? I've pulled trains before.*

Zay shifted in his seat. Equally coolly, he said, "All right. Let's find her."

So we went looking for Karen Bell—which meant, essentially, that we kept driving just as we had been, but now we slowed down at every parking lot to narrow our eyes and peer out of the windows to see if we could spot her. At one point, off the main strip, we passed a little grocery store. Its lot was empty except for a familiar pickup truck that stood tall on massive, jacked-up wheels. "Ain't that DeVaughn's ride?" Zay said.

I wheeled into the lot just in time to see DeVaughn exit the store sucking on a Big Gulp. DeVaughn stood tall just like his truck, and he had big feet, big hands, a big, sleepy-eyed face, and nice big lips. Despite his laconic, easygoing demeanor, DeVaughn struck me as one of the nastiest, most lascivious individuals in the school; and I just knew he had the school's longest, nastiest dick. Most of this fantasy was based on what I and everyone else and their grandmother must surely have noticed—his huge balls, like little planetoids, bulging in the crotch of his pants, so tightly packed, tucked, and zipped up you figured they had to hurt him when he walked. A man like that would be insatiable, I was sure; so much testosterone was swimming in his system that he wouldn't be sated unless he came three or four times every time he got laid.

"Whusup? What you two niggas doin out here this time of night? Looking for trouble?" He cast a dubious glance at me. DeVaughn generally kept his distance from me, and something in his attitude was mocking. I always had the sense that he knew the little game I was running, and that he was watching, waiting for me to be unmasked.

Zay gave him a slow smile. "We're looking for Karen Bell."

DeVaughn had been leaning into my open window, but now he stood straight up. The straw from the Big Gulp fell to the ground. "Naw! *You?!*" He stared at me.

Hesitantly, I nodded.

"Really?"

"Yeah, man," Zay said. "You know where we can find her?"

DeVaughn only laughed, which made me so upset I stopped breathing.

"Why don't you come with us, man?" Zay said in a low voice.

I looked up at DeVaughn with sudden hope: to see Zay and him, together . . .

But he shook his head and smiled. "Naw, I don't think so. I'm busy. You ain't gon find that girl tonight anyway. Her daddy probably has her shit locked up, with all those Negroes sniffing around." He looked away and seemed to consider changing his mind. Then he shrugged. "But then if anybody can find that ho, you can." He turned to me. "You know who you got driving around in your car, man? This boy is the pussy magnet. Lucky motherfucker. You just gon get to dip yo shit in *everything*, huh? He tell you about when he had those two girls at the same time? One white, one black? Shit." At that he stood up again and thumped the side of my car with his knuckles. "You let me know what happens," he said, and with that, climbed into his truck.

After he was gone, Zay suggested that we head toward the school. "I think she lives over in that direction."

"What's he talking about?" I asked. "This black-white two-girls thing?"

Zay made a face. "It's not really anything," he said at first, but eventually he gave in. Zay liked talking about sex nearly as much as he liked engaging in it. "Aw, it's no big deal, man. Last summer I was playing in a baseball league, and you know Delia Williams? And Cassie Davenport, the white girl? They were cheerleaders for our team. So one night after the game the three of us was hanging out, and I don't know, we got drunk, or *they* got drunk, and before you know it, Delia was challenging me. With this *dare*. She dared me that I couldn't have sex with two girls at the same time. You know, that I couldn't come twice." (It sounded like a stupid dare to me, but then I guess Delia knew exactly what she was doing.) "Soooo— they came over to my house and took turns sucking me off. In my front room."

He smiled, perhaps reliving the memory. I tried reliving it myself: Did he stand and did they kneel before his hairy belly, one after the other, or did they kneel together? Did he flop himself on his mother's red-cushioned Queen Anne chair and flip it out so that they could kiss the tip as it hung below the seat of the chair? Did they deep-throat him or just lick him like a lollipop?

He shrugged, and preoccupied as I was, I almost thought for a moment that his gesture was in answer to a different, more urgent question. But instead of turning to me with his hand gripping his crotch and saying, "You want to suck it, Darieck? Yes, you do. I know you want it," he said, "DeVaughn got all excited about it. Acts like it's a big deal."

DeVaughn and I were in agreement.

We traveled quietly for the next several minutes; with a point or a grunt, Zay had me taking turns onto streets I had never seen before, dimly lit and framed by rows of silent houses, vague and decrepit as if covered in moss. As we passed by each one I began to panic. I couldn't picture myself fucking Karen. What if I couldn't follow through at all, if the only thing that excited me was Zay's naked body, and everyone could tell? And then there were logistical quandaries: Was she really so horny that she'd spread herself out in the backseat as soon as she saw us? (I was mystified by the question of how girls got sex when they wanted it; I figured that if I were a girl, spreading out and getting right down to business would be pretty much what *I* would do.) Or were we going to have to talk her into stripping down—and how were we going to do that?

I took another turn and Zay directed me to slow down; we came to idle across from a wide, gray, clapboard two-story house with windows seemingly draped in gauze. A single light shone from the house's lower floor.

My throat was dry and I didn't bother to ask whether this was the place, at last. I started trying to will my cock to get hard, but by then I was shuddering with fear.

Zay leaned forward and squinted through the driver's-side window. "This might be it," he said.

We both watched the door of the house, as if Karen Bell was going to smell black dick from across the street and come running, panties at her knees. I don't remember how long we sat without moving. Zay seemed to waver; all of a sudden he couldn't be sure this was her house. Shouldn't we check the name on the mailbox or something? I suggested. "Hmmm," Zay said, but still he didn't move, and I sure wasn't going to move if he didn't.

I guess the spirit of Norman was with me that night, just as he'd been two years earlier when Angelo had asked for his going-away present. In far too short a time for my purposes, Zay told me to take my foot off the brake and drive on. We cruised slowly down the street and made a turn. I hoped that maybe he had remembered where she really lived, or that he'd thought of some other girl that we two studs could recruit for a backseat ball. But soon I began to recognize the neighborhood; we were headed for Zay's house.

Maybe he would invite me in, I mused, or maybe he had something else up his sleeve. But Zay's mind was still on Karen Bell. The farther behind we left the mysterious gray house, the more his vigor and confidence rebounded. "I'll get her number from Phil; he's got it," he said happily. "I'll call her, and then we'll go pick her up. We'll make her work for that shit. Take it out and slap her face with it."

Zay's last words on the subject took me by surprise. Slap her face with it? I had never heard of such a thing, not even in the raunchy letters of *Penthouse Forum* magazines I filched from beneath my father's bed. My excitement about Zay increased. Any guy who thought that much about and that much *of* his own dick was my kind of man. I craved a chance to watch him use it for real.

Yet unlike Angelo, who wanted the company of his fellow males to make heterosexuality worthwhile, Zay, I think, preferred the pleasures of telling his friends the tales of his sexual adventures. For him, maybe, it really was all about his dick. He loved it, thought it magnificent, the source of unexpectedly incredible joy, and like any-one with a great natural gift, he wanted people to appreciate it—girls up close and guys at a distance. I'm sure he would have liked to demonstrate its prowess to me in the flesh, and showing off must have been a part of the allure of pulling a train with me. But where Angelo had found a way to manage his need for male attention and erotic camaraderie and keep it safe, Zay flirted with the idea but couldn't quite bring himself to follow through. Perhaps he sensed the risks of showing off his "nice one." I would have dropped to my knees in his front room if he asked me to, and maybe he knew that. I think by that time, finally, even I knew it.

At the end of that summer my father was transferred to Texas, and from there I went off to college in California, never to see Zay again. However, I did call him one evening a few months later from my dorm room. In the midst of a conversation about his decision not to go to college—which shocked me—and my decision to quit the university track team—which shocked him—he told me he had finally hooked up with Karen Bell.

For some reason, I felt anger rather than excitement. "Oh? Just you by yourself?"

"What?"

"By yourself?"

"Oh . . . yeah."

"So. What happened?"

Maybe he caught the glint of something sharp in my tone, because he didn't offer his customary detail. Instead he let the low purr of his voice illustrate what he wanted to reveal. "She came over to my place. . . ."

I pictured his front room again, though I had never actually seen it. "And?"

"Well, she showed me what she had . . . and . . ."

"And you showed her what you've got," I completed the sentence for him, unable now to conceal my fury at having been betrayed.

Soon after, we hung up.

We talked once more, the next summer when I was supposed to take Greyhound up to Kansas for a visit, but didn't.

I did not learn in our subsequent conversation whether or not he'd slapped her face with it.

Fantasy:

We find Karen Bell leaning in loneliness against a video game at the arcade. Looking for love and convinced that nothing resembles love so much as a big black dick jammed up inside her (oh, how her father would die if he knew!), she is easy prey to Zay's cajoling whispers, his insinuating little grin, the pat of his palm on her flat ass. The mere smell of him as he stands close to her, the curly wisps of hair at the open neck of his polo shirt—they're enough to make her want to jump him right there. Me, she's not so sure about; but I'm dark and I have nice pecs, and aren't skinny guys supposed to have big ones?

We park on a dark stretch of road in a quiet place on the outskirts of town. I've been driving and Zay's been in the backseat getting Karen revved up with his knobby fingers digging in her snatch and his tongue darting into her mouth. Now that I'm no longer limited to glances in the rearview, I turn around and watch my boy pull Karen's pants down to her ankles and then over her feet. Her bare butt rests against the soft bucket-seat cushions of my Trans Am. Up on his knees above her, Zay works his Wrangler boot-cut jeans over his hairy, delectable little ass and hard thighs. I'm salivating over his ass but can't see that twice-sucked-off-in-the-front-room super-dick until he shoves his hips forward to her mouth.

It comes into view, slender with a large, fat head like a huge walnut. Then she wets it with her lips, and the head and half the length disappears. He takes the hair on her head into his hands and begins wildly to fuck her face, while I hurt my neck straining to see and almost catch the skin of my dick in my zipper fumbling to jack off. I listen to his breath, thickening like my cock, and yearn to kiss his mouth, to smell his ragged breath. He jerks his ass forward, hard. I see his hairy balls like two dark kiwis flail at her chin. He grunts and comes and I can feel it; I can feel the sensation of her mouth on the head of his dick, the overpowering need thudding in his chest and tight in his throat, the thrill of having a dick and having it be so monstrously, pulsatingly hard, the feel of his fingers twisted in her hair at the back of her head, the pushing, the force, and the rank, intoxicating smell of his pubic hair at her nose.

"Now you, man," he says, beckoning. Just the gesture of his hand in my direction makes me hard. With the wetness of her mouth and the memory of the sight of him as I relive the scene over and over in my mind, I blow a big load on Karen's tongue and buck uncontrollably against her face in ecstatic orgasm.

I can feel Zay's eyes on my back. As he watches, he strokes his dick hard and slow.

Awkwardly, I withdraw. Zay moves me aside and shoves his sticky dick far up into Karen's wet cunt. She squeals, then starts grinding in time with his nasty corkscrew strokes. I watch his ass and balls until I can no longer resist. I get down on my knees like a dog. I grab his hairy cheeks in my hands and thrust my tongue between them. The musky aroma of the sweat there and the taste of his butt-juice overwhelms me. I ream his ass in a frenzy, trying to keep up with his thrusts as they come harder and harder and faster and faster. I swab his bouncing balls with my tongue. He lets out a long, gurgled moan as if in pain, and so does she. His spasms peak and then slow, and I dip down and pull his dick from her cunt so that I can lick the bulbous head as it spews its last gobs of thick white cum.

. . . After we recover, Zay gets the idea to have me stick it to

Karen while he crawls up from behind to give his dick a taste of black-boy butt.

We drive Karen home, and make a date for next Friday night. Then I drive Zay home. We say nothing. I'm afraid of what he's thinking. But just before he closes the door of the car and goes into his house, he bends down and looks me in the eye, winks, and flashes me a welcoming smile.

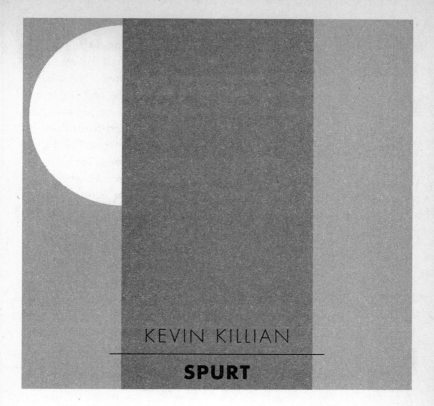

KEVIN KILLIAN

SPURT

"The blood is the life."
—Renfield, in Bram Stoker's *Dracula*

MY LITTLE CAR VIBRATED UNDER ME, AS THOUGH ITS ENGINE
were announcing exciting plans to fall apart, but I didn't pay much
attention. Tears were drying on my face. I was preoccupied, you
might say; I simply hadn't the time for car trouble. For a week the
temperature had stayed high above ninety degrees, and the radio
announcers kept saying it was going to rain. Even at night the heat
was thick and hot, like a soup, but I kept driving, for when you're
drunk, no challenge is quite beyond you. Traffic was light on the
Long Island Expressway. Full moon, and moonlight revealing huge
purple clouds scudding east, always before me, moving faster than I
could. Squinting, I tried to read the hands of the dashboard clock.

It was either 4:00 A.M. or 4:00 P.M. I was driving east, into the moonlight, away from the belt of lights that surround New York, and I was so drunk I could hardly keep my eyes open. My lids felt heavy, as though while I was crying some evil genie had implanted them with iron filings. My face felt like one of those cast-iron spigots that pour water into old-time zinc-lined, claw-footed bathtubs.

"I'm spent," I mumbled—that seemed dramatic. For luck I grabbed the bottle of Glenlivet that stood propped between my thighs, its long glass neck tapping the vibrating steering wheel. Single malt whisky that had lain undisturbed in some Scottish cavern for more years than I'd been alive and now, *glug glug glug*—created just for me, on my dumb day of grief. On Monday morning I'd start cracking the books and really put my nose to the grindstone and work on the dissertation. You must keep going, I said to myself, like a coach giving a pep talk to a reluctant player. All the same, tonight, I would try to imagine that I wasn't returning to school; that I was done with writing and thinking; that I'd never met Tim Baillie.

Something magical about really flogging your car, and the clear stretch of highway ahead; and feeling the motor and its complex accoutrements shudder under your heavy foot. And dipping an elbow out into the hot summer night and watching towns go by like reflections in shop windows—whole towns and neighborhoods, gone, gone, gone. You lose touch with the world—a car is an island all its own, another world; a world from which, perhaps, you might never return.

The radio, staticky and shrill, burst out with bass-heavy Motown, then the abrupt, insinuating guitars of the Eagles. A low-slung, dark car passed me on the right, gleaming like a streak of phosphorescence under a Jamaican sea. Sucker must be doing a hundred easy. Lotus. Then the driver seemed to slack in speed and I was passing him. I saw his face—couldn't help it, he was staring right at me.

Cute guy, in a sleeveless T-shirt, tanned, beach-boy look, shock of curly blond hair on top of his head, big pink rubbery lips and dark eyes staring at me. Like he'd seen a ghost.

One hand rested on top of the wheel, lazily, as though he could drive without looking ahead. I sped up, and he sped up too. Cruise

control. I caught him looking at me, again and again, and he flicked
on the driver's seat light, a plastic dome that filled his car—for a
brief moment—with a thin plastic light, like cheap statuary of the
Church. I guess he knew how hot he was. His lips parted. I could
see him trying to speak, or signal. Eighty miles an hour and his
mouth was saying, "Wanna fuck?" I nodded, he nodded, I got hard,
I shifted the bottle, the Eagles wailed, over and over, about how
dangerous life was in California. Our cars kept passing each other,
and his image faded in and out of the open passenger seat window.
"Let's," I heard him call, and my car leapt ahead a length or two.
Then he was beside me again. A sheen of sweat made his upper body
look wet, as though someone had pulled him out of the shower and
thrown him into a moving car and said, "Drive!" He was my dumb
guide race-car stud boy, come to lift the cover off this hot sultry
night and show me love's underside. Or something.

I swung in behind the tail of the Lotus and we slowed down
to a sedate 65 mph into the right-hand lane, and a few interchanges
later fishtailed out onto an exit, by a gas station and a diner. Under
the purple neon lights of the diner we parked side by side. The Lotus
was a gorgeous lime green, a color that the purple neon and the
purple clouds overhead kept remarking on, whispering among themselves. Buzzing about. *Bzzzzzzz.* "Where we going?" I asked—don't
even know if I asked in words. When I jumped out of the car, the
air smelled of burning rubber, and he was pulling off leather driving
gloves. He was six feet tall, disheveled, with long ropy arms, supple
with muscles and fading tattoos. Steam covered the parking lot to a
level of about four feet high, up to our chests. The net result was I
couldn't see if he was hard, but knew he was. A thick white steam
like dry ice, or the hot air that pushes up Marilyn's skirt in *The Seven
Year Itch.*

"I'm Scott," said my new boyfriend. "You know where the
Meadowbrook is?" "The motel?" Calculations spun in my head like
the apples and oranges in a slot machine. He shrugged, and the
muscles in his shoulders rippled. He said to follow him. But first he
kissed me, his big lips pressed flat against mine. When he broke
away my mouth was aflame. "How old are you?" Scott said, like a
challenge. I couldn't think if he wanted me older or younger, so I

told the truth. "Twenty-five." One time in life when truth seemed to do the trick. "Grand," he said, sliding into the Lotus butt-first. "It's room 813," he said. "We've got it all night." Foolish me! I thought "we" meant me and him; boy, did I ever get that one wrong! I got back into the Maverick and took another slug of Glenlivet, checked my wallet, then followed Scott down an access road past strip malls and gas stations and into the huge, eerie, almost empty motel lot. They should have called it "Salem's Lot."

Any of you ever been to the Meadowbrook Motel? I don't even know if it's still standing. In 1978 it was a sex motel, catering to the needs of suburban adulterers who could steal an hour from the PTA and the IRS and rent by the hour—what my cop pals called a hot-sheet pad. The Meadowbrook reared up its proud head like some Vegas monstrosity, its huge lobby studded with Italian crystal and a marble fountain. On either side of this lobby two endless wings extended, big rooms joined by a kind of faux-balcony with wrought-iron railings. Privacy and discretion a must.

I couldn't see the Lotus, but I saw room 813. The door was ajar, and bright light edged the crack of the doorway. "Hello?" I mumbled, tapping, and slowly the door swung open. I stepped into a dazzle of whiteness and was grabbed from behind by a big burly guy: a thrill shot through my lungs like pure oxygen. "Hi," said a voice, teasingly. Big arms like bolsters against my chest. "What's *your* name?" His voice was dark and low, like some underground stream choked with weeds. When he ordered me to shut my eyes his words came out in a gargle. He twisted my wrists behind my back and held them there with one tight fist. I suppose I helped a little. "Where's Scott?" I said.

"Shot," said my captor.

"What?"

"I call him Shot," he replied, pinching my nipples through my white Brooks Brothers shirt. "I guess his name is Scott, but I call him Shot."

I relaxed a little and surveyed the room. "Why?" The salient feature of the Meadowbrook rooms was, and maybe still is, the walls—every available wall surface covered with mirrors, like the end of *Lady from Shanghai*. Mirrored ceiling, too, hung with the primitive track lighting of the seventies. Again and again my reflection gleamed back at me, and I could see the face of my captor. He shut the door with his bare foot, *slam*. Even the back of the door was a mirror. I guess there was a thermostat on one wall, but other than that there was only me, him, a TV and a bed. Endlessly. And silent air-conditioning—its thin metallic smell seemed to bounce back and forth between us. The TV was showing some closed-channel sex film starring Marilyn Chambers. Marilyn was laughing her fool head off while jerking off one white guy and one black guy. The sound was turned down so I couldn't catch the dialogue.

"Because he's, like, well . . . he's shot," said the man behind me. "Didn't you see his eyes?" I'm thinking, God, I'm supposed to have sex with *this* guy? He was about fifty-five and must have weighed three hundred pounds, wrapped in an oversized white terry-cloth bathrobe, its sash underfoot on the red rug. "What is he, your scout?" "Ha ha ha," he laughed, as though I were joking. His unruly beard and jolly grin would mark him today as a Daddy type, a big bear, but back then we didn't have that type: to me he was just fat. But I was drunk enough to not really care. Weakly I held up the bottle of Glenlivet, waved it around. "Want a drink?"

"Shot's into bondage," said Bear Guy, making a face. "But not me—I'm only into eating beautiful ass. How about you?"

"Whatever," I said. The ruined king-size bed looked good to me. On TV Marilyn's face beamed, dripping with cum on her temples, eyes, lips. Okay, the linen wasn't exactly pristine—a thin strip of blood streaked the top sheet. "First I just want a drink."

Suddenly solicitous, Bear Guy led me to the bed and vanished into the bathroom. "Don't run off now!" I sat on one edge of the bed, removing my shoes and socks. Soon he reappeared with a glass of ice. *Glug glug glug.* He said his name was Schuyler but all his "friends" called him Sky. "You've been crying," he said. I wondered if he was some kind of counselor in regular life. His big kind brown eyes. "Yes," I said, as I helped him insert his big hand through the zipper of my pants. "I've just been to a wake."

Sky squeezed my balls in that tender way some big guys have. "Ah, one of those long drunken Irish wakes. You look Irish."

"Yes," I said. I could see my face in the mirror, and beyond that I could see my own back. Everywhere I looked I saw me, sipping this motel glass full of that wonderful Scotch. Sophisticated. My dick was hard. I saw it. I saw it in the mirrors. It was everywhere, sluicing up and down through his hand. "This'll make you feel better," said Sky. He grabbed some change from the nightstand and put a couple of quarters into the frame of the water bed. Instantly the bed started sliding and shaking up and down, to and fro, like an ocean liner on stormy seas. "Whoa," I said. "Relax," said Sky. Obediently, I shut my eyes and rolled onto my stomach. I didn't want to see his belly, tons of flab folding over and reconstituting themselves as he bent to work. I lay slumped amid the big coverlets and stained sheets, hid my hot face in a pink satin pillow, ruffled with black lace. "Good night," I said sadly. I didn't want to puke. Sky tugged my pants down to my ankles, then peeled off my tight white underwear, ooh-ing and aahing like a connoisseur, touching and nibbling. The bed kept shaking as he parted the cheeks and licked the crack. At his muffled request—"Mmmftlmm?"—I raised my hips. I imagined my legs sprawled, my bony ankles dull under the weight of his knees, his bearded face buried inside my butt, a buffet. Comfortable. His tongue darted in and out, in time with the whirring vibrations of the water bed, licking the walls of my asshole. Nothing could have surprised me at that point, so when I became aware there was another boy in the bed near me, already passed out, snoring, I wasn't shocked, only pleased. I held on to his waist, pressing my cock along his long thigh. Hispanic guy with nubbly little pubic hair surrounding this enormous flaccid organ. His body was warm, he was naked, zzzzzz. An hour later, when I came to, he was gone. I've always wondered who he was and what became of him. The bed was still. Sky's quarters had run out.

And Sky must have run out too. Inside my ass I felt a little stretched, but not much. My mouth was parched. 5:30 a.m. Scott was sitting on the other end of the bed, by the mirrored nightstand, fully dressed, making a phone call. "You're up," he said to me, scratching the bridge of his nose. "Grand."

There was still about an inch of my drink left—thank God. Scott had two grams of cocaine that he said were worth a hundred dollars. "On me." This was his hint for me to fish them out of his clothes. They were in the right-hand pocket of his blue jeans. I slithered to his end of the bed while he talked on the phone, I think to his girlfriend or wife. I patted him down to find them, to find the tiny lump the vials made in those slick blue pants. The inside of his pocket felt warm, greasy, like sticking a hand into a Joseph Beuys sculpture of fat. I looked over his shoulder and saw our two faces. I could barely make mine out; it looked like the mirror was melting it, like rain on spring snow. But his face glistened, tan and sweaty, brilliantly smiling. His eyes were blue, like mine, but darker, almost black. I pulled the stash out of his pocket and dropped the vials, lightly, on the big sloppy bed. He hung up and then we scarfed the coke. What the hell. After we kissed some more he jumped to his feet to remove the belt from the loops of his jeans. "You work in a garage or something?" I think I said. "Your clothes are dirty, man." Even his boxer shorts had grease stains, as though he worked on motors in his underwear, then wiped his hands on them.

Ever been really drunk, in a room full of mirrors? Liquor, brown and warm, slops down the side of your mouth. You can't swallow fast enough. Your kisses get sloppy; your vision too. All of a sudden there's a little click in your head, and the first person turns into the second person. That's you—Kevin. Have another drink. Don't mind if I do. You stroke the warm cock in your hand, you can't decide if it's yours or another's. Click. The second person slips into the third. Kevin rose suddenly, the chenille bedspread sticking to his butt, and made his way unsteadily toward the far end of the room, where a picture in a neo-Rosenquist style hung on the wall of mirrors. He thought it was marvelous.

Fine scars striped Scott's chest and back—thin shiny veins, like long gleaming tapeworms—and across both cheeks of his butt a thicker scar, of rough skin, as though he had backed into a hot pipe. Inside his head Kevin was, like, ????, but he kept grinning as though it was nothing out of the ordinary to see a guy whose outsides looked like insides. "So, you're into bondage?" Now it was Scott's turn to make a face. "Who told you that—Sky?" "Oh, no," Kevin said sarcastically, "Lana Turner told me."

He wore Kevin's hands around his waist like a belt, but Kevin took them off and lit a Parliament, backwards, nonchalantly lighting its "recessed filter" so that acrid smoke filled the air of the mirrored room. Scott walked nude to the bathroom and flipped on the light, and, blinking, he tipped a plastic glass sideways in its holder, one limp arm pointing at it, his fingers working, weakly, as though he wanted to grab it. "I'll take a drink too, you got any to spare." Like any other alcoholic, Kevin measured what was left in the bottle and tried to figure out if, indeed, there was any to "spare." Scott was naked in the threshold of the bathroom, and Kevin kept ogling him blearily. His body had the extraordinary angles of the junkie, the bumps and bones, the big thick red cock like a windup handle for the toy it set to motion. "Turn around," Kevin said. Scott complied. Kevin peered at his ass. It was big and full, a whole novel's worth. I could eat breakfast off that butt, thought Kevin, scar and all. He saw Scott's elbow working, moving like a piston from behind. Like, he's jerking off, kind of. When he turned again he had a hard-on bigger than a mackerel, and Kevin had seen a lot of fish. "Want another drink?" Scott said, pointing to the bottle that stood on the bedside. The alcohol sweat from Kevin's body gave him a chill on this hot, humid night, just before dawn, and he shivered as though —as though, he thought, a goose was walking over my grave.

Brrrrr.

"Let's take a shower," Scott said. "I'm filthy." He told Kevin he liked being tied up to the shower pole. Is it called a "pole"? Whatever it is that holds up a shower curtain—whatever it is that he was now tapping like a woodpecker, in a rare burst of excitement. "Nah," Scott said flatly. "It's called the rod!"—a word he seemed to find excitement in, as did Kevin: a phallic word, concealed yet radiant, like Poe's purloined letter, among the bathroom's pedestrian fittings. Then Scott wanted Kevin to take the knife he held out, and slice him with it. "After that it can be *your* party." Trouble was there wasn't any rope in their mirrored motel room. On all four walls, on the ceiling, their faces, multiplied to infinity, represented an infinity of puzzlement, thousands of eyes darting around drunkenly to look for rope. Finally Scott gave up, shrugged. "No rope—let's improv." Improv? Very Second City, that boy! Very Lee Strasberg! For a few minutes Scott pretended he was tied, but that got tired. He stood facing away from Kevin, wrists crossed above his head, clinging to the rod as though lashed on. He kept looking back over his shoulder, trying to panic. Trying to feel trapped.

"Hey," whined Scott. "I really could, you know, use some rope. And I'd like to do this before Sky comes back, if you don't mind."

There was a second click in Kevin's head—a click of clarity. He saw clearly, vividly, where he could find some rope—in the trunk of his Maverick. Viewed the mental image in 3-D. It was like getting sober. The third person vanished. The second person lasted only long enough for you to whip one of the motel towels around your waist and prop open the door with your pants. Then you were out in the parking lot, and pop! I opened the trunk, staring down at the rope Tim Baillie had hung himself with.

A tiny wind whistled under the thin cloth of the towel, tickling my balls. I bent over and took the extra rope. The leftover rope. Tim Baillie was dead now; I had just come back from his wake. He was my advisor in grad school, and I had slept with him to pass my orals. Do they still call them "orals"? I guess I used him, without many qualms: just did it, set him in my sights and knocked him down like a bowling pin with charm, Irish whiskey, and my big basket in the front row of Victorian Studies. "Kevin," he said, "you could have been a real scholar if you had anything in your mind." And now Tim Baillie—"*Dr.* Baillie, if you please!"—was dead.

Coiled loosely on the floor of the trunk, among pieces of an oily jack, the rope looked harmless enough. But just looking at it made me jittery, as though it concealed cobras. I remember fantasizing about an inquest where I would have to get up on the stand and some Perry Mason type would be snidely asking me, "Didn't you know he would use that rope to hang himself?" "No! No! I've gone through this a thousand times! Dr. Baillie said he wanted to pack a trunk!" "A trunk to death?" "No, no, an ordinary trunk!" "Mr. Killian, may I remind you that you swore to tell the whole truth and nothing but the truth?" What could I say? I knew I didn't love him, but wasn't giving him all that head enough for Tim Baillie? He had been closeted for forty years or more; I thought I was bringing a little sunshine into his elderly life. I remembered lying in his bed in his awful condo in Rocky Point with all his books on Alfred, Lord Tennyson stacked sideways on the bookcase, as though he didn't care enough about them to stand them up straight. I remembered listening with him to Willie Nelson's doleful *Stardust* album again and again—his favorite album, whereas mine was either *Radio Ethiopia* or *Sexual Healing*. Maybe I should have loved him. But nobody respected him, why should I have? He was just this flabby fool with spots on his face that might have been freckles. He left a note, they told me: "I can't stand this heat." I didn't know, when he asked me to get him some rope at Smithtown Hardware, what he'd use it for. I remember his pursed lips when I showed him all the rope I'd bought, saying to me, "I only need about twelve feet, it's just for a trunk, I'm not Christo wrapping the Eiffel Tower." He cut off what he needed with a pair of cooking shears. Least he paid me for the whole hundred feet. Always this sarcasm, always the mockery, the checkbook, the despair. I thought *I* drank a lot till I met him—his eyes were the color of grappa, all the way through, no white, just this sick luscious purple tinge color. *Gulp.*

When I heard about Tim Baillie's suicide, I was sitting at a table in a bar in Port Jefferson, reading a book and nursing a bottle of beer and a glass of rum and Tab. The bottle kept leaving wet rings in the pages of the book. You know how Seurat worked? Placing millions of tiny dots of color into pointillistic masterpieces? I began to think, well, maybe you could do this with the wet rings of a beer bottle, and later Chuck Close took my insight and became way famous doing so. Oh Tim! If I made you feel second best, Tim, I am sorry I was blind. Maybe I didn't hold you, all those lonely lonely times. Little things I should have said and done, I just never took the time, et cetera!

Room 813, Scott was lying on the bed whacking off, keeping his dick hard and his heels cool. "Grand," he said when I showed him the rope and mimicked lassoing him. Expertly he tied himself up, lashing his wrists to the shower rod and needing my help only for the last knots. The rod was L-shaped, to match the contours of the bathtub below; its two ends screwed into two different mirrored walls, and a sassy full-length shower curtain of hot pink vinyl hung from it dramatically, the drag queen of all shower curtains. I stood behind Scott, kissing and biting his neck and shoulders, my hard-on poking between his thighs, his big butt. I gripped the knife in one hand, my knuckles white around its heft. He was on tiptoes, arms braced tautly against the frail metal rod. I flipped a hand between the part in the pink vinyl curtain and turned on the shower; a rush of cool water beat on the other side of us. "You know what you're doing?" he said sharply. "I'm not a piece of meat, I just want to let some blood out. You don't hack me like you're at some butcher's shop." I saw him full length in the mirror facing us, on the other side of the tub. The hair under his armpits was blond, darker than the thatch on his head. His nipples were brownish-red, spaced far apart on his magnificent chest. "Right under my ribs," he said. "Let's start there." I could see how hard he was. His erection lifted his balls right along with it—everything pointed to the knife. I just wanted to fuck him but thought, Well, later, later it'll be *my* party.

I took a deep breath and lifted the knife to his skin. First I heard a kind of screech, like two cats fighting. Then another screech, more protracted, from above my head. The shower rod screws sprang half out of their sockets in a noise of splitting glass and metal. My instinct was to jump back, anywhere, but there was nowhere to jump to. The knife fell from my fist. I tightened my hold round Scott's middle, his skin a blur. Another screw flew out of its seating and the shower walls collapsed. "Uh-oh," whispered Scott, and we began to drop, he right on top of me, he getting the worst of it for sure. Splinters of glass shot through the air, then whole panes peeled from the bathroom walls, sticky with glue and loud with crackling and smashing. The room was imploding. With a sudden crack, the rod bent again, into three broken parts, and all the curtain rings fell to one end like poker chips clicking on a croupier's table. Scott's body, still knotted to the mangled metal rod, fell to the bathroom floor with a heavy thud, though I tried to cushion his fall. Hot pink vinyl fluttered and descended over our heads. Slumped to the floor, Scott's torso sprayed blood, pink mist erupting up the side of the bathtub, mist that grew red at its edges. His hands were still tethered, with the hemp now wet, swollen. I sat on the floor, afraid to move, for the glass was everywhere—on the rug, on the pink tiles, strewn across the tan of his naked body like sand. And also I was afraid of sitting on the knife I had let go.

Mirrors, with bright colors zigzagging across them; his dick seemed a thousand feet long, like a string of sausages in a Chuck Jones cartoon. I kept seeing him bleeding out the corner of my eye, the way you might think you're seeing something when you're really paranoid. Peripheral vision.

"Guy, you all right?" I said.

His eyelids pulled up to reveal blue irises swimming in twin seas of pink. His lashes were incredibly long, and from overhead the gaudy light of the motel's fluorescent tubes threw long shadows onto his picked-over cheekbones. One large shard of mirror stood, like Stonehenge, embedded directly in his stomach, about an inch above and to the left of his navel. Another shard toppled over on his right thigh, propelling a piece of pink flesh that looked like dog food across the rim of the bathtub. The blood was everywhere. I was covered with blood: spots, streaks, puddles. But somehow I hadn't been hurt. I ran back into the bedroom to grab a drink and to fetch a pillow to stanch Scott's blood; I had the word *tourniquet* in my head.

"I'm all right," he gasped. "Wow, I just wanted a little cut, dude, but you brought in the whole artillery, didn't you?"

"FX," I said.

"Now help me," he said. "Help me come now."

I sat back on my haunches and used one hand to stroke my cock. With the other I held his dick, which hardened and throbbed to a vivid red brightness—its natural pink intensified by desire. I studied it before I began to pump: it looked angry, swollen, as though stung by bees. Blood and pre-cum, greasy in my loose fist.

The aroma of blood: stale, tangy, older than either of us. Scott stirred, smiling, moved his head across the wet shiny tile. Gently I placed the pink satin pillow between his head and the floor; its black lace ruffle grew instantly darker with blood and water. This is like some Mario Bava film! I thought, scared to death, but horny, too. Scott's dark blue eyes fixed on some point on the mirrored wall, from which another face gazed back at him, mine or his. His tongue protruded from his mouth, like a dog in summer lapping up water. "Cool," he said.

His tan flesh, which should have been lightly dusted in sand; his beach-boy look, spoiled or accentuated in scars; and everything pricked with glass, like a St. Sebastian I felt so sorry for, yet couldn't help. All I could do was jerk him off. That's all he wanted from me. His tongue touched the tip of my dick as I labored over him. Lick. Rustle. Spurt.

Again. Spurt. Presently I straightened up, creaking from my knees, and tossed a towel into the bathtub, so I could stand in it without cutting my feet on the broken slices of mirror. Then I stepped over his body and into the shower, let cool water rinse the blood from my arms, hair, crotch, legs. Through a streaming veil I watched Scott sink into sleep, as blood continued to pool up in all the concave sites of his fading body. Was he sleeping? Unconscious? His blond hair matted red, brown, black; his smile gave no clue, his big lips slack, happy, purple and gray as the petals of a sterling-silver rose. I nudged him with the Glenlivet. He didn't seem to want a drink, again I'm like—????? Then I dressed, found my keys, left the motel. I guess.

C. BARD COLE

MICHAEL M___:
A CASE STUDY
OF DOORBELL
TRADE

THE SUBJECT WAS FIRST ENCOUNTERED ON FRIDAY, JANU-
ary 29, 1993, at Crow Bar on East Tenth Street, New York City:
"1984" night. I don't go to bars much, as I am bad at cruising and
small talk. I don't have sex much and when I do I like it to be with
a boy I think is cute. My somewhat atypical judgment of cuteness
absolves me from any accusations of snobbery or prejudice. The night
in question, I had met my friend Astrid, her stepsister Rachel and
my friend Amy at Vazac's bar on the corner of East Seventh and
Avenue B, and we'd drunk a pitcher of Genessee Cream Ale, plus
assorted mugs. This was to get into a pleasantly intoxicated state
before facing Crow Bar's overpriced bottled beer.

When we arrived at Crow Bar, the girls were hassled for ID as
usual (they do not look underage). It was still early—maybe eleven

o'clock—and the bar was pretty empty. We played some pinball and danced sporadically to Blondie, David Bowie, and Public Image Ltd. I noticed a kid standing in a dark corner who seemed to be looking at me, an occurrence rare enough to draw my attention. Skinny and tall, he had on a long overcoat and a knit hat. What I could see of his face from between his scraggly dreadlocks looked sort of clean and all-American, almost bland except for his nice lips.

He hardly moved from where he was posed, and being unused to being stared at, I kept my eye on him but didn't approach him. Ten or so minutes later, with the boy still checking me out, Amy asked me for a cigarette. I pulled out two and handed her one, put one in my own mouth, and lit them. The boy approached: his face looked even better out of the shadows, definitely grade-A, and his hair was an appealing shade of light reddish-brown. He asked Amy for a cigarette. When she said, "I don't have any . . . ," he turned and headed for the door at a rapid clip, interrupting the ". . . but my *friend* here does" that I knew she intended to add. Now, pressed and lacking a more reasonable alternative, I yelled, "Hey! I have a cigarette!"

His name was Michael. I told him I lived in the neighborhood and he said that he didn't. He told me he was in art school and I told him I drew cartoons. I had one of my cartoon minibooks in my pocket and I gave him one. He asked me to write my phone number on it. Before I knew it, we were making out, standing in the middle of the dance floor while the deejay played "We Are the World." He kneaded my hardening dick through my jeans while I slid my hand down the back of his pants, hidden from public view by his long coat. I grazed his asshole with the tip of my finger while we tongue-kissed. He said he would call me real soon but he needed to catch the train back to his house. I went to sleep smelling his butt on my finger.

Two weeks later he hadn't called. "This shit happens," I said to myself. And to my friends Astrid and Amy, who were wondering, I said, "Cute boys never call me when they say they will." Once again, I would not be getting laid.

Saturday, February 27, 1993, I had been out drinking with my friend Danny, spending most of the night talking about a mutual friend's problem with heroin. I returned to my home at 700 East Ninth Street and went to bed at approximately 2:21 A.M. I awoke in confusion to a flurry of beeps from my answering machine, and this message: "Hey, this is Mike. I met you at Crow Bar. I was wondering . . . what you're doing . . . 'cause I really wanna . . . you know, get together . . . but I guess you're not around. . . . I'll call back in a few days." While he spoke, I went nuts trying to figure out what time it was (3:48 A.M.) and where the phone was (the living room). By the time I had traced the telephone line from its outlet to the actual set, he had hung up.

And he didn't call back in a few days.

Thursday, March 11, 1993: He finally reached me at home. We made a date for him to come over the next day. I was not confident, at this point, that he would actually show up, but close enough to the appointed time my doorbell rang. By this time I had pretty much forgotten what he looked like. He was taller and skinnier than I'd remembered, with a bigger head. I'd embellished my image of him as sort of a Gothic type, but he was wearing a Timberland jacket, a turtleneck, sweatpants and those very padded high-top sneakers with white tube socks. He called me "kid" and said "whassup." We didn't kiss then, and I wasn't sure what the terms of our interaction would be, whether it was to be hot sex or "first-date." I decided to act "first-date," at least for the moment. I suggested we get some movies and some beer. At Kim's Video I picked out Andy Warhol's *Flesh*, because Mike was studying film at the School for Visual Arts and he said he'd never seen it. We bought some forty-ouncers and, walking back across Tompkins Square Park, I was very satisfied to be seen walking with this kid. I didn't run into anyone I know.

I put in the movie and we started watching. I was on the couch and he sat down on the floor to my left and started talking nonstop, about going to film school and his old apartment in the Bronx and how sucky it was to have to live with his parents. He talked about the ins and outs of bicycle messengery. (My friends tell me that I have a tendency to ramble on endlessly about myself; I supposed this was my comeuppance.) Suddenly he shut his mouth and looked at me, and I scooted down on the floor and started kissing him. He was already hard. We got our hands into each other's pants, and I wrapped my fist around his cock and started jerking him off. Kicking off his sneakers, he pulled his pants and underwear entirely off, unzipped my pants, pulled my dick free and started sucking it. His dick was really thick but comparatively short, maybe four inches long, with bristly clipped blond pubes. I hadn't pegged him for a pube clipper. I rubbed beneath his balls, moving toward his asshole, and he arched his back like a cat, keeping my dick in his mouth. He wasn't that good a cocksucker. I said, "Let's go into my room." I was afraid my roommate John, the twenty-three-year-old heterosexual associate editor of a prestigious Marxist monthly, would show up soon.

Once in bed and thoroughly naked, Mike and I sixty-nined for a while, but it was clear that his butt was where it was at: he moaned and squirmed whenever I got near it. While he kept sucking me off, getting better little by little, I poked and licked his butthole, which was smooth and hairless without much pucker around it, just a clean pink hole between his cheeks. It was surprisingly loose, too; I could get three fingers in it almost right away, and the more I fingerfucked him, the prettier and puffier his asslips became. Without saying a word, he got on his knees, rubbed his ass in my face and braced himself against the head of my bed. I picked my recently purchased package of Trojans off the bookshelf by my bed, got one out, opened it and rolled it down my cock, lubing it with spit. I slid it right up his ass, and he pushed back at me, his bony ass pushing against my groin. I ran my hands along his torso, making him grunt appealingly as I pinched his nipples. I could feel his ass twitching as he got ready to shoot his load onto my sheets, and he thrashed wildly as he came. I pulled out then. When I used to get fucked I always thought it hurt to get fucked after I came, so I was trying to be considerate. I hoped he would suck me some more and try to get me off, but instead he started talking again.

He told me that he was a dread—not a Rastafarian, he made clear, because he was white and thought it was stupid that white

American kids thought they could become Rastafarians just by smoking pot, listening to reggae and growing dreads. But he respected that philosophy, for the most part. There were some things he disagreed with, of course. "Like a lot of Rastafarians think that if a person is gay, what you should do is hit them in the head with a rock. I don't agree with that," he said in an unusual, detached tone. Then he began explaining his theory of sexuality while I lazily jerked off my half-hard cock: "I'm bisexual. I think that when you want to fuck, when you want to do it to somebody, you go with a girl, and when you want to be the one who lets go, who gets done to, you go with a guy." He expressed the desire to dress up in women's clothes "sometime," because sometimes he wanted to be a woman, and get fucked. He was sliding closer to me on the bed, and I was jerking his dick a little too. He pushed against me close and the head of my dick started to feel warm and snug: I realized that the poor, unlatexed thing was nestling just slightly inside his poop shoot. He said that he wanted to feel feminine. I thought about fucking him a little without a rubber, because he wasn't asking. I bent down and sucked on his dick some while thinking about it. Doesn't he notice that I'm up his ass? I wondered. But I put on a condom—hooray for me— before I started drilling him again.

He said, "I've never let anyone do this to me before. You're the first guy that's ever fucked me." I didn't think he was lying. Some boys just have naturally loose buttholes. He needed five bucks to get to the train station on time.

Saturday, April 17, 1993: Mike called me just after I had announced giving up hope. He was in his bedroom at his parents' house on Long Island, thinking about me (circa 2:10 A.M.). We talked small talk for a while. He asked me why I didn't talk about myself very much. I said I was shy and he said that was no excuse, he was shy too. He told me he had run into a friend who was a girl he used to go out with and that they had had a fight, which had made him sad. Somehow we got back on the topic of women's clothes. This is what he said he wanted to do:

I was to pick out a dress for him. I thought a snug black dress like my girlfriends wear to go out would be nice. (Astrid has a very pretty one by Michael Kors, which she wore when we lurked outside of Cafe Tabac, looking for Madonna on the night of her birthday party there.) But no—Mike wanted a leather miniskirt with fishnets and high heels. He wanted me to take him out dancing to a nice straight nightclub, believing, at a great stretch of the imagination, that he could pass as a real woman if he tried. I would let everyone see that he was my woman, he said. We would make out on the dance floor and he would rub my dick. Then we'd go to a dark corner and I'd slide my hand up into his panties and feel his secret surprise that was just for me. Then I could finger his hole and get him all relaxed and loose. Then I could take my big hard cock and stick it in him, push it in and pull it out, screw his pussy, let him feel it, fuck his pussy so hard, make him come. . . .

We came. I shot a load of runny white sperm over my stomach and thigh as I held the phone to my ear, sitting on the edge of my bed. He was panting, with three of his own fingers—if his description can be trusted—firmly shoved up his ass. He asked me, "Can we really do it?" I said sure. He said, "I'll have to shave my legs. . . . Would you do it for me, baby?" I said sure.

Friday, June 4, 1993: He called me from one of those weird bars on Bleecker Street where straight people who live outside of Manhattan come to drink. His friends were all drunk and heading home. He wanted to see me. I told him come on over. I was depressed and tired because I hated my latest job, working on a porn magazine production line. Though I had been employed there for five months, I still felt awkward and unliked in a very junior-high-school sort of way. In a last-ditch gesture of camaraderie, I had contributed my own story of the weird bisexual boy I had slept with to my co-workers' makeshift conversation of sexual adventuring, and it did not seem well-received. My boss told me that there was no such thing as bisexuality. I did not understand how a workplace devoted to the production of something as scandalous and unrespectable as homo-sexual pornography could possibly be so uptight and unpleasant.

This time when we got together, I tried to stick it in too soon, and he complained that it hurt. We sucked each other's dicks and masturbated until he was ready for me to try again. I had to lick out his little butthole for a long time before he said it was okay. "You got a jimmy?" he asked. I did ("jimmy" is a word for condom, prevalent in hip-hop argot).

Again, he needed a token and a few dollars to get home. He left me his beeper number and told me his last name, Carlisle, and his age, eighteen.

Friday, September 17, 1993: I hadn't heard from Mike in several months. I beeped him a bunch of times but never got a call back. I called information and they had no Michael Carlisles listed in any of the Long Island towns I vaguely remembered him mentioning. Then I gave up.

"I've been in the hospital," he said when he called. "I got run over by a bus and broke my arm." He still had a cast on when he came over, and I had to fuck him facedown with his arm hanging off the edge of the bed.

He was tired and wanted to spend the night, but insisted on sleeping on the couch, so I wouldn't bump his arm. When we left the safety of my room, I ran into a girl in the hallway. Apparently my roommate John was getting some that night too. Neither Mike nor I was that naked or anything, but our appearance confounded her: a couple of long-haired tattooed boys in their underpants. I know all this because she's now my friend Sarah. I ran into her at a queer film festival a few weeks later and she said, "Hey, remember me? I slept with your roommate!" Sarah was a Riot Grrrl at the time.

After we got to be friends, she told me this story: "I asked John who those boys were hanging out in your living room, and he said, 'Oh, that's my roommate and his friend.' I said, 'I thought you said your roommate is gay,' and he said, 'Yeah, he is, that's the guy he has sex with.' I said, 'Wow, I just thought they looked like weird straight boys who'd listen to Pearl Jam or something,' and John said, 'Bard maintains a critical distance from gay culture.'"

Saturday, October 2, 1993: Mike called me at 2:45 A.M. He was at a friend's house "in the city" and wanted to come over, but needed directions. It turned out his friend lived in Far Rockaway, about as far from Manhattan as you can get on the subway. He was sloshed and it took hours for him to come over. He called again at about 5:05 A.M. and said he'd forgotten my address. I looked up from the phone and out the window and saw him talking on the pay phone on the opposite corner.

I sucked his dick, he sucked mine, I rimmed him, we fucked. We were getting into a routine. Afterward he told me a story about his boss at the bicycle messenger service. The guy always talked about porno movies and, Mike said, "he's always talking about how big the guys' dicks were, how great they looked sliding in and out of the girl's pussy or her mouth, always just really obsessed with the guys' dicks. I asked him if he ever watches the movies where two girls do it to each other, and he said, 'No way, man. That shit is a sin. I don't watch that gay shit.'" I liked that story. I felt that it demonstrated an innate intelligence, a sense of irony that had been lacking in his earlier comments about the Rastafarian perspective on homosexuality.

The next morning we sucked each other off and lay around in bed. Suddenly at eleven o'clock he jumped up and asked to use the phone. He found out that his friend who'd driven him to Far Rockaway from Long Island had already gone home, so then he called her mother and left a snotty message about how "he really appreciated her waiting for him like she said she would."

Not too long after (Tuesday, November 9, 1993), I got fired from my job and had to give up my slick East Village apartment. I moved into the crawl space under the stairs in Amy's apartment. Mike didn't have a beeper anymore, since his accident had forestalled his career in bicycle messengery. I went to Boston, then to San Francisco for a while—where, to my chagrin, I found no Cute Boys—and worked my way back east on the trains, visiting Astrid, who'd left New York to go to graduate school in Milwaukee, a city bubbling over with weird straight boys who looked like they'd listen to Pearl Jam, and finally returning to New York City on Thursday, February 3, 1994. Amy told me that Mike had called looking for me. He had tracked me down.

He came over for a slap and tickle. I could not lure him into my cozy cubbyhole, as he claimed to be claustrophobic, so I had to duke him all around the living room. For a while, he was coming over as frequently as every two weeks. He was starting to get on my nerves. I'd discovered that his last name wasn't Carlisle, and when I tried to recall why exactly I thought it was, I couldn't come up with anything (I do know what his last name is now, but since it is actually his last name, I feel it only proper to withhold it). We were always being caught doing it by one or another of the five people who shared the apartment. I was liking fucking him facedown or doggy style just so I could look at my dick sliding in and out of his ass thinking about the boys I really wished I was fucking.

His sexual demands were getting increasingly irritating. He tried on clothes from Amy's closet and made me fuck him with her panty hose around his knees. He decided he might be into S/M a little and demanded that I tie him up and drip hot wax on his nipples and down his butt crack. Unable to ride his bike or play basketball, he'd put on weight and had developed a little belly. I smacked him around a little after he bugged me to. I got really pissed once when he asked me if I was finished with my beer—there was an inch or so left at the bottom of the bottle—and I said sure because I thought he wanted to drink the rest. Instead he stuck it up his butt and tried to put on a show. He had gotten a job dancing at Show Palace and performed once, not sure if he wanted to go back or not. He told me about the old guys touching his dick. Some of them had made offers. He asked me if I thought that was dirty. I said, I don't know. If you want it to be.

We were doing it on Amy's futon when she came home with some of her friends to watch *Saturday Night Live*. Mike demanded to know who was out there. "See if anybody wants to watch us." Totally whipped at this point, I ventured out into the living room. "Amy," I said, "Mike and I are having sex. You wouldn't want to watch, would you?" She raised her eyebrows, burped and said, "Why not?"

Mike and I just fucked for a while, but he was intent on pulling her into it. Anyhow, I always had the fantasy of fucking a boy up the ass while he ate out a girl. I think he may have fucked her after I fell asleep; she's said a couple things that sound vague and slightly guilt-ridden. The next morning, our roommate Ann-Marie opened the door to ask Amy a question and was surprised to find the three of us in bed. Her boyfriend, Barney (an exceptionally handsome East Village squatter recently dispossessed from the late lamented Glass House, a renowned squat that had been shut up by the police), soon popped his head in too, made himself at home on the floor and began talking with Mike about what kinds of guns could pass through metal detectors. Barney expressed interest in getting his hands on a Glock—for self-defense, of course—and Mike told him that he knew how to set him up with one cheap. There was a certain evident kinship between them. It was not reassuring.

The next couple times he came over, I'd only listen to him talk for a few minutes before I'd get him on his stomach and stick it in his can. I thought about other boys I'd have liked to screw while duking him, and I'd try to get him out of the house as soon as I could. I am not a callous person by any means. It's just how I felt. The novelty had sort of worn off, and was not yet replaced with any other consolatory sentiment.

On Saturday, April 23, 1994, I fucked him on the couch until I came, then slid down onto the floor to suck him off. My couch, incidentally, is wicker—not like the crap you see at Pier One, but heavy and solid and square—and a single futon fits just perfectly into it; this detail figures prominently in a few moments. So I was sucking him off, hoping to make him come so he would put on his clothes and leave. Mike said something like, "I could enjoy you doing that for hours," which indicated to me that he was not concentrating on getting off. I got him to sit up a little so I could jerk him off better, and he looked down at my dick and said, "Whoa, was that like that when we were fucking?"

I looked down at the condom that was still on my dick. At least the bottom part of it was still around my dick; the torn part of it was hanging off. I said to myself (I think to myself; perhaps I said it out loud), "This must have just broke . . ." And before I could complete my thought, or protest, with the words, ". . . 'cause it's still filled with cum," all of the runny, transparent semen dripped to the floor in one runny gob.

I concluded that the condom must have dried out during the twenty minutes I was sucking his dick, caught on the wicker of the couch and torn. Unfortunately, Mike did not see the little pool of stale, runny semen hit the floor. He was upset. He wanted to know if I had any diseases. He said that this was a matter of life and death and called me "bra."

I explained what I thought was my exceptionally likely interpretation of events several times. Then I realized that, despite its logic, it sounded like a fat lie. That made me sound anxious and, therefore, like a fat liar. I was not happy.

The easiest thing in the world would have been to say I don't have any diseases, but I couldn't bring myself to do it, despite the fact that I don't have any diseases except occasionally athlete's foot. The right answer to "Do you have any diseases?" is "No. I got tested a few months ago and I'm clean." In my case, this would be a lie. I do not have the required certification. I have never been tested for HIV, have had very little in the course of my sexual history to make me think I should. I mean, I've never even had crabs. In my opinion, this is an altogether reasonable outlook.

So here I was, finally faced with the consequences of my beliefs: I am aware that any sexual act has the potential for putting you at some risk. But this is not a comforting thing to say to someone who thinks a condom has just broken in his ass. It sounds like a used-car salesman saying, "Well, you should have checked the carburetor before you paid me three thousand dollars for it."

To put it succinctly, I was fucked. There was nothing I could think of to say that didn't sound like a lie.

I said that I'm pretty sure I'm okay, but that this is something we should talk about. That having sex with guys means thinking about stuff like this, and that if he doesn't want to think about it, then he shouldn't be doing it.

He agreed that maybe he shouldn't.

I told him that he absolutely must call me in the next week or so and we would talk seriously about it. I said I have never asked you to promise me anything but you must promise to call. He said he would. He didn't.

I guess I had enjoyed the thrill of embodying the strange, mysterious world of queersex. This was its opposite face, and I did not enjoy it. I said to myself, he's the one who used to be heavy into dope, he's the one who fucks strange girls all over town, and maybe does a lot more I don't know about. Why do I get to be the wellspring of HIV? When he didn't call me like he promised he would, I decided I wouldn't see him anymore.

He did not call again. However, four months later, on Friday, June 17, 1994, he came by without calling and we had sex, despite the decision I had made. This was about the same time that a song entitled "Self Esteem," by the band Offspring, which dealt with precisely this situation, began being played on the radio a lot. Mike doesn't like that kind of music, but I filled up my five-disc CD player with all of my hip-hop albums—House of Pain, Gang Starr, Beastie Boys, Digable Planets, Lords of the Underground; not necessarily your hardest collection, but all I had. He didn't mention the ripped-condom incident and neither did I. However, I did make sure to have nice new Ramses on hand, rather than LifeStyles, which I've decided are crappy. When Mike came over, he wasn't drunk at all. Myself, I had gotten a job, and when Amy moved out to go to California for a couple of months, I took over the lease and her bedroom. It had been ages since Mike and I had gotten to mess around in my own bed in my own room, and I stripped him of his clothes and we rolled around naked, sucking each other's dicks. At a certain point, he pushed me down on my back and straddled me, holding my dick and guiding it up his ass: he'd never been quite so aggressive in getting fucked before. It sort of hurt. My dick wasn't being rubbed the right way and I kept hitting his pelvic bones at a bad angle, but he was hard as a rock, biting his lip as he slid up and down on my cock. The visuals were great—I've been able to masturbate numerous times remembering his facial expression, the way his stomach looked as he arched his back, the way his small, hard nipples felt between my fingers. I could lick the head of his dick as it poked out at me, and after a few loud groans, he shot a load onto my chest. I moved his ass a little so his weight was resting more on me, and fucked him fast and furious at a more satisfying angle and came pretty quick after that. I told him that sometime I might like him to fuck me. He said, "I don't know. I've never done that before."

I came home from work a few weeks later—Thursday, September 8, 1994—and was surprised to find him sitting on the couch talking to my friend Spot, who I was letting stay with me for complex reasons really beyond the scope of this essay. It was almost still light outside, and I don't think I'd ever seen him so early in the day. He was back in school, and told me about one of his teachers who had it out for him, who believed that he was "always stoned." He said he was trying to get his shit together, was going to quit drinking, quit smoking ("except for herb, which is natural") and quit cutting classes.

When Spot left, I shut my bedroom door. Mike had on girl's underpants, black satin with lace trim, when I took down his jeans. I accepted this without inquiry. I rubbed his dick through the satin and he took off his shirt: his chest was shaved. He said some guy he met was paying him $100 to take pictures of him and asked him to shave his chest smooth. As a dread, he felt that cutting hair was wrong, and felt some conflict about having done this. He said he'd never do it again. "I want to make you come," he said. "You never just let me suck your dick until you come." He took off his panties and knelt down between my legs, hauled out my cock and started sucking on it. I held the back of his head by the dreadlocks and fucked his face a little harder than I'd done before. He was really good at sucking dick by this point, and pretty good at sucking my dick in particular. He was jerking off while giving me head. When I was about to come, I said, "I'm going to come," hoping slightly that he wouldn't take his mouth off. He did, though, and I shot my wad onto his hair, neck and chest. Then he stood up and put his butt in my face, jerking off while I licked his asshole and balls. I pushed him down on the bed and sucked his dick while moving three fingers around in his ass. He came all over his stomach.

Smoking cigarettes afterward—he had two Newports left in a pack and said he wasn't going to buy any more after this—he told me he wasn't sure how he felt about getting fucked anymore. He was starting to think that sex for the sake of pleasure was wrong.

He said he was fucking a lot of girls and felt bad about it; that he shouldn't be fucking with people and not loving them. Sex is for having babies with the person you love, he said, and he didn't want a baby or anything right now. He said he didn't know if the person he would love would be a girl or a guy. He said that just because he had to live in Babylon didn't mean he shouldn't keep the rules he believed in. After school, he wanted to go to Africa: That's what was important to him right now.

He said he hadn't planned this or anything, but he wanted to change his life and live according to what he believed. What we'd had was cool and he really liked me a lot, but we shouldn't have sex anymore. He said he would stay in touch and would peep me later ("peep" is a word from the hip-hop argot, meaning "to get in touch with, greet"). He gave me a long tongue kiss at the door.

Afterward I told my roommate Chris that I'd gotten dumped. He said that he doubted it. "He'll be back."

Saturday, October 8, 1994, I was watching a movie that I'd rented from Kim's Video with my friends Jodie and Spot. Chris was getting dressed to go out, and the doorbell rang. Our doorbell rings lots, because poorly raised children and drunks hang out on our stoop. I never put any credence in our doorbell. I said, jokingly, "If that's a cute boy, send him up here for me."

A few moments later, Mike knocked at the apartment door.

He was shitfaced, and flopped down on one end of my bed, pretty much passed out cold. We watched the rest of the movie.

After everybody left, I had a hard time moving him so that I could lie in bed. Finally, I woke him up a little and got him to lie on one side of the bed. I took off his shoes, covered him with a blanket and went to sleep.

I woke up when he started taking off his jeans. My dick was hard, and he pushed his butt back against it. I slid my hand under his shirt and started feeling his stomach. He pulled down his underpants and I felt his dick. He was hard too. I jerked him off and started rubbing my dick between his butt cheeks. He was really grinding his butt on it, and I stuck one finger up his ass. Then I sat up and put my face near his butt, spit on my fingers and really started poking at his hole. I kept poking until I got three fingers way in it, and just looked at his asshole all stretched out. I kissed his butt. I could feel him squeezing my fingers with his ass and knew he was wide awake. I lay back down and turned him around and started kissing him. "Are you going to let me do it?" I asked.

"Do what?" He smiled faintly. He knew damn well what I meant. I could tell he wanted it, but I wasn't going to allow him to think that I stuck my dick in his ass without permission.

"Can I fuck you?" I asked. He shrugged.

"What do you want to do then?" I asked. He rolled over and put his arms around me, burying his face in my shoulder.

We fell asleep for a while. When we woke up a little later in the night, I sucked his dick and he came on my face. He turned on his side, facing away from me, and I jerked off, spewing come on his butt. When it was finally morning, he put on his clothes, kissed me and left. It has been a month and a half since I've seen him; it's now Monday, November 21, 1994. I say it is done now; Chris says, again, "I doubt it."

Some questions for further study:

1. So what is this boy's deal? Do you think I'm really the only guy he sleeps with?
2. What makes him look me up on particular nights? Does he think about me at other times? If so, what does he think?
3. Did it turn him off when I told him I wanted him to fuck me sometime? Did this disrupt his internal rules for having sex with a guy?
4. Sometimes I think I'm sort of in love with him. I told him that once, that I was sort of in love with him. Do you think he's sort of in love with me?

MICHAEL LASSELL

GNAT

"Remember that I am thy creature; I ought to be thy Adam, but I am rather the fallen angel, whom thou drivest from joy for no misdeed."
—From *Frankenstein* by Mary Shelley

I AM WRITING. AGAIN. FINALLY. YOU LIKE THAT, DON'T you? You like it when I write. It makes you think of yourself as a good influence on me, as if you help me to overcome the . . . difficulty I have in being alone long enough to string the words into sea foam, each bubble a single thought, a single cell of . . . loneliness. All right, of you.

I am writing because no one understands, because I cannot *get* anyone to understand why it happened. And if I can't get anyone else to understand, perhaps I don't grasp it myself. And if it's not knowable to me, how can I expect you to understand? It's important to me, that the entire affair be explainable, communicable. In words . . . and even "affair" isn't right, with its connotations of mutual, or at least of simultaneous, involvement.

It isn't rational, of course, I know that, thinking that I can ever understand it. But the affair that was not an affair was never about reason or restraint, and neither is the need to explain. Maybe it was about salvation. I know you have no use for God or gods. That's fine. Neither do I, not after you—not *other* than you.

But if I can't at least describe it, what's left to me?

I met him in daylight, an afternoon in late fall, November, just before Thanksgiving, that's right, because he went home to St. Paul right after we met. His hair was long and dark—but not as long as it would get, and he had not yet grown the goatee that would come to make him resemble a Mexican outlaw in league with Pancho Villa. Even from across a room I could see his lips were dark cherry red; they matched the deep letters of his tattered HARVARD sweatshirt. His eyes were the lightest, most intense blue—the color of the Madonna's robe in Renaissance paintings, the color of forgiveness.

I was living in a duplex I couldn't afford anymore because I'd lost my job a year earlier. I was paying the rent with credit cards I knew I had no hope of paying off short of a miracle. I had been single for five years—long city years without so much as a weekend in the country. I was working as a freelance editor and knew I was just biding my time until I'd be French-kissing bankruptcy for the second time. I was out of everything I had ever relied on for survival: hope, fantasies, dreams. Even humor—hard won at best—had deserted me. I was forty-five.

Gnat was an atheist, a student of philosophy, a bulimic, and twenty-four.

I wanted to fuck him on the spot. I wanted to fuck him so hard the head of my dick would come out his mouth. And I wanted to hold his balls in my hand the way a child holds an Easter chick— in awe. To brush his hair after a shower. To lick him wherever there was hair. To hold him in my arms until he cried out every shard of pain the museum of his body still sheltered. To shovel snow with

him and write poems about his nipples, to fold him into the musty
suitcase of my love and carry him forever with me.

Perhaps I told him my name.

And when did I touch you first? A handshake in the first moment,
I suppose. But when the first *touch*? Odd that I can't remember. And
how many thousand touches since, both simple and complex, like
sentences, the commas marking moments when innocence slithered
into provocation? And when the first kiss among the many thousand . . . ? No. You see, I slip into the lie. There were few kisses,
and none more passionate than a business card proffered by an Asian
banker. All the deepest kisses of my passion for you I have kissed in
the dark of my own room, alone, feeling you in the absence where
you would have been had you been there.

"I hate people who kiss with their lips closed," you said as we
stood in line for a film about a Catholic boy obsessed by obese older
men. My arm was around your waist, my hand on the raised eyebrow
of your hard hip. Cars driving by slowed, and the curious caught us
in their confusion. "And they flick the end of their tongue against
your lips," you said. "I hate that. And they keep their lips hard."

"And how do you kiss?" I asked.

"Like I want to crawl inside them," you said. "With my mouth
open as wide as I can get it."

And my breath begins to come shallow even now, imagining
the playground of your open mouth. I nearly tripped over the garbage
piled at the curb as I stared at the column of fat men hoping to
meet a Catholic boy guilty enough to want them, to take their semen
onto an outstretched tongue like a liquid Host.

NEW ANGLE
"Do you see that man over there?" I ask. A car slung low as an open-
toed pump crawls by, its Puerto Rican passengers ogling. "The one
in the purple shirt?"

You nod.

"He's the director of the film."

"How do you know?" you ask.

"I met him at the peep booths at Christopher and Greenwich.

He was on his knees in the next booth. He wanted me to go home with him."

"Did you go?"

"No."

"Why?"

"I don't know. Because I was so fat at the time, I guess, and hated myself so much. I figured anyone who would have sex with me had to be sick. I don't want to have sex with someone who's using me to punish himself. It's a self-esteem issue," I say, turning the truth into a joke with my tone alone.

You laugh your ironic, irreverent bad-boy laugh. The one that starts with a shot placed high on the hard palate and falls like a stream over ever-smaller rocks, into the soft, wet opening of your throat.

Another Movie:

You sit in the dark theater. Gnat shifts into you, his body hot on your body. Your hand is on his thigh. His arm is around your shoulder. Your hand is on his. You can feel his rib cage, frail as a female bird's, as it rises and falls under the flesh of your right arm, the bellows of his torso against the muscle of your arm, the tattooed muscle you hope will attract other men.

But you do not desire other men. He is the only man who can share a thought with desire.

Soon, he uncrosses his leg and your forearm rests in his lap. Now, near your elbow, you can feel him swell, can feel the rise and fall of his hardening cock while the gangsters of Reservoir Dogs *pump bullets into the bodies of their fellows. You are hard for an hour imagining what is happening in his lap, under your elbow as it rests on his leg, as he wraps his fingers around the muscle of your arm, pushes his face into your shoulder when the gore goes beyond his limits of witness.*

You see: He gives you strength.

Here are the things they say he is (and they all have an opinion): a sexual compulsion; a romantic obsession; a distraction from problems I am trying to flee; a means of avoiding intimacy; a self-destructive indulgence; a midlife crisis; a symbol for lost youth.

————

Here are things I say you are: fire, flesh, and the power of flight; the eyelash of a winking imp; truth.

He was—and still is—of course, beautiful and, of course, thought he was ugly. He was . . . oh, all the usual: bright, articulate, curious. I flattered myself that he found me endlessly fascinating, and for all I know he actually did. I believed him when he said anything, even when it was a compliment. He was so . . . young. And that was part of it, the innocence, the incredibly deep cynicism he thought was unique and that seemed to be the same as my own. But mine had been working since he was born. He took a bite out of enameled bitterness and made love seem possible. So I thought it was love; that's how desperate I was.

I loved looking at him, talking to him, teaching him, learning from him. I loved loving him. I mean, it's not as if there was anyone else to love or even to fuck, just the men and boys I paid for sex because I couldn't have sex with Gnat.

And we laughed. We shared this deep, idiotic sense of humor and the same dismissive irony. Sometimes we even rolled our eyes at the same time, which made us laugh even more. I forget to mention the laughter . . . how easy it was to laugh when I was with him.

I was good for him and he was good for me, at first, and I knew it. Until I wasn't anymore, and neither was he. And I knew that, too.

Was there a time before you loved him? You can't remember. You can't remember the moment you realized that you were a man who would love other men every day of your life. But one moment you can remember: the moment you realized you loved younger men, and how perilous a road you were about to go down.

You were not yet old yourself that day, on the bluffs above the beach at Laguna. You looked down at the beach and saw a male form that roused your interest and your blood. You watched him walk toward you on the beach as a cormorant flew low just beyond the surf: diving, rising . . . diving, rising. And then he was coming toward you, closer and closer, this male presence that turned you instantly on, and soon he came close enough to see he was not a man at all, but a boy—fifteen? Maybe younger, maybe not.

And you looked at him and the soft, hairless chest of a beach-town boy in midsummer, the slightest hair on his arms gleaming orange now as the sun began to set, the long hair still stuck to his neck, his smooth belly a nest for the face of your desire, a raspberry scrape along an ankle—which? inside right ankle, as he looks you right in the eye with the challenging, curious, contemptuous look of every boy you have ever seen in the world.

And as he dismisses you with a sneer that is almost a smile, you feel the grip of transgression slip around your heart like a band around the throat of a cormorant—captured and trammeled—always diving, never satisfied, the catch pulled from his gullet by the man who controls him now, who feeds him what meager food he needs to survive so that he can pull what he desires from the sea and surrender it, his desire constantly inflamed by having what he desires as far inside him as his throat, but never permitted to swallow. That's what Gnat was. And God.

We walk. You hold in the loose cradle of your left hand two fingers of my right, the bare ring finger and the pinky. These two fingers fit your loose grip as if Michelangelo had had something to do with it.

These are "our fingers." You always know when you have the wrong ones and shake them loose like a child whose father doesn't understand the importance of rectitude.

We walk hand in hand in Greenwich Village and Times Square. In Boston.

In the cool, dark museum that morning of sculpture from the Golden Age of Greece. All day long. Hand in hand.

"Everyone thinks we're lovers," you say with a grin.

"You don't," I say without one.

You order wine while I draw irises on the white butcher paper on the table between us.

A chin hair ingrows in his trimmed beard. You love the subtle rupture of his skin. Your skin has this memory, too, the memory of a chin hair that ingrows in a trim beard, that ingrows without healing.

The first and only time I ever saw him naked . . . nearly naked, he was at my apartment, on Grove—before the debt caught up with me and I moved to the studio by the river. I don't remember what he was doing there. He asked if he could take a shower. "Of course," I said, and he did. I hovered in the bedroom, hearing the water, watching the steam slip out from under the bathroom door like a come-hither.

Carl took showers in my apartment, too, in L.A. Six-foot-six, heterosexual bodybuilding Carl who is now a Chippendales calendar boy, who was the Arnold Schwarzenegger to my Danny DeVito, who came into my apartment and ate bread after working out and showered, and wrapped my towels around his fat-free waist, and then lay on his back on my bed, his hands behind his neck. And my mouth wanted him so much I had to leave the room, because I could not risk the rejection. I didn't see it as an invitation, I saw it as a test.

So why did I risk it with Gnat? Because taking the risk was less painful than avoiding it, just as getting sober once felt less painful than staying drunk. And I thought—idiot that, it proves, I was . . . am—I did not think he would reject me. So there's an irony: afraid of Carl, who might well have welcomed me; unafraid of Gnat, who was everything I have ever wanted and who seemed to want me, or at least to be . . . open? available? amenable? And he *was* open to all those things, just not to sex . . . to love, *romantic* love. My mistake. My . . . limitation.

So I mistakenly believed that Gnat came to my apartment to make himself available to me, to offer his body as a prelude to the symphony of his soul. I am a sucker for boys who wear their wounds in their eyes.

Gnat was thin. It was the bulimia. He was pale, too, Midwestern white-boy pale, and the possibility of him vibrated through the bathroom door, as I lay on the bed waiting for him to come out of the shower, wondering if he would come out of the bathroom, and if he would be naked. And he did come out of the bathroom, a towel wrapped around his waist. Here was another chapter of the book of his body: He was thin, yes, but there was a muscle system there, with a scattering of dark hair on his lower legs and arms, between his two perfect nipples. I stared at him, and he grinned at me. Then took the two steps it took to sit beside me on the bed. He put his hand on my stomach, looked into my eyes as if everything he had ever been looking for was to be found there, and said, "Thanks."

And then he got up and got dressed. And so I never did see him naked, never laid eyes on the dick I desired as much as I wanted to hold him in my arms all my life long. Instead of no one.

These are some of the reasons I got confused: He brought me flowers; he sent cards; he left notes with the receptionist where I work; he wrote poems about sticking spoons down his throat to purge every meal and about having sex with his mother, and he showed them to me, anxious for the approval I was anxious to give; he touched me whenever he could—gently—and agreed with everything I said; he told me everything—that he'd slept with his sister's husband when he was still in high school; he called me every night before he went to sleep and we would speak until we were both tired enough to sleep without drugs.

Here is why I guessed he was never going to be the great love of my life: He never said "I love you" even when I said it to him.

And . . . he told me.

"I love you," I said one night. He shifted on his feet.

"That's a word I never use," he finally said, sinking down into his jacket—not nearly warm enough for . . . December? January?

"Why?"

"I guess because it's such an abused word, it's just meaningless," he said, but I could tell he was evading.

"Well, I love you," I said.

"I know," he said.

And once, after yet another meal at the health-food joint where the waiters fawned on him in a mad flirt, ignoring me, and I gave him a good-night hug for his trek east, he stood there staring into my eyes while I stood staring into his, and he said:

"Sometimes I just feel so . . . I don't know. It's like, I know this is the point where something more is supposed to happen, and I know you expect it, and I just come up against my own limits or my own . . . inadequacy or . . . maybe I'm just a withholding bitch, which is what my shrink says, exactly like my mother. But I come up against as far as I can go, and I know it hurts you."

"It does hurt," I said, never able to lie to him, ever.

So we stood staring until I thought I was going to cry right there on the corner of Sixth Avenue and Tenth Street. "We're never going to become lovers," he told me. "I decided that after the first few days."

Well, if he was trying to hurt me, he was succeeding. He was succeeding even if he wasn't trying.

Those were the clues.

But I dove, even with the fisherman's band welded around my neck.

Loneliness, it turns out, has its own logic.

Loving him is like wind—a city's chemical wind that blows a bit of grit into your eye, not sweet country wind with the smell of mud and manure in it. Loving him is a winter city wind. Remembering him is a country wind in spring. And you do remember him, even now, as you walk down Christopher Street and pass a shop where you bought matching bracelets together on a whim, where he stood looking at the multitude of socks on the display rack and said, "I'd like to buy one in every color they have," and—to this day, every time you walk past this shop—you think, "I'll buy a pair of socks for Gnat one day, every color that they have." But you know you won't. It's just grit in the eye, and you know it.

"I felt like the Hunchback of Notre Dame," you hear a friend say. Well, you think, who doesn't?

INT. BROADWAY THEATER. NIGHT.

Here you are at the opening of a play about angels, AIDS, confusion, and death. The air is thick with anticipation and homosexuals. He is your . . . say it . . . date. He is looking coltish, perturbed . . . perfect. You sit hand in hand near the stage-left aisle. You are glad to be here with him, just to know him, much less touch him, this deeply flawed, still unformed and perfect man.

"This is so great," he says, turning his mouth quickly to your ear, his hair following a nanosecond behind.

And this, too, you love about him: his capacity for excitement, wonder.

He is reteaching you this, and you feel like a vampire for it—a mother who will not let a son have an unshared emotion, but seizes it and makes it her own.

At the first intermission, you introduce him to Rick, who has heard every detail of your love for him. And you all smile, because this is how it feels to introduce a lover to your friends.

"Who is that gorgeous man you were with at the theater last night?" Carter asks on the phone, his voice incredulous.

"Hello, Carter. Don't you mean, 'Hello, how are you, who is that beautiful man you were with last night?' " you reply.

"Well, who is he? He's *gorgeous!*"

"He's a friend of mine, and he's also extremely bright, articulate, and talented."

"Fuck that. What is he doing with *you?*"

"He likes me."

"Are you sleeping with him?"

"You know, Carter, I once knew a man who never talked to me unless I was talking to someone he wanted to fuck, and this is reminding me of him a lot. What's your point? That I'm such a fucking troll no one could possibly love me?"

"Not someone who looks like a Calvin Klein model."

"Carter, Calvin Klein is a self-hating, homophobic piece of capitalist shit, and anyone with an ounce of self-respect would be organizing a boycott of Calvin Klein, not jerking off in the men's room to Marky Mark in his underpants."

EXTREME CLOSE-UP.
So, you see, you are not making this up, this feeling that you do not deserve what you desire. It is the lesson life teaches: The best is not for you. The best exists only to torture you by its inaccessibility. This you learned on your mother's knee: Happiness is for your betters, not for you.

Then there was Washington, the March, the twenty-four-hour nonstop being with you, and you in a poor mood, and both of us exhausted from lack of sleep, and too many emotions in too large a crowd. What happened that day? I realized I'd never have you. A friend of yours stepped between us and turned his back on me to talk to you, so nothing was I to him in your life. You couldn't believe he'd done it. I could. The world teaches us lessons our own hearts are too hard or too full to learn. Even if you'd been willing, we'd have been doomed. The lonely pain of others—their desire—they would superimpose it on us, and we would suffocate from the weight of it.

"My passion for beauty . . . ," Gnat reads, ". . . was almost a violence."

"The self-destructive kind," you say as you wait for the light to change at Sixth and Tenth and think of the cool dark mitigating kiss of the Hudson in the slate night, the skeletal remains of the piers where men groaned naked in the belly of whales. It's like Melville writing Moby Dick *because Hawthorne wouldn't have him—or the ear van Gogh sent Gauguin to reclaim the wandering painter's attention when it strayed from his friend's madness to the soft bed of women—the moment when you know you will never be truly loved and the rules no longer apply, not to you. You have stepped somehow, forever, outside.*

It's like the blue of your young friend's eye as it twitches to the left (a glitch in the tape of your conversation) to find a blessing in the glance of a stranger just beyond your shoulder.

It's like writing poems in a midtown plaza at lunch, while an old geezer canes his way across the brick to warn you all out of the sun. "I-have-melanoma," he says, a one-word song between drags on an unfiltered Camel.

And you watch as Gnat disappears down Seventh to whatever awaits him this night that does not wait for you.

"Don't ever be middle-aged, gay, and single at the same time," you tell Seth, who is twentysomething and so full of hope he still smokes and goes to Europe.

Hope is ugly in the old, you think, and wonder why your mind hurts.

Then you hear that Seth has moved in with a man twice his age, and you know.

———

"Take care of yourself," the waiter says, as you pay your bill for a too-small order of pasta puttanesca without anchovies, then head out in search of low-fat frozen yogurt made with artificial sweetener, so totally without Gnat you'd think you once had him.

You choose the chocolate mint, another Friday night alone, the eternity of Gnat's unreturned love and your own inflamed stupidity: to fall in love with beauty again, at this idiotic age when loneliness fits like hand in leather. And the Hudson as cold as Gnat's seductive, nonadoring eyes.

March is a memory. April and most of May somehow pass. Alex pays a visit from Boston; then Bradley from L.A.

You lie in bed awake. Alex is sleeping at the farthest extreme of the mattress. He moves often, but sleeps silently, desiring you asleep no more than awake. You lie awake all night—insomniac? No, you do not sleep because your body is alive with your desire for Alex.

"Because he does not desire you?" your mind asks.

"No," it answers. "Because Gnat does not desire me."

June: Bradley's in the shower. I return your call. We speak at first about nothing. I do not care what we say. It is the sound of your voice I need today. As always, there is a surprise slung between the hammock poles of your vibrant baritone.

"Can I tell you something?" you ask.

"Of course."

"It's sexual."

"That isn't *less* reason to tell me. You can tell me whatever you want."

"Last night Rasheed and I were in bed," you say, "fooling around." I shift in the chair I bought when Bradley and I stopped being lovers, five years and three thousand miles ago. "And he got it into his head that he wanted to stick all five of his fingers up my ass."

I do not say a word. What can I say to so excellent an idea?

"I mean, it was like it was so important to him?" you say. Your voice—undamaged by the forks you stick into your throat to induce vomiting—rises at the end of your statement like a question.

"Did it hurt?" I finally ask, the vision of your asshole open to Rasheed's hand enclosing me like a fist (sound track of insanity in a film).

"Well, there are other things he could have done that would have been more pleasurable."

I say nothing. My hand reaches into the air for your open ass but comes across the bulge inside my own shorts. Bradley returns from his shower. I am suddenly ashamed. But this is not a new sensation at all. It is like going home for Thanksgiving dinner, the shame familiar . . . and familial.

"Tell Rasheed when he gets tired of you he should come over here," I say, conscious that I do not support your succession of infatuations (because they are not me), though I pretend to. I am a daughter's father in this, a jilted lover of my own fabrication.

"I thought you didn't like anything up your ass."

"I don't," I say. "It's always been the great central fact of my inadequacy: I'm a gay man who doesn't like getting fucked. Add over forty and overweight to that and you can imagine what a high premium is placed on my presence in our highly spiritual and emotionally evolved gay world. Of course, it's why I'm still alive. If I liked being fucked, I'd be dead."

"So what do you want with Rasheed?"

"Because if he wants to stick his hand up your butt it may not be just because of the macho rush he'll get from it. It may be because he knows how it feels, and wants to give you that pleasure as a gift."

"But you just said you don't like being fucked."

"I didn't say I didn't find it pleasurable."

"God," you say at the end of the phone, laughing, "I can't believe I know you."

In the vault between my nipples and knees, you are an absence so deep I am famished. I lie beside Bradley, who is naked and wanting me, but I feel only the appetite where you belong, and the heat from Bradley's body is my own shame in being rejected by you.

I want . . . only and always . . . *you*. I want to slice you from chest to balls and crawl inside for warmth, like a man lost in a snow-

filled wilderness, the way a Jack London hero lost in a blizzard can
—without a wince—cut open the belly of a wounded stag, drink its
blood for rehydration, and wrap the carcass around him like a hut.

It comes in waves, you see, this loving of him, like weather. Suddenly
a continental high-pressure center sits above Canada pulling equa-
torial air and misery up from the Gulf of Mexico. Temperatures and
passions soar. The city swelters in a brownout for days, then black-
outs that last for hours, days, weeks. Truck tires fuse to the soft tar
of melting streets. Uptown, fire hydrants are opened and water pressure falls to dangerous levels. The price of ice rises gradually, then
rapidly. An immigrant grocer grasping the law of supply and de-
mand is murdered in Brooklyn. A riot ensues. Century-old tenements
burn in the night. Glass shatters. And there is no escape, no relief
in sight. The isobars of the twenty-four-hour cable weather station
promise only more of the same and worse to come. In this respect
the weather is exactly like my loving him. And the river seems the
only answer.

(*That's what it's like, loving you.*)

And then, suddenly, and with no more warning than a random bullet
in the night, it breaks in a breath of cooling air off the Hudson.
Without so much as a rainstorm, the mercury drops to tolerable
numbers—that cooling week in August when I was on jury duty.
Sanity returns. I am not in love, only envious.

(*Loving you is like this, too: gentle, knowing, kind. And the revolver of my
resolve is wrapped up again in bunting and put to the back of the closet. For
a time.*)

And then one day you notice his skin as if for the first time, his pale
white skin and few dark hairs—the random marks in ink of an angry
child on eggshell pages; no, the abstract etchings a whaler makes in
scrimshaw, the millennial fissures of a walrus tusk on which the
secrets of a century are recorded.

————

It occurs to me to think: If I can't have Gnat, I don't want anyone at all. Everyone else is pure sham.

"That's exactly what I'm afraid of," he says, "that you spend so much time with me you'll never meet anyone else."

"Gnat, I'm not going to meet anyone else. It's been five years since I had a *date*, for Christ's sake. It's something you're too young to understand. Nobody is running around trying to meet someone like me. You are rare. The alternative to being with you is not being with someone else, it's being alone."

It occurs to me to think: If I can't have Gnat, I don't want to live.

I tell this to the Hudson one summer night at dusk. It says nothing. As usual.

"If I can't have Gnat," I say to the river, "I want you."

And the river says, "Kiss me."

I look into the filth the Hudson has become and it seems cool and healing. The pilings of the pier are green and slippery. This is the pier where the survivors of the Titanic arrived. I feel the chill of those shadows who survived the drowning, those men, women, and children who are dead now, despite their survival.

Once in, you cannot get out. There is no escape. That's how it is. The river. Gnat. Desire.

And so you sit in the chair you bought when you and Bradley stopped being lovers, how many years and miles ago? Bradley, the sweet and gentle man you thought you loved again, until you felt what you feel for Gnat and realized you had never loved or felt before, and can never desire Bradley again the way you did before. And you watch a videotape for hours, of men more attractive and desirable than Gnat, who suck and fuck each other with abandon and with vengeance. And you are naked now, as you have so often been since he told you about Rasheed fitting five thin fingers of a single hand into his willing asshole.

You are in training, you see. You are training your ass to accept a bigger cock than you have ever seen.

You start with rubber. Dildos. A small one at first you can barely get inside you no matter how much lubricant you put on it, but you do get it in—again and again until it slides inside without so much as a sensation.

The twelve-incher looks so big in the store on Forty-second you can't believe it will fit inside anyone, much less yourself, but with determination—and visions of Gnat groaning with pleasure in the night—you manage it, sooner than you might have guessed. It isn't long before you can get five fingers up your own ass all the way to the last knuckle, and you could get up there farther if not for the awkward angle, and you keep it working inside that warm, wet place for so long, so amazed at the velveteen walls, the sliced litchi disk of your own prostate, felt so often in others, that when you come it is from a place so deep you practically scream in the night, as the stuff flies around the room, and you are one contracted muscle thinking that this . . . this is how Gnat feels when Rasheed has a hand up his ass. How you would feel with Gnat's hand in yours, or just to lift his not-yet-stiffened prick from off his leg with your tongue on the underside of his glans.

And none of this is a problem for you, except you are running out of cash for boys to break up the loneliness of the nights Gnat is not with you, which is every night, and it all makes you so . . . hungry, no matter how much you eat.

And then I write it. I write the letter.

Why?

Because he continued to be himself instead of who I wanted him to be. Because he left me flowers with the receptionist where I work, with a card. And when I spoke to him, I asked him where he had been for two days, and he said: "I met someone at Boy Bar and went home with him and had sex all night, and it was really shitty, so I went back last night and had sex with someone else." Then he giggled. Truly. And, yes, this is what he needed, and I said so, to explore his body while it still responded in human fashion, to enjoy himself and his young world as much as he could so there would be no regrets when he was my age. That is what I said.

And then I sat and stared past my reflection in the window of the forty-first-floor office I despise, looked past my face at August in New York and wondered how I could break the glass so the diving through it would not be so painful, and that is when I wrote the note and told him never to call me again.

As simple as that.

And he never did.

Unless those calls were from him, the ones where someone called and never responded to my hello.

I sat in front of videotapes and put my hand into my asshole as far as it would go, and thought I could easily keep doing this for thirty or forty more years until even my pioneer longevity genes were weary.

And did I mention that I cried?

Until . . . October? No, Thanksgiving. Maybe longer.

I wanted to exorcise him, but I wanted to love him, too, to love him and have him, and fuck him night after night until there was nothing left to do to him, nothing left in my head to do that I hadn't done. And then I wanted to do it all again.

And then the cooling winter comes and cools you down, cools down your eyes, and you are fine, actually. Lonely, yes, but fine. And then, just before Christmas, you open a batch of mail vaguely remembering a return address and in the envelope is a card in the shape of a tarantula, and it says:

"Wishing you peace and some semblance of happiness for the holidays and New Year. With Love, Gnat."

And there it is: Love inside a tarantula, that poor, abused word he would never speak when we spent every day together, inside a poisonous spider.

You do not call him, against the wisdom of every cell and sinew. You have a new life now. It just doesn't have him in it. It has no one in it. And that is what the not calling of him tells you again and again every day: Your life has no one in it, and will have no one in it if he is not there.

So winter passed, and spring. I worked. I went through the bankruptcy. There was some fleeting peace.

That's when I saw you at the library, as I was coming down the steps toward Fifth Avenue. There you were, sitting beside a pillar with another boy. You jumped up onto your feet, and— impulsively—threw yourself into my arms. I didn't object. You were so flustered, I had to introduce myself to your . . . friend? lover?

"Is that a new tattoo?" was all you could manage, as you pulled up the short sleeve of my shirt.

"I got it in Honolulu," I said.

"This is the arm where you have the crane, too, isn't it?" you gushed.

Your friend was looking ill at ease.

"Yes."

You looked into my eyes with that impish look of yours and said, "Well, now I want to see how they both look together."

"But you can't," I said, as lightly as possible. I was punishing you softly, for public consumption.

Then neither one of us knew what to do, so I left.

Time passes. It does not fly. It's summer again. And again it's fall. Here is the thing I miss: I felt so alive when I was loving Gnat. The desire made me feel real. And my fantasy . . . my hope *was that the consummation would . . . crack through every fear I ever had and I could actually live, for the first time in the world.*

Suddenly, you are on the bed with Gnat, a larger bed than you are used to, and softer. You do not know how you have come to be there. Perhaps there was a sofa and a move across a floor, but, no, you have not yet kissed. You are simply on a larger bed than you are used to, as you were on a bed that night before you went to Washington, D.C., on a bus that left at 3:00 A.M., and you were just napping before catching a cab to the bus, yes.

You are in a bed in a room that is your room, but does not resemble a studio by a river that pretends to heal. It is a larger room than yours, and you can see nothing about it but shadows, as if the room is lit only by a candle in a distant corner, behind a wall . . . or bookshelf, perhaps, where everything you have ever read is arranged alphabetically. But it is still light enough to see.

You are both dressed. It is warm . . . no, not exactly warm; there are, in fact, no sensations that are not Gnat. No temperature. No sound.

He lies there propped up on one elbow, facing you as you face him, propped up on an elbow of your own.

No one moves, except to smile, slightly, and yet your face comes closer and closer to his—or his comes closer and closer to yours. You feel his breath, hear the click of his eyelashes as his eyelids flutter open for the last time, then close, as your eyes close. You can feel the heat of him before you are touching. There is a moment before touching in which you think, "Are we touching yet?" And you do not know the answer until a fleck of dried skin from his winter-chapped lips touches a fleck of dried skin from your own lower lip, and you suddenly need the moisture of him inside you.

Finally, your lips touch. Together, you sigh. You can feel his chest rise into his sigh, as you hold this barest, still dry kiss and your breath at the same time; then you both let go, exhaling into each other and pressing the kiss into the kiss.

His lips are softer than the lips of any man you have ever known, softer than a woman's lips, softer than any part of anyone you have ever known.

And they open slightly at first, and yours do, too, and there are tongues soon enough, the first touch tentative, but soon you sidle closer together, shifting your weight to bring your bodies closer together, soon, the kisses are wet enough, and lips and mouths are open, and your hands are up and down his side. You feel the material of his plaid flannel shirt, the one that used to belong to you. Under it, you feel his ribs, the hollow of his waist, the hillock of his thigh. His hands are on you, too, on the same denim shirt you wore that day in D.C. Under his touch everything you have ever hated about your body floats away, like the need to hear music or sate hunger.

You touch his hair, his long, dark hair that is soft and sweet from your shampoo. Is it still damp? No, it is fully dry, yet sweet as herbs in spring, and falls across your face and his, across your deepening kiss. He opens his mouth wide and pushes his softest of all tongues into your mouth, this man who has never so much as uttered the word "love."

And you feel the crowding of your clothes and the pressure of growing cocks to see the light of day . . . or the candlelight of night, and there is a pulling back, and a further smiling, and he puts his fingers to the first closed button of his shirt, and you reach across to unbutton it for him, as you have unbuttoned it so many times when you wore it yourself, and he lets you unbutton them all as he tugs at the tails of the shirt and pulls them out of his black jeans. You pull your denim shirt up over your head without opening buttons as he pulls off his white T, and you are bare-chested now, two nude male torsos schooled in touch. And so you do, you touch his narrow chest, the dark and gleaming hair that grows sparsely on his sternum. You place your open palm over his heart, and take a nipple's imprint as a right-hand stigmata.

When he shakes his hair from side to side, it brushes his neck. He sighs. He takes your head into his hands and kisses it everywhere: nose, cheeks, eyes, eyebrows, forehead at the center of your third eye—then runs his unshaved cheek across the buzzed stubble of your head. You hear and feel the rasp and rhythm of it. He takes out his tongue and licks and licks again the shortest of all possible hair on your head and moves down into your ears, first one and then the other. You retaliate, and you are bobbing for apples now, each ear a prize to be swallowed whole, to be washed like those of some four-legged newborn by its untutored dam.

You feel everything in a spinal line from your neck and chest to your groin, the expanding muscles of your thighs as you flex and unflex them, feel his muscles flex and unflex against them, down to your bare feet against his bare feet, toes attempting to interlace like fingers.

You rise to the challenge and push him down onto his back, then push up on an elbow, exposing the patch of dark hair under his arm, and you take your tongue to it. You lick and he groans, he groans with deep, deep pleasure and tries to bring down his arm, but you put them both up now, above his head, and you lick them in turn. Your mouth is running saliva now, like a miraculous stream from a stone, and you keep on licking his boy-sweet armpits, and he has fistfuls of his own hair clasped in his fingers now, when you move on down to his nipples, and you take them in turn into your teeth until they are hard as a good hard dick, and then take the hair between them and pull it out with your teeth and swallow, as he reels up and flips you on your back and bites a small trail across every moment of your chest and shoulders and arms, his teeth on your tattoos.

And he climbs on top of you and grinds his hips into your hips, and you run your hands through his hair like fingers on harp strings.

When he stops, and pushes himself up on his hands to get a look at you, you put your hands on his waist and look up into his face draped in hair. You pull that mouth of his down again onto yours, then turn him in a grand gesture onto his back again.

You straddle his hips, and open his belt, which is eager to assist you. It opens almost of its own accord, and so do the button and the zipper below the button, and he arches his back enough for you to slip the belt right out of its loops. You can see the hard cock of him under his white cotton briefs as the flap of the jeans opens, and you put your mouth to it even while you pull his jeans down over his hips, moving off him and lifting one leg into the air at a time to pull off the pants, and to lick the back of his knees.

When he lies there hard in his underwear you drop your head into his lap, and through the cotton take his cock into your teeth and lips. It is no huge thing, nor as small as he told you before . . . before this world of him began. The size of it is irrelevant in any case. It is the being him of it that makes you love it and want it inside you.

Finally, you cannot take the teasing of it any longer, and you pull this blunt object free of its net. It is dark and red; it points, a narrow head above a tapered shaft, the vein at the bottom of it pulsing, all of it nested in untrimmed hair the same gleaming coarseness as that on his chest, but more plentiful here. You stand and pull the briefs off him roughly. You want him naked. And you want to be naked too, and you drop your jeans in a single gesture that says it is all for him, and it is, this wanting him, this pleasure you take in him; and the pleasure he takes in it is as much for you as it is for him.

You touch now, as you lower yourself onto him, cock to cock, tentative at first, then pressing down on him. And the grind coming up out of him as it presses down on him from you, like the meeting tides of two oceans at the south end of a continent—waves of it up and down your spines.

You slide your tongue, then, from inside his mouth, over his rough dark chin, you take his trachea in your teeth and bite gently, wishing your bite could make him immortal, but you do not waste time on fiction, you drop one lick into the hollow at the base of it, and slide down, grazing each nipple with your lips before taking them into your fingers. Your mouth has another object in mind, and finds it, touches it, touches it harder, begins to lick the shaft of it, the balls, licks the groin alongside the balls until he moans. Your teeth take the hair of his balls and pull down hard on the scrotum. He is moaning. You go further, and pull up his legs and hold the asshole a moment before you blow into it as soft as you know how, as if trying to extinguish the smallest candle you have ever seen. You put the point of your tongue to it, softly, and then the moisture flows out of you and you push your way in. You lick that hole and the whole of his ass, and every inch of his crotch and groin and when he is fully wet with your saliva, you pull yourself up and thrust your own throbbing cock into the wetness of it, and your breath comes heavy, and so does his, and the power of it makes him arch and push you off him, and he flips around in a sudden gesture, taking your stiff prick into his mouth, and doing for you everything you have for him, and managing to offer his ass to your mouth at the same time.

And the sight of his white ass is just what you had always imagined. You take the hollows in the sides of his thighs into your hands and lick the underside of his balls, and his ass crack, and the hole, teasing the hair alongside, and you dig your tongue deeper and deeper into him, as he tries to get his tongue deeper and deeper into you, and you push your thumbs into the flesh of his asscheeks and pull them apart from the crack and hole, and move them closer and closer to the crack and hole, and press your chin up into the space between his balls and the hole, and then press against the hole with one thumb, until the movement of his hips against it opens the hole, and you slip in, while he takes your whole cock into his mouth, and then your balls, then cock again, then balls, his hands pushing outward on your knees as you pull the halves of him open to get a better taste of the pit.

When you think you cannot bear it anymore, he turns on you and pushes the wet face of himself onto your wet face and all the tongues you've ever known push into your mouth, and you push back, the hairs on his lips scratching on the hairs on yours.

That's when you gently push him onto his back, and reach across him to a drawer, and pull out a dick-shaped tube of lube, squeeze a glob of it into your hand, and slather it on his dick, his balls, the whole revealed part of him, and a finger slides so easily into his asshole, you try another right away, and that finger goes in easily too, and you take out your hand and grease your cock and let him take your cock in one hand as you put two fingers back inside him and then three, and then you stroke his cock awhile while he strokes yours, and then you lie down again on top of him and slide your greased-up dick on his, and all the time you think you haven't even gotten near the time to come, so you head back for his neck, for the neck in which his thick veins bulge, and you take one of these veins into your teeth under his skin, then put your mouth to his chest again, and waist, and lift your arm again for him, and let him bite the tattoo that was hidden under your shirt that day on the library steps, and your shoulder, too, where you mean to shave but never remember.

But the ass of him so calls you, you are soon back to it with three fingers and four, and now he is beginning to wince and you speak for the first time: "Should I stop?" And he says no without hesitation, and so you keep going, as gently as you can, with a sure and determined hand, until you have all five fingers inside him, and that is as far as you want to go, until you find your fingers begin to shrivel inside him as they used to do in those long hot baths when you were a child, until you feel that soft, sweet, nut-sized disk and run your longest finger across it and watch a slow drool ooze from his dick, which is dark now, as purple as royalty.

You slip into a condom and then enter him. He grips you. How long has it been? How long have you lived without this most necessary sensation on earth? How grateful are you that here finally is the oasis in the desert of your loneliness? You are on your knees and worshipping and pushing at the same time, you push until his head is bumping slightly against the wall where the headboard would be, if there were one. Then you move back and pull him with you, putting a pillow under his head, which he reaches up and throws aside.

You keep pumping and pumping into him, and you have his dick in your one hand, the other holding him up behind one thigh, and then you slip your shoulders under both thighs so you can get your mouth on his mouth, and yet you have decided you will not stop here. You pull out of him. He opens his eyes, surprised, disappointed. You reach for another rubber and slip it onto him with your mouth. Then you throw a leg across his lap and take him into your own slippery hole. You are alive with wanting him, and you take him in with a single downward push against his groin.

He begins to push up, and you rock against his pushing. He slips out of you twice; twice you slip him back in and readjust the angle of your joining. You pinch his nipples and take his pecs into your fists as he moans and grunts until he nears the climax. And he rips the rubber off it and has your cock in his hands and is pumping into you as you pump, and then he draws a sharp and sudden breath and throws back his head, and you can feel the hot fluid of him even through the rubber in the overheated hole you have offered him, and you beat at your own dick as his pushes himself farther inside you, and when you come you roar so loud, he laughs and puts a hand across your mouth, and you shoot, past his shoulders, splattering the walls, and onto his neck, and chest and stomach, and into the coarse and gleaming hair of his groin and he slips suddenly out of you, and you fall onto him, and he takes you gently into his arms, and you put your face to his ear, and say, "I love you," and he says, "I love you." And you have never been so happy in your life.

BRUCE
BENDERSON

JAMES

I HAVE A DREADFUL FASCINATION FOR JAMES, A HUSKY,
depressed nineteen-year-old with skin the color of tobacco.

James has a fixation for his dead father, who taught him to shoot
heroin when he was twelve and whom he watched die from an over-
dose three years later in an abandoned lot.

James refers to his addiction as "my wife" and to me as "the only
friend I ever had." On one occasion I decided he needed a methadone
program to save his life and took him to a profit-making clinic in
midtown after a major hassle getting him ID. The plan after that
was for him to move in with me. The methadone made James even
higher than the dope does, and he fell asleep somewhere for a day
and a half.

Since my father was on his deathbed, I left town without finding out exactly where James had nodded out. The death of my father shortly after and the sleep of James are permanently superimposed in my mind.

Though James bathes infrequently, I've never noticed an unpleasant odor coming from him. His smooth skin is often clammy and of so fine a grain that it reminds me of latex coated with seawater. On the other hand, his armpits, each with a tiny clump of coarse black hair, smell like honey, though there is a slight staleness that makes me start licking and biting.

Under James's coarse, shiny pubic hair is a large, torpedo-shaped penis of a liverish color. His balls are surprisingly full and hearty for someone his age, for I've noticed that many adolescents have testes that are small, hung high and extremely sensitive to handling.

One thing that makes James comfortable having sex with me is that I remind him of the older guys he encountered in jail. This is merely a reference to my dumpy, middle-aged body and to the fact that I seem to him to conduct myself with a certain amount of authority.

I've suffered extreme anguish at the various symptoms of James's heroin addiction. More often than not when we meet by chance in a midtown bar he is sweaty and shaking. The assumption at such times is that I will "help" him. This never seems like the optimum moment to stop being an enabler. One would have to be a better philosopher than I to see the larger purpose in not rescuing him from the cramps, vomiting and diarrhea that take hold of him in the sleazy washroom.

Reverse peristalsis has become an established circuit of James's heroin-infused digestion. We can be anywhere, with the music playing and the quips flying, a surly smile gashing his handsome adolescent face, when—oops!—James spins quickly to the side, grabs an empty glass and vomits into it, coming back refreshed.

Despite these constant exudations, James's body and even his breath never lose their pleasant odor.

Upon my return from my father's funeral, I went to our midtown bar carrying my suitcase. My intention was to see if James appeared so that I could immediately take him home. Eventually he strolled into the bar but in much worse shape than I'd imagined. I'd assumed that he'd continued with the methadone for which I'd made a week's advance payment. Instead, he'd gone back to shooting after only two days. With logic typical of the addict James blamed me for being gone when he finally came to. He said I'd broken a promise about letting him move in with me and that he'd had to spend several nights in the park.

As we talked his mouth became sullen in the bar's shadowy mirror. His scowls leapt at me in white-toothed flashes from the mirror's muddy water. His butch clarinet of a voice honked rude answers to my prying questions. I attributed his touchiness to his having been homeless for the better part of a winter week.

Because James didn't like the schoolmarmish tone of my voice, when I tried to touch him, his meaty forearm convulsed. It jerked back to strike me . . . but caught itself just in time.

He hoisted my suitcase, and we walked down the block to a hotel frequented by hookers and drag queens. I studied his arm's recent puncture mark, with its ragged collar of purple. James said he'd stayed at the hotel last night on the basis of a deposit and could only redeem his clothes or watch or wallet by paying the balance.

So he went upstairs, and I forked out the sixty-four dollars. Then he came down holding a few worthless clothes, followed by a slim young gay guy wearing new clothes and blond hair cut in a longish style that looked provincial. This made it clear that I hadn't paid for James but for his friend, who kept the room for another night.

I told James he might as well spend the night at the hotel. When he eagerly agreed, I said I hoped that "you two faggots" would sleep well in each other's arms. His blunt hands clenched into fists and began swinging. The fists made wet smacking sounds against my cheek and temple and screeched across my teeth like fingernails across a blackboard. The blond shrieked, "No, James!" as I stumbled toward the exit stairs. But James followed and swung one more time, making me tumble down all six steps.

I picked myself up and he pursued me into the street, after which the blond came running and managed to drag him back inside.

My lip was only slightly cut, but my calf suddenly inflated, sections turning a hideous purple. I began a fast hop to the corner, fearful he would reappear. Then he came toward me holding my suitcase, one arm spread out in a gesture of supplication. His coat was shedding stuffing in the places where I had wrenched it. His pale face was furrowed and suctioned by sobs.

The blond was trying to tug him away from me by the hem of his coat, but James put down the suitcase and wept into his hands. Neon from the lingerie sex shop saturated the drop of blood on his knuckle with extra color. This made him look like a statue of a hermit transfigured by some awful revelation. Drag queens on their way to a club picked their way daintily around him, while the blond decided to settle for the free room and went back inside.

We fell into a cab. My calf throbbed, but my mind didn't dwell on the beating I'd provoked. Anyone who knows street people knows never to challenge their image. People from James's world own nothing but the strength or appeal of their bodies, which must always be represented as decent and of value to society.

What shrieked in my thoughts was the realization that James hadn't bothered even to ask how my father was. So I told him he had died. James exploded into girlish tears again, burying his wet face in my

armpit. His bruised hands clutched my sleeve, staining it with blood.
His pulse was racing and his body oozed sweat. We headed for the
copping block on East 113th Street where he could put a stop to his
withdrawal.

The cabdriver refused to wait. With a curse I climbed out and sat
on my suitcase, perched against a store window. My ankle had inflated to such girth that the pressure of my pant leg smarted. I
hoisted it and removed the shoe and sock. Junkies passed by with
only a sideways glance at the chubby white guy with the dark bladder for a calf. There I sat, propped on an Eddie Bauer suitcase in the
middle of an East Harlem copping block.

At my apartment, James cooked up the dope. I lay on the bed with
my leg raised, balancing a load of ice cubes in a twisted towel.
Though the pain began to freeze away, the leg had become macabre.
Concussed blood had swelled into so dense a pool that the skin
seemed thin and ready to burst.

James grazed the leg with a kiss. The spike was still hanging from
his arm by a pinch of skin. When his nervous system catapulted into
the rush, he pulled out the spike and spilled out of his clothes, then
onto the bed. I rolled on top of him, and he began to devour my
face with his wet, cushiony lips. His mouth gaped open, and our
tongues began to wrestle. I let my bad leg hang over the edge of the
bed for fear of placing pressure on it.

Those who have had sex with junkies know about their hypersensi-
tivity. They compensate for dulled nerves with a taste for meticulous
pleasure. James's flesh pricked alive to contact like a leg that has lost
circulation and is suddenly massaged. As I gnawed his nipples, I
imagined the sparks shooting through him like hot sand. His head
felt welded to mine as I yanked at a handful of his short, kinky hair.
When his arms fell above his head, I licked his armpits with the flat
of my tongue. His dick hardened against my belly in the "dope stick"
phenomenon: The penis engorges more slowly than when the body

isn't high; but once there, it's stuck. It can take endless stimulation, and orgasm builds slowly. The waves increase and break like the proverbial multiple female's.

His cock in my throat was like an electrode that seeped some of this slurred desire, which it rushed into me so that I, as well, felt I was becoming high. On and on I played the game of feeling and desensitization, leaving behind the thought of my hurt leg. James's necro-withdrawals alternated with sudden surges of feeling. My hands and mouth trampled his beached body in a simulacrum of his earlier battering of me. He began to groan.

Street people have topsy-turvy personae. His voice, which was usually a growl, had become a thin, womanly moan. There were hulks with long prison records who'd lurched into my bed and somersaulted into the passive role in much the same way. It all had a certain logic as the thrust of machismo broke through the membrane to its sub-conscious opposite. The piercer became the pierced.

He hopped off the bed and posed before the mirror, separating his ass cheeks with his callused hands. His cock wasn't hard but his haunches undulated. Energy coursed through my thighs and into my groin.

I fucked James for the first time, though we'd fantasized about it. But we never thought I'd be one-legged. All I could do was lie on my back while James slipped on a condom and sat on me. Then I pumped my pelvis upward as my calves hung over the bed.

Like a switch flicked to off, both of us popped into unconsciousness. I jerked awake a couple of hours later, around dawn. My leg throbbed as if blasted by a blowtorch. He stayed passed out beside me, his breath fast and shallow in the junkie sleep.

With the light my anger had ignited. I saw myself limp to the closet in search of a baseball bat to smash the sleeping body until every bone was broken.

But I hadn't even gone home with James—though I *had* been beat up. The second part of this tale is a fantasy. He'd gone to bed in the hotel with his blond faggot and I'd hopped in cowardice to my cab. I spent the night alone in anger and shock with handfuls of ibuprofen. The next morning I went back to find my suitcase.

The fantasy is a symptom of what I wish I were, something more masochistic that is larger and more open. But even then I'd need a James who'd want to come back to me, and who would know how to transform into a model of remorse, after viciously wielding his fists.

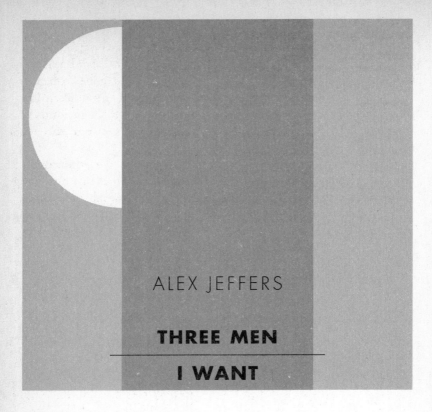

ALEX JEFFERS

THREE MEN

I WANT

I AM ENAMORED OF A MAN I'VE NEVER MET. PHYSICALLY, facially, he doesn't appeal to me at all—I've seen photos—being one of those square-faced northern Slavs, washed out, tepid, boyish in a way that's faintly repellent. He resembles Mikhail Baryshnikov. Not his body . . . well, I don't know about his body, but it seems unlikely: he's not a dancer. Not to say that a dancer's body would appeal to me more. Too much muscle makes me nervous; big thighs especially I dislike. The truth, shameful as it is, is that I like scrawny men. Men with big hands, prominent, bony wrists, and skinny arms. Men who, when they take their shirts off, you can count their ribs. And my erotic compass points south, toward the Mediterranean; east, toward the Levant. Blond, brawny, blue-eyed Swedes and Teutons and Poles need not apply.

This man, the man I'm enamored of, is at least not blond, but he has a very bad haircut and his eyes appear to be blue. He's German and, going by his surname, Polish. His eyebrows are conspicuous for their invisibility.

I think I need to say (it distresses me) that *my* eyes are blue and as far as I can find out all my ancestors were northern European. I am, however, not brawny (five foot seven, hundred fifteen pounds) or blond, though I have a blond's useless, fair complexion. It is a great disappointment to me that my parents couldn't have arranged to be Italian, Greek, or Turkish. I'd settle for Spanish. But no.

This man I'm enamored of, I don't want to sleep with him. Dear God, no. Actually, the thought of it, rather than making me hard, makes me feel dizzy and a little ill, as though a migraine were coming on. There's another man I've never met whom I do want to sleep with, although, again, this isn't a specifically sexual urge: I want to hold him and cuddle him (he's considerably younger than I), kiss his bruised-looking eyelids, his poignant mouth, comfort him. We might fuck or we might not. I want to leave that up to him. I won't say more. I have some hope of being introduced to him one day.

The one I want to fuck is completely hopeless. I've never met him either. To begin with, he's some kind of priest, or a monk—I don't have Catholic regalia down. Not having been raised in the Church, I missed out on developing a fetish for Holy Orders, and it would seem to me rather more bathetic than liberating or transgressive to be the cause of his breaking his vow of chastity. The notion is in any case beside the point, because he's dead. Has been dead for a long, long time: El Greco painted his portrait in the first decade of the seventeenth century. It hangs in the Museum of Fine Arts, Boston. I go to see him a couple of times a year. A postcard from the MFA's gift shop is pinned up next to my desk—I need only turn my eyes to the right, away from the computer screen. In a 1966 monograph Leo Bronstein writes of Fray Hortensio Félix Paravicino: *Blood red is the silence that here seals up the too-ardent, perhaps too-dangerous lips. Red (in Byzantine fashion) is the outline of the sensual fingers.* In a novel my agent hasn't managed to sell yet, *I* wrote: *Of course he was a Spaniard, ascetic, ruthless—and, with his broad, cruel mouth and long, paradoxically delicate hands, beautiful in a way that was ter-*

rifying. He'd chew you up and spit out the pieces. He'd burn you at the stake.

I don't know what all this says about me. The man I'm en-amored of, the first one, is a singer. It's really his voice I'm in love with. This is all quite recent—I only bought the CD last week. It's on the stereo right now. He sings in Italian, so I don't have any clear idea what he's singing about. Anyway, you can't describe a voice. In a sordid story about a castrato soprano, I wrote: *There are words to describe beauty, to describe perfection, every one of them halt, imperfect, un-beautiful unless they were to be scored for the castrato's voice.* . . . Jochen Kowalski is not a eunuch (so far as I know) but a countertenor with an unusually high tessitura, up into the mezzo-soprano range. Sing-ing an aria from Telemann's *Flavius Bertaridus*, he hits the same pitches as the high, bravura horns, with similar precision, penetra-tion, and brilliance. His top notes make the hairs on the back of my neck to prickle, my ears to ring. This is a very definite, physical, sensual reaction. I get hard in my shorts.

Well, it's true. If I go out walking with Jochen on the portable disc-player I have to wear tight briefs and baggy trousers or embar-rass myself completely. Bad enough I'm bopping along, waggling my chin and rocking my shoulders . . . to Baroque opera. I mean, some of it's got to leak out under the headphones, people can tell it's not rap or funk or house.

But tonight it's late and I'm sitting alone in my oppressive little apartment, no one near but the cats, who don't care. The last two days have been warm, Indian summer (it's October), and an excellent thunderstorm just finished up outside. I've brewed myself a double espresso—hot, bitter, invigorating. Hortensio gazes either right at me or over my shoulder with those huge, dark, lucent eyes. I'm really a very sentimental, soppy, vanilla sort of person—rough sex, in the flesh, doesn't appeal to me. I have my suspicions about the kind of sex Hortensio's after. He looks cruel. His fingers are very long, very slender. I think he would not be satisfied with necking and cuddling and rubbing, maybe a little mutual wanking. He has the most beautiful mouth, however, which I would really like to kiss. (The mouth of the man I'm not going to talk about, now that

I think of it, is rather similar.) The lips are quite pale but very red against his olive skin and below his straggly black mustache; the upper is broader than the lower. I like the idea of his big nose getting in the way. His eyebrows are very black, very thick. His ears are too large. (Greco had a penchant, if not a fetish, for large ears, which I must say I don't share.) I like the fact that he's wearing these huge, bulky robes but you can still tell he's really skinny. Big Adam's apple.

Jochen on the stereo on endless repeat has just come around again to that Telemann aria. It's warm enough that I'm sitting here in just boxer shorts, plenty of room to maneuver. As if it were a leaky pen, my prick draws a sticky line up my thigh. The silly thing wants to find the boxers' fly, but it's not very bright so it's pointing off at the wrong angle. I'm quite fond of my prick. It's not exceptional, I suppose, but it's certainly not exceptionable. A fair handful. Cut—not because I'm Jewish or Muslim, but because I was a postwar American baby. Jochen hits one of those supernal high notes, drags it down, and then rides it up a spectacular arpeggio, and the thing jerks, jumps, pokes its way out. When it's headstrong like this I like to refer to it as *my member* . . . my engine of desire. Still, I'm not going to touch it—I'm typing. Well, I probably will end up touching it, but not yet.

One of the rites of adolescence I skipped was measuring the length and girth of my dick. I really can't judge. At my age (as long as I'm being honest: thirty-eight), it would seem inappropriate to pull out a ruler now, if I owned one. One of the preoccupations of the modern gay man—one of quite a few—that I don't buy into is size. I see these hard-up fellows in skin magazines and they just look uncomfortable, as if their teeth hurt. One can imagine where their partners hurt. Mine, on the other hand, is the right size.

I'm practically ready to swoon—or to come—but I can't get any further with Jochen, his voice, his singing, on the keyboard. Damn the inadequacy of words. If only he were a hairy-chested Palermitan with a big nose who talks with his hands. I could think of a lot of other things he might do with his hands, if he were. Alas, as I said, I've seen photos. Puzzlingly, too, although the high male voice was practically invented and certainly brought to its peak of

perfection in Italy (*viva il coltèllo!*), there seem to be no Italian coun-
tertenors currently recording. They're mostly suavely French and dif-
fidently British. I'm as little in sympathy with Britain and France as
with Germany.

Just keep in mind that the divine German's still going great
guns in the background. If French is the language of romance (another idée fixe I won't buy), Italian is the language of passion. Nobody ought to sing in any other language. The words might as well
be pernicious nonsense—something about the joyful sound of martial
trumpets; so long as they're Italian and Jochen does them up proud,
I'm his. Every so often he achieves something with that voice that
—if you heard it without being told—you'd probably take for a
woman's, something that makes me quiver from head to toe, that
inspires a little twitch or tremor of my cock. I'm sitting up straight,
on the edge of my seat, legs spread, so it's poking more out than
up. My shorts are white with green stripes, an odd, not unattractive
contrast with the pinky-beige flesh of the shaft. Thin, branching red
blood vessels crawl up from the base, halting short of the circumcision scar, a brownish grosgrain ribbon tied all the way round some
ways below the flared rim of the head; but the thicker, ropier, sin-
gular blue vessels burrow under the ribbon and bulge up again beyond before they peter out. The head itself, the crown, is bulbous,
globular, and quite red. In porn stories they're always describing it
as *spongy*; I don't know what that means. It looks slick, almost glassy,
glazed, as if it would ring like porcelain when you flicked it with a
fingernail. In fact, the shape of it, the way it flares out so decisively
below the tender swell, reminds me of an English bone-china teacup
I own. The glazed white interior of the cup displays a chinoiserie
kingfisher perched on a flowering branch, but the outside is solid, a
color fleshy and nearly obscene—Pompeiian red, or oxblood.

It's amusing and idyllic to imagine Hortensio creeping up under the desk to poke his excellent nose into my crotch, but I suspect
he'd really rather tie me down first. He snuffles around down there
for a bit, then draws back, lays his lovely hands on the tops of my
thighs. Palms sliding against the friction of my leg hair, the fingertips push the fabric of my boxers toward the hips, pulling it up
between my legs to form a cunning bag or basket for the balls.

Lowering his head, openmouthed, he breathes coolly across the crown of my cock. The lucent little pearl of pre-cum clinging there trembles, jiggles. His tongue, which I imagine long, meaty, pointed, stretches out to lap it up but doesn't get it all: a liquid strand like opalescent silk or spit hangs a perfect catenary curve between his lower lip and my prick. Then, as he licks his lips, it breaks, trails down over his chin into his beard, and then he leans forward again.

The crown of his head, with its curly, flyaway black hair, being in the way, I cannot, unfortunately, see what he's doing. At first he simply kisses the head, his lips hot, dry, silky. Then the tip of his tongue dabbles at the vertical slit or eye. Then the lips part and I'm in. I imagine that the inside of any man's mouth is much the same as any other man's, and while a cock is extremely sensitive it's not especially discriminating. Hortensio is a competent cocksucker. He takes it all, doesn't scratch me with his teeth, it's hot and moist in there and he performs clever little tricks with his tongue, but his heart's not in it. Where he wants me is flat on my back, spread-eagled. My hands tied to the bedposts. He kneels up between my legs. First he pushes the black stole back up over his head, tosses it away behind him. He's smiling broadly, his eyes narrowed. The heavy white cassock drapes down from his shoulders, giving nothing away.

Do other men fantasize being made love to by the figures in masterpieces of western painting? When I was a kid reading *The Coral Island* I had dirty thoughts about Jack and Ralph and Peterkin shipwrecked all alone. Even then, I had my suspicions about young Peterkin, a queen in the making if I ever met one. I was deeply infatuated with competent, manly Jack. Of course, as a kid I didn't have much idea exactly what Ralph and Jack were doing there in the back of my mind with no clothes on, those lissome brown boys' limbs tangled together in a tropic bower, but I was quite sure they were up to something naughty and exciting. More recently, I wanted Lovelace to scheme and plot to ravish me, rather than Clarissa. What a splendid villain Lovelace is! I suspect I'm hardly the only man whose romantic expectations have been deformed by literature. But painting? I'm not a visual thinker—I don't *see* things with the mind's eye: I describe them to myself with the mind's word processor. When I remember my dreams, it's in the form of sentences and paragraphs.

In all of western art, the only hand more beautiful than Hortensio's two appears in another Greco portrait (*Man with His Hand on His Breast*, in the Prado), but this observation is beside the point. Hortensio's hands rise to the neck of his cassock. He's no longer smiling, his lips in repose, disdainful and passionate at once, his black eyes glowing mutely. They're very long, his hands, weightless, delicate, almost translucent—one might characterize them (one might characterize Jochen's voice) as feminine. Grasping the heavy, soft, white wool with surprising confidence, they tear the fabric down the front in one motion, one sustained, satisfying ripping noise, and he shrugs the thing off his shoulders. Of course my eyes go first to his cock, but one narrative convention to which I cheerfully subscribe is the payoff postponed, the climax delayed . . . until my readers whimper. He lifts his right hand to his breast in much the same gesture as that of the Man in the Greco portrait referenced above. Hortensio's breast, however, is now laid bare, just as I imagined it. He does not possess distended weight-lifter tits. There's a sufficient layer of flesh, just enough, to either side of the decisive sternum. The growth of thin, feathery black hair sketches an upside-down capital T, its stem reaching for the defenseless hollow where his clavicles meet. He pinches his rosy left nipple between two of those pointed fingers.

I've forgotten half the Spanish I ever knew and what's left isn't nearly adequate to let him speak to me. A pity, since I've always found the Castilian accent sexy. His left hand at the end of an elegant gesture reaches between his thighs, gathers up his balls in a serene grasp, hefts them, weighs them. I would score this next passage for trumpets, fast violins, unearthly oboes, and of course Jochen Kowalski's miraculous voice, tripping up the artificial conventions of eighteenth-century Italian verse and the da capo aria with a passion no less affecting for being affected, dramatic. What I'd hope for Hortensio to do (myself being helpless, tied down, my prick straining, aching, leaking) is either to toss my ankles over his shoulders and with no mercy or compunction ream out my ass; or, carefully, to straddle my hips, thrust his knees into my armpits, and sit on my cock.

That's what I'd hope for. What he does is, the fingers of his right hand trail delicately down his long torso to grasp his handsome prick. The horsecock of the biggest discovery-of-the-year porn star would appear clumsy, inadequate in that lovely hand, but his looks just fine, just right, dark enough for contrast against the olive pallor of the bony hand, sturdy, fleshy enough for contrast against the spindly fingers. All the while he gazes down at me with cruelly tender eyes, his upper lip lifted just slightly off rapacious teeth.

The hand starts out clamped around the base, buried in thick black pubic hair, cutting off the blood flow so the cock expands still more, thickening, lengthening. Crepey olive-beige foreskin shrouds the head, making it look blunt and soft, which it's anything but. He bounces it a little, then loosens his grasp. A phosphorescent dribble of pre-cum drools from the wrinkly lip. He milks it, drawing along the whole length as he shoves his hips forward, until there's just a little collar, like the tied-off mouth of a balloon, pinched between index finger and thumb, and a strand of the sticky stuff dangles, swaying like a pendulum, the terminus of its arc being the tip of my own fine, upstanding prick. It slips, and breaks, and drips. The coolness of the slime eases hot flesh.

Suddenly rough, rearing, he pulls the foreskin back to expose the glistening, shiny head. With his left hand he tugs on his balls, grunting hotly, with his right fiercely pumps the shaft. Those lovely lips draw back in a snarl, nearly ugly, showing his teeth; eyes squint, brows draw down to meet on the bridge of his patrician nose, its nostrils widely flared. He breathes raggedly, heavily, the ribs showing on his flanks like the ribs of a Japanese paper lantern. He's glowing, gleaming, sweating, flushed, illumined. The hands keep working, one tugging, twisting, pulling, the other thrusting in little pistonlike strokes, rabbit punches. Me, I'm just where he wants me, just how he wants me. All I can do is strain appealingly at my bonds, moan, roll my hips from side to side, cock flopping like a faulty metronome.

The violinists are sawing away, the bandleader pounding at the keys of his harpsichord. Two trumpeters raise their horns to pursed lips. Jochen Kowalski steps forward a little, tucks his chin into his throat, parts his lips. The sight of him's so disillusioning I can't bear to look. As if just testing the waters, he commences at the bottom of his register, a vibrant contralto, but almost immediately plunges right in. Plunges up, I should say, in jolts and quavers and swoops of stunning velocity and virtuosity, a cascade of brilliant notes, a Roman candle.

The first hot drop of semen strikes my belly; the second—as if a mallet had struck a brass gong—my sternum; the third, acrid, salty, my tongue. As I lick and savor and swallow, Jochen takes his top notes through a sustained run of extravagant fioriture and Hortensio continues to spurt, peppering my belly and chest with hot little splats. Two tiny droplets, one, then another, light in the corners of my eyes, like tears.

I said I wasn't going to talk about the other one, that man I haven't met of whom I'm honestly afraid to become enamored quite yet, and I won't, except in terms so specific as to be meaningless. After I run the spell check on this document while smoking my last cigarette of the night, after I shut the computer down and turn out the lights so I can no longer watch Fray Paravicino watching me, after I slip Herr Kowalski's disc out of the CD player (such stimulation I don't need) and replace it with the angelic concerti grossi of Arcangelo Corelli, turned down low to lull me to sleep, after I toss my soiled boxer shorts into the laundry hamper, I'll pull back the comforter and lay me down on my ascetic futon. The cats will curl up by my feet. I'll lie for a little while on my left side, my head aching slightly, as it does after working too long. I'll sigh, satisfied with my labors, but unsatisfied, unfulfilled.

And then I'll roll over, into his cool, skinny, boyish arms, his whispered confidences, his raspberry-sweet breath in my nostrils, his lips like sweet pomegranates pressed first to one eyelid, then the other, then my mouth. His slippery tongue recoils from the taste of stale tobacco, then pokes right in, impulsive, parts my lips, touches my teeth. The stubble on his lovely little chin rasps against the bristles of my beard and the tip of his nose caresses my cheek. One small, soft hand traces a path down my flank, dragging over corrugated rib cage to the hip. One knee nudges between my thighs as he draws me closer. Only one of us can sleep with his head resting on the other's chest, hearing the slow constant of the beating heart, monotonous thoroughbass for Corelli's virtuoso strings. Will it be I? Will it be he? Good night, sweet prince.

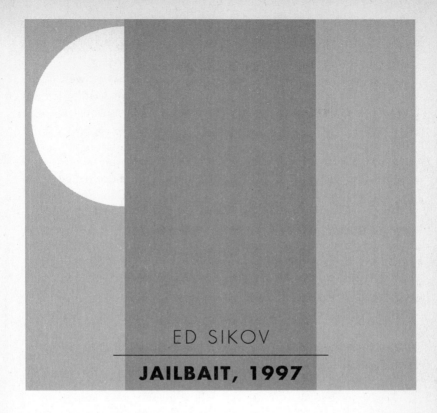

ED SIKOV

JAILBAIT, 1997

FIRST THE FACTS, THEN THE THEORY. THE DIRT COMES LAST.
I'm a film critic, and I often think about what it would be like to
fuck a movie star. No big deal, right? Well, I'm a film professor,
too, and I often think about fucking my students. This presents
problems.

I can't help but notice that in both areas of my professional life
I often develop an erotic fixation on the objects of my attentions.
Frankly, I don't see any need to be cured of it. But as a college
professor in the 1990s I stand some risk of wrecking my career for
writing about what a lot of us feel but few of us can cop to: we want
to fuck or get fucked by our students. I'm an itinerant and part-time
academic, so the question of a tenure battle will never arise, and yes,
this gives me some extra latitude in writing about student-teacher

fuck fantasies. Still, I have to admit that there might be unpleasant ramifications down the road. My feeling is, *let 'em try*.

As long as I'm in the confessional mode, I may as well go all the way: I'm also a professional pornographer. I've written mildly sleazy but basically clean-cut sex stories (swimmer boys who might like to get tied up once in a while, hunky professors who like to fuck young men, etc.) for *Honcho Overload*, *Torso*, and other skin magazines, and for the last few years I've penned a monthly video review column for *Inches* (under the name of my libertine alter ego, Joe McKenna). I like writing porn. In its own way it's the most honest writing I do. It's immediate and unapologetic—a quick, intense dream. Porn is utopian, but it has a practical purpose: I write porn so other people can have better jerk-off sessions. It's cheap dirty literature, and that's why I write it.

Naturally, I'm particularly turned on by stories about profs and students. They speak to me:

> "Professor Stokes was telling me about Walt Whitman, and while he talked he kept moving his leg closer to mine. I could feel the heat coming off him. . . ."
>
> Or, "All the other guys had left by the time I hit the showers. Then I saw the other team's coach, all by himself, soaping up in the corner. . . ."
>
> Or, "My GPA is incredibly important to me, 'cause of med school and everything? And I was just wondering if there was anything I could do to get a better grade in your course. I'll do *anything*."
>
> Or, "Before I knew what was happening, I was splayed over my psych professor's desk and he was sticking his tongue up my hole!"

And on and on. (By the way, the third example is true—an exact quote, in fact. But since I'm a real professor, not a porn fantasy, I gently steered the poor kid back to reality and told him the best thing he could do would be to study a little harder.)

Most men need porn to bring them closer to twenty-year-olds, but I just need to walk into class. Still, there's a price to be paid: I'm never allowed to talk about what it makes me feel like—not on campus anyway. Teaching requires me to turn off everything that turns me on.

Now, anyone who has ever been in college knows that a male professor's attempt to hide his hard-ons is a joke, but the need to do so still lives on as a kind of religion. You find yourself thinking about sucking some student dick? *Thou shalt not.* But perversely, the biblical force of the prohibition only makes the taste for student cock seem filthier and more appealing. Just try spending some time on a college campus. Each night, hundreds or maybe even thousands of nineteen-, twenty-, and twenty-one-year-old men are lying in bed, their balls working overtime. You can't help yourself—you just have to wonder where all their stuff goes. Every day guys come into your office for a private chat—jocks, nerds, studs, shrimps, guys who write, guys who wrestle, actors, guitar players, future Wall Street hotshots and librarians—all throwing off sex vibes like mists of sweat. The sensation can be overpowering. It can make your head roar.

But don't even think about acknowledging it in public. Keep it secret; avert your eyes. Only at night, when nobody's looking, can you slam it into them 'til they beg for mercy. When you see them the next day, you have to forget about having imagined everything from the precise amount of hair on their asses to the noise they make when they cum.

I suspect every professor on earth has thought about some student's ass, or dick, or cunt, or tits, or feet, or belly button at one point or another, and I don't think it has anything to do with gender or sexual orientation. College teaching doesn't provide great financial rewards, but it makes up for it by offering up a buffet of sexually aggressive men and women, all at the dawn of their adulthood. The scent of sex is in the air on college campuses, and sooner or later every professor has to smell it.

On those all-too-rare occasions when a professor hits the jackpot and actually fucks a student, it becomes a kind of private lore—an oral tradition of special secrecy. Sex with a student is a very different experience from sex outside of school because the professor in question isn't supposed to mention it; if he does, it's only in the form of occasional guilty whispers, and then only to another faculty pervert.

In contrast, students treat their affairs with faculty as conquests. Amazingly enough, they see themselves as having some power and integrity as individuals. A lot of professors may hate to admit it, but students always have more authority than we give them credit for.

For the professor, though, it's much more dangerous. This is especially so in the 1990s, which is in some ways a greater reign of sexual terror than the notorious 1950s. Professor-student sex is the communism of our era: you draw the blinds, check the doors, and ease your way tentatively into the conversation (let alone the fucking) because you don't want to take any chances. What makes the nineties worse than the fifties is the fact that the commies generally don't even have the guts to stand up for themselves. We live in fear, students and professors alike. Students learn that sexual harassment begins with an invitation to lunch. Professors know that every class-room contains a career-destroying lawsuit. Freud is truly dead: re-pression, once our enemy, has again become a reassuring safety net. We welcome it as a way of life. And we do so with no less cer-tainty—and with no weaker a grip—than Americans of the 1950s welcomed the hydrogen bomb.

It would be less surprising if students themselves weren't so overheated. I can assure you that sexual energy between students and faculty flows in both directions. I've had several guys in my classes pull up their shirts to show off their chests and stomachs to me— in one case, right in the middle of my lecture. It was the first week of September, a muggy late-summer afternoon, and I was standing in front of a remedial writing class at a college in New York City. I was introducing the concept of the sentence when the door banged open and a lithe, hard-bodied Italian kid swaggered in, planted him-self in the front row, and snarled at me. When forced, he told me his name was Nick.

Within moments, Nick felt the need to scratch his back—by reaching under the front of his T-shirt and riding it up all the way over his muscular belly, his angular pecs, and finally his slim right shoulder. Nick had the barest, downiest patch of chest hair right on his sternum but nothing on his stomach. His navel was deep and dark, a mean-looking gash cut into hard muscles.

Nick watched my expression closely as he showed off. I don't know what he saw in my face. All I remember is that my mouth went dry and I felt an all-but-overpowering desire to lick everything I saw, all while trying to remember what a sentence was and why I ever thought it was important to impart the information.

After a few languorous moments, Nick pulled his hand out and his T-shirt fell back into place. And that was all I saw of Nick's body; I seem to have passed whatever test he gave me that first day (damn it). After that, Nick settled down, kept his clothes on, and became one of the better students in the class.

At a much richer, prepped-out school in the Midwest I actually saw a guy's cock in class, and I didn't have to try very hard to do so. The course was Shakespeare on Film. Sean, one of my star students, was a WASPy English major with a fine light complexion, sea-blue eyes, and a thick shock of golden, inevitably tousled hair. The whole package was effortless. He took himself totally for granted.

One day in mid-spring when the temperature was supposed to hit 50 and the students were all energetically jumping the gun on summer, Sean showed up wearing Birkenstocks, a T-shirt, and a pair of baggy surfer-boy shorts. I was seated at my desk in front of the class, and in the midst of a sentence about cycles of despair in *King Lear* I noticed that Sean's legs were splayed wide open. I looked right up his pants and saw his dick hanging down his left leg. It was pale, like the rest of him; not too huge, I was glad to see; and it rested in a field of rather sparse blond hair.

I'd become a more confident teacher since the Nick incident, so after a muted double take, I continued addressing the question of despair and madness in *Lear* while privately reaffirming my own faith in life. Seeing Sean's cock was as satisfying a voyeuristic moment as I've ever had. His good looks hit an aesthetic peak as far as the classic male figure is concerned, and all without a speck of self-consciousness on the part of the figure. This relaxed, self-confident kid had absolutely no idea that his cock was making my mouth water. Perfect.

Do I even need to say that I've had demonstrably straight guys come into my office and flirt with me for reasons that I cannot comprehend? I still can't fathom what they want from me, but that doesn't mean I'm oblivious to the techniques they employ: the stretching, the hands rubbing their bodies all over, the sleepy-lidded eyes, the flirty smirks. They know what they're doing. The captain of the baseball team, a star soccer player, a lacrosse player, a former high school diving champ—these are only some of the highlights. Smart kids, dumb kids—they've all come in, sat down next to me, thrown open their legs as wide as possible, slung their arms over the back of the chair, thrust their hips forward, scratched their bellies, adjusted their balls, and discussed their grades. Their summer vacations. Their girlfriends. Their final papers. Whether or not they should bleach their hair.

That one was my favorite. I've rarely been so absorbed by a student's personal anecdote as I was the day a very friendly, inadvertently studly math major came into the office and proceeded to tell me about how he dyed his hair blond by dousing his head with chlorine at the pool where he was lifeguarding over the summer. Then he added, "I don't have to do anything to the hair on my body 'cause it bleaches naturally in the sun." In those moments there's really nothing you can do but let the mists wash over you.

So is it surprising that I think about how much fun it would be to fuck them?

But wait a minute. This is 1997, and on college campuses in 1997 the repression of any sexual spark between teacher and student is institutionally mandated. The sixties are over, there is no love, it's all sexual harassment. We are living in an era when a hand on a shoulder is Exhibit A in a lawsuit. If a professor becomes even barely physical with a student, he's in trouble. Our affection for the people whose lives we help to shape has become grounds for dismissal. With terrifying moral and intellectual certainty, academics are convinced that even the mildest expression of affection by a professor toward a student is just another form of power, that power is abuse, that abuse is sex, and that sex is rape.

So here we are, earnestly regulating our own sexual drives and the drives of our students while simultaneously teaching Foucault. I don't teach much poststructural theory, but I do agree that sociocultural life is dominated by empty codes of power, and nowhere more so than in academic life. Does the carving of a rule and the issuing of a threat diminish the overpowering lust many of us face week after week in seminars and lecture halls full of young people at their sexual peak? Hardly. Threats of disciplinary action do nothing to alter the fact that we have students who admire us, at least a little bit, and that we sometimes react by wondering how much fun it would be if they would express this admiration by sucking our dicks.

Or maybe we want to suck theirs. Maybe we enjoy their youth and vitality enough to want to taste it. Even the most desiccated professor can scarcely remain unaware of the imbalance of power involved in teaching. For some of us, it's not too much of a leap to fantasize about ways of balancing this power through sex. In practice, I'm constantly trying to rework classroom dynamics so that my students can express themselves better and more often. And late at night, or in my office, or even in the middle of my classes, I daydream about having them teach *me* a thing or two.

It's difficult for me to maintain a dominant role in a lecture hall without pushing the power-trip aspect of teaching to its logical sexual end, at least in my own endless mental porn loops. I think about how great it would be to strip one of the many studs whose attentions I'm trying to hold while lecturing on the subject of gender dynamics, pin him on the floor, throw his legs over my shoulders, slap him around a little bit, and give him a hands-on lesson on the subject of phallocentrism. I can teach gender issues until I'm blue in the face, but to most of the straight guys it's pure theory. I say this: until those boys get fucked, they can have only the vaguest clue what phallocentrism means and why the current gender wars aren't likely to be resolved anytime soon.

I only fucked a student once. To be more precise, I've only fucked, and been fucked by, one student. We did it over the course of a year and a half, but then we did all kinds of other things as well—travel, shop, watch TV, snuggle, cook dinner, argue, wash the dishes. Drew wasn't just a student fuck fantasy. He was my lover, and he's still my friend.

We met in class. As usual, I told my students that if they wanted to invite me to lunch, go to a movie with me, get some dinner, or have a drink or a cup of coffee, all they had to do was ask. I got four offers that term—three from women, one from Drew.

The women all picked lunch. Drew, on the other hand, popped into the office one day and asked me if he could pick me up at ten-thirty on Saturday night. I thought he was handsome—tall, thin, dark-blond, Nordic, very Midwestern—and I liked the idea of going out on the town with a gorgeous young guy. I said, "Sure."

Our courtship took a little more time than he imagined it would. When Drew told me he wanted to kiss me—about midnight that first night—I pulled back. I said I thought we ought to table the discussion until after the course had ended. I really don't think profs should sleep with students until their professional relationship is over, and besides, my long-standing fantasy was suddenly and implausibly coming true, and I had a lot of trouble dealing with it. My hands were shaking as I tossed him a farewell wave, but when I was alone and under the sheets about a half hour later, I wasn't nearly so anxious about the idea.

The class eventually ended. I gave Drew a B+. (Hey, his paper was late, so I downgraded him. He's still pissed off.) Then I asked him if he'd like to meet me for a drink again. This time *I* was the one who lunged—and he the one who pulled back. But after some discussion, reassurance, and quiet snuggling, we got it on. And we kept getting it on for the next seventeen months.

Drew and I had an old-fashioned monogamous relationship. We spent most nights together. I introduced him to my parents, and they all got along fine. My parents were glad I'd found someone to be with, and if they had a problem with how we met they never let me know about it. And Drew was everything I'd ever wanted in a boyfriend. I had the status; he had the vitality. I was thirty-seven; he was twenty-two. I had the endurance; he had amazing amounts of cum to spend on me. I'm (mostly) a top; he's (mostly) a bottom. And he was smart. We'd lie in bed—my hand on his stomach, his hand on my chest—and talk about Martin Duberman.

What I had with Drew went well beyond student-teacher porn fantasies, but like any good relationship it still had its moments of filth. Sometimes when I'd be giving it to him I'd think about who he was and how we met and I'd give it to him a little harder. I know Drew liked it, too. We had a particular position that worked best —Drew sitting very far forward on the couch, leaning back against the cushions, while I fucked him from a kneeling position on the floor. It gave me the best view of his lean torso, which I could run my hands over endlessly. And I also liked watching him at close range as he shot his stuff all over himself.

Our relationship ended when Drew, always restless, decided to see what it was like to live in Germany. We talk on the phone now. He writes postcards to my parents.

I don't think I'll find another Drew anytime soon, but luckily for me the exercise of desire isn't confined by an all-too-dull reality. Often, what makes the idea of fucking my students hot is that I'll *never* go through with it. It's the exquisite ache of wanting what I can't have. College students are thus the ideal fantasy objects; I can look but I can't touch. And I *do* look. *And they look back*—with a certain respect, which only adds to the sexual buzz. They look up to me. They want something from me. They like me, but they fear me. I tell them a joke, they laugh; they think they should. I give them an assignment, they complete it; they think they should. They're compliant without being terribly aware of it. They're ready to be taught. And yeah, I admit it—I like it when aggressive youngsters turn out to be just a little submissive.

Do they notice that I steal quick glances at the spectacular physical effect created by every breath they take? Or is it that they *want* me to look at them and lose myself in their images? Honestly, I don't know. What I can tell you is that they've given me material for jerk-off fantasies that will last a lifetime.

Armpit Boy is my all-time favorite. He still shows up at night, eight years after he took my Intro Film class. I first noticed him in the weight room at a college out West. Dark-haired, brown-eyed, and insufferably handsome, Armpit Boy was wearing a tank top and a pair of navy-blue gym shorts that had obviously been used in place of coveralls during a painting job over the summer. White paint stains streaked down his thighs and across his ass. I began to put together a little story from the details:

He'd been in a paint fight with one of his buddies. They were outside in the heat of July, shirtless. They'd finished up for the day, and as they were putting the paint away, one of them—*my* guy, I liked to think—accidentally spilled some paint on his friend, who retaliated in a perfectly boyish way by swiping his paintbrush across the sweaty navy-blue cotton that barely covered my guy's hard round butt.

That was the story, and as I said, I still use it often.

I wondered if he liked it. I wondered how far the scene could possibly go. I was the friend sometimes, but usually I just watched.

I especially liked the idea that this kid had *worked* over the summer—that he earned some honest sweat and didn't just lie around the pool and read books. That's what the paint stains on his gym-trunked ass meant to me. I loved looking at them. I still do.

But as fine and firm as this kid's ass was, and however much the paint stains lent an air of a real working life to him, what really did me in was the hair in his armpits. He had a fine set of wrestler's shoulders. His arms were developing well—they'd be killers in a few more years if he kept up his biceps-heavy workout routine—and the hair underneath was jet black, thick and coarse but smooth and straight, wet with sweat, and suffused with the kind of salty-sweet funk that only a twenty-year-old can produce. In the gym I used to get right up next to him and do more than the usual number of curls, just to see how long I could stand being next to him without getting hard.

What was it about the hair under this guy's arms? There's always something nakedly carnal about armpits. They have no redeeming value other than as a place to pay attention to—something to smell and taste, to twirl and lick and maybe even yank with your teeth when their owner least suspects it. Armpit Boy's were overpowering.

I was teaching an unusually large course that semester, and it took me another few class sessions to realize that Armpit Boy was actually one of my own students. With a sweater on, he was handsome, but he was in a sea of handsome guys wearing sweaters and thus was invisible. But in the gym in a tank top he was *David* about five years earlier—less of a god, more of a boy. And he was swarthy and human, not white and stone. This one had olive skin and black hair. He had sweat and smell. And he didn't just stand there posing—he breathed and flexed. He liked to look at himself in the mirror. So did I.

I had him in my class, but he had me the rest of the time. The relationship, though entirely imaginary, made a great deal of sense to me. It still does. As the obsession grew, I began hanging around him at closer and closer range, to the point that I eventually realized I was simply trying to sniff him. I wanted to befriend him—the way a dog in heat tries to befriend other dogs. But Armpit Boy wasn't a dog. He was my student. He admired me.

"Hello, Professor," he'd say with a slight dip of his head whenever he'd see me. It was a nod of deference, but I liked to read it, especially in memory in the years that followed, as quite the opposite—as his way of saying, "Yeah, I know you want to suck my cock, and I also know you can never have me."

Sweet god, please? I thought. *Please?!*

Armpit Boy was also Straight Boy. I never imagined otherwise. This meant I was never going to get him no matter what I did, and of course that only made him hotter. And it didn't seem to matter in the slightest to Armpit Boy if some faculty faggot was lurking around the weight room watching him do shoulder presses. Still, I became concerned. Was I so far gone over him that I'd become an object of pity? What if I started to drool? What if my gym trunks suddenly tented? These pulses of shame only added to the erotic tension. I loved it. *I loved him.*

Each encounter with Armpit Boy began the same way: the quick nod of the head and "Hello, Professor," or sometimes just "Professor." He acknowledged my authority every time he saw me, and by doing so he acknowledged his own. Each time I saw him he admitted that I was his superior, and each time the acknowledgment only made my daydreams raunchier. Harder. Longer. More spit, more sounds. I thought obsessively about what his cock must look like with cum shooting out of it. I wanted to lick his balls. I wondered which girls on campus already had. I thought about sticking my finger in his ass while I sucked him off. I wondered whether he'd like it. No—I *knew*. He *would* like it. I was his prof. I would *make* him like it.

I gave Armpit Boy a B— in the course and wanted to apologize to him for it—to ask him what I could do to make up for ruining his GPA. Maybe I'd get lucky. Maybe he'd punish me.

I'm sorry, Greg. I'll make it up to you, I swear. You can even call me names if you want.

Take off your tank top. Stretch your arms over your head.

Please don't take a shower.

I want to lick you.

Teach me.

ROBERT GLÜCK

A FALSE STEP

A MAN WATCHED ME SHOWER AND FOLLOWED ME INTO the sauna. He said, "I'm always watching the clock."

"The clock?" I looked around.

"The time."

"For work?" He was a little man with large features, glossy black curls, and a narrow waist fanning into cheeks as cantilevered as the drawer of a file cabinet.

"Work," he confirmed. He settled onto a bench below a small yellow light and a temperature gauge. I wanted to interest him in me; I began to see him as a destination.

"You work at night?"

He considered this. "The night shift." His voice was precise and deep. He spread his legs and the tip of his cock rested on the wooden slats. My skin prickled; we began to sweat.

I said, "I used to work at night. In New York. On the night shift unloading trucks at the Grand Central Station Post Office."

"Oh, and you went around New York during the day."

I wanted to interest him, but he was not being very interesting himself. Was talking in the sauna inappropriate, dumb-friendly? Three citizens filed in, smiles from the outside still unfaded, and draped themselves on the benches; in ten minutes they were dazed and suffering, their genitals poaching on their white laps. I could not smell my own sweat, but I watched the shine on a drop that for some reason didn't evaporate. Sighing, the men hauled themselves to their feet and left as one. The metal furnace made shifting clicks; the flame popped.

He continued to look at me. I began again and told him I was a writer, but that didn't get us very far. I told him I'd left New York, but that was obvious. As though to defend myself, I told him about my ruinous love affair.

He said, "You always complain!" That was too accurate. He'd known me, what, twelve minutes? Perhaps he was referring to something in his own life? I asked him what he did.

"I'm a nurse."

"Where do you work?"

"At St. Luke's."

"Oh, I have a good friend who worked there . . . who just died." Suddenly I couldn't remember my friend's name. I felt a jolt of fear.

"What's his name?"

"Terrance." Terrance returned as though entering the little room, his gestures, his plump face and enthusiasm. I saw his roses, bleak lollipops in the cloudy suburb.

"Terry"—he gave the ghost a nickname. "I didn't know him. In Pharmacy?"

"Administration. He died quickly."

"My brother did."

"Your actual brother?"

"In a few months. He didn't want to take anything. He thought his mind was strong enough."

"To cure him?"

"He had a belief system—the moment is all you have, why put a condom on it?" His brother had explored his own death. I am interested in people who believe the spirit has orientation. What I understood: his brother could project himself into an ectoplasmic medium through a calm that had direction (like the needle of a compass) in the eye of a sex storm, then spiritually freeze the medium and evaporate it until he was sort of freeze-dried and displayed as an essence. Like any fanatic, he needed to show the world what he had become. A glimpse of a shadow fucking hard and sped up.

The system of the brother's thought is a story for another time, but I was amazed to hear the name Michel Foucault, his brother's friend and mentor, so wildly out of context.

In the sauna we were silent for a while. His body seemed complete—the moons of his fingernails. I thought this talk of AIDS had shifted us hopelessly away from each other. I lay against the wooden wall, my head tilted back as though relaxing into the empty heat, the arousing sedative. That was so he could look at me. I muted my own judgment of my soft larval body and let fear speed up my heart and pleasure flow in the skin on my chest, belly, and thighs. I would face him; we would be on our knees, impossible, face-to-face because of the emotion there, his legs spread, out of the way. My cock slides in just a bit farther, I feel great, aware of a perpetual whirring, the beginning of sweetness on a broiling day. We're sweating freely, mightily awake.

Meanwhile we sat quietly with my old familiar cock and his, like a mood ring, a bag at one point, floppy, the connection to his body a slim hinge, then surprisingly blunt and meaty, an assertion. I smelled hot wood and chlorine. He was in charge of being sexually attractive and touching him intimately equaled eternal life. Oil from the backs of countless men had stained a dark wainscot on the wall I leaned against. I would push him around a little, push him over, then raise his torso so his ass unfolds, a place where everything is visible. It must be seen to be believed—don't avert your eyes: the party's at Hairy's. He would not struggle against me, but against his own openness, jaw dropped, grunting as I shove a finger in.

My fantasies sort of replaced my man. To my surprise, he slid over onto the bench below mine and said, "Is this okay? I couldn't tell." He barely touched me.

I barely touched him, touched his shoulder, we were sort of folding into each other without touching, like the two halves of a tackle box. I thought he was going to blow me. The human race fixed its eyes on that possibility. I blurted, "Would you like a date?" It was such a random thing to say that we both sat stumped for a minute. I tried to regain my footing—"That is, you're a handsome man." My locker key was burning the skin on my thigh.

He said, "My heart is beating so fast. It's so hot in here."

"Mine is too. That is, I'd like to sleep with you." Why didn't I say "have sex"?

"Sure," he offered, "that would be fun."

He looked a little caved in, teary. He raised his head and I tipped it farther back, holding it, and brushed his lips with mine. His position emphasized his size; I could lift and hold him.

"Sweet," he said. Then, after a moment, "My name's Pete."

"What?"

"Pete."

"Oh, Bob." But now my voice sounded strange, high and taut, Dudley Do-right.

"I'll be here the same time for the next three days," Pete said.

"The same time?" Weird voice.

"For the next three days." My ears were starting to burn. Rills of sweat ran off his face and chest. He seemed to be getting up, but when I suggested we go out together he seemed to be staying. First the heat aroused us, then it punched a hole in that arousal, though we both had semis. He stood up; all the flesh on his lean body was intelligent and knew what it was doing except for the mounds of his ass, which were ignorant and required tenderness, direction, education. That's the penis orating as it disorganizes its—owner? I slid my hand down Pete's slick back. My lips brushed the most beautiful mouth in the world. I could have stayed, touched him, no problem, but I was urgent to go, to contain this rather than fall into it.

"Bye, Pete." Cold air and a rushing noise flowed in.

We sort of avoided each other, though I watched him shower,

and the two parts of myself that debate were in agreement. When
he blew his nose it echoed. I laughed, possessing a little of him as
though I'd got a private joke. There were factory clangs, the odor of
deodorant. Pete's ass was cheerful and unreal, like balloons. He might
be too much of a twinkie, I warned myself. Well, I've always been
attracted to shallow men: I saw myself explaining that to my current
ex-boyfriend over my shoulder as Pete and I stepped into the future
together. Pete doesn't read but that's okay. I had presented myself
as a Boho, confident in the power of a simple heart, comfortable with
my self-worth and inevitable failure. Someone who writes in cafes
and is charmed by the weather. In a way, HIV and the death of his
brother were the most neutral things we could discuss.

Hello, hello? Gluckmann?
    This is Robert Glück.
    Gluck? Gluck? Just a minute. Yes. That's right. Mr. Gluck, you
are familiar with the Beth Shalom Elementary School many Russian
immigrant students? But with funds cut looking for fellow Jews to
support?
    No, I—
    You're Jewish? You are Jewish?
    I can't give you anything—I give to AIDS and I'm—
    To the Federation?
    On unemployment. Good luck and—
    So next year?
    No, I—
    You're *not* Jewish?
    A *fallen* Jew.
    You don't give?

I squeezed the bud and fell asleep. I dreamt that young men are kept
in a sunny and weedy corral. It's summer, the shadows are hard. The
men are sort of ancient Greek in that their flesh glorifies itself with
luxurious butts. They are kidnapped without force and shown a
Golden Age to which they acclimate quickly. When they arrive,
electrodes are planted in the walls of their rectums—in the nerves
of voluptuousness, as my dream commentator explains. The electrodes emit gentle encouragement, as though a tab of mild acid were

inserted there, but an ever-stronger thrill eventually replaces the young men's memories, goals, and self-regard. They are on hands and knees in the dust, fucking air with rapt expressions. One with a cock in him: his sense of his ass is not closed. It's a dark room vaulted with pleasure and the blurred lights of ornate chandeliers—his eyes are wide open, empty.

When I apologize to Pete, he says, "Those things happen some-times," implicitly agreeing that I had been inappropriate. He softly punches my stomach, says, "Don't worry about it." But where does that leave us? Later he lingers in a rectangle of winter sunlight in a corner—so I can walk over? He looks like Mickey Mouse with his simple face and legs that are muscled but basically sticks. Pine's out one window, pen and ink, and Market Street out the other, a postcard.

"I'm trying to get my endurance up," he says.

"Up how?"

"Twenty minutes."

I don't really know what he's talking about. His profile is more delicate than his full face. All around us machines and limbs guide each other in half circles while music wells up and implores desper-ately. "So would you like to get together—have coffee?"

"Sure."

"I can't do it today—Friday?"

"I'll put it on my calendar."

"At one o'clock?"

"Bye, Bob."

Later I catch sight of him, a waif in street clothes, all muscles gone.

It's late Tuesday night: my eyes keep closing on their own. I wonder why I didn't go off with Pete the day we met, and why I didn't have sex with him on Monday. Would everything be better if I hung faded cream wallpaper in my little yellow bedroom? Although I'm eager to see Pete, I have to remind myself that our Friday date exists. In the dark I look forward to the Wednesday *Chronicle*, to the Food and Home sections and to the horoscope, so intensely that I feel a welling-up of love.

I wake up crying, a sense of consequence flitting away like bats.

I'm trembling when I go to the gym on Friday. I feel my heart beating through my chest—why?—even in my hands and groin. I look for Pete, trying to estimate the damage. Is he avoiding me or just spacey? His disappearance has appeared. Suddenly some part of myself tries to "save" me and I become attracted in my mind to another guy I thought I had stopped liking. I watch the attraction assemble itself and take the form of my face between his thighs, etc. I like the way his quick shallow orgasm furrows his brow and makes him frown as though it were a math problem, and gives him ten seconds of respite from the overwhelming tension of his libido. But I use his tension as more excitement to aim at Pete. A refrain sticks in my head, the hook of a disco anthem. A drag-queen diva has a message for me from beyond the grave—I make her feel real. The monotonous beat is a wind pushing me, You Are Happy You Are Happy You Are Happy, till I feel exhausted and oppressed. There is a distance. I move through the gym trembling, saying to myself what I would have said to Pete, and I go home and pinch the skin of my cock a little, toying, deciding if I want to feel pleasure in order to secure what I almost had. Failure reveals itself as lust. Pete says, *"That would be fun,"* but it doesn't amount to much, some huffing, spurting. It doesn't raise the dead. Pete's eyes roll, he's talking on the phone, "And then he asked me for a date!—*random.*"

I read the first part of this story in a literary evening at Good Vibrations, a vibrator store. Afterward, William tells me he recognizes Pete from our gym, in fact he's had sex with Pete. We outline Pete's butt in the air, smacking our lips subnormally. Then William says, "He's very sweet," as though defending Pete against me. I process the information that Pete is active, while trying to size up the differences between William and me from Pete's perspective. William says, "Pete has a lover," as though that explains everything. William and I had a fling many years ago, old, old news, somehow reconciling.

The rest of the story takes place in my head, where Pete joins a central casting. I call him out to jack off with or to think about like a wish; he grows more perfect, more a monster, he is only the curve of his ass and some contorted expressions. I make him the deity of his brother's beliefs, a misshapen god with a few attributes: the tilt of his head backward without resistance, an unprotected ass, a mouth elongated by spasms. I spin the Gumby God like a pinwheel, stretch him out like taffy.

Pete passes me on the street and does not acknowledge me. I feel a moment of weird exaltation—I almost throw back my head and laugh. I desired him in a stale, self-conscious way. Don't make me real: let me be a porn sketch of five thick lines by Joe Brainard, or the two on screen whose flesh is powerful light. Do I want to, what, marry a man whose butt says, Have a nice day? I wanted to put off our date, and his interest appeared strong for only a moment. The link between lust and action. His absence (the rigor of it) reveals my own inertia. Loneliness makes me a shadow, yet loneliness makes me too gigantic to climb out of bed. I'd cry *save me* if there was something to save.

As if to confirm our lack of rapport, I imagine settling into sex with Pete and then hearing the mailman's footsteps on the stairs and the small crash as mail falls through the slot onto the hall floor. I am licking Pete's nipple but I can *see* the thin blue airmail envelope from Sally. I had asked her for a favor and later regretted it, scolding myself so severely I brought tears to my eyes. Although I want to believe in sex with Pete, anticipation crashes through. I long to read Sally's letter and I abandon him with mild regret and relief, as though we were having a boring conversation.

VESTAL McINTYRE

MOVING STORY

Boston, 1995

ON JUNE FIRST, WHICH WAS TWENTY-SIX DAYS BEFORE
David was to move to San Francisco, I quit smoking, joined the Y
and cut down to one cup of coffee per day. It was going to be a hard
few weeks, and I needed some diversions. Somewhere to spend some
time. A new achy craving in my chest for cigarettes that would
detract from other, bigger aches. A little battle that I could win
every day, then sigh to myself before falling asleep at night, "I am
so fucking healthy."

So this is the first thing I've written without a cigarette in my
right hand, jerking back and forth between the j and k and making
ys hard.

I had smoked Camel Lights for a year, although my true devotion always lay with Benson & Hedges, which I had smoked for

the preceding four years. David smokes Merit Ultra Lights, which always taste like they're broken, letting air seep in. Occasionally, when I was upset or anxious, I would buy a pack of Marlboros, which make your face tingle from the first drag and leave your throat feeling sunburned.

David still smokes. The last time we talked on the phone, which was over a week ago, I lost his attention and heard a rustling of papers on his end. I stopped my story.

"David?"

"Hold on a sec. I'm looking for a lighter."

I am *so . . . fucking . . . healthy*.

And so, with my right index finger free to strike the y and again and again, y y y, this story begins. David has been gone forty days and forty nights. I will be gone in twenty days and twenty nights. Two-thirds.

I joined the Y, received my membership card in the mail, and began to get healthy. After my third workout, I visited the upstairs steam room. I sat down in the corner, wrapped in a towel. There was an old man, hazy in the opposite corner, next to the door. There was another man sitting closer, maybe late thirties with a blond buzz cut and big tanning-booth orange muscles. He stared at the wall in front of him, glanced at me without turning his head, stared at the wall again. I leaned back against the tile, opened my legs as if relaxing, laid my hand across my thigh. He glanced, glanced, then allowed his head to turn slightly. The door opened. The mist swirled. A stout middle-aged man entered but sat across the room. The orange man bent his knee and drew one foot under him to shield his crotch from the other men's view. His towel fell half-open, and I saw the line high on his hip where the orange ended. He didn't close the towel. My dick was half-hard and bobbing against my towel. I got up, took off the towel, folded it in half and sat on it.

Now I had the other two's attention, but they soon looked away. I looked at the orange man and let him watch my dick rise. Then I gave it one slow stroke. He quietly scooted over so that I was within reach. Again he put one knee up, draped the towel across it, but this time he opened the other half. His cock was tiny and I understood his build differently. We both began to jerk off—I, slowly, because

I was the young, cocky exhibitionist and he, quickly, because he was the nervous older one. His hand moved across my thigh, and mine moved down to massage my balls while he jerked me off all wrong because he was right-handed. I held one bulbous, Day-Glo pectoral with my free hand, which made him nervous because of the other two, but they'd realized they weren't involved in this one and were acting like they didn't notice. His chest was stubbly. I pinched one nipple hard. His hand left his dick and pressed down beneath my balls. I opened up and one finger pressed my asshole. I took over jerking my cock and he returned to his. The tip of his finger pushed inside. I opened my legs more, pulling one foot up onto the seat, and I noticed the old man leaning forward, peering through the mist.

The door opened again and a head poked in. It was the man who distributes towels at the desk in the downstairs locker room. He saw me sit up and cover my cock with my hands. He saw Orange Man move away and pull up the towel. Beside the door, level with the man's head was a sign: SEXUAL CONDUCT OF ANY KIND IN OUR LOCKER ROOMS WILL RESULT IN CANCELED MEMBERSHIP. The man glanced around the steam room. "Five minutes, guys," and he was gone.

The two others left and we jerked off quickly, his finger up my ass. We both came onto my towel, him gasping, clenching his teeth and turning his head slightly away from his crotch as if his hand were caught in a trap and it hurt.

He stretched and massaged the back of his neck, and I left him pulling on his towel. I walked naked through the showers, past two stragglers, down the stairs to the locker room. I stuffed the cummy towel down the chute and got a clean one from the man. He gave me a blank look. No arched eyebrows. No averted eyes.

I was twenty-two and David was twenty-nine when I first brought him home and we talked and had sex all night. Even though I was drunk and stoned I had to think of cats and the Bible to keep from coming the second his dick slid inside me. He kissed me on the bridge over the Mass Pike on our way to the Kenmore IHOP at 6:00 A.M. I had to be at work at nine. Now I am twenty-three and David is thirty. He lived three blocks away in a studio apartment.

Both of us lived, and I still live, across the street from the Fens, the park where Boston's loneliest and horniest cruise for blow jobs in the bushes. David has light brown hair that always looks neat. He has a tiny pair of scissors that he uses to trim around his ears, so that he always looks like his hair was cut recently. He has clear blue Disney eyes—like Pinocchio after he becomes human. Everyone comments on how young and fresh-faced David looks. He gets carded. David has the charm of looking like he only recently became human.

David buys jeans with thirty-two-inch waists, which is exactly his size. He wears them belted up neatly at the hips. He used to make fun of me for wearing my jeans low. He'd pull them up to my waist and cinch them, which looked ridiculous. I would push him off. But, of course, I loved the embrace of his grabbing the back of my pants.

We planned to move together. We talked about where we should move. I wanted to live anywhere but California. He wanted to live anywhere but New York. So he moved to San Francisco forty days and forty nights ago, and I'm moving to Brooklyn twenty days from today.

The morning after he left it was bright and warm out and I walked across the park to the Y. My face ached from crying and I was still a little dizzy. I dutifully climbed nowhere on the Stair-Master, then did my rounds on the machines, avoiding people's eyes, not really able to think.

By now I know the protocol well. I sit on my towel. A handsome businessman rises from his seat and walks through the mist and seats himself beside me. He touches himself gently while everyone sweats in unison to the endless hiss. He eyes me sideways. I wipe my head lazily. Some other faceless muscle guy emerges from the fog and now I am cornered. I am glanced at askew, I am erected and taken down, I am so very touched, I am so touching.

I've only blacked out from drinking once in my life. I went out that Sunday and drank in the upstairs of the club where my friend tends bar. This time I was teetering and confident. I walked at a smooth rate through the crowd with a suppressed grin. I noticed more men than usual looking. So I did a little experiment. I walked around like I normally would have, sober, slow and frowning. I got the regular casual glances. Then I convinced myself of how ridiculous all these men looked and walked rudely with the snotty smile. I was suddenly twice as attractive. I had the vague thought, "I have to think more about this later."

At 1:00 A.M. I stumbled into the bathroom to piss and the kid next to me was jerking off. We had a conversation I have no recollection of. I dimly remember walking toward my apartment. My memory is clearer on what happened once we got in. I sat on my couch and he yanked down my pants. Still fully clothed, he started sucking my limp dick. He was a year or two younger than me. He had shoulder-length hair and crooked teeth. He must have been a college student; he needed to be back at the club by two for his ride home. His name was Brent or Brett. He wasn't attractive, but I got off on treating him like he was younger. "Lick my asshole," I said. I had never said that to anyone before; I would just let them do it if they wanted to. I lifted up and his face shimmied down. I noticed he had opened his fly and was jerking off. My dick was fully hard.

He came very quickly. It dribbled onto my floor. I was jerking off and had to close my eyes and concentrate hard to keep things going. Finally I tensed, came onto my stomach and let my legs drop. His face was there, smiling, his jaw receded and hanging open. I breathed for a while and then asked him, "What was your name?" I meant it as a joke, but it sounded mean.

"Brent [or Brett]."

"Do you know my name?" Hoping to make that, too, a joke.

"Ves."

David had been working as a waiter, and he usually got off late. One night, during that awful time after he had decided to leave and before he left, he came over and we talked for a minute before he fell fast asleep with his head against my chest. I looked at him and looked at him. Now that he wasn't looking back, I could cry. I sat there in the most perfect sadness I've ever felt. I had to breathe smoothly not to wake him, which was difficult. I had to catch my tears in my hand, or else they would have fallen on his face. I sat there catching them and wiping them on the sheet beside me. Catching and wiping. Inhale exhale.

David has been gone for fifty-two days and fifty-two nights. Someone has moved into his apartment. David left without telling the landlord, and for a while the apartment was dark and empty. Through its second-floor window I could see the silhouette of the dresser he left behind. But I walked by there yesterday and there was a lamp balanced precariously on the windowsill. The walls were empty except for one small picture, I don't know what of, pinned up. They were suddenly the nervous walls of a new apartment.

Last Saturday I took someone home from the Y. He was cute, early thirties, with compact little muscles. He sat next to me in the crowded steam room and immediately let his hand drop onto the seat, touching the side of my leg. I massaged my cock through the towel and he opened his towel to me. I saw that his cock was very long. He smiled. I liked him. With the others looking on, I took it and held it for a moment before I began to beat it slowly. It felt rubbery and I wondered if it's more difficult for really big dicks to get hard than it is for normal ones. Someone from across the room came over and stood next to the door so he could see. Even though a guy in the corner was leaned over sucking off the guy next to him, most of the attention was on us. I wanted to have this guy alone. I leaned over and whispered into his ear, "Meet me in the lobby in five minutes."

His name was Ted. He didn't have a lot of time. "I live right across the park," I said. He was a designer and lived in the South End. Whatever. As soon as I closed the door, he was getting naked. He rolled onto my bed and, smiling, began to jerk off. I climbed onto the bed, put a pillow behind his head and began to fuck his face, my hands supporting me against the wall on either side of the New York City street map I had hung at the head of the bed. It was there so I could memorize the neighborhoods and to remind me that soon everything would be different. I looked over my shoulder and watched him beat his cock, push it down, let it slap back against his belly, beat it again. I tested how hard I could fuck his face before he would push me back again. Then I lay down and we gave each other head in a 69. I jerked off and came onto his face because he asked me to. He came on himself. He asked if he could use my shower. While he was in there I started getting stoned. He left and

I got more stoned. The room was warm and the breeze was coming through the window and I could hear people passing on the sidewalk and kids yelling in the park across the street. That's summer.

Last weekend I took half my stuff down to Brooklyn. I returned to Boston to live out the week leading to September 1. In the living room there are garbage bags full of winter clothes and a pile of papers to sort through. They won't let me close my bank account until I pay off the credit line.

Is it just summer, or is sex always there, waiting to happen? Crossing a bridge on my way to the grocery store I see a man down in the reeds beside the river, shirtless, gazing up at me. I wander off the sidewalk into the bushes. He approaches, stops ten yards away and begins rubbing his crotch. I unbutton my pants and do the same. I can see he's a burly townie type, but cute. He loosens his belt and slides a hand in. I nod him over. He looks around, hesitates, then retightens his belt and disappears. Not his type, I guess.

A friend takes me out for a good-bye dinner. I arrange to have my phone service cut off. I go out with the women from work for margaritas. I take the pictures off my walls. I give the guy in the apartment next door some shirts I don't wear. The building manager's four children divvy up the contents of my change jar.

I find myself at 2:00 A.M. in an area of grass between lines of dark bushes in the Fens. There are many men here, some on their knees sucking; some jerking each other off; some jerking themselves; some watching with their hands in their pockets. Somehow I am face-to-face with a beautiful Latino man with thick, dark eyebrows and eye sockets so deep there's just a glimmer. I lean forward and begin to kiss him again and again and now our tongues are licking each other. Our pants are all the way down and there are hands jerking us off, but they aren't our hands. I put mine up his shirt and feel his chest where there's thin hair, and then move to his armpit where the hair is thick and wet. I lick his soft cheek and his rough chin and then kiss him again. He touches my face and my hair. Then I begin to breathe harder and his hand moves down to catch my cum. The man who's been jerking me off from behind looks over my shoulder and now Dark Eyes is coming. It squirts across my bare leg. I'm still catching my breath. He embraces me and the men around us embrace us. I am so very moved. I am so moving.

I have been here for ten days and nine nights. My room is painted and my clothes are put away. My windows overlook a canyon of tiny, sectioned-off backyards with bird feeders, sundials, a children's wading pool. There are confused blotches of ivy on the back walls of brownstones across the yards. I have no job, and I've already spent most of my money.

    Here's something I started on the subway and finished at the Laundromat. It contains information useful if you're planning to move here. I proclaim it a good-bye poem to Boston, to David, to the empty space David left in Boston. Good-bye to missing you. It's entitled "Postscript with Subway Emergency Exit Instructions":

> *Listen for instructions from crew.*
> There's a place on Sixth Avenue in Chelsea where you can climb stairs into the dark and wire into a tangle of thirty men and conduct nothing.
> *Do not pull emergency brake.*
> There's a shop on Thirty-eighth Street where you can enter a small black room with a magic hole. Spread your arms. Press hard. Nothing gets you off quicker than the wall.
> *Remain inside train. Subway tracks are dangerous.*
> There's a church up near Columbia where you can climb up and up, past loud bells to the steeple. And you can look down and see both rivers and the rectangle of green, and everyone and everything in between. And Broadway lobotomizing the island. And everyone in New York looks up and gives you a mannequin smile and a beauty-queen wave.
> *Exit only when directed.*

Postscript, New York, 1996

I know part of the poem's name was "Postscript," and no story deserves two, but it's months later now and there's another end.

    There's an ashtray next to me, a lit cigarette in the ashtray and a rope of smoke swaying in front of the computer screen. (Some

things change and stay changed for good; other things change back
to the way they were before. All the same, I'm planning to quit
again soon.) Next to the ashtray there's the heart-shaped box Aaron
gave me for Valentine's Day. Pasted on the front is a magazine cutout
of Crystal and Nomi, the main characters of my favorite movie from
last year, *Showgirls*, eyes locked, faces close, about to kiss. They are
surrounded by cutout red and yellow flowers, and written beneath
them is "The Good . . ." If I flip the box, there's the despicable Rod
and Bob Jackson-Paris embracing. Beneath them is a broken heart
and the words "The Bad." As if this weren't proof enough that he
knows my taste, Aaron had taken out the center chocolate and replaced it with a small bag of pot.

He gave me the heart and I thanked him with a hug. We ate
the dinner I had made in his oven. We pulled down his Murphy
bed, and before I pushed him back and unbuttoned his pants, I might
have looked past him, out his window, and seen the peaks of the
burnt-out church, topped with snow, and beyond that the projects,
and between the buildings of the projects, the Williamsburg Bridge
with the red and white lights of cars coming and going.

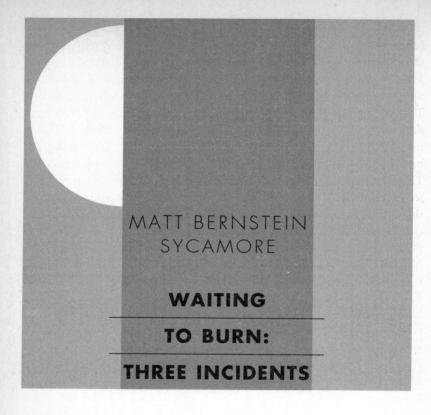

MATT BERNSTEIN
SYCAMORE

WAITING

TO BURN:

THREE INCIDENTS

How I Got These Shorts

IT'S MY FIFTH TRICK. HE CALLS AROUND ELEVEN, SAYS DO you go to Concord. I say 100 an hour, 250 for the night, wash up, catch the last train, and of course he isn't there. So I'm standing there waiting, thinking he's not going to show up and there isn't another train 'til morning and what the fuck am I gonna do. Finally, this man comes up in Speedos and a windbreaker, says are you Tyler, like there's anyone else around with pink hair. Then we're driving along, he's pushing my head to his crotch saying *suck my cock suck my cock* and I'm sucking his limp cock, he's doing Rush every few minutes and squeezing my balls and we're driving in the pitch dark—I don't know *where the fuck* we are. Tells me he's been up all weekend on crystal, met these two straightboys and don't I wanna fuck these straightboys. I say yeah, I really wanna fuck those straightboys. Says he gave the straightboys his Mercedes and they're gonna show up at his house, I'm thinking hell yeah the straightboys are gonna show up with your Mercedes. We get to his house and he's flying off his ass, chasing me around, trying to get me to do crystal. Then this straightboy shows up, but he's by himself—and he's some *flaming* fag, just flaming. I pour him a drink, I'm standing there in my boxers sort of flirting with him. The trick comes in, I'm sucking his cock and the straightboy's watching, I'm kind of embarrassed. The straightboy takes out his cock and I'm thinking that was easy so I suck his cock and then the *real* straightboys show up, turns out the other guy was another whore. The real straightboys aren't so cute—one of them has a potbelly and he's only about eighteen. I say you wanna drink. The trick takes me in the other room, says you like Ecstasy does it make you horny. I say X *oh* it makes me *so* horny. I take the X and I've already smoked a lot of pot and had some Xanax and Valium and niacin and a few drinks. So I'm Xing my brains out, hiding in the kitchen. The straightboy with the potbelly comes in, says are you watching a video. I say *you* wanna watch one and I turn one on. He watches and I squeeze my cock, he gets scared and runs into the other room. I go into the bathroom to take a shower. I'm spacing out in the mirror and the straightboy comes in, looks both ways, locks the door and says shh. . . . Takes out his cock and pretends he's gonna piss, starts jerking off. So I help him. He comes twice, says keep this between us okay. I say don't worry, *honey*, go into the bedroom and the trick says did you make any progress with the straightboys. I say I just jerked one off. The other whore is trying on all this underwear, it's like everything from the *International Male* catalog *and more*. He's trying on this leopard print metallic thong, swinging his hips in front of the mirror, saying things like shhh*wank*. And that's when I put on these shorts.

Pulling Taffy

"Since I had my prostate removed," Dave says, "I can't get hard, but I can still have orgasms. I think I'm in touch with different nerves. When I come, I don't ejaculate and it feels almost like a female orgasm, from how I've heard it described. Now if you could just bend over me with your head that way, I could get a good look at your bottom."

We're at one of the bathhouses downtown, in a tiny room lined with wood paneling from the seventies, metal siding to protect the walls, an alcove with a mattress squeezed into the corner. We're on the mattress. I try to watch my reflection in the siding as I bend over Dave, my ass in his face, fingers rubbing his balls. He puts his lips at my asshole and I get hard, thinking *eat my ass* like in a porn video. Thinking of another Dave, thirty years younger and a whole lot cuter. I was with him last night when I got paged. He said, "Do you want to call that trick?" slid his lips around my dick, arms under my ass, and I moaned, held the back of his neck. Pulled his head off my dick and kissed him, tasting my own pre-cum. I said, "I can't decide whether to come all over your chest or make that call."

This Dave says, "Let me show you how to get me off—it's kind of like pulling taffy. You put a little lube on it and pull hard with one hand after the other." He demonstrates. "We'll do that in a few minutes, first just pull on my cockhead like this." He's pulling gently on my cockhead with two fingertips. I'm standing over the bed, his hand underneath my ass, and I'm getting hard again even if I'd rather have a firmer touch, the other Dave on top of me. I picture last night, when he bit my neck while I held his head with one hand and my other hand slid down his pants to his asshole, and he said, "This is a great way to be a bottom."

This Dave says, "Yeah, now could you work on my cock," so I put some lube on my hand and start squeezing his dick, alternating hands. Feels more like milking a cow than pulling taffy. He says, "Yeah, a little harder," and I'm squeezing really hard now, one hand then the other, closing my eyes and breathing in with each pull, out with each release. He says, "Could you spread your legs a little . . . great," and I'm pulling on his dick, it's getting slightly longer. He has one hand on my dick and the other between my legs. I'm sweating because they've got the heat on 95 or maybe it's because of the sauna. I can feel the sweat rolling down the sides of my chest as I spit on my hand and keep pulling.

He says, "Oh that feels *great*, could you squeeze a bit harder on my cockhead? It might seem like it's too hard, but believe me it feels good." Now I'm squeezing harder, pulling up and down, up and down, thinking I hope I get a tip for this. He says, "Oh that's just right, I love that extra slide on my cockhead," so now I focus on the cockhead, squeeze and slide, squeeze and slide. He says, "That's great, it takes a few minutes—that feels just great." I open my eyes and look at him, hair rising off his chest, his face bright red, eyes half-open and fluttering. I think: what would happen if he died here? He wouldn't have enough money to make me want to take his wallet and run, so I'd have to deal with the cops, they'd take all the cash and then hold me for questioning.

I'm pulling on his cockhead, squeezing with one hand and then the other. He starts this high-pitched moan, sounds like he's going to die but I know he's loving it. He says, "Oh could you touch my balls a bit, not too much." I touch his balls and then move back to his cockhead, spit on my hand again and squeeze, slide. He's not touching me anymore, eyes closed, just squealing and moaning. I'm watching him like some strange creature—it's amazing and not quite funny, almost hot, and he grabs my hands, says, "Just squeeze gently now." I hold his dick and squeeze the head. He sits up, says, "Oh that was wonderful, just right. Do you think we could make it a once-a-week thing? When someone learns those techniques, I feel like it's an investment."

Heat

I wake up too early because I drank too much last night. Spend two hours lying in bed then getting up to piss, drinking water and then back to bed, back up to piss. In the bathroom for the third time, I look out the window and I can't believe how bright and soft it is outside; it gets me kind of high. I lean my head out the window and start licking one of my armpits, tasting the sweat with the wind and the sun against my face. I go back to my room and lie down but now I'm too horny to even try sleeping. Hornier than I've been in a while, weeks or maybe even months. This great full horny feeling, not just driving lust for someone else but driving lust for myself as well.

I think about Christopher and the boy he picked up last night, asleep in the living room. I got home and saw them there, said I'll just change into something more comfortable. Put on this ankle-length black wool dress with black vinyl men's stack heels from the seventies, sat down next to them and said let me see the show. Christopher was naked and semihard, the other boy was down to his briefs and the two of them were laughing at me and moaning at each other. Christopher said honey, come join us, but I was too drunk, I said let's do that in the morning, kissed them good night and went to bed.

Now I lie in bed thinking about Christopher fucking me while the other boy sucks my cock or fucking Christopher while the other boy fucks me. I wonder if the other boy likes to fuck—he's seventeen and I didn't like to fuck when I was seventeen. He kept mentioning condoms last night so I wonder whether he only sucks with a condom, whether he'll get sucked without one. I picture Christopher holding his dick all the way in my ass while I come into a condom in the other boy's mouth. I hope I don't shoot right away.

I wait until I'm not so hard and pull on my boxers, listen at the living room door and it sounds like they're awake. I go in and they're sleeping but I say are you two awake? Christopher says what time is it? I say it's early, ten o'clock, but I woke up at seven-thirty and I'm wired, do you mind that I'm talking to you? He says no but keeps his eyes shut and the other boy barely stirs, so I go back into my room; masturbation sounds sexy enough.

I pull the curtain down and turn on the lights but it's too dark without sunlight so I tie the curtain back up. Sit down and start licking one of my armpits again; for once I wish I wasn't so neurotically clean because I want a stronger taste. Then I start biting and chewing my underarm, sucking up and down from my shoulder to my elbow, flexing my muscles and biting them, grabbing my dick through my boxers.

I start to get hard and I lie back, slide off my boxers and hold my dick with one hand, move my face to my other armpit. I hold the back of my head and twist my face as far into my armpit as I can get it. This armpit tastes better or maybe it's the accumulation of tastes. I slide my tongue in circles over my armpit hairs, gently licking the bitter sweat. I lean back and smack my chest just the way I like it, the way I saw some boy get smacked in a video and it's turned me on ever since. I hit my left tit as hard as I can, palm open. My tit gets red and my dick gets harder with each smack. I move to the other tit, then smack both at once.

I'm unbelievably hard. I hold my balls with one hand and slide the other hand over my chest and up to my mouth, stick one of my fingers in my mouth and suck on it, squeezing harder on my balls. Slide four fingers into my mouth just to the gagging point and I picture some guy fucking my face, choking me as my saliva builds. I realize I like the feeling of gagging, not just from a dick but also from my fingers. I keep four fingers in my mouth and squeeze my dick with my other hand, hold my breath and relish the feeling of my throat relaxing around my fingers. I start jerking fast on my dick and I'm about to come, I can feel the headrush, but I stop jerking and grab both of my thighs, press up against my balls.

I start smacking the insides of my thighs and I realize that I like the quick stinging sensations. I lean my ass up and I'm smacking my ass and my balls and I'm loving the gentle rushes, thinking am I having some sort of S/M awakening? I stick my nose into one of my armpits, start licking again, feeling my pectoral muscle against my eye while I slap my balls gently and breathe through my nose, feeling a bruisy feeling between my legs while I smell the mixture of amber oil and morning sweat in my armpit. I cup my balls and lick up and down my upper arm, sucking and biting and tasting.

I look up at my dick, stiff and red. I think about some guy sitting on my dick and then lying down on top of me, I can feel his whole body against me, my chest cradling his back and my dick doing spasms inside of him. Holding him and kissing his neck, squeezing him tight, running my hands up and down the sides of his chest while we make out. I almost come without touching my dick, I have to grab it to stop myself. I run my hands up and down my chest, over my hips, through my pubic hair, up to my tits.

I get my dildos from the dresser, squeeze some lube onto the small red one, lie down and shove it in my ass. Usually I like it slow but right now I'm so horny it doesn't matter. My dick goes slightly limp but then I sit up onto the dildo, squeeze my dick with both hands and that makes me moan, breathe in and moan again. I pull out the dildo and then lube up my other dildo, the one that's too big and not hard enough. I try to sit on it but it won't go in, it keeps bending, but I love the feel of it sliding back and forth against my asshole. Finally it goes in and it hurts because it's thick but today I like the pain. I sit all the way down on it and my whole body gets warm and just as I feel the dildo inside my ass equally as pain and pleasure, or the pain *as* pleasure, I squeeze my dick and jerk faster. My asshole relaxes and I feel this calm explosive rush to my head as I come, slide the dildo out of my ass and lie down on the bed. I imagine the drenching humidity of an East Coast summer and for once I wish I could go outside, lie down in the sun, and burn.

KEVIN BOURKE

"ADONIS IS WOUNDED, WHAT CAN WE DO?"

SO WE'RE SITTING BESIDE EACH OTHER ON THE COUCH, and we're jerking each other off. His dick size presents a bit of a challenge, even for a hand job, but he's very encouraging. "You're really *good* at this," he says, his voice quivering. The tight muscles on his hairless stomach ripple with each breath. He increases the velocity of his fist on me. Gasping, sputtering, he says, "You like that, don't you? You like that." Then he arches his back; his pelvis bucks in anticipation. The next words come from the back of his throat; hoarse; they're uttered with some urgency. "Watch out now. I'm going to shoot all over the place," and a few seconds later he shudders violently and cries out . . . and his cum kind of dribbles in little tapioca globs down the back of my hand. "Well, I *usually* shoot everywhere," he says. It looks exactly like the pureed banana my niece spits up.

Really, his lack of imagination is a turnoff. "Why talk like you're in porn movie," I say to him, "if you can't perform like you're in one?" Why, I wonder, bother saying anything at all?

What I want is to be seduced by a few choice phrases spoken in an amorous voice. Instead what I get are men who think it's enough of a display of their verbal skills if they brag about their oral ones.

The ideal line for the start of an encounter goes something like: "As long as I'm thinking about you I'm no good for anything else." Or, "I can't stop kissing you." It's not that romance is necessary, but sex isn't all that much fun when the other person doesn't give you even as much consideration as a cashier in a fast-food joint. One wants the personalized services of a really thoughtful caterer.

I meet one guy in a supermarket during lunch hour. He's got dark curly hair and his pink oxford shirt stretches tight across his chest. He tells me to phone him, he's in the book: "West," he says. "As in: wild, wild." It's a charming line, actually, and so I do call him when I get out of work.

He dispenses with small talk and ushers me into the bedroom, practically pushing me from behind with his hands. I spot Lee Iacocca's autobiography sticking out of his weekend bag on the floor. I take note of it because there are no other books anywhere in the apartment. He has already gotten out of his work clothes and all he has to do now is drop the bathrobe and he's ready, complete with hard-on. He's got one of those thirtysomething bodies, where he's sexier now because he has filled out with extra weight, and where going to the gym has hardened his stomach but will never make it flat. It's a body that arouses but doesn't intimidate. He's wearing a strong dose of some spicy cologne. Without a word, he pushes me down onto the mattress and begins to strip me. As he takes off my clothes he appraises each part of my body, out loud, as if I'm about to be auctioned off at Sotheby's in one piece and he wants to see if all the individual parts are worth it. I interrupt to ask him to put on some music. What does he say to this? He asks me if I'm kidding.

Inches from the foot of the bed is a twenty-three-inch television screen. He lurches out, slaps it on, and returns to me. But television isn't music, and I'm forced to listen to the six-o'clock news: a murder, an indictment for tax evasion, a border skirmish. Perhaps for him this *does* set the mood. Straddling my legs, he kneels over me and jerks me off as quick as he can, using both hands, and then collapses onto his back: "My turn." He takes forever. After a while, I have to give one hand a rest and use the other, and then since that isn't getting either one of us anywhere (apparently), I stick my nose into his crotch and start to lick his balls, and I get a little grunt out of him, finally, and interpret this as some sort of encouragement, so I use a lot of spit and roll my tongue back and forth along the flesh around his balls and his inner thighs, and he says, his voice a growl, "That's more like it." I blow a thin stream of cool air onto the parts I've just licked and he twitches a little and comes. "You know, you're a pretty good ball licker," he says afterward. My auction value is confirmed.

I find one guy who's a book-lover—finally. He spends the evening telling me about what he's been reading, but then he never fails to ID each author (yes, of course I've heard of Evelyn Waugh, you asshole) until I feel hopelessly condescended to.

One who says, "I could make love to you all night," but who really just wants to spank me.

One who can't remember which fake name he's given me, so when he phones and I ask who's calling *he* has to guess.

One who says, "Do you want me to make your first time special?" (I used to pretend I'd never had sex before so the other guy would feel like he was in control) and what he means by "special," it turns out, is that I'm to give him a blow job. *As if.*

One who responds to even the least demanding sexual request with "And after *that* will you promise to go to sleep?"

One who throws me to the floor in front of the fireplace, falls on top of me, and rips my clothes off. "I want to fuck you," he says. Well, *obviously.*

Carroll gets me under false pretenses, which is a fabulous start. (He's wearing a tight blue T-shirt that claims he's part of the fire department. He is, in fact, in advertising.) His approach is to saturation-bomb me with compliments. Entirely over the top. He's not even close to my type and at first I want him to go away so I throw all sorts of bullshit at him. I lie outrageously but with complete conviction. ("A lie well told is a beautiful thing.") But he is persistent. He says things like, "*You* know how handsome you are. *You* know you're smart and funny and attractive. I'm sure you've heard a million times already that you have the most gorgeous eyes. *You* know all the men in this bar are jealous of me for even getting to talk to you." It's a pleasure to hear such things. In no time at all I'm completely happy to fuck him.

But being complimented in this way isn't necessary. It's the tone of voice, the forceful, single-minded urgency emanating from somewhere down deep that seduces.

I would love someone to speak to me as if he were out of breath, as if he were so heightened with desire that speaking itself might cause him to burst. The words can be taken from anywhere: Once I read about a poet who was said to thrive on "stealth, toxicity, wildness, neon—'perfect mean lines.'" I want someone to say this about me, to bring his mouth close to my ear and say this, hesitantly, as if afraid of the spell he's conjuring. "Something in you thrives on stealth, wildness, perfect mean lines." It's not the truth, but that's not important. Wouldn't you give in, at that moment, to any request? Wouldn't you want to be taken then, taken with both hands? A few lines of verse will do, too. They don't have to be your own; the art of stealing words from someone else, especially if I know you're stealing them, adds a layer to the pleasure of being seduced by them. Your voice will work where oysters and magic potions have failed. Say to me: *Beat at your breasts / with hard hands, girls— / Tear your tunics to shreds!* and my interest won't be the only thing that rises. Especially when you have one hand at my waist and you've brought your face close to mine. As your verse progresses so do your hands, slipping now to the seat of my tight leather miniskirt, and pressing your naked hips against it, and the cool, smooth leather feels good against your dick and so you move your hips to the rhythm of the verse; you press your chest into mine, your muscles hard against the black lace brassiere you dressed me up in. Your face is a fraction of an inch away, so close I can feel the heat, the vibrations, the breath. Your tongue rims my ear as you come into the next line and then the next *stealth, toxicity, wildness, neon, something in you*, you tear the wig off and finally put your mouth over mine, and in being taken up with it—your lips hot and wet against mine, the softness of them and your soft goatee—in being swept along with all this you keep it up, keep up the chant, the rhythm, *Adonis is wounded/ What can we do?* the voice muffled now but I can feel the vibrations into the back of my throat until I can't resist any longer and thrust my tongue through your lips, push myself into your soft warm hairy wetness, as you tear off the skirt and push me down onto the chair, straddle my hips, slowly lower yourself *something in you* and you re-alize, as you begin to feel it, as it begins to take you over, as it begins to interrupt your train of thought so that the words having done their job blur into sounds you don't recognize, become syllables that have lost their meaning against the pure articulate demonstra-tion of lust, you know that the *something inside you, that likes perfect mean lines, this something inside you* is me.

KEVIN BENTLEY

DEEPER INSIDE

THE VALLEY

OF KINGS

I STOOD LEANING AGAINST THE WALL BY THE STAIRS AT
Sutter's Mill, eating peanuts and drinking a beer. I was feeling a rare
surge of confidence: I'd just talked Mrs. Eidenmueller, the blue-
haired owner of Bonanza Books, into giving me a 50-cents-an-hour
raise, and earlier, a German tourist who'd been reading a Grove
Erotic Classic with a prominent hard-on barging around in his shorts
had flirted with me at the register.

Sutter's was a Financial District bar; it was the middle of the
afternoon. Most people there were coming from work or were on
their breaks. A cute boy walked over and reached into the peanut bar-
rel, glancing at me. I stared boldly back at him; he looked flustered and
moved on, but a minute later he'd thought better of it and came back,
standing right beside me. "Work around here?" I said.

He told me everything he knew: he drives into the city once a week for orchestra rehearsal; he's a freshman at San Jose State; he's on the wrestling team. He's nineteen, works part-time in a film-developing lab, and collects old cameras. ("You mean they don't even *work?*" I said, unenthusiastically.) I wasn't really listening. If I had been, I might have realized sooner that he was riveting to look at, but dull as a lawn gnome. He *was* cute: on the short side, stocky; from the bulgy crotch to the compact round ass, the contents of his button-flies seemed bent on release. I could imagine his dick snapping to rigidity like an inflatable life preserver. He was wearing a long-sleeved green-and-blue-checked shirt like your mom would buy at Sears (as his no doubt had) and a blue windbreaker with the hood still attached. He looked like he'd just wandered out of the middle row of my eighth-grade class photo.

I had to get back to work. We exchanged names and as I turned to go he put his palm flat against my chest, stopping me to ask what bars I frequented on Castro. It was as if he were feeling for my heart.

A week later I was back at Sutter's on my break, slouched at a table in the half-dark with my legs stretched out. Once in a while a guy would remark on my long, Texan's legs (presumably not meaning bowed), so I indulged my bad posture, throwing out my Dingo boots like bait. I'd forgotten his name, but I remembered that he drove into the city on Mondays. I was about to leave when he appeared: light brown hair parted on the side and swooped across his forehead like a schoolboy's; big, doelike brown eyes; strong-looking thighs. He was smiling broadly: "Kevin?"

This time it really hit me: I was so attracted to him I could hardly speak. He sat on the edge of a chair he pulled up beside me and, looking around the bar, casually let his leg bump mine. My cock stiffened against my jeans, and there was a sort of buzzing in my ears. The boy, whose name was Ben, nattered on about orchestra and his German language major. I noted that he affected an ersatz German accent (he lived, for instance, in Zan Oh-zay), but I forgave this small foible instantly. He smelled of baby shampoo and fabric softener, and I wanted to yank down his jeans, stick my tongue up his plump ass, then fuck him hard and fast.

My lust was amplified by confusion: this very specific and overwhelming desire to poke was unusual for me. I'd done it with girls back in Texas, and my limited experiences with guys there were mostly reciprocal, but since coming to San Francisco I'd most often been cast as Boy to a series of late-thirtyish Tarzans. Other than some one-time tricks, I hadn't had a relationship with someone my own age or younger. I was accustomed to waking up beside some big, warm, older man who'd stroke my hair back from my forehead and murmur, "Pretty . . ." "Twenty-one? Twenty-two? Twenty-four?" they'd repeat, when I answered the inevitable awestruck question. "You're just a *baby*!"

My friend David would harangue me on the bad deal he felt I was getting from these men. "You mean he doesn't let you fuck *him*? What does he *do*, for chrissakes, just lie back and smoke a cigarette while you jack off?" I hated to admit that that was often exactly what happened. Larry, for example, was selfish, pompous, and lazy, but he looked like Alan Bates and he was as far as you could get from the queers my dad hooted at on television. I might have gone on warming his feet indefinitely if I hadn't finally figured out that his eccentric vocabulary and eerie non sequiturs weren't the result of a mild stroke: he was an est graduate. "What is, *is*, right?" he'd say with a screwy grin. "I'm just an asshole, *okay*?"

Larry looked like Alan Bates; Ben reminded me of Ray Connor, a straight crush of mine in junior high. I was always cruising men who reminded me of one of these romantic icons of my past, and it was always a mistake. For a blissful period I'd be thinking *My god, I'm kissing So-and-So, I'm fucking So-and-So*—but sooner or later I'd find myself staring irritably up from bed at a petulant stranger waving a driver's license in my face, shouting, "I'm just plain Judy Barton, from Salina, Kansas!" like Kim in *Vertigo*.

He yelped like a puppy when I tried to stick it in. He had his eyes screwed shut and he looked as if he might cry.

"Do you want me to stop?" I said.

"No. No, I want you to fuck me. I've just never done it before."

"I feel like doing something *different* tonight," Ben had said, rolling the *r*s like he was Herr Somebody. I had brought him home to the half-empty railroad flat I shared with two guys who worked with me at Bonanza: Steve, a straight boy from Tampa who holed up in his room writing long letters to his former girlfriend or strumming James Taylor songs on his guitar late into the night; and Dan, another gay boy. Dan and I routinely sat on the floor in the unfurnished living room drinking and smoking bongs, or went to the Stud on acid and dragged tricks home while Steve cowered behind his door or went for his daily three-mile run. Steve was virtuous but sexy, stepping carefully over beer cans and bongs with his bowl of Wheat Chex, and Dan and I regularly availed ourselves of the sweat-soaked blue running shorts he left draped over the shower curtain, as if they were poppers. Steve came to San Francisco expecting *Tales of the City*, but life in our chaotic Sixteenth Street flat was more like *Tales from the Crypt*. Once, very drunk and editorializing in some elemental way, I urinated on Steve's door, which probably contributed to his decision to move back to Florida.

Ben and I had climbed up the back stairs to the roof to smoke a joint and look at the city view, and before you could say *The Fountainhead*, we were necking like parched men at a fountain and I'd wedged my hand down the back of his jeans, snaking a finger into the damp and mysterious region of his asshole. I pulled him back down to the flat, and we brushed past Steve in the hall, shirttails half-out and hard-ons jutting rudely.

Now, shut up in my room, clothes scattered, lying on my unzipped sleeping bag on the bare mattress, I had his stocky, hairy legs pushed back to his head so I could see the dark swirls of hair on his pale chest and the almost-hidden tiny pink nipples. With only the tip of my dick in him, I could just manage to bend and suck hard on the red, blustery head of his cock. He had what my friend David called *the doorstop kind*, meaning one of those cast-iron Scotties up on its haunches or a weighted Coke bottle with a knit poodle head— thick and short. I wasn't really inside him yet, I was just nudging my way into the vestibule, his tight ring clenching and grabbing my cockhead. I hadn't yet passed that invisible barrier I knew so well from the other side—that abrupt, melting *give* after which even the largest of cocks could go barreling the rest of the way in without impediment.

His eyes were still closed. "Look at me," I said. I bent and stuck my tongue down his throat, then pulled back and, still staring into his wide pupils, pushed right up him. He was staring back at me, alternately biting his lip and uttering little *uhs* and *yeahs*. I was moaning as I sawed in and out, the sweat rolling off my forehead and the end of my nose; I heard Steve stomp across his room just beyond the sliding parlor doors, pick up his guitar, and start singing "Fire and Rain" in a hopeless attempt to block us out. I threw my whole weight onto Ben, rutting deep and hard, rolling and twisting in him. I felt the cum burning slowly up my cock like the mercury registering a fever on a cartoon thermometer, and I pulled almost but not quite out. I grabbed his jumpy little stump and gave it two or three jerks, and as he lost his last shred of inhibition and shouted "Yeah, *fuck me*!" his cum shot smack against my chin and down my chest and I swiped up a hot gob of it and fed it to him while his spasming asshole wrung from my raw dick the hottest orgasm I'd shot since Ricky Temple made me sit on a Coke bottle and masturbate for him in the seventh grade.

Steve was singing weakly about Carolina and I imagined he wished he were there.

We got up and went out for pizza. Wasn't I already squirming as he held my hand tightly all the way to the restaurant? And when he asked *Could I spend the night?* after we'd gotten back into bed and I'd fucked him again, his tender little asshole still slick from earlier, my dick so hard it felt like a punishment; when we lay soaked and stuck together and he told me what he hadn't till then, that it was his birthday; when he said through half-shut eyes, "I think I'm falling in love," what iron force seized my resisting jaw and made me utter back, "Me too"?

I *thought* I wanted a lover. The bars on Castro, Polk, Haight, and Folsom were like the pastel-colored squares on the Candy Land board, with LOVER at the end, the pot of gold. I approached every trick as the potential love of my life—but in fact, I relished the exciting, encapsulated event of a one-night stand. *Who am I?* I'd think to myself: I'm this sexy, unknown, completely new person that Jim or Bob or Rick is treating like found money. I'm whoever I tell him I am. Later, of course, he might rise and, donning a caftan, light a cigarette and start to tell you about this really good book he was reading (*Don't Say Yes When You Want to Say No*, or *Reclaiming Your Inner Child of the Past*), or you'd step into the bathroom and find yourself in the stifling dark heart of the Judy Museum, surrounded by chrome-framed blowups of the twitchy, hand-wringing star. Or you might be lying there dewy-eyed and smitten, the cum still cooling on your chest, while he, having sized you up postorgasm as underemployed disco trash, was yanking on his tight black jeans and, looking meaningfully from his watch to the door, saying, "I've got some calls to make." There was a particular feeling of satiety and exuberance I treasured, walking home sticky and rumpled in last night's clothes, lips swollen and cock chafed.

I'd march right home and, sitting at the table with a cup of coffee, write it all down. It was no coincidence that prior to beginning a journal in college, I'd last kept a little red diary around the time I reached puberty and spent a steamy Texas summer fucking and sucking a neighbor boy in a rickety backyard fort, and I'd resumed journal-keeping when I came out at nineteen and began having sex with men again. Sex made me want to write, and I wanted to write about sex.

When we'd kissed good-bye for the last time and he'd backed down the block to his car, waving and smiling sadly, I turned back to the flat, my mind agog. I felt inexpressible relief at being away from Ben after twelve hours of his rapt gaze—and I couldn't wait to see him again. What if he blew me off? *I'm in love*, I thought, to see how it sounded—but a nasty little voice piped up sneeringly from outside the Valentine heart: "*Zan Oh-zay?*"

All the pretty ones to the front! Last call at the Stud: the deejay's smirky amplified words cut through the ear-splitting Blondie ("And if I *do*, will anything happen?"). I'd been thinking about Ben with lust and anxiety all week, but it was Friday night and I could only sit at home mooning over him in my silk-bound China Books diary for so long. Beer-blurry in the jarring brightened lights (*Gentlemen, the bar is now closed!*) I shuffled once around the rectangular bar, kicking trash and cigarette butts, *looking*.

"You—I'll take *you*!" I turned to see the tall, strapping, Michael Yorkish blond who'd grabbed my arm. "C'mere." We kissed drunkenly. "You're cute—the shy type, right?" One hand played over my crotch; he tilted my face back in the light with the other. I thought he might ask to see my teeth. "How'd you like my big cock up your ass?" he said, halting the flow of traffic around us for a moment. He registered my angry look. "Hey, don't get all insulted. You want to get laid, don't you? Just come home with me; you don't have to do anything you don't want."

The interior of his Camp Street flat looked like the inside of Jeannie's bottle, all dirty velvet and piled drapery. The gauze- and ruffle-laden furniture and windows were like homeless people wearing every piece of clothing they owned. The air was thick with patchouli, pot, and the inevitable litter box, and I felt like I'd just stumbled into a musty side room in the Valley of Kings, as if the walls might be covered with fading murals of bird-faced homosexuals walking sideways—but there was no way of knowing if this was the case because every inch of wall was covered with large and small framed photographs of Marilyn in every phase of her career. The cluttered bedroom was dominated by a wrecked canopy bed, swathed in dirty netting, a pith helmet artfully tossed over one post.

Then we were naked and rolling around inside his sultan's tent. He was on top of me, pinning my shoulders with his elbows and kissing me in a way I didn't like, dredging his tongue around my mouth and then slavering my chin and nose with saliva, like a drunk applying lipstick. He'd been grinding what felt like a very large cock against mine, pushing my hand away when I tried to reach for it, and stretching my arms back over my head; now he moved down and took my dick in his mouth and started sucking elaborately, loose and slobbery all the way down and up, and then jacking it with one hand tightly gripping the base and sucking hard on the swollen head. I forgot my momentary annoyance and started thrusting into his mouth. I'd purposely not been jacking off till the next time I'd see Ben, and I felt a dramatic load on its way.

"Not so fast, cowboy." He flipped me over, spread a gob of Vaseline across the crack of my ass and in with his finger. Then, pushing my face down into the mattress with one hand, he jammed the fat head of his dick inside me and kept on pushing, though I tried to squirm away with a muffled, "Wait a minute, it's hurting. . . ." It was all mechanical then: he was pistoning in and out of me, yanking all the way out and then slamming back in from different angles. Each time I reached for my own cock he grabbed my wrist and wrestled it back to the bed. He seemed not so much to be fucking me as performing the act of fucking someone, like he'd stepped into a porno film. I'd relax my way into liking it for a while, and then, after another ten minutes of rough pumping, my butt would start to clench up and hurt. Finally he slowed down, ground as far up into me as he could get, and leaned around the side of my head, slobbering in my ear. "You're real hot up inside, you know that? I'm gonna fuck you real hard some more, and then I'm gonna squirt a real big load way up inside you, and it's gonna be so much and so hot you're gonna feel it shoot. Now open up for me, baby."

The soreness had abated some while he was still; now he slammed it in and out like a bully jabbing at your shoulder saying, *Yeah, you want to fight, you gonna do something about it?* and my insides were fluttering and out of control and I thought *Christ, I'm going to piss myself* and then some crucial bit of tension broke and I was jutting my ass back to meet his hammer thrusts and he seemed to come straight through me and I was ejaculating, one, two, three, a gush with each lunge and then he yelled and dug into me, arms locked around my chest, shaking and gasping.

"Hey," he said, head propped on his arm, "you're sweet. Why don't you stay and just cuddle awhile?" I was yanking on my socks, my legs shaking, pulling my Tom and Jerry sweatshirt on wrong-side-out.

"I really have to go."

He watched me from the bedroom doorway as I started down the hall. "The door's the other way."

"My coat's *this* way," I said, diving back into the Marilyn gallery, and then fumbling the front door open. He yelled after me from the top of the stairs: "Why don't you do yourself a favor, huh? Just don't go back to the Stud! It's not your style!"

I didn't see Ben for a couple of weeks; he didn't have his regular Monday rehearsal, and I was busy finding and moving into a studio apartment on Polk Street, after Dan returned to school in Michigan and Steve moved back to Tampa to get married. We'd talked on the phone several times—short, halting conversations consisting chiefly of sentiments like "I really want to see you" and long sighs. I imagined Ben practicing his oboe or arranging his camera collection after we hung up, or writing me one of those Hallmark cards I'd been getting regularly ("Just thinkin' of you . . .") with "Love, Ben," down at the bottom. In my diary or in conversation with any friend who could stand to listen, I debated whether or not I was in love. Other nights I walked out to the Giraffe or the Cinch and tricked.

I couldn't wait to get him alone in my new apartment. We met at Sutter's, grinning like idiots. He looked freshly showered and glowing, dressed in stiff new Levi's and another plaid shirt, this one brown and green. "Let's go by my place first," I said. We were kissing and pulling at each other's clothes as soon as we got through the door. I slid down, unbuckled his belt, opened his pants, wedged out his fat cock, and started sucking it hungrily. He leaned against the wall, eyes shut, breathing deeply. He started to pull me up, but I pushed his hands away. "It may take me a long time to come like this."

"That's okay," I said, and went back to work, jacking it with my thumb and forefinger and slurping on the head, tugging lightly on his heavy balls. I had the delicious feeling of debauching a youth—though in fact he was only a couple of years younger than me—because his Jockeys smelled slightly of talcum powder, because he was so awkward and inexperienced. After maybe ten minutes, his legs started to quiver and he clutched at the sides of my head, hanging on to my ears—"Oh jeez, you're gonna make me come"— and my mouth was flooded with hot, pungent sperm that brought to mind the odor of modeling clay. He sank down to kiss me but I pushed him lower to the carpet.

"Let me see your ass," I said. He was all tangled up in his jeans, which were only pulled down just past the curve of his buttocks. I'd been jacking my cock while I blew him; now I stroked it slowly over his pale, plump, damp butt, which was half-obscured by his shirttail and white T-shirt. His ass smelled sweet and just slightly funky, little pubic tendrils of black hair plastered down with sweat. I spit several times into my palm and stroked my dick, scooted onto him with the open fly of my jeans pressing at the base of my scrotum, and pushed it slowly up him. "Aww man, aww man," he muttered as I stretched myself full-length, skewering him, turning his head so we could kiss. His asshole felt tight and rough with just the spit for lube, and I kept my thrusts deep inside him, reaching under his hips and pulling him closer against me, trying to climb all over him, inside him. Then I was just pumping and kissing his neck while he lay still and shivered each time I thrust, goose bumps rising on his sweat-slicked back. Then the semen came jerking out of me, and I lay breathing on top of him, separate, jolted from a violent dream, the taste of his spunk still sharp on my tongue.

"I don't have class again till Wednesday. Can I stay over?"

"Sure."

"I love you."

Later, after going out to dinner, we both sat with notebooks on our laps, writing, though I found I couldn't be very frank in my journal with Ben shifting and sighing five feet away. I glanced over, and couldn't help noticing something strange about his loopy printing. He looked up. "I write in German, for practice," he said.

He was still there when I came home from work the next day. "My car wouldn't start. I took it to a Datsun place on Van Ness. Guess I'll just have to miss class tomorrow."

Two days later, his car fixed, Ben went home. "In a way, I'm almost glad my generator went out, because I got to spend all this time with you."

"Uh-huh," I answered. I was walking him down Polk Street to his car, and I wondered if anyone I knew in the Giraffe would be looking out as we went by holding hands. I felt guilty and crabby, shocked at my own brisk transformation: three nights of adoring glances and camera talk, of Ben poring over and underlining passages in his copy of *Loving Someone Gay*—three nights of unrelieved Daddyhood—had killed my sexual obsession. Whatever I'd been projecting onto him had dissolved, leaving behind a clinging stranger. He was just plain Judy Barton, from Salina, Kansas.

"I've never been so happy," he said with a misty smile as he got into his car.

"Talk to you soon," I said, almost looking behind me for the long, scaly tail. I'd put him out of my mind before I got a block away. A hustler standing against the Bagel Deli with a torn tank top and a snootful of speed stared at me appraisingly. Both our heads jerked as a horn beeped a few yards away: Ben, frantically waving one more good-bye.

I got another one of his cards the very next day: "Words are coming easier to me now. You've brought so much into my life. . . ."

I dodged Ben's phone calls all week and distracted myself with an old fuck-buddy, Dennis. Dennis would call up every six months or so, I'd bus over to his Mission flat, and I'd fuck him or he'd fuck me. He was in his late thirties, skinny, with thinning hair and glasses, but he was kind, funny, undemanding, and he fucked with the attention and passion of an aging man who takes nothing for granted.

I lay stretched out lazily on Dennis's bed, staring at the red lights on the Twin Peaks tower blinking through the condensation on the long windows, reaching for another slug of Budweiser while he sucked on my cock. Dennis's straight-boy fantasy of me almost required that I be lazy and selfish; I could lie back and be adored and ravished. When he pushed my legs back over my shoulders and fucked me, it was long and slow and sweet till he paused, trembling on the verge of coming, jacking my heavily lubed dick in his fist: "You ready? You want to shoot it for me now?"

The following Monday I agreed to meet Ben at Sutter's.

"You seem bummed out," he said, trying to take my hand. We went straight to the Grub Stake; I sat glumly while he chattered about his job, his classes. "I've told my parents I may start spending weekends with a friend in the city," he said. "Hey, what's wrong? Are you mad at me?"

"It's not your fault," I lied. "I just get depressed. That's why I'm living alone. I just need to be by myself sometimes."

And then, to my shame, I stopped returning his calls.

I got a letter from him after a couple of weeks, block-printed on a sheet of lined notebook paper: "I never knew anybody could be as cruel as you. You've broken my heart. I hope you really do love somebody someday and he hurts you like you've hurt me."

Dennis lay panting on top of me, sweat and cum coating our chests. My eyes filled up suddenly and a couple of tears spilled out. "Sweetheart," he said, pushing my hair back from my forehead, kissing my closed eyes while I sobbed. "Sweetheart."

One Saturday morning six weeks later, the phone rang as the door clicked shut behind Dennis. "Hello! Is this *Uncle* Kevin?" I lay on my stomach listening to Mom in Texas talking excitedly about the birth of my older brother's first child.

"Yeah," I said. "That's great. How many pounds?" Grandma got on the phone, and I was daydreaming through a litany of doctor visits and diabetes when I heard the front door swing open. Dennis must have forgotten something, I figured. I half-turned, hand over the mouthpiece. Ben, staring at me impassively, was kneeling at the foot of the mattress. "I'll be off in a second," I said, thinking I'd better get him out of the apartment. "Let me just get some clothes on and we can go somewhere and talk as soon as—"

"*Nein.*" He was unbuckling his belt, pulling open his button-flies, a strange little determined smirk I didn't recognize on his face. I shook my head emphatically and started to pull the sheet up. He yanked it out of my hand, shoved me back onto my stomach, and threw his weight on top of me, one arm in a serious choke hold around my neck.

"I don't know if we're driving to Abilene for this year's Stone family reunion or not. . . ." My mom was back, talking surrealistically in my ear; the receiver was now mashed against my face. "It'll just be a bunch of fat people standing around a graveyard talking about dead people." I still had a crazy half-idea Ben just wanted another hug. When he pushed a wet finger up my butt, I struggled in earnest to throw him off, but he'd locked his thighs around me and was making it difficult for me to breathe.

And then, amazingly, he rammed his fat, short, plunger of a dick in my asshole with one rough movement and started humping fast without another word, without releasing his hold on my neck.

"Daddy's having those bars put on all the windows; I said it's like *we're* in prison, but he wants to do it, so that's that—What are you doing, washing dishes while I'm talking?"

You can tell when someone's fucking you with tenderness, however brutally he may be socking it in, and when his whole excitement is a kind of contempt. This was something new I couldn't place. Ben was jabbing his dick in with a determined coldness, but his death-grip on me conveyed something else. It was uncomfortable; he was *hurting* me, he was telling me something I didn't want to hear. I felt as if he were trying to break me open and peer inside.

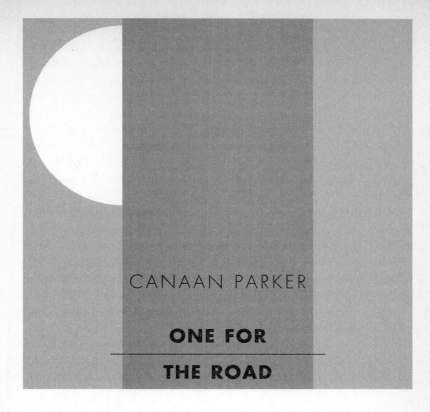

CANAAN PARKER

ONE FOR
THE ROAD

I

KNOCK ON WOOD, BUT MARCO THE MAGNIFICENT MAY
have saved my life when he fucked my brains out fifteen years ago.
It was the last time I was ever screwed, perhaps the last time I ever
will be, but, honey, it was one to last a lifetime.

Fifteen years! I miss it in the ass. I often dream about it vividly.
I remember *thunderclaps against my buttcheeks*. Marco pinning my prostate gland to the bulletin board. I could use condoms, but my experience hasn't given me enough faith in them. In the early eighties,
we didn't know quite how to use them. (They are tricky little things;
it does take a bit of finesse to get one on.) And so my memories
sustain me through these dry years of abstention.

Thanks to Marco, I was able to change my sex habits (as far as passive anal sex goes) in the early days of the plague. I still got horny, but once Marco was done with me I was no longer in heat, which is a very key difference. When you're horny and a guy refuses to put on a condom, you kick his nutty ass out of bed; in heat, you fuck anyway. You feel incomplete; you are *searching* for sex. You are "on a mission." Better to stay out of heat these days. Fortunately, I found what I was searching for *once and for all* with Marco, whom I think of as His Majesty. It was May of 1982 when the Great King fucked the Holy Molies out of me, and all these years later my bunghole is still content.

Well, perhaps not content, but I'm not going nuts like my friend Nicky either. Nick is buzzing like a queen bee for a good boning, but he too is wary of men who don't like or don't know how to use rubbers. Five years ago a man promised to use a Trojan to fuck him, but as soon as Nick was facedown in the pillow the guy tried to sneak his unsheathed prick into Nick's ass. "They make me lose my boner," the trick complained when Nick turned around and caught him just in time.

Nick hasn't had a dick in the bum since. He was doing his "fuck-me" walk last week—his hyperkinetic swish, fast-forward knock-kneed zigzag with panicked shoulder glance *bend my pelvis pop my cherry* splayed jellyfish salmon wriggle *yes yes* high-step jump out the window *oh God Christ Jesus please*—and Nick is not especially fey.

"What are you doing to me, Nick?" I asked, fighting the urge to mount him right there in the street. Nick is in heat, you see. His primal mating instincts are driving him mad. There's two theories about this. One, a virus gets into your brain and its reproductive instincts become your own. And two, when the mortality rate in an ecosystem is high, reproductive urges intensify to make up for the losses. Nick's butt apparently doesn't know he can't get pregnant.

I worry that Nick can't hold out forever. One day "Top Man" Johnny is going to follow him into an alley, and when Top Man won't use a condom, or tries to but the damn thing turns inside out and sticks to his dick like chewing gum, and the plastic lip tears off and gets tangled up in his pubic hair, Nick is going to fantasize that Top Man is "probably negative" just long enough to get lovingly seroconverted. I could easily do the same, but Marco let the hot air out of my balloon, so to speak, a long time ago.

II

I had beautiful legs when I was twenty-two. I lived in Boston then, and every day after a run along the Charles River I'd finish with a sprint up Beacon Hill. Neighbors hollered from their windows, "Lift! Lift!" as I kicked up the hill most normal people had trouble walking. I also lifted weights, but sparingly. I didn't want too much muscle. I was in my oral phase then. All I wanted was to give head and I wanted my body to look like a dish of pudding. Up and down the Esplanade I walked in barely legal corduroy cutoffs, shredded in homage to Tina Turner. I hadn't been screwed yet, but the idea must have been germinating in my brain cells. Bobby, whom I knew from music class, came walking toward me from about a block away with an abandoned-in-the-desert look on his face and didn't look up from my crotch until he was a step away. His face beamed when he realized he knew the person in those shorts. He took me back to my apartment, opened the living room window, turned me around in my recliner, and tried his best to get inside of me, but I was too tight, and Bobby couldn't hold it.

Kevin May lived across the street. He was weird and obnoxious and vulgar, and hot after my cherry. No one else talked to me the way he did. Sitting on my doorstep, eye-level with my hip pockets: "These buns will suit me fine." In the bathroom at Buddies disco: "Wait 'til you see the log I got for you."

I had never been pursued so aggressively before. I told Kevin to drop dead, but he kept after me. "I'll fuck some of that snot out of you." "Shish-ka-buns, shish-ka-buns." He had to be joking, I thought. Why would I let someone crack open my ass and pump cum inside of me? After all, I wasn't a girl. Kevin paid no attention to my male ego, which was a red herring. He ignored my prissy rejections like so much irrelevant red tape. "Damn, I want your big butt," he sputtered, speaking directly to my body. "Shish-ka-buns."

It took me a year to figure out that I liked Kevin. After months of insulting him, I sent him an anonymous letter asking if he wanted a hot piece of ass. Somehow Kevin knew I had sent the letter. When I came downstairs he was waiting for me, a doubtful but smoldering look on his face. My roommate was still upstairs so we went over to his apartment.

He hadn't lied about his log. It was heavy as a big-job wrench, black, solid, and industrial. It would have hurt if he hit you in the head with it. While I fretted and fussed like a baby Kevin wedged it into me.

"Stop crying, it's all the way in," he said.

All I felt was numbness. "Easy. Oh please, easy," I whispered. I scrambled away, trying to pry myself off his cock. Kevin pulled me back, but I bucked and lifted him up off the bed. Fed up with my nonsense, Kevin gave up and pulled out. I felt a gusting vacuum where his cock had just been.

I complained about how rough he was. "You have to go slowly. I'm a virgin!"

But Kevin didn't appreciate my blessed state. "You're just a piece of ass to me," he said, giggling with an eccentric glee.

I was exasperated. "I let you be the first, Kevin!"

He put his arm around my shoulder, his eyes vital with a private joke. Resting my chin on his chest, I looked down a long, rippled brown landscape past nipples, knees, an iron mine in a loose bag of skin, and tall feet in the distance. I felt like crying—I wanted Kevin so badly, but he was too much for my cherry. My ass felt damaged and raw. Kevin saw my eyes wetten and smiled impishly.

"Nothing special. You're just another piece of ass," he laughed.

I spent the summer after my last term in graduate school in Boston so I could be with Kevin. I was scared to let him fuck me again, but there were other things we could do to enjoy ourselves. Though I fucked Kevin several times, emotionally I felt I was his wife. That was the relationship I wanted with him, and it was true in all ways except mechanically. It didn't matter to Kevin who fucked whom. "It's like having sex with myself," he told me once, so the difference was ephemeral. Kevin and I were practically twins. I was slightly taller and my skin a shade lighter, but we were the same age and built alike—brown, leggy, and lean. He was a painter and I a musician. He was more talented, I was more educated, but we were both eccentric, young, and broke. I saw him once on the corner by the Greyhound station, where he turned tricks when he needed money. "Come here," he said, grabbing at my belt as I walked past. He held me warmly against his crotch, one leg on a standpipe, his arms comfortable around my waist. A man walked past, stopped at the corner, and wiggled a finger at him.

"Wait here," he told me, and walked with the man around the corner toward the Boston Public Garden.

After he made money, we spent the day together, strolling the length of lovely Boston, toe-dancing in the grass on the Esplanade. Down by the edge of the water we hugged and French-kissed, hidden from the straighties by the thick hanging leaves of a tree rooted in the riverbank. "Let's go home," Kevin suggested. He was enormously hard and I could tell he wanted to finish the job he had begun on my butt. But I was in a fickle mood—a cockteasing mood—so I said no.

That afternoon I wanted to drive Kevin to a dreamy level of unrelieved horniness. If possible, I wanted to make him come in his jeans in public. In Kevin's pool-hall hangout, in front of several of his friends, I brushed my bum on his zipper, rolled up my cutoffs, spread my legs, unbuckled his belt. I rolled up his shirt and licked wax out of his navel. The bartender, letting soda run on his hand, looked on the verge of tears watching us. Under Kevin's shirt I played patty-cake with his penis.

"Come home with me," said Kevin.

"No," I answered, to my eternal regret. Kevin was ready to turn what was left of my cherry inside out and peel the pits. I was tempted, but fearful. I didn't want to fail again. Was I just too tight, a lousy lay? Not woman enough? What was I supposed to feel anyway? Perhaps I should try again and tough it out? But cockteasing was also an intriguing experience and I wanted to explore it a while longer.

Two days later I left Boston with an unanswered question a foot deep in my behind.

III

Marco, the Great King, adorned his neck with a small gold chain—
flat, soft links that brought out the undertint of his skin, *gold shining
through mud*. He was built to fuck, ass in particular. The shape of his
hips, rump, and thighs implied a great chemical potential of power
lying in rest, like plastique or nitro. His fat, Cajun penis was the
bait in his mantrap. His brown boy's eyes, both blinding and sooth-
ing, prepared his sex partner emotionally for a natural, moral ag-
gression. His golden skin. Lightly tinted pubic hair.

Once inside his circle of reflected light my mind slowed and I
groveled. I wanted to be fucked by gold. I hoped to become gold
next to him. Marco's gift was to conquer gently, and yet presump-
tuously. Which is to say, he had a regal bearing.

I was with him twice, a sonata in two movements. The first,
Allegro cantabile. The last, *Allegro con fuoco*.

Our first time came in the bathhouse on the Upper West Side of
Manhattan. I was living there, night after night, having failed at
coexisting with my parents. I saw Marco in the steam room, and
even through a cloud of vapor he was beautiful—compact, powerful,
the young middleweight champ. I groped him, but he slapped my
hand away angrily. Afterward, by the heated swimming pool, Marco
took my hand and led me upstairs to his private room.

"Did you think I was straight when I said no downstairs?" he
asked.

"No," I said. "I thought you just didn't like me."

Marco's body felt like a warm bath. His pubic hair was fresh
and sweet. He was nineteen; he didn't live anywhere. And he came
from so far away, Louisiana of all places (he talked while I sucked
his cock). I wouldn't have guessed. He had no drawl. He reminded
me of no one and no place.

He seemed conspicuously untroubled for a homeless gay youth
on the streets of the City of Predators. No one, I sensed, had ever
fucked him over. He was luckier, so far, than Baldwin's Giovanni.
The hardened tricks with spare rooms or a carpet for him to sleep
on, who might have wounded him, preferred to adulate him. He was

their favored guest. For Marco had a reputation, I later learned, in Greenwich Village. He gave priceless anal sex, the best in the world. You couldn't buy a more wonderful screw with a million dollars. Men smiled at him as he walked the street. Some poked their faces in his path and made tentative gestures, bids for his interest. Everyone wanted to lie beneath him. Which is to say, Marco enjoyed the royal prerogative.

"Nice ass," he said as I crawled toward him on my knees. He had grown bored with the blow job and nudged me onto the bed. "How old are you?"

"Twenty-three."

"Twenty-three?" he asked, as if that were ancient. "You got a nice ass for twenty-three." He brushed his hand up and down between my cakes. Then he swiped lightly at my down, giving me a start.

"Do you want to get fucked?" he asked politely.

Of course I did. I wanted to get stitched into the mattress. But I answered with that tired, silly cliché:

"Only if you promise to take it easy and pull out when I say." Which was nonsense *and* a lie.

Action: Marco fucks me in a dozen positions—on my belly, on my knees, standing up, upside down. He shoves my legs over my head and tells me my asshole looks just like a pussy. "I'mah get some of this pussy," he says. I whisper in his ear, "Oh Marco fuck me," as I wrap my arms around his chest and my knees around his neck. "Please fuck me." Someone knocks on the door and interrupts the warmest, richest pleasure I have ever known. Marco stops and opens the door. It is his friend, a tall, older man with a bushy Afro. I sit up on the bed with my arms crossed on my knees and grin with embarrassment; I can tell he heard me. Marco glances at me and then smiles at his friend, who looks at me with jealousy and hate. Evidently he had expected to be with Marco. Later Marco tells me his friend had paid for the room.

After his date left I wanted to start right up again, but Marco leaned toward me with a worried look on his face. "When did you become so, uh, feminine?" he asked. He seemed concerned that he might one day enter a feminine phase himself. After all, I was an athletic young black man much like him, perhaps physically stronger and only a few years older.

"*You* made me feminine," I said. "Usually I'm the one that fucks."

Marco winced, mistaking my meaning. "I don't give ass," he warned.

"I wouldn't want to fuck you," I said. "You're too masculine." He smiled like a ten-year-old. To make him smile again, I told him his cock was really enormous. Jumbo-sized.

"This is nothin'," he said, with absurd modesty. "Down in Louisiana they got those *big* dicks." The image of Marco in bed with a giant knee-dangling Creole (doing what?) was terribly provocative. From his curiosity about my feminine urges, and his statewide survey of Louisiana trade, I could tell he had budding questions in his own bottom. Marco was no schoolboy on top. He was dominating, long-lasting, egotistical, and experienced. But in his strong, round ass, he had not yet been, but clearly one day *would* be, fucked, which made him, technically, a virgin. (This wonderful paradox, the virginal stud, exists only in gay sex.)

On the subject of dick, true, Marco's wasn't the biggest I had ever seen. It was the ideal size, as big as one can get without being impossible. It was surely enough to dry your mouth on sight, to shut your brain off for the night. No one would ever say, "I wish it were just a bit bigger." Thankfully, it came to a pointy tip so it could slide through a frightened little pucker and smoothly split it open. If it were a person, I'd say Marco's dick had a slight weight problem.

It had softened during our conversation. "Make it hard," he insisted, expecting me to use my mouth, but it was coated with shit and so I used my hand. Marco fucked me beautifully on my back for a long while and then came inside of me. It was 1981.

A year later, in the spring, Marco found me sitting on the stoop of a dumpy hotel off Christopher Street, where I had moved. "Don't I know you?" he asked. I nodded and he sat next to me, still remembering me only vaguely. As his memory returned in detail he winced with guilt, then smiled. We talked a bit. Marco had on his gold necklace. I complimented him on it and ran my finger down his neck. *Gold in shadows.* "Where do you live?" he asked. I pointed overhead, indicating my room upstairs. Marco's hair needed combing. I took out my Afro pick and undid a tangle in back of his head. The sky was clear; it wasn't too hot. I could smell dead fish in the Hudson River just across the highway. The drone of four-lane traffic only yards away was calming. There were queers everywhere, pushing their luck in early spring, wearing hot pants, going topless. I took off my sneakers and socks, pulled off my T-shirt, undid the top button on my shorts.

Marco leaned over and whispered in my ear. "You want to do something?"

"All right," I said. We went upstairs.

IV

Marco fingered my rump as I bent over his thigh and blew him, unraveling my fleshy curlicue. It was my favorite thing, too, when I was the top; to twirl a few shit-caked hairs between my fingertips, to press that pouty little button like a doorbell when you're caught in the rain. Using his whole hand, Marco brushed and smudged like an artist working in pastels. I knew firsthand how good that felt. Who cares about the blow job? I can do better with my hand. But to scrape and pinch and tickle and poke. Up to the knuckle and shake. Sometimes fingers are the best things in the world.

That's what I mean! It was wonderful to give ass. I stuck my rump out until my back hurt and my big cheeks opened wide to Marco's touch. I knew he would love that. Marco scratched me with his fingernails. He didn't slap me, though I would have let him. "He's not mean enough," I thought, prematurely.

"Do you want to get fucked?" he asked, just as before. How sweet. It was the unfucked virgin in him, his darling nature, a schoolboy raising his hand for the bathroom pass. Asking permission to fuck me to pieces, as if there were any chance I might say no. This time I didn't ask him to go easy. I thought I could handle this.

I didn't know yet that, our first time, Marco *had* been taking it easy with me. I thought he had fucked me as hard as he knew how, ignoring my plea for lenience, but no. As I had asked, Marco had held back a good half of his strength.

But not knowing this, I answered simply and directly, "Yes." No conditions. Marco made room in my bed for me to lie down. Then he gestured with his hand where he wanted me to stretch out. He wanted me to lie on my stomach, though I wanted it on my back. I tried to roll over but he coaxed me back down on my belly. That ancient gay dilemma: On your back feels more like you giving than him taking. You feel more skin, and you can kiss and wrap your ankles behind his neck (behind your own if you're very good). On your belly you can't see much, so other senses perk up to compensate—in this case, the feelings in the rectum.

Facedown, blind in my pillow, I felt revolutionary nuances of pressure. An alert, graceful insinuation past folds and curls, sticking hairs. Marco hitched and locked me with his thigh. A snakebite deep inside me, then pop! and a trickle of fluid as Marco crushed a tiny, inflated, fleshy obstacle. What finesse, I marveled. Marco was experienced to the point of being sage. He was an enlightened despot, brutal right up to but not past my breaking point. But he was not considerate; he simply knew what he was doing.

My philosophy of anal sex

In music, jazz drummers play drumrolls on fresh eggs. The violinist shuts his eyes and cocks his head to hear the resonant frequency—one cycle per second off and the whiskey glass won't shatter. In painting, it is the invisible point where blue is no longer blue but green. In my hotel that May afternoon, it was Marco's fine, measured blend of lenience and stabbing, splitting violence. He was looking for an invisible point on the spectrum of physical sensation. I could relax just enough to make penetration possible, but no more—Marco wanted it to hurt. It should hurt until my squinting eyebrows touched the tip of my nose, but not a bit more—Marco wanted me to enjoy the pain.

Finding his fine balance, he made pain register in my mind as pleasure, fantastically transformed into its opposite through a trick mirror in my nerves. Which is to say, the aim of art *and* anal sex is the realization of paradox.

I did scream. I screamed to make room for more agony. I heard myself grunting desperately. I wanted to say, *Oh fuck me Marco*, but I no longer controlled my voice. Marco did. He played me like a saxophone, pressing my keys, blasting air out of my lungs. This noise was what he was really after. He fucked not for orgasms but for the dance on his eardrums, the quaking vibration in his solar plexus from involuntary squeaks and honks, groans and frightened squeals. Perhaps as a baby he had heard his parents fucking. Did his toes spasm in his crib that night?

I was his musical composition, a rhythmic tone poem. Oh (THRUST) OH (thrust) (thrust) (pinch) Ouch! Sheets of sound. Marco played conga drums in my ass. He made me sing like Leadbelly, like Sonny Rollins's horn in low register.

My rib cage rattled. The shock waves escaped through the top of my head. My eyelids flapped like a window shade in a windstorm. Then came gale-force winds. Then a typhoon.

I thought he was in all the way. He wasn't. He had a secret weapon, an extra inch, an inch I would never have consented to. An inch that wasn't funny anymore. A lonely inch that even great cocksuckers couldn't suck, a shortchanged youngest child. A neglected inch of cock filled with rage. Marco was blind and deaf. He was humping, pounding, grappling, jiggling.

Blast off! With one thrust, he speared me with that last inch of cock and added depth from his furious hips. The pain surprised me, and I hollered in great alarm. But it was over, and before I could resist he had come. It was an instant of true violence, unendurable if it had continued. . . .

It was just a flash. A vicious half-second I've relived a thousand times in all the years since . . .

In my memories, I don't feel the pain. I remember it but don't feel it, and so I can alter the sensation; I can change it into gold. I squiggle in my chair. I flex my cheeks and sap the energy out of a blind, old moment. I nurse the memory to keep it alive. . . .

Marco was enough of a virtuoso to have tricked me on purpose. Holding that last stretch of cock in reserve, knowing I would have hurled him off the bed if he had tried to get it all in sooner. And I'm sure he had done it to other men. Waited until they were drooling and thankful, their legs limp, their thoughts trapped in a box. Then launched a missile up their ass and came and was done, before they could object.

It was rape, calculated from the start behind a mask of grace, more childish than criminal, but still brutal. That single, splitting, foot-long thrust was Marco's aim from the minute he sat down next to me on the stoop, smiling with the sweetness of ancient sugarcane. Still, I would have happily consented again if I had ever had another chance to be with Marco. I would have asked him to take it easy, though.

A Spanish man who had been after me in my hotel for some time must have been listening at my door. He gave me an amazed look later in the hallway. Maybe the sound carried in the stairwell and he followed it. "Can I do that to you, too?" his eyes asked. There was envy in his eyes as well. I felt like a celebrity—I had put on a concert of sorts. I took his amazed, almost incredulous look as a testament to Marco. *Sorry, but I belong to the Great King.*

Dear Marco, Amon-Ra, sunburst shadows and golden mud of the Nile, Your Majesty, for a thousand nights, until death will I serve you.

V

That was the last time I was ever fucked. By the next year AIDS was on television and I saw my first friend who was to die, Mark, twenty-two years old, struggling down Christopher Street with a cane. My passive desires vanished, though I'm sure they are still buried somewhere in my unconscious. I'm in an odd state now. I fantasize about Marco and about Kevin. I've been with Marco perhaps a thousand times in the past ten years. Yet I have no actual desire to get fucked. I'm not fighting temptation constantly like Nicky, zigzagging his way up the street and trying to stay alive. Though much less than a perfect solution, it is enough for me to remember Marco.

I suppose if I had never been with him, I would be much more confused about the epidemic. But I look back over nearly half my life, I look into what I hope will be a distant future, and say *I had it really good at least once.* My sexual regret is not so profound that I would risk my life for a hot cock in the bum.

Whereas I might for a fresh, beautiful ass.

My deeper sexual regret is that I've never done to anyone what Marco did to me. I haven't screwed a man I found truly beautiful so fantastically, so long and hard and strong, that it exceeded my fantasies, and his. Anxiety, awkwardness, a lack of finesse, and now a lack of practice, all due to the plague, have interfered every time. It is a hard thing, to feel sexually cheated by life. It presses me blindly. It stirs in my bonnet. If I get another chance—to lay a virgin, or to throw the fuck some teenager will remember in *his* middle age— will I stop if the condom breaks?

Pray for me. My dick is still out there, on the riverfront, on Weehawken Street, out in the gay wilderness, searching. My ass, though, has been put to dreamy sleep.

MICHAEL
BRONSKI

DOCTOR FELL

Part 1
Journal
October 5, 1995
MADE NOTES ON "FLESH AND THE WORD" ESSAY. NOTH-
ing feels right. I have no idea of what tone to strike—lurid, medical,
religious, psychological, confessional? The whole thing makes me
uneasy. It should be simple: for six years, in several relationships,
part of my sex play with my partners was that we cut each other
with razors, scalpels, X-Acto blades. Sometimes we did temporary
piercings with needles—usually to draw blood. No big deal. Assume
an honest tone and simply describe the experiences. Mention the
potent sexual stimulation. Leave out the drugs (you wouldn't want
to give cutting and blood sports a bad name).

October 17, 1995

Essay going nowhere. Realize the problem is that it is supposed to be sexy. The actual experiences were sexy, but how do you convince readers who may well be appalled by the very idea? On the other hand, everyone likes gory movies, slasher films where sex and anxiety are bound together and released in the oozing and splattering of red fluid. The problem with writing about cutting and blood is that nothing much happens: cut and bleed. No thrashing legs, pulsating cocks. It is not the stuff of pornography but of dreams and unreason; the fairy tale, fearful myth; the elliptical spaces left unarticulated.

> I do not like thee, Doctor Fell,
> The reason why I cannot tell;
> But this I know and know full well,
> I do not like thee, Doctor Fell.

I've always loved this nursery rhyme. It resonates with dread, which is so often sexual. Odd that the man—Jim—who introduced me to cutting, whose scars I still carry and who died more than a decade ago (with the scars he carried from me), was a doctor and a Vietnam vet. Sometimes on acid he would remember the horrors of battlefield surgery and cry and praise me for having protested the war. And then we would cut each other. I would try not to cry because this was *his* time, his way of finally gaining control. He was not simply transferring the bloodied flesh of men from the battlefield into his living room, but shedding the shame and humiliation that were the constant companions to his sexuality when he was in Vietnam: he was making his desire real, palpable. The intensity was suffocating; heart-binding. "Do you trust me?" he would ask. "Do you trust me?"

The question felt superfluous. Trust, like love, is diminished when articulated. Fear, like love, can vanish when examined. The cutting and the gradual flow of blood—first a trickle, then a tributary; never more than that—was a physical and emotional release. And it was so sexy, so *driven*: I have a hard-on writing this. The fifteen years between then and now slip away, I can feel my heart beat, place my hand on my breastbone: a tattoo, a pulse: blood, blood, blood. I still love thee, Doctor Fell, the reason why I cannot tell, or even remember clearly, but I remember those long nights with hot black tea laced with bourbon, lemon, and MDA, and the almost unimaginable intimacy of scalpel to skin, of steady hand to willing flesh.

Essay (part one)

The living room in Jim's South End apartment is dark, candle-lit. A hard music beat on low volume comes from the radio. It is 3:00 A.M. We came home from the Ramrod twenty minutes ago, high on energy, cruising, MDA, a little acid, and each other. We've been going out for four months. Walta, my lover of six years, is at home; Jim is my other life, my nondomestic dark side, where the wild things are. At home I feel loved and secure, bookish, smart, even respected. Here I feel beautiful, desired, wanted, needed. I am no longer the friendless high school kid jerking off thinking about juvenile delinquents and hoods, James Dean and the wild ones with their antisocial attitudes and slicked-back hair. In Jim's eyes I become someone who lives in the world, lives in my body. With Jim I move through the bar like I should be there, like *we* should be there. Ripped dirty jeans, T-shirts, leather jackets: these were the uniforms of the rebels of my youth. I have become my childhood dreams. I have become the men I feared.

We are alone. The room is hot, the heat turned up against the winter outside. On the far wall, above a low, long chest, is a mirror—seven feet by seven feet—that dominates and enlarges the room. We move the candles in front of it and the cavelike room becomes magical. We make tea and carefully doctor it with sweet bourbon and sugar to mask the bitterness of more MDA.

We talk and laugh about someone at the bar, my arm around Jim, his hand under my shirt. We kiss and allow ourselves the pleasures of small movements, affectionate gestures. I feel myself both leaving my body and entering it. Like a transformed beast in a fairy tale, I can feel my flesh changing around me—it is a body I like, that I want to touch, that feels right. Jim's hand is on my nipples;

my hand is in his pants, kneading his cock through the jockstrap, feeling the foreskin shift and move with my fingers.

We kiss again and Jim gets up to piss. I begin to rearrange the room, moving candles away from the mirror, adjusting the music to increase the volume and lower the bass, and take the scalpels from where they reside, hidden deep in the drawers of the antique captain's desk. The instruments are meant for healing. In my heightened consciousness I think about the "art of healing"—a derisive term Jim uses to blaspheme and dismiss his experience in Vietnam.

Jim comes from the bathroom as I turn on the crane's-neck lamp and focus its 150-watt bulb on the mirror. The effect is mesmerizing; the intense illumination seems to radiate heat as well as light. The reflected room has become a stage on which we are to perform as actors playing ourselves, fantasy projections who are both us and not us. Jim has taken off his shirt and jeans. He wears only boots, socks, and his jockstrap; his six-foot-five-inch body—long sinewy arms, flattish ass, slight potbelly, shaved head—moves in and out of the mirrored light.

I remove my shirt, pants, boots and cast them into the corner. Jim opens a sterile package. The plastic crinkles; my body responds. I stretch my arms. I've done this before. You have to get the blood moving through the skin, bring it to the surface. I run my hands over my pectorals, down my thighs, play with my nipples, watch my body in the mirror. I am beautiful, I think. Who is this person? Not me, surely not me. Not as I know myself in the real world, the world of books and politics.

I stand in front of the mirror and inhabit the warmth from within and without. I run my fingers through my long hair and throw my head back—half Garbo in *Camille*, half Brando in *Streetcar*—and feel Jim's hand roam my chest as he chooses where to cut. I reposition my head and, staring at the body in the mirror—my body—watch as Jim makes feathery cuts around my nipples. I flex my pectorals. Pink lines form on my upper chest—Tina Turner chants "What's Love Got to Do with It?" in my subconscious, or on the radio, I'm not sure which—the pink turns rose, then vermilion, then crimson as it gathers and trickles, eddies and flows. I flex and breathe deep, stretch my arms above my head, savoring the pull of muscle and the tightness of skin. But most of all I watch. Watch as the blood—my blood—begins to run down my chest, glistening and gesticulating with a life of its own. This is who I am, I think. This is my body. Jim whispers in my ear, "Look at it look at it I love you look at it." I am in my body and beyond it, I have made it do what I want it to. I am transfigured, scarred, and left wanting more. More cuts, more pleasure, more warmth, more refuge from the hard life of the real world, from my past, from the person I was as a child, an adolescent, yesterday. I am the man in the mirror, the man standing next to me, holding me and cutting me, the man in my body and the man outside of it watching it live and bleed, move and breathe. I am . . .

Part 2
Journal
November 3, 1995

Essay is too difficult to write. I'll be misunderstood, misinterpreted. I would think that I'm beyond worrying about most of that—after years of cultivating a reputation as a sexual renegade. But what here is making me uncomfortable? My depictions of my cutting experiences are detailed and verifiable (I just looked at the fading scars on my chest and legs, running my fingers over them in memory and dispassionate awe), but the essay feels false to me. Is it overromanticized? All those candles and references to fairy tales? Is it too consciously spiritual, with its insistence on high-Catholic kitsch? Or is it that it is simply too, well, literary?

November 7, 1995

Journal entry of four days ago is complete shit. I know perfectly well what is missing from the essay: honesty and truth. Not that the cutting didn't happen, and (at its best) was romantic, affirming, potent. What am I leaving out? That as much as I loved Jim, I thought he was fucked up about sex? That his S/M practices—including cutting—were mostly vain attempts to break through the crushing repression of his southern boyhood and his horrible feelings about himself? That in our first year together he would have to leave the room after coming so he could be alone and cry? Or that Jim died of AIDS in 1987? Acting out doesn't always bring you through to the other side. And what does this mean in an essay that is promoting sexual experimentation in the name of freedom and health?

What else am I leaving out? That while I was seeing Jim I was involved in a deeply committed relationship with Walta Borawski, a relationship that lasted twenty years, until Walta's death in 1994. Walta and Jim and I spent a lot of time negotiating how to be nonmonogamous. Sometimes it worked; sometimes it didn't. But what does it mean that while I rhapsodize now about my cutting experiences with Jim, I *never* talked about them with Walta? That I would wear sweatpants and T-shirts to bed for weeks at a time to hide the fresh scars, as if Walta couldn't figure it out anyway. What does it mean that I trusted Jim—my boyfriend, my fantasy—enough to cut my flesh with scalpels, and yet I couldn't trust Walta—the man who gave my life meaning—enough even to speak to him about this? Was I lying to Walta?

The idea of what is truthful and what is not is arbitrary; an approximation. We write to give the appearance of truth and hope readers believe us. But even careless readers must realize that these "journal" entries are fake, a literary device used to move my story along. All, of course, in the pursuit of "truth" and "honesty."

Moments after Walta died—at 9:05 P.M. on February 9, 1994, at home in the bed I'd inherited from Jim, in which he had died eight years earlier—I sat next to him and talked to him for the last time. My first thought was to apologize for all the times I might have hurt him by my relationship with Jim. Why is *this* harder to confess than precise details of erotic extravagance?

Should I also mention that while taking care of Walta during his illness I accidentally gave myself several sticks with potentially contaminated needles? That if I am HIV-positive—I've never been tested—it is because transmission occurred (accidentally, incidentally) while nursing to his death the man I loved? That the blood running down my chest—the blood I shed for Jim—conflates in my mind with the blood of my dying lover? That the romance of the scalpel slicing through my skin is nothing compared with the sharp, frightening reality of the needle's jab in the thumb, the fear that pierces the heart and disorders the mind?

Essay (part two)

The living room is glowing now. Not only with the candles and the reflected lamplight but with the heat of our sexual energy. I stand in front of the mirror and watch myself. A simple flex will increase the trickle of blood down my chest; arching my torso to one side will change the course of the fluid, now carmine in color as it oxidizes and finds its way in the world, outside of the body. Jim lies on the couch watching me, enjoying my self-involved pantomime. I pull on my cock. It is soft, but full of feeling. I can feel the sexual excitement in my belly and down my thighs; I feel dazed by my own lack of inhibitions and overwhelmed by desire.

My self-entertainment lulls and I go to the kitchen and begin to make us more tea. Waiting for the kettle to boil, I look at my chest and marvel at the patterns, now crusting. Jim is in the bedroom looking for the restraints (tossed beneath the bed after he took them off last night's trick) and appears in the kitchen wanting my help fastening the buckles. We adjust the black leather cuffs, finish making the tea—sugar, lemon, bourbon—and sit on the floor, our backs resting on the couch. We hardly speak. We are lost in our own worlds as well as our shared one, and words seem superfluous. The tea is hot and sustaining; its heady fragrance intoxicates. Jim says it smells like hibiscus; a memory of his youth. We kiss and I run my hands over his chest, pulling the skin taut and relaxing it like a moire silk or the most subtle of velvets.

Tea finished, we stand in front of the mirror. I flex and watch the now-dry blood crinkle and flake. Jim holds up his arms, and I stand on a chair to slip a long rawhide cord through the D-bolts of the restraints and around the not-so-subtly placed hook in the ceiling. I pull the rawhide taut; he raises his arms, relaxes. The cord holds tight and I deftly knot. Climbing off the chair, I readjust the light—Jim is taller than I am—to highlight his form in the glass. He plays with the tension—up on his toes, down again, shrugging shoulders, and then forcing them down—until he is comfortable. I stand to his side and run my hands over his skin, play with his nipples. Jim's eyes are closed. What is he thinking? About me? About last night's trick? About being a teenager and the smell of hibiscus and the terror of sex with other boys? About Vietnam? He

sways and I hold him still with my hand and then carefully open
the hermetically sealed package and remove the blade.

"Open your eyes," I whisper. He does. "Where?" I whisper.
"Here?" I touch the skin above his nipple. "Here?" I run my hand
along his breastbone. "Here?" I touch the flesh on the uppermost
part of his abdomen. "Yes." "Where?" "There." I press on the soft
center, pinch the skin, knead it, redden it, make it ready for the cut.
"Watch," I say. "I love you." I steady my hand and slide the blade,
ever so gently, across the expanse of white epidermis. A three-inch
arc appears. We both look in the mirror amazed, confounded by the
beauty of it. From pink, to rose, to vermilion, to crimson (who knew
there were so many shades of red?), it rises to the surface magically
and begins to weep. Slow at first. Jim tenses his body, holds it,
relaxes. Tenses and relaxes. The blood rises and then begins to run:
rivulets almost afraid to give in to the gravity that pulls them down.
"Do you like it?" I ask. "Do you want more?" The question is need-
less. "Here." "Here?" "Here." I create a feather pattern over his
nipples, alternating light with deeper strokes. Jim likes to see a lot
of blood. It is not a matter of cutting deep, just of time and tension,
patience and gravity. I cut lower on his belly and we watch. Wait
and watch. "Shave me," he asks quietly. There is a hospital safety
razor on the chest. I reach for it and remove the stubble of his pubic
hair—we did this two weeks ago—with short, quick strokes. Around
the soft cock, the inner thighs, the top of the scrotum; carefully,
carefully. He is clean, more naked then ever. And suddenly he tenses
his whole body: once, twice, again and again and again. This is what
he wanted. What he has waited for. The blood runs more freely, past
his nipples, his rib cage, each one showing as his body stretches, over
his belly and down onto his cock and balls. It runs down the foreskin,
slowly. He watches in silence, rapt with the extraordinary grace of
it. This is what he wanted. This is what he always wants. Suspended,
displayed—like some martyr in a Renaissance painting—unable to
help himself, and watching as rivulets of blood dam at the tip of his
gathered foreskin and then fall, drop by drop, to the floor. You can
almost hear the droplets, tiny amounts of precious, jewel-like fluid,
fall and shatter as they hit the floor. I look in the mirror. It is like
a dream. But whose? And then I see that Jim is crying.

Part 3
Journal
December 2, 1995

Have just reread what I have written after putting it away for a few weeks. Does it work? Is it sexy? Or sexy enough? Is it "truthful"? Is it truthful enough?

Jim and I had an intense sexual relationship for almost five years. The dynamic between us was that I took care of Jim—sexually, emotionally, psychologically. The last time we had sex, I had him tied to a chair and beat his chest and arms with a switch, and then cut him with a scalpel. There was much blood. We were angry at each other, yet he still trusted me to enact our old rituals. After we broke up, my fury at him was nearly out of control. How could a man who trusted me to cut him not trust the depth of my love for him? We broke up and continued speaking, if only to argue. Walta was both upset and relieved. Jim left me for another man—Patrick —who loved him without any demands. Maybe in the mirror, Jim's dream was to find the perfect lover, the man he did not have to be tied up to love, the man who would not remind him of his guilt about Vietnam. Where had we gone wrong? Can you trust with your body and not trust with your heart? Walta felt more betrayed by my grief at losing Jim than he did by my sexual relationship with him. It was easy to hide scars in bed with T-shirts and sweatpants; it was nearly impossible to hide my desolation when Jim told me, "I just want to be friends."

December 12, 1995

Can I write about "honesty" and "truth" without writing about Vince? I started seeing Vince after Jim and I broke up. I never mentioned it to Walta. Or rather, Walta and I never talked about it. Vince was a distraction from my loss of Jim. Our sex was energized and extravagant. He let me beat him, tie him up, cut him. His capacity for this abuse and pain was endless. He fell in love with me—a fact he never felt permission to state—and I used him to get over Jim. My grief and anger fueled the affair. Was I hitting Jim when I hit Vince?

Once, in the middle of a long, somewhat drunken night, I said that I loved him. The words hung in the air. He had never said these words but it was true for him. I did say them, but it wasn't true for me. The next week he asked tactfully if I had uttered those words. He remembered I had, but thought he might have made it up. I said I didn't know. We continued the intense sex for another year and a half. Did I love him? I don't know. Was I using him? Probably. Was he using me? For what? Attention, sex, love? I gave him some of that. When I cut him it wasn't like cutting Jim—it was exciting but perfunctory, surgical. It was about Jim. It was about me wanting control again. "Trust," "love," "honesty." Is it enough to say that those words have no real meaning detached from actions and intentions? Is it enough to say "I'm sorry" now?

My last date with Vince was June 13, 1986. The day Jim was diagnosed with PCP. I was at the hospital and stayed there for the night. His body was so depleted that he needed red blood cells immediately; he had ignored the fact that he was sick for at least six months—was this the doctor-in-denial or the saint-in-the-making? I watched the blood—thick and heavy concentrated plasma—drip from the plastic bag into the clear tubing, through the large-gauged needle into Jim's vein. I never slept with Vince again, or tied him up, or beat him, or cut him. Jim needed me. I won. I was back in his life.

December 28, 1995

I sit here running my fingers over the scars on my chest and legs. They are fading now, most of them gone. Here or there is a line, a bump, a bit of raised skin, perhaps whiter than the surrounding flesh. I touch my flesh and pull at it. I look at the bed next to me—its brass in need of polishing—and think of Jim and then Walta dying in it. I look at my life and think, "It's not too bad. I'm here. I am writing this." My fingers roam my chest, pinch my nipples, I think about Jim's white, fish-belly flesh; Walta's hairy, darker skin; Vince's pliant scarred arms. I think of Walta and Jim and love and trust and where we fail and where we succeed, but sometimes, in the end, fail. Flesh is what brings us together, what joins us, and what keeps us apart.

I always thought Hamlet's line was "Oh, that this too, too solid flesh would melt." But someone just told me it is "sullied," not "solid," and that made sense. Flesh isn't solid, it isn't marble, but tender. Like "truth" and "honesty" and even "love," it can be inexplicably ruptured, torn apart. It is ripe for decay on its inevitable journey to become lifeless, what we—as a last resort—call "dead." Like "honesty," "truth," and "love," it is negotiable: we can make it do what we want (sometimes); we can do to it what we want (often); we can misuse and abuse it; but we cannot deny that it is there, that it is us.

I think about cutting Jim, about being cut. I feel my scars and think about cutting again. But with whom? Jim is dead. I never even talked about this with Walta. Vince is sick; we haven't spoken for a decade. Feeling my skin, I decide—one last time—to cut myself. Will it be sexual? My cock feels nothing. Would it be an experiment in remembrance? I can remember. I have remembered. Is it an easy way to end this essay? A cheap, exploitative shot? What do I feel writing this? What does my skin feel aging as it is on its journey to death?

Essay (part three)

I've turned up the heat in the house. It is cold outside. I've made a strong cup of tea with bourbon and sugar and lemon and have warmed myself within and without. I find the needles I saved from when Walta was sick and look at them in their sterile paper and plastic wrappers. I forget which is thinner—20G1, or 25G5/8? These are things I used to know. How odd to hold these slim packages in my hand. Three years ago I would deftly open them, remove the needle, and irrigate Walta's Hickman catheter or flush his feeding tube with saline and heparin. Fifteen years ago I would open these packages and carefully push the needle through Jim's and Vince's flesh. Which has more meaning for me now in memory? I nursed Walta and at times even made him better; he needed me and I was there. I gave Jim and Vince pleasure, at times even ecstatic joy. Did they need me? Could someone else have done this for them? And me? I learned, I received pleasure, I grappled with the mysteries of flesh, my own and others', I entered worlds I never dreamed

existed—of sex, of fantasy, of fear, of AIDS, of death—and I became
who I am today. Oh, that this too, too sullied flesh would melt.

I am lying on the brass bed next to my desk. I rub my chest,
my nipples, warm them with my palms. I unwrap the needle and
breathe deep. I've done this before. I can do this now. I hold the tip
of the needle—the thinner of the two—to the almost pink-beige
areola of my nipple. I breathe, I look at my chest and remember the
whiteness of skin, the tension of muscle, the love of other men, their
bodies and their trust. I trusted them, and why not now? Why not
myself? I hesitate and then I push without thinking, without feeling,
without memory. The needle slides, clean, and then sticks. I see the
skin on the other side of the nipple poking pointed; the needle has
not broken through. I breathe and push again. There is little pain,
a poke and that is it. The tip of the needle is exposed and its shaft
emerges clean and bright. My breath comes back and I stare at the
gleaming needle. What does it mean? Have I re-created a moment
from my past? Did I think this would bring back Jim or Walta?
Bring back some sense of their presence, of their desire? Or is it to
bring back my own desire for them? Will it ignite my passion, which
feels long asleep, quietly resting in my flesh, my heart, my cock, my
past? The needle feels hot; the skin surrounding it feels warm. I
rotate the tiny steel rod and feel nothing: a slight pull, a tiny tug
deep inside my flesh.

I reach next to me and open the single-edged razor from its
package—not sterile, but clean, shiny—and hold it up. Can I do
this? Without pausing or hesitating I reach down with my left hand
and stroke the skin around the pierced nipple. I can feel the tension
from the needle below. I stroke and warm the flesh and again without
pausing I look down, and with the blade in my right hand sketch
—delicately—an arc across the skin. There is no pain; there is no
feeling at all. I breathe and wait. Nothing. I breathe more. My hand
trembles: tension, anxiety, fear? I remember Jim in the mirror, Vince
on the floor, Walta in bed sick and frail, hardly able to talk or help
himself. Do I cut again? I'm too tense. There is no blood because I
can't relax: tense, relax, tense, relax. There is no gravity; I am lying
down. Tense, relax, tense, relax. I am holding my breath as I remember Jim in his hospital bed, his face gaunt; Walta at home

holding my hand so hard it hurt. Tense, relax, love, trust, truth, pressure, tense, relax, trust, truth. All of the men I have loved, really loved, in my life are dead. I am here. I think about Vietnam and Jim and dead boys covered in blood. I think about the needle in my thumb, my panic. There is no blood. Tense, relax. Tense, relax. I stand up. Breathe. Tense, relax. I look in the mirror on the wall across from the bed. The room is dark. I see Jim's picture on the wall above my desk. Walta watches from across the room. I feel hot and look again in the mirror. The arc is pink, almost rose. I breathe, tense, relax. Suddenly the rose turns deeper—a lovely color—and almost imperceptibly a new color emerges from the top of the arc and slowly travels to its end: as if by will alone a single drop of crimson, scarlet, carmine blood forms and runs down my chest. It stops and I stare at it in the mirror. I don't feel like a saint, I don't feel beautiful, I don't feel sexy. I just feel alive.

AVRAM
MORRISON

BROWN PARTY

"Fair and foul are near of kin, / And fair needs foul," I cried. . . .
"But Love has pitched his mansion in / The place of excrement. . . ."
—W. B. Yeats, "Crazy Jane Talks with the Bishop"

I FOUND MY WAY TO THE BROWN PARTY OVER A JOURNEY
of many years. Even as a boy I had been turned on by men's underpants. Briefs or boxers that showed signs of human habitation—piss
stains and skid marks—were my special favorites. I was fascinated
not only by the semen that flowed from men's cocks but by the urine
as well, and by the well-rounded buttocks that hid the most secret
of human places. Once I was old enough to put my fantasies into
practice, rimming became my favorite sexual activity, reaching with
my tongue as far inside a man as I could, and finally it seemed almost
natural to want what lay within.

It was never easy to find men willing to go as far as I wanted to. I'd cruise Christopher Street in the predawn hours. When I'd encounter a likely prospect and we'd pretended to stare into shop windows long enough to say hello, our conversation was usually brief:

"Nice night."

"Yeah."

"Live around here?"

"Mm-hmm."

"What do you like?"

"I like it dirty."

Most guys politely excused themselves at that point. A few were game. Some of them were simply hungry for sex and it didn't matter what kind; some of them hoped to get me to settle for what I considered mere preliminaries so they could have it their way; and some of them were willing to explore any new and kinky experience. Almost never was it something they desired for its own sake. So I usually contented myself with deep rimming and wondered if there were many others like me and where they might be hiding.

Psychologists were never too keen on coprophagy. It's one of those fetishes that lie beyond the pale. Books that mentioned it usually did so only cursorily, so it was hard to get a reasonable understanding of the mechanics of my mind. Even if my self-esteem was low when I was in the closet, that problem disappeared in the glow of gay liberation. Along with other gay men I began to explore my fantasies more fully as the 1970s progressed. What before had been totally unmentionable was beginning to be discussed in specialized magazines, and men began to gather in groups that shared the same predilections. At first I wandered into the world of sadomasochism, but even in that black-leather-clad fraternity I was a kind of freak. Eventually, by going to the right bars at the right hours—like 3:00 A.M. on a Wednesday morning—I began to encounter the underground network of men like myself.

It was fairly popular in clubs like the Mineshaft for men to sit in bathtubs and be pissed on. I tried that pleasure myself, carefully keeping my clothes dry by dangling them over the edge of the tub in a small cloth bag. On a good night, I would be surrounded by shadowy male forms, the mingled spray from their dangling cocks playing over my body from one end to the other, at first warm from their insides, then suddenly cold as my skin was left to dry. I hung out near the urinals as well, drinking the generous offerings of anonymous men, one after another, until my own bladder felt ready to burst. But even in this illicit world, scat was hard to come by. Although an occasional freak was into it, most of the clientele weren't inclined in that direction, and the management discouraged it because of the cleaning problems it presented.

I answered suggestive ads in mainstream gay publications, which directed me to private-circulation magazines. I eagerly read their pornography and answered some of their ads, which led to some memorable one-on-one encounters, so I had already become something of an adept by the late 1970s when I received an announcement of a private party to be held by the Brown Oval Group (BOG) in a loft in the northern reaches of Greenwich Village. It was years before the AIDS epidemic would terrify most willing men away from any unsanitary practices. No one claimed that playing with shit was healthy, but the only risks we thought we were taking had to do with hepatitis and amebiasis, which were more readily obtained from simple rimming, so it seemed a risk of degree rather than kind. I was willing to accept that risk. Following William Blake's dictum "The road of excess leads to the palace of wisdom," I was pursuing not only sensation and gratification, but some sort of truth about the human condition.

I had no idea exactly what to expect, but in my fantasy, the men I would meet were garbagemen or hog swillers or sewage workers. Later the host informed me that although men traveled from half a dozen states to be there, a surprising number of them were lawyers from Philadelphia, but that didn't matter. Whether it was a daily lifestyle or a one-night adventure, we were all escaping from the compulsive cleanliness of middle-class America. By our standards, anyone who washed his armpits or wiped his ass was a fool, and anyone who objected to any aspect of the human body was some sort of traitor. I had not showered for two days, and I had eaten carefully timed portions of rice and cheese the day before so that I would be able to dump during the party and my offering would have the right consistency.

As I climbed the stairs, my imagination was working overtime, and I thought I could sniff the promise of the hot night ahead, but the party had barely begun, and I was just smelling my own anticipation. I had been to orgies in this loft space before, featuring plenty of rimming and pissing and fisting amid the general suck and fuck, but this was the first time that the party had been dedicated specifically to scat lovers. The Brown Oval Group would host about half a dozen such parties over a two-year span, but the first experience would remain the most memorable. The man at the door checked to see that my name was on the list before taking my money. Everyone had to get there between 11:00 P.M. and 12:30 A.M., when the doors would be shut for the night.

The loft was divided into six rooms. The first one was for stripping down to the required raunchwear. Most of the men wore grimy jockstraps or briefs, some with stained tank tops or T-shirts that were strategically torn to reveal a nipple or to suggest ripping them further in the heat of passion. I wore the cruddy long johns I'd been carefully ripening for the last month. They clung like a second skin and smelled like the bottom of a swamp. I stored my street clothes in a cardboard box with my name on the outside, making sure to tuck my poppers into my sock for easy access.

My head was already expanding with the THC I'd dropped earlier as I entered the second room, a lounge with sagging couches good for casual relaxation between jam sessions. The lights were reddish and dim, and the music was loud and eerie—a mixture of the kind of earthy soul they used to play for die-hard disco dancers at 8:00 A.M. and vaguely religious incantations suggestive of secret monastery rituals. A few men were grouped on the furniture, eager to relate to like-minded people and in some cases to make one-on-one dates for future nights. There were forty or fifty men there. They weren't the drooling trolls one might expect at such a gathering. For the most part they were attractive and well-built, ranging from their mid-twenties to their late forties. Once the door was locked everyone got friendlier and friendlier, and by the end of the night, practically everyone who wanted to make it with somebody in particular got around to it. It didn't take too much patience. There were plenty of interested guys to keep us busy while we waited.

I wandered into the next room, which contained a well-stocked help-yourself bar, filled with beer and soda. Sometimes there was a bartender, who didn't mind if you ate out his ass (also on a help-yourself basis) while he was working. Men lined the walls in this room, checking each other out in the dusky light, beginning a little suggestive foreplay by brazenly fingering each other's asses and sniffing their fingers, and following each other into the deeper recesses of the loft.

The other three rooms were for sex. The first one was a large space containing several points of interest: a simulated jail cell; an overturned urinal, a bathtub and a trough for pissing; a cluster of slings for fisting and rimming; a few dark corners for free-form grappling; and a couple of regulation toilets. The second room had some bunks and mattresses for the romantic types, and a machine that looked like a bicycle turned inside out: instead of a seat, there was a backrest where one guy could lean back, spread his legs and rest his feet on a tubular chrome framework, while the other guy sat on a lower seat that gave him perfect access to the first guy's ass. The floor was covered with plastic sheets, which seemed like a dainty touch to me, but as the evening progressed, I could see that it showed real foresight.

The last room had plenty of uncovered windows, which faced the street some four stories below, so while we went about our bizarre business we could look out at that other world where ordinary people were going to ordinary bars to meet partners for ordinary sex. Some guys chose to stand in front of the windows as if daring someone in that more normal reality to notice them, but our lights were so dim that it would have taken an eagle's vision to discern what games our shadowy figures were playing. The walls tapered to a narrow corner, as if the whole loft were shaped like an arrow pointing to the unknown. There were some mats on the floor, and a few "rimseats" (toilet seats mounted on short legs) scattered around, and just at the tip of the arrow there was a raised platform.

As I walked into the final room, there was a show in progress. An audience of enthralled guys were sitting in front of the platform, where a man was lying on his back with his legs in the air so everybody could watch the turds slip smoothly out of his ass. His ankles were straight up, and he spread his cheeks with his hands. When the tip of his turd began to dilate his asshole, the audience cheered, as if they were witnessing a royal birth. In slow, unbearably sexy rhythm, it oozed its way out, an inch at a time, dark brown clumps compressed into a log that looked like braided clay and gave out a rich aroma that filled the room. The men held their breath until it was out, and then they all relaxed into a collective "Ahhhh." The turd was like an idol on an altar to them. A few guys knelt before the open ass, begging to see more shit, and we were soon rewarded by a second turd, almost as big and lumpy as the first and steaming with a sumptuous perfume. I could hear the other guys sniffing it in, sharing the aphrodisiac musk that reeked of human insides, inhaling it the way congregants in a church inhale incense. The three guys who knelt there picked up the first turd, passing it back and forth, sniffing it, licking it and finally biting right into it. They shared it ceremoniously, like a holy sacrament, and that set the tone for the rest of the red-lit evening. The audience began to rise and scatter in search of ecstasy.

I wandered from room to room, losing myself in other men's fantasies and rituals and the darkest kinds of human male beauty I had ever dreamed of. Wherever I wandered, I heard the incantations, "Worship my shit. Worship your master's shit," and I saw men kneel to obey. Most guys went whole hog and gave forth their shit as well as taking it from each other's asses, bonding themselves to one another as communicants in loving celebration of their common humanity. Although most of them remained strangers socially, they were united in an intimacy I could only admire. Then I felt hot breath in the seat of my long johns, and two hands gently opened the trapdoor. A tongue licked slowly up the crack of my ass, and I spread my legs, using the face as a stool. I didn't care whose it was. It was anybody's. It was everybody's. It was all humanity's face, and I loved it and treated it with respect. I felt my asshole widen, and my hot shit slid down past his greedily sucking lips and into his hungry mouth. I felt his throat as he swallowed. His mouth was so good that I wanted to give it everything I had, and I stroked my hard-on while I fed him. He was grateful; I could tell by the way he moved his hands under me.

Shadowy forms wandered past us. Some stopped to watch, and some began reaching behind to share in the feast. I wished there were enough for everybody to have some. Finally I shit the last of my load into someone's hand, and I turned to find him rubbing it into the face of the guy who'd done the eating. The recipient was a small, wiry guy with close-cropped hair. He sat back on his heels patiently while the man with my shit in his hand began to rub it all over his face. Like a painter, he dipped his forefinger and middle finger into the stuff and anointed the small man's forehead with a wide streak, adding smears to both of his cheeks, his nose and his chin until he looked like a savage ready to rise and dance around the firelight in a quest for magic. Then the second man kneeled down and began to lick my shit off the sitting man's face until both of them were smiling widely with the shit-eating grins that almost every man there would wear by the end of the night. I kissed them both. They tasted of my shit, and I loved it.

I stopped in the barroom for a drink and a rest, but while I was standing there, a short well-built guy in a grubby athletic undershirt and Jockeys appeared in the doorway for a minute. I put down my drink and followed him into the dark middle room. Standing next to him, I gently put my hand on his ass. He turned and put his arms around me and nestled his head on my chest. In a few seconds we were on one of the mattresses, caressing and cuddling and kissing like two monkeys in love. I massaged his ass with my hand, running my fingers up and down his crack. Then I put my finger in my mouth and wet it to make it smooth. I returned it gently to his asshole. It entered without resistance, so I put another finger in and rummaged around, feeling the blunt end of a turd just beyond my fingertips, all the while kissing him and writhing excitedly. I brought my shitty fingers out from his ass and held them between our two noses while we both inhaled. Then I put them in my mouth.

In a moment he reached behind himself, saying, "I've got something for both of us." He came out with a plum-sized hunk of shit and held it in front of us to be admired. I licked it and took it into my mouth, and then he kissed me. His turd slid back and forth from my mouth to his until our spit was all brown with it. It didn't seem to taste acrid as I had expected. Somehow its status as a special treasure lent it a pleasant taste, and both our tongues twined around it lovingly while it slowly disappeared like a peppermint in a happy kid's mouth. When it was finished, we sucked each other's asses for a while and licked each other's cocks, but neither of us wanted to have an orgasm because we wanted to enjoy the rest of the party. We went into the lounge for some talk, proud of the shit that streaked our mustaches, and we made a date to meet later that week, so we could sleep together smeared with one another's shit.

I decided I could use a drink, but I wasn't thirsty for fresh beer. I like the recycled stuff and had been known to order a glass of the bartender's piss at my favorite bar, always offering a grateful tip when it was supplied. In the corner of the first sex room, I saw a dark-haired guy standing in a dark corner, rubbing his hand across his dingy jock to keep himself hard. I made my way to him and put my hand over his, and he drew me into the shadows, pulling his jock pouch aside to offer himself to me. I could taste the smegma beneath his loose foreskin, and I tongued it lightly, savoring the Limburger cheese flavor while I waited for his erection to fade. Then I held his softened cock in my motionless mouth as a signal that I wanted him to piss. He tried his best to cooperate, but after several minutes he withdrew, saying, "This isn't a piss party; it's a shit party. Come with me." Of course, I did.

He led me into the front room, where he found a rimseat. Then he took it and me into a corner, where we could have some privacy. With a little pressure on my shoulders, he got me down on the floor and then carefully placed the rimseat over my face and sat down. I rimmed him for all I was worth, trying to reach for his heart with my tongue. After a very few minutes, I was rewarded first with a smelly fart so strong I could feel its breeze, then with a turd that entered my lips slowly in the beginning and then in a big rush until my mouth was so full that my cheeks were puffed out. The initially bitter taste was soon overwhelmed by the logistics of dealing with its volume. It was dense and well-formed and not about to melt away. "Swallow it," he said. "I want you to eat my shit. Worship what's inside me."

I had played with shit plenty of times—smelled it and smeared it and taken it into my mouth—but I'd never actually swallowed a hot turd. Eager to explore a new frontier, I tried to answer with a "Yes, sir," but my mouth was too full, so I just obeyed his orders, thinking hard about sweet chocolate while I chewed lightly and gulped it down in three or four big swallows. I could feel it sliding down like a deep-throated dick, and then suddenly it was gone. When I was done, he lifted the rimseat off and bent down on his knees to kiss my shitty mouth. At that moment I think I would have died for this man, but a few minutes later, after much gentle whispering and stroking and reassurance, we were on our separate ways, looking for still more.

Wanting to wash out my mouth, I went over to the trough, where a stocky man was pissing through the fly of his loose boxer shorts. I took his cock from his hand, allowing it to wet me down while I got my mouth on it and swallowed greedily to slake my thirst. His piss might have been as strong as a horse's, but I couldn't tell after all that shit. Then he blew his nose into his hand and gave me his snot to lick. I really enjoyed that. I would have taken more, whatever he wanted to give, but he walked off without a word, and I felt like a used handkerchief, carelessly tossed aside. I waited at the trough for a while and tried to get some more piss, but everyone seemed too busy, so I made my way over to the tub, where I could shower in the stuff. After fifteen minutes of that, I had to wring out my long johns and hang them on the radiator for a few minutes because they were weighing me down. After I had a beer to rinse out my mouth, I put them back on again, enjoying the way they stuck to me.

The next guy I met was Don, who wore a leather motorcycle cap and black chaps that outlined his naked crotch. He had just finished taking a shit and was standing with one foot up on the toilet seat, so I naturally went over to clean out his ass for him. "Come here," he told me, and took me into the jail cell. He sat me in the urinal and turned around to present his ass, which I swabbed hungrily with my tongue, pleased to be putting on a show since we were under a red lightbulb and a few guys had stopped to watch. But Don wasn't fully comfortable yet. He lifted me up and took me into the next room, directing me onto the lower seat of the inverted bicycle contraption, where I must have then spent half an hour eating out his ass. There was no more shit left inside him, but we were happy, and when we were finished he gave me his phone number, which I used a couple of weeks later when he came to my place and gave me a whole load of shit for myself. Nice guy.

I went to the barroom to refresh myself, and there I met the host, whose curly white hair matched the white tank top that, aside from his boots, was all he wore. He was having a ball. While we talked, he reached behind himself and came out with a shit-covered finger, which he held in front of my face. I naturally took it into my mouth and returned it to him clean. He worked his finger into my ass and looked a little disappointed when he found it empty. "Get down," he said. At that moment, in the red light, my head full of THC, I could have sworn that he was not the same man I had been talking to a moment earlier, but Satan himself. (I would have laughed if I had stopped to remember that I don't even believe in the devil!) Intrigued by the forbidden, I lapped his asshole clean. Then he turned around and offered me his big cock, which I took deep into my throat, sucking for all I was worth, while everyone in the barroom stood around us. This turned him on enough to flood my mouth with his semen, and I drank it down, wondering if I had just lost my immortal soul. He asked me, "Do you want to come by and help clean up this place tomorrow? It's an honor I save for special guys." I told him I would if I could, proud of the invitation, and I bent to kiss his cock good-bye.

After that I thought I might have had it for the night, but I couldn't stop wandering around to watch the festivities. I ended up in the front room, the one shaped like an arrow. One guy stood in a window with his foot up on the sill, in full view of the streets below, offering his cock to a man who knelt before him, and a stream of piss glistened in the dark air between them while I watched. Then I heard someone else say, "Don't move. I have to take a piss." He wasn't talking to me but to a guy he was fucking right next to me. They both waited patiently for all the piss to flow into the asshole, and I waited beside them, bearing witness. When he was finished, the top man pulled his cock out with a little plop. He turned to me as if I had been part of his plan all the while, and he put his hand behind my neck, forcing me to my knees behind the guy he'd just fucked. I offered no resistance. "Drink my piss out of his ass," he ordered. Wanting to please him, I put my lips to the desperately clenched sphincter. The piss came out mixed with traces of the other guy's shit, like warm broth pouring into my toilet mouth.

When I had finished, the two of them went their way, and another man, wearing dungarees without a shirt and smelling like a sewer, took their place before me. He unbuttoned his fly to reveal the Jockey shorts beneath and then turned around with his ass in my face. He pushed the underwear down so I could see the load of shit that nested in the seat, and then he ordered, "Don't touch my shit. Just clean my asshole." I complied gladly. He tasted wonderful. He left as suddenly as he had appeared, and I rose to my feet, slightly confused.

Nearby were a couple of guys using a rimseat. I stood and watched, entranced at how beautiful the whole dark episode was. The bonding of the two men seemed complete. A few people gathered along with me to encourage them: "Give him your shit. Let it out. Take your master's shit inside you. It's beautiful. Worship it." As if planted by some psychic force, that word *beautiful* kept echoing in my mind—*beautiful . . . beautiful*—and when at last the bottom man slid out from under the rimseat, his face all covered with shit and wearing a smile as wide as a chamber pot, he simply said, "It was so beautiful." I felt that all of us had been mystically united for that moment.

Next to the rimseat there was a man with a shaved head, kneeling on a mat. He had been watching all the action and letting loose all control of his body fluids. There were piles of shit and puddles of piss beneath him. Tears streamed from his eyes and snot from his nose as he forced his hand down his throat, reaching for some ultimate letting go. It came when he puked up his guts, then let the vomit dribble down his chin and chest, covering himself in his own humanity and for all his abasement looking like a saint at prayer. His road to spiritual enlightenment was through the acceptance of every aspect of his physical body, and he relaxed into total serenity, having achieved his own version of nirvana. For me, he embodied the words of the Roman writer Terence: "I am a man; nothing human is alien to me." I went over to him, knelt down and quietly kissed his vomit-covered lips, and he opened his eyes, which shone brightly even in the late night gloom. His gentle smile and the nod of his head were barely perceptible, but I knew that he was acknowledging me as his brother, and I bowed my head in accord.

I thought I was ready to leave at that point, but across the room I saw a handsome bearded guy in a smeared T-shirt, just sitting down on a rimseat with no one beneath him. It was already nearing dawn, and I had thought that every ass in the place would be empty by that time; but he waited patiently, and I couldn't resist. Without saying a word, I went over to him and smiled and slid myself under his seat. A small turd came from his ass, still hot. He leaned down and said, "I could tell how hungry you were by the way you slid under my seat. Want to come home for some more?" Of course, I said yes.

As I tried to pull myself together so I'd be at least reasonably presentable in the streets, I could have sworn that every available surface in the place, including the ceiling, had a thin covering of shit, but even with all our efforts I knew that was impossible. I could see other guys getting ready to go. If not for the friendly reminders of the doorman, some of them would have walked smiling into the night with shit streaked all over their faces. After a night of such pleasure, we all found that our standards of civilization had changed. We wore our shit streaks like badges of honor, and our sensitivity to the aroma had long since been overwhelmed, so we didn't smell a thing. But everyone had to pass basic inspection at the door so the neighbors wouldn't complain. I made it out into the cool predawn air with my date, feeling like I'd just witnessed a miracle. He agreed. We walked to his place a few blocks away, where he had a big drawerful of his old piss-stained, shitty Jockey shorts. He rubbed some of them in my face and put some of them on me. Then he sat on my face and gave me his load of hot shit, which I chewed and swallowed gratefully. We fell asleep that way, with my mouth full of his shit and his ass in my face, and I woke up the next afternoon a fulfilled man.

That was nearly twenty years ago, and the world and I have journeyed far from that moment in history. I tried at the Brown

Party to embrace all things human, to find nothing revolting, to accept the deepest implications of having a body; but when I pondered what the next step could possibly be, I realized that it was to accept the inevitable decay of human flesh and to embrace death itself. The loss of a great many of my friends to the AIDS epidemic has given me more experience with mortality than I could ever have wanted, and so I took my explorations in other directions. I had gone as far as I could into the sexual frontier, farther than most people even think of going. I learned lessons there that continue to shape my life today, and I did have a wonderful time in that mysterious realm. Although such adventures are not part of everyone's experience, I feel that they should not remain an esoteric secret. Our antiseptic society, obsessed with its deodorants and mouthwash, is too fastidious to openly acknowledge such forays outside the boundaries of civilized behavior, but I believe that somewhere they should be chronicled as an authentic part of human history. It is the responsibility of those who travel to the outer limits to draw their maps clearly, because there are others for whom that journey is just beginning.

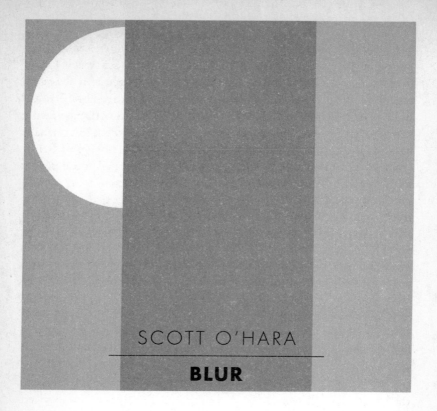

SCOTT O'HARA

BLUR

BY THE TIME I ARRIVED AT . . . WHERE DID I GO? DOES IT matter? A sexclub, one to which I'd never gone before . . . I was sweating: the evening was surprisingly warm for San Francisco. Pleased with the layout of the place in a cursory once-over, I decided I'd stay for at least an hour (despite the fact that this was a week-night, and I had appointments first thing in the morning). To my amazement, though, it didn't take an hour. I'm used to a certain hesitancy at sexclubs, a reluctance to engage: though there may be many aching gonads in the place, there is seldom very much action until "critical mass" is reached and the crowd suddenly combusts. If there are too many trolls in the place, it's unlikely to happen at all; but if there are none, the prettyboys will probably stand around waiting until dawn for the other guy to make the first move. It's a frustrating situation for someone who considers himself neither troll nor prettyboy, who loathes being pawed by someone who doesn't know the meaning of tact, and who abhors the thought that he might be behaving with such tactlessness toward someone else. . . . Where was I? Oh yes: it didn't take an hour. Within two minutes of my walking through the door, a man smiled at me, walked over, and, with no hesitation whatsoever, kissed me. Would that all men could be so direct! I didn't reject him. He was enthusiastic, a great kisser, and just my kinda guy: not pretty, but easygoing, self-confident, and self-aware. He knew what he liked. We stood in the center of the kitchen for a while, just kissing, then made our way downstairs to the play area, and played. I sucked him off (What was his dick like? Would that I could remember! But, ultimately, it doesn't matter. He was appreciative, and that's what counts), and he sucked me for a while too; and then there were other men in the darkroom, and I moved from dick to dick, as my long-term Ultimate Erotic Fantasy of Heaven would dictate, coaxing a load out of more than one pair of balls.

There was one, though—an obscenely fat, black sausage, on a heavily muscled and quite athletic man—that defeated me. With all appropriate modesty, I have to state that there aren't a lot of dicks that give me much problem. I think it's a psychological thing, more than anything else: when the guy's attitude about being sucked matches the attitude I have (and that does change with the weather, I admit), then he could probably shove the Empire State Building down my throat, and my only response would be a spontaneous climax. Sex takes place in the mind; and if my head is in the right space, my body cooperates. I mean, the fact is, I *like* being manhandled. Face-fucked. Controlled, manipulated, USED. But when it becomes mindless brutality, punishment for punishment's sake (and the dividing line between these two behaviors is so thin as to be almost invisible), my interest fades, the fantasy pops like a soap bubble, my throat closes down, and I usually flee. That's what happened with this man. (Well, I assume there was a man attached to the dick.) Was he really interested in getting off? It was hard to tell. It seemed he was more determined to prove that his dick was too big, too fierce, for *anyone* to suck successfully. Sometimes it's hard to tell the difference between sex-passion and revenge-passion. I eventually tore

myself free of his demanding hands, groped my way out of the mass
of bodies that had coalesced around us, and left him to some other,
more eager cocksucker than I. I felt finished for the night. A little
bit worse for wear, but I knew I'd sleep well.

But the night was young—four dicks in my throat, and I don't
think I'd been there twenty minutes—and so was my body, relatively. I flopped on a sofa in the video room, next to two guys who
were jacking each other off, and watched the video. Within five
minutes, a guy came in and sat down in the overstuffed chair next
to me. He was fully dressed, but he soon had his dick out; and all
it took was my realization that he was working a foreskin back and
forth over his head . . . well, my salivary glands went into overtime.
Again. Suddenly my jaw no longer felt tired. Isn't it amazing how
that happens? And I started jerking off, and we were both hard, and
in short order I was on my knees in front of him, and his dick was
down my throat. And this guy really did get brutal, holding my
head all the way down to the base, yanking it up and then slamming
it down again without the slightest concern for how I felt about it.
The damn tab on his zipper practically lacerated my chin. You
wouldn't think he'd have that much leverage, sitting down in a very
comfy chair; but he held my head down on his dick until I saw stars.
It was all right, though, because my throat muscles were working
their magic on his dickhead, and I guess he saw stars, too. My gag
reflex did eventually kick in, and I guess that's when he came. I
missed a few moments there. And when he came back to earth and
let go of my head, and I extricated his dick from my throat, he
quickly zipped himself up and hauled ass out of there. While I massaged my jaw (dislocated, I was sure) and tried to figure out if that
was the best sex I'd ever had, or just rape. The lines, like I say, blur.

Well. That was definitely it. I was beat. I didn't want any more
sex; I just wanted a nice warm bed. I headed for the front door. The
guy who'd taken my money when I'd arrived was there to let me
out. He handed me a pass, and said, "Here—this is for the next
time you come." And I looked down at him, all five foot six of him,
and my determination to leave just evaporated. Suddenly I didn't
want to leave at all, ever. I was halfway out the door, but I couldn't
make myself move one way or the other, and he said, "I'm about

ready to take my break . . . ," and I was back inside the house in an instant.

And so Paul (despite the fact that he looked like he'd come straight from Guadalajara—cholo streetpunk appearance, short curly black hair, big liquid-brown eyes, and that classic Aztec nose—he preferred the Anglo name, and had no trace of an accent) took me to a room, a private room that he could lock, while his co-worker took over the job of managing the door; and I think we spent the first fifteen minutes doing nothing but kissing. A man with more sensuous lips would be difficult to find. And yes, we eventually made it out of our clothing, with the usual awkwardness and fumbling; and, yes, we engaged in all the appropriate foreplay and exploration of each other's bodies; but it was when I moved from sucking his dick to nibbling on his balls to seriously tongue-fucking his asshole—and he started to do the same to me, as we were clasped together in 69 position—that I suddenly realized I was going to get fucked. It was the first time in months, and I wanted it SO badly; and finally, here was a man without inhibitions, a man who I realized wanted me as much as I wanted him, and wanted me in more or less the same way.

Sometimes—not often, but sometimes—this information can be transmitted by body language. It's a lot more reliable to use good old-fashioned words; but the proper words are so difficult to find. Yes, you can imitate art, and say, "Fuck me with that big dick"; or you can sound like a romance novel and say, "I need to feel you inside me." But the most intense sex is often the result of silent communication: when you need it badly enough that you come close to telepathy, broadcasting it to him from every square millimeter of skin.

Paul didn't use lube. He didn't need to. He got me on my back (and oh, I was an eager and willing co-conspirator) and got my legs up in the air, and then got down there and rimmed me until I was squirming, and my hole was sloppy and spasming around his tongue. Then he moved up so his dick was resting against my ass, sat back on his haunches, lowered my legs a bit so they were over his shoulders . . . and waited. Moved his dick back and forth a little. Rubbed it against my asshole. Jerked off, slowly. All the while, he was staring into my eyes, with a knowing smile on his lips. And after just ten seconds of this, with my asslips trembling and gaping and quivering, I started hunching myself back against his dickhead.

He moved farther away. I started whimpering. His look turned serious. He still didn't say anything, and neither did I. My eyes were wide and staring, probably downright maniacal; I had passed beyond the possibility of formulating words, into a world of pure need and physical sensation. I just reached back and grabbed his buttcheeks, holding him in place as I pulled my ass down toward his dick.

He knew what I wanted. There wasn't a doubt in his mind. I wanted his dick up my ass. I wanted it relatively dry, without lube (hey, it wasn't so big, really, that he needed it; besides, it had a good healthy foreskin to lubricate me as only a foreskin can) and definitely without a condom. And he locked eyes with me, and started to push back gently, and his dick slipped in so easily that I wondered if I was the same guy who'd always whimpered in pain over any insertion (but wanted more, once the pain subsided). And Paul kept staring me in the eyes as he made that first plunge, and then lay down on top of me and fucked me as savagely and deeply as only a man with years of pent-up desires, and a whole battery of thou-shalt-nots to keep him frustrated, can fuck.

I was on my stomach, some fifteen minutes later, when Paul (who'd been nibbling on my neck, when I didn't have my head turned around, deep-kissing him) started slowing down the pace of his thrusting. Then he'd freeze up completely, not moving for several seconds, dick pulled most of the way out of my ass; and then resume his slow and gentle in-and-out. I could tell what he was doing— I've been in his situation often enough: being stimulated beyond bearing by the way a bottom's ass is devouring my dick, but wanting to satisfy him before I shoot my load. But frankly, with Paul, the knowledge that he was holding back made my ass all the itchier: it needed to be doused, salved, healed with a dose of his cum. So I reached back, again, and pulled his butt down, so that his dick slammed into the short hairs, and he started groaning, and I finally turned my head and stared him in the face as I broke the nonspeaking pact: "I want it," I said. "Shoot it." And he did. He went wild on top of me: bucking and thrusting and spasming. And I held on to his buttcheeks the whole time, making sure his cum went as deep into my ass as it was possible for it to go. I wanted it to stay there awhile.

And of course we lay there, connected, his dick still up my ass, for a good twenty minutes, while both of us drowsed—and this is the time, with many men, when I enjoy sex the most; but with Paul, the entire sex act had taken on this rosy glow of intimacy, and this was just the desire to prolong it as long as possible—before he roused himself and realized that he needed to get back to work. His dick slid out of me with the usual "pop," and suddenly I was a single man again, instead of half of a two-backed beast; and we got dressed (Paul a little more slowly than I; he'd run a hard race) and we exited the room and found that no, the rest of the world hadn't gone away for good.

And this is not 1980 I'm talking about. It's 1995. Why am I able to engage in condomless fucking with such abandon? It's very simple: I'm HIV-positive, have been for most of my adult life, and I have a prominent tattoo to that effect on my left bicep. It says to potential sex partners: do what you like with me, you can't harm me. Is it possible that Paul was fucking me at a risk to his own health? Yes, it's possible. As a sexclub worker, however, I think he's likely to know the risks at least as well as I; and as a San Francisco resident, he knows firsthand about the epidemic. He'd already told me he was caring for a dying ex-lover. If he was in fact still Negative, he was obviously a Negative who was tired of the limitations imposed by Negativity. Being Positive allows me the freedom to engage, frankly, in whatever sex I feel like, without worry. And it's a great relief to meet and fuck with partners who share my attitude toward safety and sex, to wit: there is no safety in sex, or in anything else. There can, however, be varying amounts of pleasure. Our job is to maximize the pleasure. It's the Negatives' job to minimize their risk—that is, if they're determined to stay that way.

Need I add that when I walked out of that sexclub (Where was it? Oh yes, I know, intellectually, where it was; but it seems to me that it was in some other dimension, some other world entirely, a never-never land with artwork created from Found Boys. . . .), I was walking on clouds? A cliché, perhaps, but that's exactly what it felt like. I swear I couldn't feel the pavement beneath my feet. The street-lights coruscated and danced as if I were doing drugs. Who knows, perhaps I was. Cum probably contains leftover chemicals, much as piss does; such chemicals are easily and quickly absorbed through the rectal lining; who knows what Paul had been taking over the previous twenty-four hours? All I really know is that I couldn't stop smiling—occasionally at moments that seemed totally inappropri-ate—for at least twenty-four hours afterward.

If there is one thing I've learned about sex, over the many years of my debauchery, it is that sex takes place entirely in the mind. I know, of course, that the physical sensations of being fucked by a rubberized penis are not all that different from the physical sensations of that much-vaunted skin-to-skin contact. And of course, for many men, after a decade of propaganda, the thought of being fucked con-domless is enough to wilt the hardest dick. For others, it's the one fantasy that makes a dick stand proud and tall.

There is likewise no physical difference between being fucked by Raoul and being fucked by Norman; if I were blindfolded and conducting a taste test, I probably couldn't tell the difference. The difference is all in the mind: when I know it's Raoul fucking me, my pussy gets wet in an entirely different way than when it's Nor-man. Every man has his own set of such keys to arousal; I don't necessarily value the same things as other men. I seldom come during sex, physically, but I often experience a sort of psychic orgasm at the moment of my partner's climax, if he and I are particularly in tune and he comes down my throat or up my ass. Having him shoot on my chest, though stimulating, doesn't have the same effect. Having him shoot in a condom while fucking me leaves me, frankly, cold.

It's the knowledge of being possessed by him, of possessing a part of him, of being truly connected, that gives sex its special frisson of perfection. And this has nothing whatsoever to do with safety. When a man's dick slips into me unprotected, I know that he's taking me in a way that is stringently forbidden by our so-called civilization; and my heart leaps up with a special joy at the thought of flouting the rules. Rebellion, I've always thought, is healthy—and, yes, erotic. The rebel, in our society, has endless fantasy-potential. And oh, there are many other things that give me pleasure:

kissing is essential to good sex, and a comfortable bed (or lawn, or beach) helps a lot; foreskin, as previously mentioned, makes fucking a helluva lot more comfortable. (For both parties, I suspect. Alas, I'll never know for sure.) But the one thing I know is necessary to good sex is simple: trust. That doesn't mean I have to know him; he can be someone I just met at a sexclub. But he needs to be someone with whom I'm willing to share all my bodily fluids, someone with whom I want (however temporarily) to merge. That's not a halfway sort of thing.

Six months have passed since that night. Yes, I've been back to that sexclub; yes, I've spoken to Paul; no, he hasn't invited me back upstairs. I'm a little disappointed by that, but I also know the wisdom of leaving well enough alone. Perfection doesn't need to be repeated; pleasure is sometimes greater if not multiplied. But I'm certain that, by writing about it, I've made it real to at least a few other people; and that gives me another level of satisfaction. Memory is a traitor in my life: writing something down, sharing it with others, is one of the few truly honest ways of preserving the pleasure of reality. And by sharing the experience with an audience whom I'll probably never meet, I've given pleasure to one of my favorite groups of people.

It's hard to tell, sometimes, how much of sex is in the happening, how much in the telling. If I'd looked up, halfway through the sex, and seen Paul's co-worker standing in the doorway beating off, how would it have changed the experience? Given the dynamics of working at a sexclub, I'd know that they'd be talking about me later that night; that knowledge alone would give me pleasure. Presenting the story to you does much the same thing. You don't have the diamond-sharp memory of the event that I have; your picture is, necessarily, a blur, filtered through my impressions and my imperfect descriptions. You've altered it to fit your own fantasies. Had the evening been videotaped, it might have been more exciting to some of you, less exciting to others; I'm just as happy to provide my personal version of it as The Truth, and leave Absolute Truth to documentarians.

I guess the mere fact that I write about my sex life, exposing myself to all of you, qualifies me as an exhibitionist. Writing is sex;

sex is writing. Every writer loves being Lady Godiva. (The towns-
people's refusal to look has always struck me as sheer perversity.) I
revel in this exposure, however blurry. You are the voyeurs, peering
through a grimy back window: the scene on the bed is for your
benefit as much as mine. Exhibitionism . . . or sex? Rape . . . or
sex? Suicide . . . or sex? Welcome to Club Semantics, home of the
neverending mindfuck. Where you draw the line is up to you.

JUSTIN CHIN

GOO

YOU HAVE THE KIND OF CUM I LIKE, THICK YET FLUID, WITH-
out the strange lumps that plague some ejaculates, a fine blend. Mine
on the other hand has the consistency of the unnamed white stuff
that you might find on tables in vegetarian restaurants. Walking
down the street with you, people assume that I'm your little boy.
Would they be surprised to know you let me put you on a leash and
take you to public rest rooms where men suck each other at urinals,
masturbate each other under the partitions, leaving their jism in
careless splatters on the tiled floors? You obediently go down on all
fours and lap up the spatter, some turned liquid, some gray with
shoeprint tracks, left by men whose urges have long subsided and
gone. I call you on the phone and you rush to a designated rest room
in a quiet office building where I have procured a decent puddle of
cum for you. I place the collar, with the spikes turned inward, on

your fleshy neck, attach the heavy chain to it—both pieces picked out by you—and take you to sex clubs and adult bookstores where you dash about like a naughty puppy, vigorously licking at every spot of cum you find. Often I have to jerk on the chain to calm you down. I take my task with some amount of gravity and would like to bring you on a good methodical sweep of the premises. You would prefer to dash at every glob that you spy in any corner.

No, people would not assume anything of that sort when they see how you rush to buy me drinks at bars, how dapper you look in your expensive clothes, how you fawn over me and hold my hand at the symphony. Your slowly receding hairline, your slightly pouchy belly, the lines in your face starting to show, your homosexual cravings sure, you look like a kindly uncle, an older professor indulging in some nonacademic fancies.

You are a connoisseur of your craving; you approach each spot of cum as if you were a zoologist in search of some elusive animal: This one was spat out, this flicked from a hand, this one tried to dash to the safe place to prevent a mess, this was in a rush, this one hadn't come in days. How much of this is fancy I do not question. This one went to the market, this one cried wee-wee-wee all the way home.

Once, I told you my theory of Mormons and how their cum would taste somehow different because Mormons were the human equivalents of free-range chicken—all that clean living and loose underwear must have some effect on those testicles—and you promised me that you would find out the truth.

Once, just once, we stumbled upon a rare find, something you never found again: a midsized puddle of cum with a spot of blood in it. Perhaps the poor bloke had a urethral nick; perhaps there were bleeding gums. You put your face so close to the pool, and instead of your usual vigor you very slowly dipped the tip of your tongue into the spoog. You took more than five minutes to finish lapping that small puddle. After that, you developed a deep fear of your craving and you wrote fifteen letters to sex advice columnists in several magazines and newspapers asking for some counsel. For weeks, you scanned the columns to try to find your letter, but the ones that made it into print were always the same: small dicks, large dicks, burst condoms, fear of intimacy, can't find small enough dicks, can't find large enough dicks, regrettable sex, want to do something the other doesn't and vice versa. You took this as a sign that all was well and that your deviance was well within the range of normal deviances, and in celebration of this epiphany I took you on another feeding.

Once, in a private moment, I asked you what those puddles of jism tasted like, if each was in some way better than the other, if I should lead you to fresh splotches and forgo the ones sitting for so long till they become indistinguishable from snot. Your answer surprised me: You said it all tasted the same. It tasted of all the men you never had, you said. The urgency in your voice scared me and I told you I had a dream about nachos.

You tell me I am a faggot piece of shit and that I do not deserve your dick. You snap your finger and point to your boot. I go down and lick the tip, allow you to step on my face, to cram the tip of your boot in my mouth. On my knees, I look up at you; you purse your lips and a gleam of spit forms on your mouth that I take willingly into mine. You fuck my mouth in slow sharp thrusts. Sucking your dick, my mouth fills with the sour sting of your piss, which I choke down. I let you pinch my nipples until they hurt for days.

I adore your large balled fists as they smack across my head, each blow a token of your affection and my worthlessness. I teach you how to cut into my flesh with a sharp knife like so many words. You say that I am your dog and I say *Less than that*. You wrap your big hands around my neck. I have seen how you snap barbecued beef ribs into two at dinner tables, a messy display of strength to split a treat for us to share. You close your hands around my small neck, my face turns red, I come hard and you eat the jism off my hands, off my thighs and off the floor like a gentle goat at the petting zoo.

With my hand up your ass, I can feel the strange squish of your colon. The rubber glove, cool against my palm, is not large enough to shield my forearm from your warm sphincter or from the blood and juices staining my arm a medicinal pink, the color of fresh kill. I uncurl my fist and snap it closed again like a sea anemone inside of you; I run my arm in and out of you as if I were digging crab traps on a soft beach. You wince when I grab the nub in your pelvis where your spinal cord ends, a hard lump that hides bundles of nerves and arteries, the stuff ripped apart by tragic car accidents and snapped bungee cords. With my free hand I caress the front of your body, fingering the nipples embedded in your hairy chest, running my hand down the bristly extent of your body; I say hoarsely, *Breathe, relax. Take a deep breath.* But whatever drugs you have punching your heart through your bloodstream don't even allow you that comfort and I refuse to take my hand out of you even as you plead with me to. I lean over to place your cock in my mouth and you say *Bite my dick.* I clench my teeth down in the middle of your shaft, I draw your foreskin under my teeth and nip into the elastic flaps, you flinch and bear down on my fist, sweaty from the heat of your body and the tight constraints of the rubber glove. I pull my hand out, turn the glove inside out and hold it up to you, the insides of the glove now filled with traces of your shit and anal slime stained by your internal ruptures. You slip your hand into the glove, retrieve your own fluids and devour them like a stupid dog that would slurp at anything placed in front of it. I wipe the bloodied mucus on my forearms off on your back and go home to my cat, my computer, my books.

You clean up, put on your clothes and return to your lover, your ex-wife and kids and job and politics and upper-income life, you call to make plans to meet again, you drop everything when I call you, you do everything I tell you, you buy me gifts and take me places I cannot afford to go, you tell me your problems with life, work and love, I listen and make no judgments or comment, I feed you my cum on occasion though you never ask for it and I seldom offer, and with each tender caress, each deeply done kiss, we slowly become the objects of our hate so much that we wish for nothing more than to see the other dead in someone else's arms.

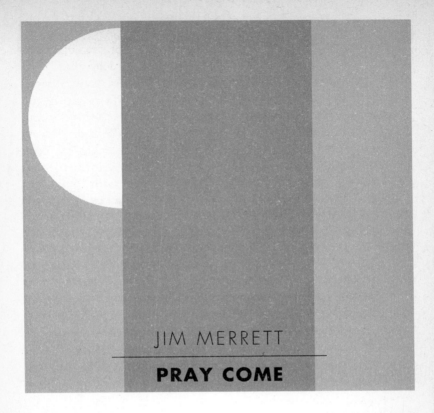

JIM MERRETT

PRAY COME

I TOUCH MY THUMB TO THE POUTY MOUTH OF IVAN'S UN-
cut cock, source of a lazy river of pre-cum. When I take my thumb
away, a tiny strand attaches like a spiderweb to my fingernail, glis-
tens like a bath bubble, and disappears.

Before I met Ivan, deciding whether to suck or not was simple. After
I had tantalized a man from head to toe, all the while pretending
that his cock was an exotic land I *might* someday visit, I would touch
my thumb to the tip of his prick. If it came back dry, my lips would
go down next. If, on the other hand, my thumb came back moist,
it was my unfortunate duty to disappoint the one-night stand or
fuck buddy. I had my cocksucker's creed: I would eat no pre-cum.

　　There were times, mind you, when this simple test failed. In
mid-suck, alarms would sound in my throat: *Cum Alert. Cum Alert.*

After I'd finished him off with a handjob, I'd disappear to the bathroom for an emergency dose of Listerine. I chalked up those dicey sips to the risk of fast-lane sex. Even if you look both ways, you still might get hit by the truck.

Then one day the love truck hit me. I won't bother with courtship details except to say that the truck has a body to die for. All muscled up and *piel canela*, which means "cinnamon skin," in other words "walking cinnamon," from the hue of his smooth chest to the aroma that rises from his crotch. The vanity plate reads "Ivan."

The accident happens on the stretch between his long-lashed eyes and his merengue-bopping midriff.

"Come home with me," I plead when we meet in a Spanish nightclub.

"*No puedo,*" he replies.

"Can't, or won't?"

"*Es que. . . .*" He loses me in rapid-fire Spanish. Only the last part is clear:

"*Mira,*" he says. "*Tengo SIDA.*"

Ivan visits every day for a week after that, regular as church. One day he brings a gift of plastic roses reeking of incense. Another day he sneaks up and rests his chin on my shoulder, baring his perfect white teeth. But he won't sleep over, won't part his lips for a kiss good night.

"You're terrible," I say.

"*Sí, soy Ivan el Terrible,*" he says.

Then one day he springs a six-pack and a proposition: teach me English. I salt the necks of his beer bottles, split the limes with a steak knife. I'm no teacher, I say, don't even know how to begin. Ivan makes martyr eyes. They bewitch the knife. Okay, I say, sucking lime-flavored blood from the cut, but not in the kitchen.

Upstairs in my room, he points to the crucifix on the wall above the bed: "*¿Católico?*"

"*Sí.* You?"

"*Claro que sí,*" he says, blessing himself the Central American way, reverently touching his thumb and forefinger to his lips.

The lesson begins: "Hello." "My name is Ivan." "I am fine." He murders every syllable, but I tell him he's great.

"Teach me something nasty," he asks.

"Like what?"

"Cocksuckee. What that?"

"Cocksucker," I correct, kneeling, bowing into my cupped hands to demonstrate. He giggles; he's getting drunk.

"You cocksuckee," he says.

"You're getting the idea," I say.

"In my country, they say, *'rezando el rosario.'* " Saying the rosary.

"That's great," I say. "As in, 'Jim wants to say Ivan's rosary.' "

He swings his bluejeaned legs onto the comforter. I unlace and take off his shoes so he can swing his feet up too. His white socks are immaculate. His blue-black tresses seem to float across the cloudy pillowcase. After a mild protest, he lets me rub his thigh.

"Por favor," I plead, running my finger over the bunched denim. He takes a sip of beer and closes his eyes. He lets me pull up his T-shirt and lick his smooth nipples, his neck, his jawline. His head arches back; he reaches down and unbuttons his trousers. I pull them down and off, snagging his socks too, take the pilgrim's route back up kissing his ankles, calves, thighs, kiss the cupped softness, kiss away his bikinis, unwrap his cock like a dime-store cinnamon candy.

"Te la mamo," I say.

"You crazy," he says.

"Crazy for your cum."

*"Pre-*cum," he corrects, leaning on the Spanish-accented first syllable. Pray come. My lips twitch for it. I finger-paint it across his belly. My dripping hand makes the sign of the cross: *"En el nombre del padre."* I pretend to suck each finger like a kid mopping up after a Popsicle, rub my nose in it till all I can smell is pre-cum, even as it winds along the fresh cum-shiny nick on my middle finger.

"Did you hear the one about the sloppy basketball player?" my patrol leader, Mitch, asks the scouts huddled around the campfire. Mitch waits a beat, then imitates sinking a basket: "He dribbles before he shoots." I don't really get the joke but laugh anyway because, though he's only a year older, I like Mitch a lot. In the tent we share with two other scouts, Mitch whispers: "I got *Playboy* books in my knapsack." I'm not exactly sure what that means either, but the hush of Mitch's voice thrills and scares me at the same time. The four of us go through a Boy Scout ritual of undressing inside our sleeping bags, usually a modest affair that ends with uniforms balled up against the toes, but not with Mitch. Mitch hums "The Stripper" as he shimmies out of his skivvies, then twirls them around his finger before flinging them into a tentmate's face. Amid comments about "skid marks" and "toaster burns," Mitch trains a flashlight on the *Playboy* centerfold. But I don't need the *Playboy*; the sound of Mitch beating off inside his sleeping bag is quite enough. "Wet your hand," Mitch coaches. As I lick my palm, I try to imagine what his dick looks like. Is it hairy? Then he zips down the flap and talks like Mae West: "C'mere, big boy, I wanna show ya somethin'." It looks like a big brown hatchet buried up to the middle in black pubes. "Ohhh, I'm gettin' there, I'm gettin' the . . ." He shivers. His dick dabs clear gel on his belly, then prongs back, slinging a viscous vine. I burrow into my sleeping bag. Skin sings against nylon. Mitch and Scout 2 let loose; Scout 3 climaxes so loudly he draws a "shut up" from the next tent. I'm left jerking haplessly alone in the dark till both of my wrists hurt.

That summer I develop my first real crush, on a boy named Christopher, who is the assistant director of the Catholic Youth Organization variety show. "Only adore Jesus," the nuns teach us, yet I can't resist a competing adoration when, during rehearsals, my eyes wander to Christopher's angelic face. Every time Christopher leaves the church he blesses himself with holy water; I follow his example, then try to get his attention by pretending to drink from the font. "Don't do that," he yells. "It's sacrilegious." Home in bed, still stinging from the rebuke, I close my eyes, pump my dick, and think about Chris. It feels prickly in my groin like when my leg falls asleep.

The next night, still thinking about Chris, I feel a rush like a million soft pine needles sweeping across my body. My dick twitches

deliciously and the pisshole fills with fluid. I race through my bedtime prayers and smile myself to sleep.

Bedtime beatoffs become a habit, in time producing a rice-
puddingy mess copious enough to make future tricks marvel, "God,
you come a lot." But after those first few months, I don't pre-cum
at all.

I won't let Ivan come in my mouth. But will I let him pre-cum in
my mouth? Or more to the point, how can I resist sucking that
beautiful uncut cock? As a cockmeat purist, I've already decided not
to suck rubber. What would be the point? Instead, I try to become
America's preeminent expert on preorgasmic emissions. I read every
safe-sex pamphlet I can find. One article calls pre-cum the "million-
dollar question." It's the question "on every gay man's lips." Is it
safe? Possibly safe? Unsafe? Does anybody really know? Are the sci-
entists on our side? They've found HIV in seminal fluid, but gay
saliva seems to do it in. So say friends who've been sucking cock for
years and are still healthy and still sucking. With all this uncertainty,
a peculiar charm attaches to pre-ejaculate, not unlike with skydiving
or eating sushi—99.9 percent safe, but what about that other .1
percent? We all hear about the guy whose parachute fails to open,
or the fellow who croaks taking a bite of fugu. Scariest of all is the
HIV-positive gay man who claims he only sucked pre-cum cock.

The spell breaks in a motel room near the Chesapeake Bay. I've
worshipped Ivan for more than a month now, buying him clothing
and driving him each dawn to a construction job, always *a la orden*
—at your service. For this he grants me an occasional audience with
his dick. In the afterglow of one such visitation—he'd let me lick
his balls while he jerked off—he regales me with tales of his other
boyfriends. I laugh till I realize the joke's on me, 'cause I'm just like
them: a pilgrim at a very popular shrine—queue up, kneel down,
then gangway for the next sinner. I ask Ivan if there's *anything* that
would make him fall in love with me.

"A miracle," he says.

Now that he's recovered, he delights in taunting us mere mortals. Wait for me, he promises one Saturday morning, I'll slip into your bed tonight after last call. "Yeah, *right*," I say. Then I go ahead and buy champagne and fresh condoms anyway and fantasize a luxurious Sunday morning sleeping in, which only sets me up for the inevitable anticlimax: falling asleep with the light on, waking up alone with my piss boner. When he finally calls three days later and asks what I'm doing, I try reacting coolly, telling him, "I'm kind of busy right now."

He laughs it off. Seems my chief rival for his affection—a guy who lives in Brooklyn, with whom he'd spent the last couple of days—had pushed for sex once too often. About an hour ago Ivan had instructed the guy to lie naked on the bed with his legs in the air. "Now don't move; I'll be right back," Ivan had said. Then Ivan slipped out the guy's front door, and for all Ivan knew the guy was still lying there with his bare ass pointed at the Verrazano Bridge. "*¡Qué barbaridad!*" I admonish, then I drop everything to pick him up at the station.

On the drive home I invite Ivan on a road trip I've been planning. Why not, he says; with a flip of the middle finger he's quit his job: he's going to enjoy life. I drop him off at his home fully expecting to be jilted again, but two days later he shows up in a pair of holey cutoffs, and for most of the road trip lets me rest my free hand on one of the holes. He falls asleep with his head in my lap as we soar past the Chesapeake shipyards.

In our motel room, Ivan lays a pair of fresh white underwear on the bed, undresses, showers, comes out dripping, and stands in the middle of the room drying himself—chest, armpits, legs, heaven between his legs. I avert my eyes but they stray to his brown butt, reflected in the mirror. My hand strays too. "*Deja mi culo*," he commands, then translates: "Leave my ass alone." I tell him that his English is improving—now he can reject me in two languages—so he touches my face and explains softly, "I'm *dressing for bed*," then kisses me gently, with an open mouth so our tongues can meet for the first time. Our chests touch; I backhand his cool cock until it moistens my palm. He grins and murmurs, "*Espérate*," and pushes my hand away.

"Can't wait," I say. He leans on my shoulder as he steps into the creamy-looking Jockeys. "No use," I warn. "Just going to rip 'em off ya." He folds the dirty clothes and lays them on top of his duffel bag.

"*Now* can we please go to bed?" I ask, turning back my covers.

"*Sí,*" Ivan says with a sigh, sliding alone into the crisp linen envelope of the other bed. "*¡Qué rico!* My own bed," he says. Cotton wicks against linen as he removes his shorts and pitches them across the room. I try but I can't hide my frustration:

"Then we're *not* sleeping together?"

"*Mañana,*" Ivan says, yawning. "I am tired now. *Que sueña con los angelitos,*" he says. Dream of angels. He shuts the light and the television, fluffs his pillow, shifts around for what seems like an hour, then kicks off his covers and begins to snore. I place my palm, reeking of his crotch, to my mouth and beat off with the other hand, in the dark, until my dick numbs out; I get up, take a piss in the bathroom, gaze at Ivan resting on top of his covers, go back to my own bed, and drift off. In a dream, I eat Ivan's ass with a passion. He raises two fingers and morphs into a dashboard saint. I wake up hard and beating off again, this time with both hands, until I get interrupted by Ivan's talking in his sleep, in garbled Spanglish, thrashing and lifting his head from the pillow. I go to his bedside, kneel, and caress his brow until he's calm again. Still kneeling on the floor, I rest my head on his chest. My fingers travel across his lips, down his neck, chest, side, hips, belly, hot damp mane. I unhood his cock and pump the foreskin until he stirs and laces his fingers into mine. I wet my hand with my tongue and we work his dick over and over together, the spit and pre-cum crackling like a fire. Ivan's hips buck and his cockhead unsheaths and juts through our locked fists. The scent of his cock in the dark is driving me crazy.

"*¿Qué haces?*" he asks.

"Gonna suck your cock," I murmur.

"You crazy," he protests, rolling over onto his stomach, trapping his cock between his silky hipbone and rough linen. I snake my tongue to the head and try to coax it to my mouth. He won't budge but can't control the flow of sweet water. Blessed is the fruit.

Ivan grunts, turns over, pushes my head away, points his hard dick up like uncorking champagne, mouth open, eyes shut, and sprays Ivan bubbly into the air. His cum splats and squiggles onto his chest, spills over his cock-grabbing knuckles. I come on the carpet, rest my head on his soaking hip, savor the miraculous taste for the last time, then slip away to the bathroom and gargle till all that remains is the familiar cool mint of Listerine.

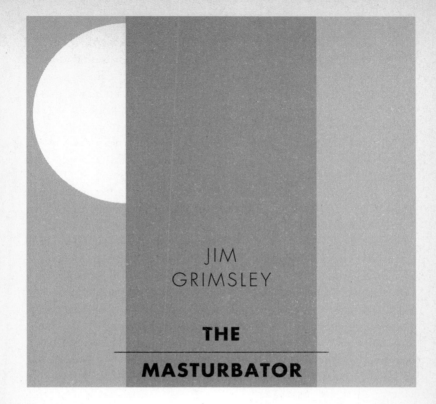

JIM GRIMSLEY

THE
MASTURBATOR

I have to get out of bed again, the stranger is growing
the green one on the dishes
I have to pick up
my clothes again
I have to breathe carefully
I have to pick up my underwear
the dishes in the living room
the carton of rice the Chinese dream
i have to pick up
the tape box with rick donovan

i have to breathe carefully, count each in and out

When I am bored I think of friends fucking friends. Lying in
bed with an ache in my eyes, I make pictures run there, my own

movie screen; I can make the images with eyes open or closed, so I start with eyes open. Adjusting the level of the hospital bed for maximum comfort, I slide my cool arms under the blanket, and, for beginning, refuse to touch my cock. I picture Claude with John. Claude has flown to Philadelphia to the apartment John shares with his lover. They barely know each other, Claude and John; John shows his surprise when he opens the door and Claude stands there. Claude enters without being asked. He smiles in the slightest way, something like a curl of the lip indicating, hinting, contempt. This offends John, since he is a butch number, thick round muscles, hairy chest, nothing to sneer at, and not used to this sort of attitude. They speak, hardly anything important. Why are you here, I came to see you, sentences like that. We skip the exact dialogue, which will change anyway as moments repeat. Claude has a long lean body, olive skin, the kind of gray-black hair that comes to some men in their late thirties. Why have you come? I came to fuck you. Claude undresses in front of John, patiently removing shirt, shoes. But John protests, Nobody fucks me, I don't go in for that, while Claude smiles and removes his socks, his pants, the final barrier. Falls out the great genetic blessing of Claude's life, his long and limber cock, full and thick, the one that I have seen and can verify, making this fantasy all the more pleasant.

While the nurse's aide rolls in her machine that takes blood pressure and pulse at the same time, John stares at Claude in utter fascination, at the handsome body, the beautiful legs, the amazing flared calves, and then at the center of him, the hanging cock. In my head I make the cock even larger than usual, a true monster, and John can't take his eyes off it. I remind the nurse's aide to take my blood pressure on the right arm and to place the cuff above the swelling phlebotomy bruise at my elbow, while Claude stands in that sunlit apartment in my head, allowing his cock to grow, lengthen and thicken, while John becomes perfectly still. But my lover will be home soon: John's slight protest. Claude shrugs: I don't care. John strips his T-shirt over his head.

I think you should come over here. Claude employs that tone of command he likes. John obeys, and the nurse's aide takes my temperature in my left ear, cool today, 97.7; she waves good-bye and

I give my best southern have a good day to her, pays to be nice to these people. While John slides toward Claude feeling some unnameable resistance in himself and Claude wraps his arms around John. They kiss and the kiss goes on and on. Claude kisses like a force of nature, like there's a volcano pouring out lava from inside him, while John kisses openly, in a detailed, meticulous way, rich as any dessert, a genius kisser, they enjoy themselves. Claude slides his hands down into John's loose pants.

This continues all day; I refuse to finish. The nurse enters bearing my noon pills while John reveals his own average dick. I am allowed the tiniest amount of water to swallow the leucovorin; you are supposed to take it with a lot of water, but I am in the hospital for low sodium, my fluids counted to the last cc. Claude's cock thickens and arcs out. John, amazed, gapes. A change comes to his face, a sheen of fever. Claude locks his attention on John, never wavers. He says, I think you should go down there. John gives that look of slight resistance, of irritation, as he has before, but each time the reality of his resistance fades a little more. He does go down there, sinking on his knees, the firm muscles of his thighs shimmering. Handling Claude's arched cock first with his hand, then, in a deep fever, taking what he can into his mouth.

I am aroused but waiting. Richer parts of the fantasy approach. When the doctor arrives to measure my daily sodium level, Claude and John have moved to the kitchen, where John blows Claude while Claude leans back against the doorframe, the long cock getting longer, a curved span of bridge, John giving head with skill, Claude making small pleasure sounds but keeping mostly silent. He looks down at John, lays a hand on top of John's head. The doctor, seated in a chair, guesses that I will be in the hospital a few more days at least, till my sodium has risen to a safe level. She leaves and Claude begins to fuck John over the kitchen counter. What I enjoy most is the point of entry, Claude's size into John, the notion that John would be very tight, the fact of Claude's big cock that I know to be true, the fact of John's strong body that I have seen. John offers no further resistance, sweaty now, thoroughly aroused, anxious that his lover will soon return; he allows Claude to turn him around, he watches Claude oil himself, he waits. When the cockhead slides in,

John makes a sound between a gasp and a cry. Claude pushes farther in, and John heaves; Claude pushes farther and John makes a fist, takes a deep breath. Claude has pushed all his cock inside and spreads himself over John's muscled back, a moment of rest and comfort. Then he fucks.

Lunch arrives. I eat every crumb, every bland vegetable, every morsel of dry chicken. The nurse visits, the nurse's assistant takes my vital signs again, and by then the boys in my head have fucked in several more rooms. Claude gives John a rest at times, they do handwork on each other, John comes once, but not Claude. Always they resume fucking in a different position, in a different room. Some combination of drugs I am taking, or maybe the dripping saline solution entering me through the catheter, enhances my ability to make pictures.

We have entered the safe part of the afternoon; no one will bother me for a while as long as I don't accidentally hit the nurse call button. I take down my underwear and lift my gown. Adjusting all my tubes, I turn over. I rub my cock against the mattress slowly, liking the scratch of the cotton sheets against my sensitive parts; Claude fucks John standing, and John attempts to stay manfully on his feet, bracing his hands, clutching the back of a chair, but each stroke of Claude's drives him down till they are both kneeling. He makes that sound, the pained, pleasured groan that rises in pitch as Claude fucks intently and urgently. They are sweating and beautiful in my mind. Claude hardly needs to announce he will come this time; we have been at this all day. We come together, the three of us. I clean the bed with a towel and settle down for a nap.

Pretty baby on the boob tube
please channel me
please understand me when I
adjust the knob to guide you open
when I single you out for devotion

Please pretty baby please on the boob tube please
I can give you

a hand you can
bob me up and down on
your wavelength

Handsome tall fair young pretty baby boy
reach out of the tube I want you to
come out of it
I will give you
power over me
pretty baby on the boob tube please
receive me

Often I am absent from my own fantasies like this, and then I suddenly return. Cycles of friend fucking friend are followed by mental sex that always involves me. I have noticed that I frequently vanish from the landscape of make-believe during periods of illness, returning later when my health returns. Sometimes I vanish when I feel depressed or simply alone. When I absent myself from my own fantasies, I vanish without a trace. When I return, I must be present every time.

During this present illness, I have few fantasies of any kind. The extended dream about Claude and John marks the first time I have come in days. At one point in my life this would have concerned me, the lack of release for such a long period. But here in the hospital I become lethargic enough that nothing concerns me except my sodium level. That I fail to masturbate successfully every day means less than it used to.

I wonder what kind of death this represents, the suspension of my sexual self. Maybe my body simply lacks the energy for sexual thoughts, for any real desire. Maybe I am not drinking enough water. Or maybe the whole impulse is fading in me, being burned away, by what is happening in my life. My idea of myself as a healthy, vigorous person fades also, to the point that I can hardly conceive of myself that way. Yet I know that health can come back, that some vigor can return. These thoughts go round my head like little planets.

Impossible Teuton
ravish me
unspeakable satyr

take off your clothes and we can get right to the
heart of the matter

chase me into the yard and have me on top
of a car
fuck me in hyperspace show me how luminous
galaxies are.

O send me a hologram, video too hot
to mention.
Impossible towhead lavish me
with attention.

When I reach home again, released from the hospital, the nights
are the hardest time to endure. I am alone again, in the dark. I cannot
fall asleep. The cat lies as close as I will let him, uncomfortable and
fat on the bed. Water drips in the kitchen. Soon water drips in the
bathroom too; I listen to the chorus. Evenings are all right, friends
drop by or I call to invite them. They bring food I do not have to
cook and provide company to prevent me from thinking so much.
But when everyone leaves and I am alone, the darkness falls on me
and weighs me down.

Someone would come now, if I called. But I would be asking
for something, for help, and I have done so much of that lately. In
the darkness there are shadows I do not usually see. The shadow of
a hand over my face. The walls receding, closing in. The longing for
the future to be better. The fear that it will be worse. The weight
of the cat against my stomach as he expands and I contract.

I have always had trouble falling asleep. Once I would have
gotten up, started reading one of the books that are piled around the
house, or, even more relaxing, I would have opened my closet and
pulled down one of my favorite porn tapes. Maybe the one where
Rick Donovan fucks Matt Ramsey across the school desk, maybe that
one, since it always seems to work so efficiently. I always come.

Afterward, returning to bed, I would feel as if I had actually touched someone, or touched some vital place inside myself.

I tried a porn tape two nights ago and the whole scene played as if through fog. Matt's fine ass raised over the desk as Rick stroked that ever-threatening-to-soften cock into him. But Matt's groans of pleasure and disbelief, which have always thrilled, penetrated me dully that night, as if he were groaning off-key. The sex looked bad, even silly. I turned off the tape and went back to bed, where the moon threw the shadow of the intravenous pump across my arms.

> The lord is not my shepherd I am not a sheep
> so I lay me down my soul to keep
> through the night
>
> the hole in the bed is my enemy
> I shall not fall through it
>
> so may I walk through
> the valley of the shadow of
> you know who
> the very last prick himself.

The catheter in my arm has become the great dick of my life these days, the only porn I need. The drug it feeds me fucks me like invisible fire, entering everywhere, penetrating every cell, leaving me pale, white, and limp in its wake. All day I wait for the gush of love, the intravenous infusion that continues the spiral of my life toward something I can't see. I watch the raging of my integers downward, the fall of T cells, the descent of my viral load. This is real, I think. This is living in fullness, and I remind myself, I can do this. I can take this medicine one more time. A person can live through this: having one's will and energy sapped by a clear bag of medicine that hangs overhead, entering my body through my precious catheter and stripping away pieces of my vitality. Fiercely, like a butch lover. Pain will be absent, somewhere left behind; taking this clear fluid into my body has proven a harder force than pain. I slide on gloves, I touch the bag of medicine that burns if it drips onto my bare skin. I load the pump, open the clamp, and the love begins; and it is good, beyond description, this love. I tremble and shake, alone in the house. I turn the light on, following its movement to the walls, slow and thick. The hum of the pump soothes me. I step into the clear stream of medicine knowing it will carry me away to a world where nothing matters except this infusion and its effect on my cells; I become no more than a system of exchanges, one substance acting on another, and I lie there limp and wait for the fucking to be over.

BRIAN
BOULDREY

WHAT'S UP, DOC?

The earaches Swift suffered from are partly responsible for his misanthropy. If I am interested in others' infirmities it is because I want to find immediate points in common with them. I sometimes feel I have shared all the agonies of those I admire.

—E. M. Cioran

I

IT WAS BUGS BUNNY.

In a key episode, my cartoon hero is having his rabbit hole reamed by a bunch of construction workers. They're putting up a high-rise, and Bugs's house has got to go. This means war, declares Bugs, and he takes it out on the big muscled foreman, a hairy-chested bruiser with a permanent five o'clock shadow and slabbed pectorals.

In the most important scene, the hapless builder finds himself standing at the end of an I-beam dangling seventy stories up, balanced perfectly by a pile of bricks stacked at the other end of the beam. One by one, Bugs pulls away the bricks, and the construction worker must compensate for the weight displacement. For each brick, he has to remove an item of clothing: hard hat, tool belt, boots, jeans, shirt, socks—until the choice is removing those boxer shorts or taking the Wile E. Coyote plunge. Of course, entertainment allows violence but not sex, but every time that cartoon ran, I'd reach into my pants and begin to play with myself, hoping that, maybe this time, that big hot lug would show me his 'nads and spare himself the broken bones.

Let me make myself clear: this was not one of those Mild Sublimated Episodes with Vague Stirrings; this was Full-On Raging Boner. An example of a Sublimated Episode with Vague Stirrings would be the time Underdog's girlfriend, Sweet Polly Purebread, is abducted by the Moon Men and enslaved to make cakes for their pleasure. As their desire for more cake grows, so do her mixing bowl and the big paddles of her electric mixer, until she stands swooningly on top of a ladder and falls into the batter—languid, exhausted, spinning ever closer to those big stirring rods. What was that tingling in my loins?

It was just a tingling, because that's a Sublimated Episode with Vague Stirrings. But for my hunka hunka burning cartoon construction worker, there was a knot in my underwear, and at night, when I wasn't fantasizing about the Hardy Boys doing it together, I gave Bugs Bunny's mortal enemy my hot load of early teen liquid soap.

I'd lie there and think of him shucking off the boots, the hat. If he wasn't three-dimensional, everything else was: I could smell sawdust, tar, wet cement. I could feel the vertigo in my ears, the wind that rises when you're in high places and makes your T-shirt whip against your nipples. What was real about him was his five o'clock shadow, the clearly delineated pectoral muscles, the curls of chest hair that looked almost like the cartoonist's afterthought.

Thinking about that—the cartoonist hunched over his drawing table, carefully drawing every cel complete with chest hairs; the scrutinous, meticulous work it takes to make a cartoon man strip to his skivvies—was a turn-on in itself. That there was an artist out there, lost in time and space, who paid as much attention to the hair on this man's chest as I did, or more, was a sort of introduction to my first ménage à trois (no matter that one of us was possibly dead, another unreal).

But the thing that sent me over the edge was more immediate, brutal, and selfish. A cartoon man was a comfort to me. Like every adolescent, I had misgivings about my body's idiosyncrasies. I wanted to blend in. I prayed to God, that bitch, to make me look normal.

My body was all right, in hindsight, prone to average amounts of acne, wet dreams, and dandruff. How do you describe yourself honestly, even in memory, without sounding self-pitying or vainglorious? Certainly, by the things that were cartoonish. My dick was large enough but it had a mean hook to it that drew the attention of my teenage suck buddies: "How are you supposed to fuck a girl with *that*?" Meaning: we boys will let you get away with it, but you think any chick will put up with something so abnormal? The tag phrase "about as useless as a bent dick" did not fail to enter my mind.

But my dick's trajectory—a selling point nowadays—was nothing compared with the freakish hugeness of the construction worker's calf muscles, the permanence of his beard, his ability to survive a seventy-story fall. Compared with that, my dick was comfortably normal.

Exaggeration and distortion stretch out the range of what's considered normal. Last year, DC Comics got in trouble with America's parents when the antiheroine Catwoman started sprouting larger breasts. Not that her breasts were small in the first place: the premier issue had a special "feely" bonus cover, so you could actually run your finger over the sensuous outline of Batman's foe in her slinky leotard. And believe me, she was no carpenter's dream. But with each issue the D-cup got just a little D-er, and the parents of comic book readers blew the whistle: our children's allowance money will not be spent on this!

We exaggerate to prove a point. We want to be believed. The advent of Catwoman's comic book series coincided with the bigger-is-better fashion trend, from waif Kate Moss to whole-lotta Anna Nicole Smith. In the same distorted way, my construction worker was all I wanted in a man: big, big, too big. Hair, muscles, the perfect mix of strength and vulnerability.

That's when I'd feel the cum rise up through the head of my crooked dick—which used to balloon out so huge and rock-hard, like the rest of my shaft, when I was a teenager—and spray my own chest: three, four, five long ribbons of it.

He was cartoonish, exaggerated, disproportionate, and dreamy. And ever since, I have loved the disproportionate portions of men. You think I'm joking, but my desire is real. Why bother to fake desire?

II

Until he died, my friend Will shared this love for the disproportionate. We were size queens together, but not your usual size queens. I mean, I'm not going to turn down a huge dick—I'm not stupid—but what thrilled me and Will were big noses, jug ears. Even the occasional protruding beer gut on the right guy pleased us enormously. When I told Will I'd had really good sex with Mark, a mutual friend of ours, Will was all adither. "Oh Brian," he said, tremblingly, in his Louisiana drawl, "his *teeeeeth*!"

True, Mark is perfectly built in every way: fine face, fine cock, fine ass, curly brown hair that looks best unkempt, redder in the pubes (which you can see in his eyebrows), not so much legs as haunches, an outy belly button you can nibble on. But his best feature is his worst feature: when he smiles, he becomes an instant poster boy warning America off British-style socialized dentistry. His teeth are a mess, a ruined picket fence, crooked like old tombstones, fluoride-grayed, patched, cheaply capped, chipped. They are hot. I wanted to run my tongue across them, slice my tongue against a misaligned incisor. Naturally, Mark gives great head, incredible deep-throating action that leaves a fine necklace of dental dents at the base of my dick. His favorite position is on his hands and knees, me up on my own knees feeding him the length of my arching dick and pushing a dildo into his happy tight asshole.

Will was always one-upping me. He wanted a guy with a missing finger. A club foot. He wanted a guy with no legs, so Will could lie back, skewer him on his dick, and spin him. He wanted to fuck a man with a high fever, so his dick would feel superheated as it plunged into the guy's insides.

I'm sorry that my own love of aberration is less Barnum-and-Bailey. Sure, I've fantasized about the leather midget who suits up in his harness and roams my neighborhood. I've considered the sinewy strawberry-bepatched burn victim who swims in my lane at the Y. But I prefer the more subtle exaggerations. Men with lisps, a slight case of oversized ballsac, tragic teen acne scars, premature gray, bowleggedness, cleft chins so deep you can store food in them. To all the boys with piercings, tattoos, meticulously shaved heads, I ask: Aren't you jealous?

III

Another example: I was staying on a ranch outside of Moab in Utah. Moab is surrounded by stunning national parks, but it is also "funpig central" for mountain biker dudes who like to risk their lives pedaling over slickrock. I had had my own day of hiking through the Needles District of Canyonlands and, weary, came back into town and stopped at the grocery store to get food.

While standing in line, I noticed a funpig boy in another lane, checking me out. He was dusty and tanned and whittled down by wind and pedaling, so that all that existed of him was muscle, determination, a body poised as if always at the starting line, skin, position, energy. He had dark curly hair cut short, a face that would have been sensitive if it hadn't been as taut as his biceps and calves. His head looked as if while it was being molded the gods had pinched it a little at the center to make it the shape of a slice of bread. Weepy down-tipped eyes like a flapper's.

He followed me out of the store with his bag of groceries. The hanging weight of the bag dangling from two hooked fingers showed off his vascular arm. He had beat-up shorts and just a little skin poked out from a ripped hole in the right leg. Scarred knees, scrapes. "I'm starving," he said, when it looked like somebody was going to have to say something.

"How many do you have to cook for?" I asked, checking out the two chickens at the top of his groceries.

"My buddies are still out riding," he said, to explain that it was okay to go over to his motel, which was just across the road.

At the motel room, it was obvious that there were at least four other guys staying there, with piles of sweaty underwear, deodorant sticks, baseball hats, bike repair kits, inner tubes, maps, used towels. My new friend took off his shirt. His pecs were solid and his shoulders wide, making the shape of a cobra's hood, a shape his body had changed into from hours of hanging over his handlebars. His bike was leaning against one of the beds. He straddled it, whipped his dick out from the fly of his shorts, and rested it on his bike seat. I put my hand over it and gripped the slender vinyl part of the seat with it, like I was grabbing two dicks. I felt him swell under my hand.

I leaned over and ran my tongue down it, like I could attach that piece of swelling fat meat to the seat with my adhesive spit. It was a wide dick that jutted straight up and out from his tight body.

He grabbed me and pulled my shirt off and we got on the bed, upending the bicycle. He liked my balls. He put both of them in his mouth and stretched them out slowly, holding on to my dick but not really stroking it. I chewed on his pubic hair, because it was short and bristly and he made more moaning noises when I licked down between his legs than he did when I sucked his dick. Besides, I liked the feel of his fat dick pressed up against my cheek, the way my nose would press deep into his ballsac, the way he spread his legs wider so I could get better access.

Things were going along nicely when he reached down to jack himself off while I suffocated myself in his crotch. That's when I noticed his arm—in two places, one where the wrist met his hand and another farther up, in the forearm, there were holes, deep volcanic craters, shaped like two anuses or the traps ant lions build to capture their prey. They were huge inverted puckers, and had to go half an inch into his flesh.

I was intrigued, distracted enough to put my finger into one of the holes. He didn't pull away. In fact, he made the scar more easily accessible, and I moved my head away from his groin and stuck my tongue deep into the scarred hole. It tasted metallic, and dusty. It was going to make him shoot. I looked at him and kept my tongue deep in the pucker on his arm.

When he came, there was that look of surprise and then gratefulness that all men seem to get after sex, as if we've been tortured hour by hour by the quotidian and our sex partner, even the most furtive fast anonymous kind, has made normalcy go away, cut the knots binding our hands together. I never knew his name.

He came violently, seconds after I began sucking on his forearm. He by turns groaned and laughed, and continued to do so with my balls still in his mouth. He jacked me off, too, and spread my cum and his together down over his abdomen, a perfect layer of gleaming spunk.

Outside the motel windows, the sun was setting on the desert, and it left those impossibly long shadows on everything. The angle of the sun even got behind the hands of the clock on the wall and cast a second ghostly time. I could watch our cum slowly dry into a tight puckering sheet on his belly.

I grabbed his forearm and held it up to him, a question mark on my face, suggesting, What happened here?

"Out on the rocks, there are these spiders, brown recluse, you know them? They've got a poison that eats your flesh. You die if you don't get it cut out of you. I had a brown recluse crawl up my jacket sleeve last year and bit me twice, and I was way out in Canyonlands and had to walk all the way back to town before I could get it taken care of. Those are the scars they left. The poison ate that much flesh."

I stuck my tongue down into it, and we both got hard, and we both came again. I was just finished dressing when his buddies came back to the motel, and he turned back into his alter ego self. He threw on a long shirt and hid his scar and urgently hissed, "You gotta leave."

I didn't want to have sex with him again. I just wanted to have one more look at his arm.

IV

In my desire for human cartoons I came across Michael, an ador-
able black-Irish chef with a killer brogue and a widow's peak that
would've shamed Eddie Munster. His smile, his jawline, his ability
to toss back half a bottle of Bushmills, these I admired. He insisted
on getting to know me first, three dates before he allowed anything
more than a kiss. He was good company, a goofy romantic like the
French skunk Pepe LePew: "le pant, le heave, le sigh." He served
tea on a warm evening at his house and he played Van Morrison and
told me grotesque stories about his "Prot"-hating grandmother and
her ability to roll her false teeth in her mouth like an acrobat (another
cartoon I'm sorry not to have seen). He kissed well, which was why
I waited for him. He wasn't virginal, I could tell that wasn't it, but
there was something he wasn't ready to show me. Tiny dick? Secret
fat? Dimpled butt cheeks? Could I be so lucky as that?

The night he let me touch him was the night he met me at a
dark bar halfway between our houses. Usually he wore a thick Irish
wool sweater and loose corduroy jeans. This night he wore a torn-up
T-shirt and a biker's leather jacket and jeans ripped at the knees,
low-slung. He grabbed me and my beer spilled on us both, and he
pulled me to him and took my hands, cold from a San Francisco
summer night. "Warm them up here," he said, pulling my hands
up under his shirt, guiding them first to the place between his
pecs—solid, muscled, lightly haired with that straight black glossy
Irish stuff—then to a nipple, under the arm to one of my favorite
places, the armpit, with another nest of whorled warm fur, and then
down through the black down (on the Irish County Down!) to his
taut belly. But there was something else going on there: all over,
like a surface of smooth pebbles, he had these bumps, some skin
problem that showed itself as tough little eruptions, hundreds of
them.

It was a moment of truth for Michael, the final test for me: he
stared fixedly at my face. Would I be revolted? Disgusted? My eyebrows shot up, and I could see the beginning of despair on his face.
But how much longer could he have had misgivings when I put the
other hand there too, and began to feel all over him—his waist, his

back all the way to the shoulder blades, down between his belted hips to his perfect ass and more of these welts, all over him.

He smiled. Naturally good-looking, wolfish, Michael is the kind of guy who draws back the corners of his mouth to smile, like he's decided to exercise just those two muscles in his face and that's all. He also reminds me of certain women who know they look good unkempt—a few strands of hair loose from a French braid. Mike would have looked terrible, probably, if he combed his hair. He murmured, "It's something I inherited from my horrible grandmother." I took a drink of my beer, kissed him, and told him it was time to go someplace more quiet.

Back at his place he insisted that I fuck him in front of a huge standing mirror, on his knees, his face looking straight in. I didn't mind. I got to pummel him and still look into those gorgeous dark eyes, and for better torque, I held tight to his hips, covered with his coarse foreign texture that thrilled me. It was like fucking a man of marble, the golem, one of those cartoon superheroes mutated by a tragic scientific catastrophe, Swamp Thing, Incredible Hulk.

Those superheroes are always cases of alter ego, by-day-by-night transformation, dark secret. Of course, fucking him in front of the mirror made it feel like a three-way. But it also felt as if a real third entity was with us, the distorted cartoon version of this incredibly handsome dark man I'd wanted in a simple straightforward way now made complicated and indeterminate. I ran my hand across the bumps over and over; the faster the friction, the more it warmed me. I lubed up my hand and jacked him off, then moved up with the oil and covered the bumps with it, slicked them on his belly, his ass, his back. He was the texture of my parents' suburban driveway, a gravelly beach on a Mediterranean island.

He seemed to like it. The more my hands roamed, oiling him up, the more far-reaching the eruptions apparently covered him. Those strong legs, calves, the tops of his feet. The nape of his neck and in between his ass cheeks. There was a muscular quality to them too, so that over his abdomen, already as ridged as the rind of summer squash, a second layer of strength adorned him, the extra muscles that would put him in the category of superhero.

His dick was perfectly smooth, though, which seemed right to me. I liked to watch him in the mirror, where foreshortening made his head bigger than his real-life ass, though the latter was much closer to me. Head and ass, that's what he was during our sex, and that landscape of swellings. He was a smear of something odd yet familiar. You see it in Picasso's paintings of his mistress, the loss of volume and proportion, an enormous face or breast, the distortion, the cartoonish view you get of your lover's body when you crave it and are lost in it.

He began to back his ass into my dick, and I jacked the cum out of his wide prow-shaped cock until he collapsed beneath me and I wouldn't pull out of him. I was still hard and wanted to stay there, and so I ran my fingernails across his back and scratched what felt now like hundreds of mosquito bites.

The relationship with Michael didn't last long, precisely because I liked his congenital inheritance. He wouldn't believe that I really liked *him*, and I wish I could have convinced him that, like my fantasy of the cartoon construction worker, it was all real desire. Did Apollo love Daphne any less when she turned into a laurel tree?

V

My late partner Jeff, the first night we slept together, sealed our bond by slipping in a videotape of back-to-back Warner Bros. cartoons, and did a heartbreakingly accurate imitation of Yosemite Sam while going down on me. In the years that followed, he obliged my cartoon construction worker fantasies by wearing his tool belt to bed (he was a carpenter, and there is no coincidence).

Handsome Jeff. Unruly brown hair I'd scrutinize for hours at a time, the way it grew out straight, then curled at the ends—how was that possible? Close-set eyes of some kind of devoted animal: in the morning he'd splay like a dog on the bed. Strength in the back and shoulders, a wrestler's sense of torque and balance, good for working and fucking. Teutonic hands and wrists, thick and meaty, hairy arms but a broad long chest, practically smooth. Equipment between his legs not huge but by no means less than average, the kind I always wanted to encompass with my hands.

Jeff took his first big full-blown AIDS diagnosis dive with meningitis, a consequence of climbing through dusty ducts in that union-man drag. Meningitis, said the doctor, is not a good thing to start out with. I hate it when doctors are right.

Meningitis opened Jeff up to a bad case of Kaposi's sarcoma, which transformed him as dramatically, in its way, as any myth out of Ovid's *Metamorphoses*. And aren't all transformations erotic?

Well, not at first. At first it was strange and awful: the newness of it, the fact that he was dying and that I could catch it, like the flu. But I couldn't help looking at those big purple sores. They were the third party again, the scientific catastrophe that created a new persona. Jeff was the Toxic Avenger with a heart of gold. It was best on sunny weekend afternoons when the sun would come through the windows onto the bed where he'd nap like a mongrel dog, his long sexy torso and short legs stretched to gather as much heat as possible. I'd wake him with my exam, running my hand along a flank and circling a lesion with my finger, zeroing in. I knew they were tender, and he'd wake up. He'd yawn.

His mouth was so wide and big. Jeff had a double-jointed jaw. As a prelude to sex, he'd grab an unattached rearview mirror from the nightstand, something he pulled off a heap at the big Pick-Your-Part automotive graveyard. He could fit the whole mirror into his mouth, and together we'd look for the spread or absence of lesions across the roof of his mouth. I liked to watch with him. I'd hold the flashlight so we could see better and he could show me the places where it was more tender than in other places.

Eventually I would lie on my back and Jeff would slide a rubber down my dick, straight to the base. He'd lube his asshole with one of those big fingers from his big hands, and then he'd lube up my cock and replace his finger with me, saddling up, moving that double-jointed jaw back and forth like an imitation of the way his guts were rearranging themselves.

Often, Will might like to have known, Jeff was feverish, so hot inside. You could feel the heat coming off him like he was a planet with atmosphere. And we'd both get hotter, flushed, and I noticed that those lesions—sunspots on his legs, his chest, the bottom of his jaw—would get even more angry and bilious. They fed off our sex too. Jeff would become one with the thing taking him over and in that fucking, I think, at least for a few minutes, he would take over the thing.

Suffering succotash, his body was beautiful, even in that disguise. I've never known a mouth, hands, torso, any and all, so well as his. Under that sheeny purple-patched coat of sores I found his skin always mysteriously smooth and lank, warm and open. When I put Jeff's flat-against-his-belly dick into my mouth it was like putting his whole body into my mouth, because that is the way he responded.

When he used his mouth on me, it was like a massage. It was a way to make me as smooth and lank as him. To fuck with Jeff made all my past seem deadened and moot. Each fuck was a repeat of that last great passionate sensation.

To fuck with Jeff was—*is*—present tense. It is like driving fast on a wet curved road with trees in the path. Now his legs are over my shoulders and I'm licking the aureoles of yellow around those glowing places. My cock is in his ass and my balls are hot and low and full, fuller than they've ever been, swinging forward against his ass, then my ass. His ass is like a muscled throat. There doesn't seem to be much difference between any of those thresholds: his mouth, the slit of his dick, his asshole, my asshole, even his ears and nostrils, a little bilious. They are all pure and part of our sucking and fucking.

He's stronger than me—he can flip me over with one of his wrestling moves and hold back my arms with those big hands, but it's still me doing the fucking. Top and bottom don't matter when there's that third stained body with us.

His skin is important. It's a different kind of skin when I touch it. Since love is an enduring close study, I scrutinize the different kinds of skin he has: the brown of nips; the roughed-up hands; the way it gathers on the underside of his cock at a certain point where the head meets the shaft, as if an invisible drawstring had pulled it there. When I take my turn and slide his dick into me, I am as smooth and lank as he has been. My body is accommodating and there's nothing even remotely like pain, only that fullness, that feeling from my waist down as if part of me is floating.

And there is that smell, that metallic smell of coins and blood, maybe a lot of vitamins sweating out from our pores. He drags his hand along my back, down to my ass, reaches a finger alongside his cock and spreads me wider. Our pumping was always effortless.

Jeff is gone now (a-the-a-the-a-the-a-That's All, Folks!), but when I watch cartoons I think of him and get horny. When I see a man with a missing digit, I think of Jeff. It's gotten to the point where I see anything less than perfect—cups with broken handles, typographical errors, a squadron of Down's syndrome children out on the town—and I dream of Jeff and very good sex.

My pleasure was for all of him. Him alone, yes, even if the virus left its own trail. The trail I chose to take: the skin, the sin in it, infected cuts, swollen eyes, the wart that never quite got burned out, the light in his eye and the yellow corona around each lesion as they spread, eventually turning into dark sores, the way tomatoes ripen.

I don't want to say that it was right, or that it was pretty. It's not like what Mussolini's son said when flying over Ethiopia and bombing it, how he said the bursting bombs looked: *come fiori*, like beautiful flowers. I was not twenty thousand feet above; I was closer. Sometimes I was in him, sometimes he in me. I don't say it was right, or pretty, to want all of him, but make no mistake: it was all true desire.

CONTRIBUTORS

JAMES IRELAND BAKER is an editor at *TIME OUT, NY*. He was the recipient of a 1992–1993 fellowship in fiction from the New Jersey State Council for the Arts and is currently working on a novel and a memoir. His journalism has appeared in *Out* and *POZ* magazines.

BRUCE BENDERSON is the author of two collections of fiction about Times Square. His most recent book, *User*, is a lyrical novel that plunges the reader into the night world of Times Square male hustlers, junkies, transvestites, and johns. Benderson wrote the screenplay for the film *My Father Is Coming*, which featured Annie Sprinkle. He is also the translator from the French of Sollers, Guyotat, Robbe-Grillet, and other writers. He lives in New York City.

KEVIN BENTLEY is a writer and editor living in San Francisco whose work has appeared in *Diseased Pariah News*, *ZYZZYVA*, and *The James White Review*, as well as being included in the second volume of *His: Brilliant New Fiction by Gay Men*. He likes to think of his writing as the place where Boyd McDonald and Jean Rhys meet. He keeps a smutty diary.

BRIAN BOULDREY is the author of the novels *The Genius of Desire* and *Questions of Travel* and editor of *Wrestling with the Angel: Faith and Religion in the Lives of Gay Men* and the annual *Best American Gay Fiction*. He is the associate editor of the *San Francisco Bay Guardian*'s "Lit." book supplement and writes often about industry and blue-collar issues, mostly because he hates hard work. He lives in San Francisco with Grace, his S/M-oriented dog.

KEVIN BOURKE's previous credits include "Welcome to Sex in the Nineties" in *Flesh and the Word 3*. He has studied writing with Jay Cantor, Frank Conroy, and Paul Carter Harrison.

MICHAEL BRONSKI is the author of *Culture Clash: The Making of Gay Sensibility* and the editor of *Flashpoint: Gay Male Sexual Writing* and *Taking Liberties: Gay Men's Essays on Sex, Culture, and Politics*. His essays have appeared in more than twenty-five anthologies and in numerous magazines. His book *The Pleasure Impulse: Culture, Backlash, and the Struggle for Gay Freedom* is forthcoming from St. Martin's Press. He lives in Cambridge, Massachusetts.

JUSTIN CHIN is a writer and performance artist. He is the author of *Bite Hard*, a collection of poetry and spoken word texts. He lives in San Francisco.

C. BARD COLE is the creator of the cartoon chapbooks *Tattooed Love Boys*, *Grievous Angel*, and *Fag Sex in High School*, among others. His fiction and essays have appeared in *Christopher Street*, *Dirty*, the *New York Press*, and elsewhere. A native of Baltimore, he lives on New York's Lower East Side, where he is at work on a novel.

TOM COLE is an artist and writer living in Cambridge, Massachusetts. His writing has appeared in *Flashpoint: Gay Male Sexual Writing*, edited by Michael Bronski; and the *Harvard Gay and Lesbian Review*. He has also written a book of poetry, *Action Adventure*.

ROBERT GLÜCK's books include two novels, *Margery Kempe* and *Jack the Modernist*; a collection of stories, *Elements of a Coffee Service*; and a number of volumes of poetry. His work appears in *The Faber Book of Gay Short Fiction, City Lights Review, Best American Gay Fiction 1996*, and *Best American Erotica 1996*. He swims with Chris Komater in a sea of love.

JIM GRIMSLEY is a playwright and novelist who lives in Atlanta. His first novel, *Winter Birds*, was published by Algonquin Books in 1994 and won the 1995 Sue Kaufman Prize for First Fiction from the American Academy of Arts and Letters and also received a special citation from the Ernest Hemingway Foundation. His second novel, *Dream Boy*, was published by Algonquin in September 1995 and won the ALA Gay/Lesbian/Bisexual Prize for Literature in 1996.

ALEX JEFFERS doesn't ordinarily write essays or autobiography and would prefer to call "Three Men I Want" a nonfiction short story. His novel *Safe as Houses* appeared in hardcover in 1995; in 1997, Gay Men's Press will issue a paperback edition. His short work has appeared in *Mandate, North American Review, Men on Men 3, Universe 2* and *3, Best Gay Erotica 1996, modern words 4, Advocate Classifieds*, and *Happily Ever After: Erotic Fairy Tales for Men*, among others, and is forthcoming in *His: Brilliant New Fiction by Gay Writers, Vol. 2*. He lives in Boston and his website can be found at http://www.people.hbs.edu/ajeffers/

KEVIN KILLIAN is a poet, playwright, and the author of several books, including the novels *Shy* and *Arctic Summer* and a book of stories, *Little Men*. "Spurt" is from a work in progress called *Bachelors Get Lonely*, a sequel to his 1990 memoir, *Bedrooms Have Windows*. With Lew Ellingham he is writing a life of the American poet Jack Spicer

(1925–65), to be published by Wesleyan University Press. He lives in San Francisco.

MICHAEL LASSELL is the author of *Poems for Lost and Un-lost Boys*, *Decade Dance* (winner of a Lambda Literary Award), and *The Hard Way*. He is the editor of *The Name of Love*, *Eros in Boystown*, and, with Lawrence Schimel, *Two Hearts Desire*. His poetry, fiction, and essays have appeared in such anthologies as *Gay & Lesbian Poetry in Our Time*, *Men on Men 3*, *High Risk*, *Hometowns*, *Flesh and the Word*, *New Worlds of Literature*, *Friends and Lovers*, *The Badboy Book of Erotic Poetry*, and *Wanderlust*.

MICHAEL LOWENTHAL's short stories have appeared in numerous anthologies, including *Best American Gay Fiction 1996* and *Men on Men 5*, as well as in periodicals such as *Yellow Silk* and *The Crescent Review*. His nonfiction has been anthologized in *Wrestling with the Angel*, *Sister and Brother*, *Taking Liberties*, and *Friends and Lovers: Gay Men Write about the Families They Create*, which he co-edited with John Preston. In 1994, he succeeded Preston as editor of the *Flesh and the Word* series. The recipient of a 1995–1996 fellowship in fiction from the New Hampshire State Council on the Arts, he now lives in Boston. He is twenty-eight years old.

VESTAL McINTYRE was raised in Idaho and attended Tufts University. His work has appeared in *Christopher Street* and the anthology *Wrestling with the Angel*. He now lives in Brooklyn, New York.

JIM MERRETT is a freelance writer whose work has appeared in *The Nation*, *The Village Voice*, *The Advocate*, *The Washington Blade*, *New York*, and many other periodicals. He was a contributor to the Lammy Award–winning anthology *Sister and Brother* as well as *Flesh and the Word 2* and *Grave Passions*. He is a contributing writer at *Frontiers*, *The Guide*, and *Metroline*. He continues to dedicate his work—and life—to Cesar.

AVRAM MORRISON lives and works in New York City.

SCOTT O'HARA is rentable at your local video store in about twenty-six different skinflicks; he also founded and edited, for three years, the journal *STEAM* ("the Literate Queer's Guide to Sex and Controversy"). His first two books are *Do-It-Yourself Piston Polishing (for Non-Mechanics)* and the memoir *Autopornography: A Life in the Lust Lane*. He is available but not marriageable.

CANAAN PARKER is the author of two novels, *The Color of Trees* (1992) and *Sky Daddy* (1997), both from Alyson Publications. His activist career has included work with the Publishing Triangle, the lesbian and gay literary program In Our Own Write, Queer Nation, the National Conference of Black Lawyers, and Outmusic. A songwriter and graphic artist, Canaan is a native New Yorker, retransplanted to Chelsea from Boston.

DARIECK SCOTT is the author of the novel *Traitor to the Race*, which should still be on the shelves by the time *Flesh and the Word 4* comes out, so please buy a copy. He is currently at work on a second novel. "Why I Need to Be Gang-Banged . . ." is his first work of erotic writing, but he plans to publish more, all of which will be completely made up and therefore more arousing.

ED SIKOV is a film historian, critic, and itinerant college professor living in New York City. A graduate of Haverford College, he earned a doctorate in film studies at Columbia University. He is the author of *Screwball*, *Laughing Hysterically*, and the *American Cinema Study Guide*, as well as articles for *Premiere*, *Architectural Digest*, and *Inches* (under the name Joe McKenna). He is currently writing a critical biography of Billy Wilder.

MATT BERNSTEIN SYCAMORE is a cheap slut and an expensive whore. His writing appears in *Queer View Mirror* and will appear in *Queer View Mirror II*. He currently lives in Seattle.